Legal deposit 2020
Library and Archives Canada
Bibliothèque et Archives nationales du Québec

Book cover image: Lee Avison / Trevillion Images
Book cover design: Lise Antunes Simoes

Original title: *La renaissance de Pemberley*
Original copyright © 2019 Lise Antunes Simoes

Pemberley's
RENAISSANCE

Written by

Lise Antunes Simoes

Translated from French by

Catherine Trollope

CONTENTS

« There is a stubbornness about me that never can bear to be frightened at the will of others. My courage always rises with every attempt to intimidate me. »

Jane Austen, *Pride and Prejudice* (Chapter XXXI)

CHAPTER 1

"Good grief," grumbled Mrs. Bennet, trying to tie the ribbon on her hat for the third time. "How clumsy I am this morning!" she exclaimed, addressing her reflection in the mirror.

Elizabeth was walking down the passage just then and stopped to help her.

"Lizzy, dear, where are your sisters?" asked her mother.

"Everyone is waiting out by the carriage. We can leave as soon as you are ready."

"Very well, very well... I must speak to Hill and his wife first."

Elizabeth finished tying the knot and smiled affectionately.

"There, how fine you look, mamma."

"Nonsense!" the woman chuckled, raising her eyebrows. "My dear, I am too old for that. It is now your turn to receive such courtesies."

Then, gathering her thoughts, her eyes suddenly widened.

"Mr. Hill!" she cried, hurrying to the kitchen. "Mr. Hill! Brandy in the sauce, do you hear me? Don't forget to add brandy to the sauce!"

Amused, Elizabeth left and joined Jane, Mary and Kitty, who were all waiting outside with their father.

"Well? Where is Mamma?" enquired Jane at Elizabeth's approach. "I thought she was tying her hat and then joining us?"

"Indeed, but she has gone to the kitchen to discuss something urgent with Mr. Hill."

"Again? Why is she so flustered? It is not the first time that Mr. Bingley and Mr. Darcy are invited here for a meal, after all! The Hills are entirely capable of handling the kitchen, are they not?"

"I suppose that Mamma will only cease attempts to impress our visitors when they are finally part of the family. And even then there is no guarantee. We should climb into the carriage. It will save some time."

The young ladies settled inside while Mr. Bennet took the coachman's bench. With a sigh more inflected with resignation than patience, he reached into his pocket for his pipe. His wife had been racing throughout the house since dawn, sternly reminding servants, daughters, and husband, to be ready on time. Everyone had made an effort and yet she was the one waited upon. If she did not make an appearance soon, they would only just make it in time for the church service, as was usually the case.

At the first puff of his pipe, his wife emerged from the house at last, half running, holding onto her hat with one hand and her shawl with the other.

"My dear, what are you waiting for? Come, let us go!" she cried out breathlessly, climbing into the carriage and taking a seat amidst her daughters.

The carriage was not designed to seat five people but, as of late, Mrs. Bennet stoutly protested the notion of one of them sitting with their father, even weather permitting. "What would people say if they saw you, hair blowing in the wind, like a common farmer's daughter?" she exclaimed. Even though the Bennet sisters had always travelled in the coachman's bench when required, they did not insist. Since Jane and Elizabeth had become engaged, their mother's whims and ploys had multiplied, and it was simply less exhausting to follow along than to argue.

"Ah, my dears, what a burden it is to have to manage so many invitations, believe me!" declared Mrs. Bennet while fanning herself with her hand in an effort to cool off. "I must think of a thousand different things without a minute to myself! Once again, I leave with the certainty that I have forgotten something of the utmost importance. When we return later with the gentlemen, it will be too late to rectify any of Mr. Hill's mistakes... Instead of having ham, we shall have turkey. Do you even know how much turkey costs? No, of course you don't, do you? The day before last it was rabbit, veal and guinea fowl. Five days ago there was a piglet and quail with mutton liver. It all costs a fortune! I did not think we would have to entertain these gentlemen so often!"

"You go to such great lengths to make sure that everything is perfect, mamma, and I am certain that Mr. Bingley, as well as Mr. Darcy, would be more than happy to enjoy a less elaborate meal in favour of a simple family affair, especially today," Jane objected softly. "It is only a luncheon, after all, not a lavish reception."

"'Non ut edam vivo, sed ut vivam edo'," Mary quoted. "The masters have said it since Antiquity: do not live to eat, but eat to live."

"Yes," added Elizabeth, for once agreeing with her younger sister, "there is no need for such elaborate displays. I agree with Jane: Bingley and Darcy do not visit us for the pleasure of eating. A good soup and a spread of cold meats would satisfy them, even for dinner."

"Soup! Cold meats!" Mrs. Bennet cried out, scandalised. "Think again, my child! These gentlemen are accustomed to refinement and they have a keen sense for anything lacking in good taste. You will become just like them Lizzy, and Jane too. I am convinced that one day soon you will look upon your poor mother and her modest house with the same critical eye."

"Mamma!" the two sisters protested.

"Yes, yes, my dears, you will see!"

Jane took her mother's hand and squeezed it comfortingly. All things considered, Mrs. Bennet did not seem troubled by the idea that her daughters might one day look down upon her. It was of greater importance to her that they be suitably married. An advantageous match was the primary source of her happiness as a mother.

"How eager I am to see you both married," she continued, "my poor nerves cannot handle any more excitement. Whatever it takes, I suppose. In the meantime, I shall ask Bragg's son to go out and shoot a few birds for us. What I wouldn't give to have a pheasant or a few partridges to serve our guests! Or a deer! A deer, can you imagine?"

Jane and Elizabeth exchanged a look and let their mother speak. It was no use interrupting her when she was lost in thought.

3

"Ah," she sighed again, "if only we could serve them tea and sandwiches. It would be less costly and work just as well..."

Despite her complaints, Mrs. Bennet took enormous pride in hosting her future sons-in-law. She grumbled loudly but went to great lengths to prove her social graces, showing how well educated her daughters were and how competently she ran her household. It was in such stark contrast with her usual conduct that even Darcy raised an eyebrow, surprised to see such a change in a woman towards whom he had been prepared to show a great deal more patience. Apart from a few blunders, Mrs. Bennet's conduct had thus far been exemplary. She took her role to heart and no one dared contradict her, not even her husband. Whenever the illustrious guests were expected at Longbourn, everyone trod lightly.

While these dinners were more ceremonious than necessary, they provided Mrs. Bennet with precious material to hold forth amongst her neighbours. Especially with Lady Lucas, to whom she would describe every dish and conversation in minute detail the very next day. She had not forgotten her neighbour's unpleasant comment regarding Longbourn. Lady Lucas had openly rejoiced that her son-in-law, Mr. Collins, would inherit the estate but thanks to the upcoming marriage of her two eldest daughters, Mrs. Bennet could finally relish having the upper hand.

After all, Longbourn's meagre income was nothing compared to Mr. Darcy's vast fortune.

~

It began to drizzle when the carriage arrived at the church in Meryton. One could not help but notice the two elegant gentlemen engaged in conversation with Sir William and Lady Lucas amongst the crowd of parishioners congregating in front of the building.

Charles Bingley, naturally more energetic than Darcy, was the first to notice the approaching carriage. He sprung forward, smiling, to open the door and help the ladies down.

The young man had discovered that in order to prevent Mrs. Bennet from taking over the conversation and making potentially inappropriate comments, one simply had to address her first. This way, she was forced to concentrate on her response, thus limiting any foolishness she might utter. Since discovering this ploy, he had made ample use of it.

"Mrs. Bennet, what a pleasure to see you again!" he exclaimed, greeting her cheerfully. "Allow me to assist you. With all this rain, I strongly recommend you take shelter inside the church. I will escort our dear Jane. She will be well taken care of!"

It was a rather graceful way of contriving a moment alone with his fiancée, but his efforts went entirely unnoticed by his future mother-in-law. Pleased by this welcome, she responded with a smile and gracious civilities. She would have continued doing so if Lady Lucas had not intercepted her and ushered her under the church porch, the latter also failing to detect Bingley's hints. She had arrived earlier and collected tantalising gossip, which she could not wait to share with Mrs. Bennet. The two quickly moved away, deep in conversation.

Relieved, Bingley turned towards Jane and helped her down. He took her arm and they hurried off a short distance, trying to take advantage of the little time they had together before the service. Darcy, less hasty, took over.

"Miss Elizabeth," he greeted solemnly, reaching out to her.

He had never been as exuberant as his friend, and the fact that he was now engaged to Elizabeth did not affect this character trait in the slightest. Nevertheless, that tender smile of his appeared, making him all the more handsome to her.

While her fiancé courteously helped Mary and Kitty down, Elizabeth noticed the inquisitive looks thrown their way by a small group of parishioners passing by. Evidently, the news that she had received a proposal from Darcy had begun to spread, prompting rather indiscreet curiosity. Were they here to see the wealthy young Derbyshire man for themselves? Or perhaps they wished to confirm whether Miss Elizabeth Bennet's charms warranted such a union?

Not knowing quite how to react, she merely greeted everyone with an awkward smile.

"Lizzy?"

Darcy held out his arm.

"Forgive me, I am distracted," she answered, moving closer to him.

"Indeed. How are you, dear Lizzy?" He asked, lowering his voice so that their conversation remained private. Have you finished reading *The Odyssey*?"

Having lent her a copy he had come across in the Netherfield library

5

– and knowing that its owner would neither miss it nor mind the gesture – he was anxious to hear her thoughts.

"Not yet, but give me time" she replied. "I would already have finished if you had not distracted me with a visit yesterday... and both days before that. My halting progress should not come as a surprise with such regular interruption!"

"My apologies, Miss Elizabeth, far be it from me to impede upon your progress... In that case, shall I return to Netherfield after the service instead of joining your family for lunch? You might then better apply yourself without the inconvenience of my presence."

Elizabeth bit her lip and tightened her grip on his arm in an effort not to laugh. She had discovered that since their engagement, and although he would deny it, he was entirely capable of handling her provocations. She found it endlessly amusing to tease him and to receive his similarly spirited replies. Especially as his once impenetrable expression softened as he looked at her.

"I beg of you, do not call off your visit," she pleaded. "Mamma will be so disappointed! You cannot imagine the scene it would cause at home!"

"A scene? Really?" repeated Darcy, amused.

He imagined Mrs. Bennet, distraught, upsetting the entire family with her cries and lamentations.

"Do you know the great lengths she goes to in order to accommodate you and Mr. Bingley? You would not want all those efforts to go to waste, would you?"

"And yet, did you not just say that you needed some time to yourself? You know I desire only to make you happy, Elizabeth," the young man continued, mischievously.

Elizabeth laughed, admitting defeat.

"In that case, I would be awfully pleased if you could join us for lunch after the service, as planned. My book will wait. After all, the words were written so long ago. If they could wait all these centuries for me, they can wait a few more days!"

Interrupted by the church bells that rang one last time to gather the remaining stragglers, the two young people hastened to join the Bennet family at their pew.

~

A few days earlier, upon learning of Mr. Darcy and her second daughter's forthcoming union, Mrs. Bennet had risen into action.

"You must be married by special license!" she cried out.

This license, which allowed for swift marriages and was only handed out to couples fortunate enough to afford it, would, in her eyes, be an ostentatious way of showing off Darcy's wealth. It would also ensure that her daughter was married as soon as possible, before Darcy could have a change of heart and call off the engagement. When it came to conjugal matters, Mrs. Bennet preferred erring on the side of caution.

Her hopes were dashed, however, for there was to be no special license. Neither Darcy nor Elizabeth had the slightest desire to obtain one, precisely because such a display of wealth and connection was, to them, as vulgar as it was superfluous. They wished to respect the natural order of things, in particular the fact that Jane had been proposed to first. It would have been unfair to the young woman if her younger sister were to be married first based on a mere whim. It was thus agreed that the required three weeks engagement period would be respected. Since Jane and Bingley's wedding preparations were already underway and a date agreed upon, Darcy had quite naturally suggested combining the two together. It would have been absurd to celebrate two weddings within days of each other when only one need be organised. As a result, Mrs. Bennet was forced to control her anxiety that one of her future sons-in-law might call off the arrangement.

That day, one of her consolations was the first official reading of the banns at the end of the service by the Reverend of Meryton. From his pulpit, he announced the upcoming weddings in a loud voice, carefully articulating the names of the future spouses along with the date and place the dual wedding would take place. The announcement was completed with a ritual question, asking any person who wished to oppose the union to manifest themselves before the fateful hour. Mrs. Bennet willingly uttered a little cry of outrage, which echoed throughout the entire church. Elizabeth and Jane shared a look of dismay, but their fiancés pretended not to have heard anything, and the other parishioners stifled some laughs. The message was clear: anyone who disrupted this double wedding would suffer the consequences of Mrs. Bennet's maternal wrath.

Once the pastor had stepped down from his pulpit, the assembly rose for the last blessing before the end of the service. Elizabeth felt a wave of emotion rising in her chest. Almost dizzy, she reached out to steady herself on the bench in front of her.

The reality of her engagement was suddenly made crystal clear.

Ever since she had been old enough to attend the Sunday service, she had listened, like everyone else, to these public announcements as they described the lives of Meryton parishioners. Birth announcements, baptisms, engagements, weddings, deaths: more often than not they involved people the young woman only knew from afar and she would listen distractedly, waiting for the announcements to end so she could leave and return to her activities. But today, the announcement was about her. It was her name along with Darcy's that had rung out in the church she had attended her whole life, flying above the heads of friends, neighbours, merchants, and other familiar faces. Her betrothal, a simple idea, a promise that had until now not left the confines of her family circle, was now known to all. It was as if the entire town of Meryton now bore witness to that which was not a dream: she truly was going to marry Mr. Darcy.

It became all the more tangible with the young man standing next to her, as upright and unyielding as usual, readying himself for the flood of congratulations he would soon face. He did not notice his fiancée's emotional state and it was only when the parishioners rose to finally leave the church that he glimpsed her discreetly wiping her eyes.

"Lizzy," he whispered, "is everything all right?"

"Of course, do not fret on my account," she replied.

She took his arm but avoided making eye contact with him and kept her head lowered, her face hidden by the edge of her straw bonnet.

~

After lunch with the Bennets, Bingley suggested going for a walk, claiming with his usual good humour that he needed a bit of exercise to digest the excellent meal they had eaten. Luckily, it no longer drizzled and the roads would hopefully not be too wet. Their parents approved immediately. According to Mrs. Bennet, fresh air was excellent for one's constitution and coloured the cheeks of young ladies, making them prettier still.

Kitty immediately volunteered to accompany the couples but Mary, who was more inclined to work on her music, had to be coerced by their mother. Sulking, she eventually joined their party. Mr. Bennet, relieved of his duties as host, disappeared into his library, while Mrs. Bennet lingered on the steps, cheering them on and advising them on which paths were best.

As they set out, duos formed: Bingley and Jane in front, followed by Kitty and Mary, whose resentment changed into a silent contemplation of the landscape, and finally, Elizabeth and Darcy, who intentionally slowed their pace to distance themselves from the party.

"I have something to show you, Lizzy," began the young man when they were alone.

He took out a newspaper from his pocket, unfolding it and rifling through the pages until he found the right one. He then folded it into a smaller square and handed it to his companion.

"There, look at the third announcement," he said, pointing. "Our banns were published yesterday. Just above, you will see the one for Bingley and your sister."

Elizabeth read them thoughtfully. It was not the reaction that Darcy had expected.

"Well?" he asked, concerned. "Are you not excited? Or, dare I say, filled with joy?"

"I will be happy when we are married and settled down, Mr. Darcy," the young woman answered with earnest gravity. "Tell me, is this newspaper distributed all over England? Or only in Hertfordshire?"

Darcy frowned.

"This one covers London and the South," he replied, "however the banns have also appeared in two other newspapers, one of which is distributed throughout Derbyshire – if that is what worries you."

"Oh, I am not worried about Derbyshire."

She handed the newspaper back to him and they walked in silence for a while. Darcy sought to understand what had upset his fiancée.

"You seem rather pensive... do you wish to tell me what is worrying you?" he finally asked.

The young woman pressed her lips together.

"To tell you the truth, I am worried about your aunt," she sighed. "We are not yet married and I fear that during our three-week engagement she will seek to separate us. Perhaps she still believes that our union is hollow and will not amount to anything more? In which case, reading this newspaper might further stoke her anger."

"What do you think she might do? Scold me like a child?" replied Darcy.

"As the daughter of an earl, I have no doubt that Lady Catherine holds sway with the Archbishop. Who knows what she might contrive to separate us!"

Puzzled, Darcy was pensive before answering:

"Lizzy, you are now one-and-twenty, am I correct?"

The young woman nodded.

"Good. This means you are old enough to decide for yourself. You no longer need permission from your parents. As for me, I have done nothing to be ashamed of, and therefore, legally, we are safe: no one can oppose our marriage. Have no fear, my aunt can scheme all she wants, call upon the wrath of God if she so wishes, but she holds no power over us. My decision is made and I assure you that my determination is unwavering. Our wedding will indeed take place."

Elizabeth replied with a nod, and they continued their walk in silence. At the sight of her fiancé's self-assurance, the young woman felt her concerns melt away a little, but she had to draw several deep breaths to release the tension in her shoulders.

"Do you think she might send someone who will attempt to change your mind?" she queried a short time later.

"Are you thinking about anyone in particular?"

"Someone of seemingly strong moral character. A Mr. Collins, for example. I believe that Lady Catherine holds him in the highest esteem when it comes to proper conduct and all things moral."

Darcy was about to answer when he caught the gleam of mischief in Elizabeth's eyes. She was teasing him.

He began to laugh.

~

In the days that followed, Jane and Elizabeth received numerous letters from distant relatives and acquaintances who, upon hearing the news, rejoiced in their future happiness. They were wished a happy marriage and beautiful children. The well-wishers never failed to allude to the fact that the two young women would soon be very comfortably settled, to the great pride of their parents.

However, one of the letters stood out, both for its contents and for the lack of care with which it had been drafted. Lydia Wickham wrote to congratulate her sisters for having followed her example and asked if she and her husband should expect an invitation to the ceremony.

"Please understand, should it be the case, we will need to plan swiftly as Wickham must request a leave of absence. For my part, I am overwhelmed with so many other commitments that I fear I may lose my mind!" she wrote.

The young girl had not bothered to write to each of her sisters. She had instead written a shared letter in which she sometimes addressed the one and then the other. She spoke of Newcastle with great enthusiasm, boasting of its parties and the lovely people she now considered her friends. She described the comfort of living in an inn and how she had no other responsibilities besides pleasing her dear husband. She finished off by declaring her eagerness to return to Longbourn so she could describe everything to them in greater detail.

Unfortunately, her attendance was out of the question. Even though, thanks to Darcy, they had been able to keep up appearances, there were many in the Bennet's intimate circle who knew that Wickham and Lydia's union had been preceded by a shameful elopement which had lasted a fortnight. It was better not to remind everyone of this unfortunate episode on the day Jane and Elizabeth redeemed their family through their own marriages. Only the passage of time would allow them to see Lydia in Hertfordshire again, without feeling any sort of shame.

Answering such a letter was not easy. Elizabeth spent an entire afternoon filling up pages that she would then burn, before finally managing to produce a satisfactory draft.

She began by extending a polite invitation to her younger sister while also worrying about the great distance that separated them, emphasising that it would not be advisable for the young Mrs. Wickham to travel alone. Indeed, Elizabeth reminded her that there were irreconcilable differences between Darcy and Wickham, which prevented her from inviting the latter. She concluded that it would be wiser for Lydia not to call on them now, but rather to use her savings to visit the Darcys when they were settled in Pemberley, perhaps the following spring. She would always be welcome to stay with them, although, once again, without her husband. Elizabeth finished the letter by expressing her regrets regarding the disagreement between the two men. Lydia did not know the real cause behind it and so, on a hopeful note, the older sister suggested that perhaps things might improve with time. Of course, she did not believe a word of this, but she felt the need to protect Lydia.

With the letter sent, there was nothing to do but pray that the younger girl and her husband would not choose to undertake the journey anyway.

Lydia, as Elizabeth knew well, was prone to whims.

~

"How about this pretty satin, Jane?" asked her mother. "Or else this silk! Good heavens! Look at this silk; how wonderful! This is a taffeta, is it not? How beautiful it is! Oh, my dears, it makes one want to buy it all!"

Since she had entered the dressmaker's shop with her daughters, Mrs. Bennet no longer knew which way to look. Even though there were fewer choices than in London, it was already more than the family could usually afford.

Elizabeth was rather amused by the way in which Darcy addressed her mother. Unlike Bingley, he let her speak without reservation, guiding her patiently back on track with some nodding or a few well-placed words, until they circled back to the main subject he wished to address. Within about ten days, Mrs. Bennet had lost some of her initial shyness around him and no longer considered him to be haughty or unpleasant. She happily sang his praises, although she maintained a clear preference for Bingley.

As a result, Darcy had been able to present the Bennets with an idea, which seemed entirely spontaneous: he and Bingley suggested offering each of their loves a new dress as a wedding gift. Elizabeth and Jane were astonished. Like any bride, they had already selected their best dress, which they planned to decorate with embroidery or a bit of lace. They had been more concerned about finding a pretty bouquet or, more extravagantly, a pair of satin shoes, so the thought of indulging in a new dress was an unexpected joy. Elizabeth, meeting Darcy's eyes, quickly understood that behind the seemingly spontaneous gift there was also the hidden preoccupation of what people might think. The wedding dresses were a way of impressing the attendees at the ceremony by elevating the young women to their roles as mistresses of large houses. The entire matter was resolved with such subtlety that Elizabeth could not help admiring her fiancé for his grace. Her mother, however, saw nothing of this manoeuvre.

"Look, Lizzy," said Jane, stroking some beautiful blue silk, "I think I shall choose this one. With puffed sleeves and a lovely ribbon embroidered along the trim, what do you think?"

Distracted by her mother and Kitty, who babbled excitedly about everything, and by sweet Jane, who had begun imagining her own dress with an almost guilty pleasure, Elizabeth found it difficult to make a choice. She eventually decided on a percale sheet in Saxon green. The dressmaker, who had come to assist her, suggested that she add white tulle coupled with the latest embroidery. Before Elizabeth could argue over the exorbitant price, the dressmaker explained that the gentlemen had already come in to give their instructions: nothing was to stand in the way, provided the dresses were suitable for the wedding, as well as any other social event that was bound to follow. The gentlemen had mentioned the receptions in London, the theatres, the dinners and balls in Mayfair, which convinced the dressmaker that she would have to outdo herself.

"Percale?" Mrs. Bennet was surprised when she saw her daughter's choice. "It is pretty indeed, but Lizzy, it's hardly more than cotton! You should take the silk! Which young woman has not dreamt of wearing a silk dress?"

By all accounts, Elizabeth was not one of those women for she unwaveringly defended her choice. Her mother, disheartened, was forced to let it go. She fell back on Jane's dress, which promised to be dazzling in silk taffeta.

Meanwhile, Kitty, who was jealous of the attention her sisters were receiving, walked around and meddled in everything. She could not tease Mary, who had stayed behind at Longbourn, nor her mother, and even less the dressmaker and her assistant. She therefore annoyed her older sisters incessantly. When she heard them speaking about London, her excitement suddenly increased.

"Will you go to town often, Lizzy?" she asked. "Mr. Darcy has a house there, does he not?"

"That is right," replied her sister, "but we are only to go to London for two weeks, right after the wedding before settling down at Pemberley."

"You shall be in town for two weeks! Oh, mamma," the girl cried as she turned towards Mrs. Bennet, "can I go with Lizzy and Mr. Darcy to London when they are married? Just two weeks! They can accompany me back to Longbourn when they go to Pemberley, it is on the way!"

"Not exactly..." began Elizabeth.

"Mamma, please!" Kitty insisted. "I would so love to go!"

"Well," began Mrs. Bennet, "why not? It does not seem like such a bad idea."

As Kitty began to jump for joy, Elizabeth turned to her mother with a look of dismay.

"Forgive me, but I have no desire to take Kitty with me," she protested.

"Why is that?" asked Mrs. Bennet. "It does not seem so absurd to me! Miss Davies did the same when she took two of her sisters with her on her bridal tour. We all know that Mr. Darcy is not an easy conversation partner. What will you do, Lizzy, if you find that you have nothing to talk about when you are alone with him? You might be glad to have your sister with you to distract you!"

"I am sorry, but no, it is out of the question," objected Elizabeth. "I am perfectly capable of making conversation with Mr. Darcy, I assure you that I have no need for a companion!"

Understanding that her dreams had shattered, Kitty stopped skipping. Jane barely had time to take her in her arms before the younger girl burst into tears. She pulled away violently and began yelling at Elizabeth, shouting that it was not fair, that she hated her, that she was never entitled to any kind of fun, that she would die of boredom alone at Longbourn with Mary once her sisters were gone, and that life was not worth living because her sisters had everything and she had nothing.

Her yelling and crying chased away two clients who had ventured into the shop but, as if that were not enough, Kitty also ran out into the street, chased by Mrs. Bennet who ordered her to calm down, while becoming angry in her own right.

"Forgive us," Elizabeth apologised to the dressmaker, as embarrassed as Jane was by this scene. "Our sister is still young and she struggles to contain herself..."

Kitty raged until evening. She even dared to enter the library in order to plead her case before Mr. Bennet, but to no avail: Elizabeth held her ground. She promised to invite her to see Pemberley at a later date.

She would finally be alone with her husband for the first time and she awaited this moment with such impatience that she had no desire to leave anything to chance.

~

"I received a response from my sister, Georgiana, this morning," said Darcy. "I cannot remember her exact words and I think even she lacked the vocabulary to tell me how delighted she was to learn of our upcoming wedding. You made such an impression on her during your visit to Pemberley this summer and she found you so captivating, that she cannot conceive of wanting anyone else as a sister but you. She is impatient to see you again."

The four fiancés had been invited to tea at the Philips and now left Meryton to return to Longbourn. Elizabeth, walking alongside Darcy, looked at him in slight bewilderment and almost laughed out loud at his impassioned assurances. Was this an attempt at humour? However, he seemed quite serious.

"Really?" she asked, surprised. "Are you certain she was referring to me?"

"Of course," replied Darcy, frowning. "Do you doubt the affection she already has for you?"

Georgiana Darcy, as far as Elizabeth remembered, was a charming yet extraordinarily shy girl, who spoke only when invited to do so. Although Elizabeth had shown great care and had managed to put the younger girl more at ease during her visit to Pemberley, they had hardly exchanged more than a few words.

She was on the verge of responding with usual civility, before changing her mind, preferring to tease him a little.

"My dear Mr. Darcy," she declared in the same pompous tone, "I thank you for your tact, but as you know, although I found your sister quite charming, we barely had the opportunity to exchange more than the usual civilities. I do not doubt her joy at the news of our union, and the sincere attachment we shall develop for one another in due time, but perhaps it is a little premature for her to be this overjoyed at the idea that I will soon become her sister..."

She then took on a look of mischief and added:

"You must admit, I am still a stranger to her. Are you not embellishing her message a little?"

The joke did not appear to work. On the contrary, instead of laughing, her fiancé appeared somewhat offended.

"Forgive me, I thought it would please you," he replied dryly. "It is possible that Georgiana does not know you as well as I would like, but I have spoken about you a great deal. Is it not the same?"

Elizabeth squeezed his arm affectionately.

"I simply wanted you to understand that there is no need for you to speak to me so formally, my dear, especially when we are alone," she explained gently. "I respect your fondness for elegant phrases but please save them for your letters, where they are more appropriate. For my part, I don't expect such grandiloquence; I prefer simplicity over embellishment."

Darcy scowled, but Elizabeth felt him relax a little. They walked on a few steps before the young man rallied once more.

"May I just say, without the slightest embellishment this time, that the entire household at Pemberley is looking forward to having a new mistress soon? My housekeeper, Mrs. Reynolds, remembers your last visit perfectly, even though she does not know you very well either."

"Oh! Yes, much better!" exclaimed Elizabeth, chuckling.

Her companion's sullen mood finally lifted.

"Nonetheless, Georgiana is indeed really happy that I have chosen you, and not another," he continued, adopting a more relaxed tone. "You are one of the rare people to have dedicated her much attention, with kindness and authenticity. She appreciated it greatly."

"And in turn, rest assured that I have found in her a wonderful sister whom I will have no difficulty becoming attached to. When I think of Jane having to contend with Mrs. Hurst and Miss Bingley, I assure you that I am quite happy with my fate..."

Darcy could not help smirking. He refrained, however, from commenting on this little taunt and they continued at a leisurely pace until they caught up with Jane, who awaited with Bingley at a bend in the road.

"Dear Miss Elizabeth, everyone tells me that you are the best walker in the family and yet here you are, late again. Is our friend Darcy too heavy to pull along?" joked Bingley.

The latter immediately flicked his friend's hat off his head. It was the only response he made to the provocation, making everyone laugh, including Bingley.

"You see," he continued, picking up his hat, which lay on the grass, "since meeting Darcy, I have never known him to ignore a provocation or leave an injustice without repair!"

"And I find you rather brash, Bingley. I doubt you would have made these comments if these ladies were not here," Darcy replied, without skipping a beat. "I suspect you are attempting to impress Miss Bennet."

"If that is the case, he is successful," replied Jane, with a chuckle.

"I have been exposed! I plead guilty!" added Bingley, wincing.

The young people had left without chaperones which gave the two couples the freedom to seclude themselves as they wished, allowing the foursome to develop their own dynamic. They exchanged quips effortlessly now, even if Jane, the most reserved member of the group, did not yet know how to address Darcy with ease.

More than once, Elizabeth wondered how Bingley and Darcy's friendship had lasted with such opposing temperaments. Bingley, barely twenty-five, was active, energetic, and laughed easily, while Darcy, who was a few years older, was of an Olympian calm and seemed always to navigate life with utmost solemnity. Yet, when together, their personalities matched well, and Elizabeth suspected that Darcy chose to surround himself with people who were lively and stimulating, like Bingley or the very pleasant Colonel Fitzwilliam, who both provided him with the effervescence he lacked. Either way, she could only welcome this friendship, which guaranteed that she and her sister would see each other often after the wedding.

"Lizzy, I would speak with you," Jane whispered, taking her by her arm while the two men continued their gentle bickering.

"What is it?" asked Elizabeth.

Jane walked away another few steps, agitated, and giggled nervously.

"He kissed me!" she laughed.

"Who? Bingley?"

"Shhh! Not so loud! Of course, Charles, who else!"

"But, when?"

"A moment ago, as we were waiting for you. I did not see it coming, he suddenly took me by the waist, and... it happened!" she said, before laughing again, both to hide her embarrassment and her elation.

Once over her initial surprise, Elizabeth was delighted for her sister and just as excited about this new development between the two lovers. However, as the four of them made their way to Longbourn once again, the young woman began to wonder.

Darcy had never attempted the slightest move, apart from a few touches on her arm and a lingering kiss when he brought her hand up to his lips. Now they were engaged, it was likely – desirable, even – that other kisses would follow, like the one shared by Bingley and her sister. Was it due to a lack of initiative on his part? Shyness? Or simply a lack of opportunity? Elizabeth did not have the answers, and, feeling slightly envious of her sister, she vowed she would do everything within her power to enjoy the same pleasure.

~

Tremendously excited to have Jane by his side soon, Bingley had set his sights on showing her the entirety of the Netherfield estate. He therefore returned the Bennet family's numerous invitations by hosting a family luncheon, following which he offered to take them out on a carriage ride through the estate's woods.

Although October was drawing to a close, the temperatures were unusually mild and prompted a change of plans. Already excited at the idea of discovering something new, Kitty requested the use of a cabriolet, so as to take full advantage of what she described as the 'pretty autumn leaves, which are never as bright anywhere else'.

"In a cabriolet? But what shall we do if it rains, my dear?" Mrs. Bennet exclaimed. "We shall have no roof!"

"And we run the risk of catching a cold, which would require us to keep a room here at Netherfield," her husband pointed out with his usual sarcasm.

Elizabeth gave him an amused look and Jane blushed crimson; but their mother did not grasp the reference.

"I don't think that it will rain, madam," Darcy intervened, speaking to Mrs. Bennet, "the sky looks clear. Personally, I find Miss Catherine's suggestion very appealing. What do you think, Bingley?"

"Upon my word, I had not considered using the cabriolets. Unfortunately, there are only two of them here, so we will not all fit."

"Perhaps we could form separate groups?" suggested Elizabeth. "You could show the estate to Jane in one cabriolet, Mamma and Kitty could use the other, and we could go on foot. Unless, papa, you would prefer to go by cabriolet, as well?"

Mr. Bennet refused energetically, claiming that he did not wish to deprive Kitty of such fun. The prospect of a walk seemed more attractive to him than listening to his wife's incessant chatter, especially since she would no doubt take delight in every pebble they came across.

"Miss Elizabeth is right," added Darcy. "I know the gardens well enough to lead the visit in your absence, Bingley."

Everyone agreed to this change of plans, although no one thought to ask Mary what she preferred and she was thus forced to join the walkers. Netherfield's butler distributed shawls to the women as a precaution while the horses were being harnessed. Bingley, Jane, Mrs. Bennet and Kitty then climbed into two elegant French cabriolets whose hoods had been folded down. Judging by the younger girl's wide smile and enthusiasm, she seemed to be experiencing the happiest moment of her life, which greatly amused Bingley.

As the carriages set out slowly along the path Darcy directed the rest of the guests towards the gardens, on the other side of the building. With Elizabeth on his arm and Mr. Bennet and Mary just behind them, he was a very pleasant host, deftly answering Mary's existential questions and bowing to his future father-in-law's superior knowledge of botany.

"I would be incapable of describing the flowers and plants in this garden, Mr. Bennet. On this subject, I defer to you," he admitted.

The older man did not have to be asked twice and, very soon, he was leading the walk, admiring the clever layout of the plants and declaring that he would dearly love to own something similar. Engrossed in his thoughts and without realising it, he began to speak of Netherfield with just as much praise as his wife, albeit more sincerely. Elizabeth exchanged a mischievous smile with Darcy. Seeing that her father took such pleasure in sharing his knowledge, the young woman encouraged the two men to spend a little time together by drawing nearer to Mary, giving them some space.

"When do you think we will go home, Lizzy?" asked the younger girl with a sigh of boredom. "Have we not seen enough of Netherfield? It seems to me that this is not the last time we shall visit. Why go to all this trouble?"

"Patience, my dear. Life does not only happen in books and music, we must venture outside at times," replied Elizabeth. "But I seem to recall Jane telling me that one of the dogs here has had a new litter. Would you like to go see them?"

Playing with a litter of puppies was considerably more tempting to Mary than observing the autumn colours and it was soon settled with Darcy. He motioned to a gardener who was passing by.

"The lady would like to see the dog and its pups," he explained to the servant. "Would you take her? Miss Elizabeth," he added, turning towards her, "I thought I might show you the grotto but if you would prefer to see the pups..."

"A grotto? You intrigue me, Mr. Darcy," she replied.

"It lies at the end of the garden, just past the large fountain. Would you like to take a look?"

Mr. Bennet volunteered to accompany Mary, and insisted that the couple continue their walk to the grotto. The little group separated again.

Now that they were alone, Elizabeth and Darcy would be able to conduct themselves more freely. Or so Elizabeth led herself to believe, before realising that being at Netherfield complicated matters somewhat. Visiting the gardens was a more formal affair than a walk in the countryside – especially since they could easily be seen from the house – and Darcy did not seem ready to abandon his reserve.

They walked in silence for a while as the young woman searched for a way to revive the conversation.

"I am dazzled by your talents, Mr. Darcy," she declared after some time. "It appears that you had a very clear idea of where you wanted to take me since we were in the house, and you have managed to get what you want without ever asking for it directly. Am I correct?"

"You begin to know me well," he admitted. "I did indeed have some idea of what I wanted, but my hopes are also quite simple: I merely wish to spend some time alone with you, that is all."

Then, with a small conspiratorial smile at the corner of the lips, he added:

"Mind you, that has been my intention for a very long time."

Elizabeth began to laugh.

"And Lord knows I did not make it easy! My poor Mr. Darcy! How I have mistreated you, all this time. You sought my company and I fled from you! I am most horrid! But please, put my mind at ease," she added, holding on to his arm lovingly, "has my attitude changed enough that you might consider forgiving me?"

"You have shown good progress, I will admit."

"I have shown 'good progress'?" the young woman laughed heartily. "'Good progress'!"

They did not come across anyone else in the gardens and as the ice seemed to have broken again, they spoke freely until they reached the grotto.

In the middle of an ivy-covered wall, inside an alcove evoking a sort of cave, stood the white marble statue of a nymph. Naked and concealing her breasts with her arm, her eyes were lowered in the direction of a stream of water, which escaped from the wall at her feet and tumbled down into a small basin.

Elizabeth quickly noticed that the area was tucked away from prying eyes, closed off on one side by a wall of trees whose leaves had not yet fallen, and on the other by bushes and shrubs of varying heights. The path they had taken leading up to the grotto was lost in twists and turns amongst the garden's plants, hiding them from sight. One had to be in close proximity to have a clear view, which made it ideal for two lovers exchanging a quick embrace.

She had already suspected something, but was then convinced: Darcy had set up a romantic surprise and she suddenly felt exhilarated.

While she pretended to admire the statue, she secretly observed her companion out of the corner of her eye in an attempt to guess when he would attempt an advance. She sensed his hesitancy and decided to make it easier for him: she leant over the edge of the fountain and stretched her hand out under the stream of water in a pose that she hoped was seductive and graceful. As a gentleman, Darcy just had to step closer to offer her his handkerchief, and, with a little encouragement, steal a kiss.

Indeed, as the icy water trickled over her fingers, he stepped forward. The young woman's hopes flared.

"I must return to London for a few days," he said. "As a matter of fact, I leave tomorrow."

Elizabeth felt as though a rug had been pulled from under her. Shocked, she was silent for a few seconds as she tried to find her words.

"You cannot be serious?" she replied, dully.

"I'm afraid so."

"But..."

The icy water was burning her hand. Elizabeth straightened.

"But our wedding is in twelve days!" she exclaimed. "You never mentioned that you had to leave Netherfield!"

"Indeed, but I have some unexpected business to handle in town. I am truly sorry, believe me."

"When do you think you will return?"

"Two days before the wedding."

"Oh..."

Forgetting all about the fountain, the graceful pose, and the handkerchief – which, by all accounts, did not seem to be forthcoming –, she wiped her hand absent-mindedly on her dress. Seeing her disappointment, Darcy tried his best to comfort her.

"Don't fret, dearest Elizabeth," he said, taking her cold, wet hand and bringing it to his lips. "The preparations are going well, you need not worry. I shall be back promptly before the wedding. Nothing will be rushed and everything will be perfect. And I will write to you, of course. I assure you, there is nothing to worry about..."

She nodded, trying to appear calm, but the moment had lost its charm. She felt disillusioned as they made their way back through the gardens.

~

Having spent the afternoon outside, the Bennets were invited to tea, which was served in the drawing-room. As night fell rapidly, candles were lit, complemented by the glow of two large fireplaces.

Jane sat on a sofa facing her mother and sisters and already looked like the lady of the house. Bingley, standing beside her, did not leave her side and showered her with charming attentions. Elizabeth's state of mind, however, was very different. Darcy also stood close to her, but he was engaged in conversation with Mr. Bennet. Besides, the young woman felt dispirited. She was not as inclined to exchange glances and whispers with her fiancé as before. Only Jane seemed to notice her change of mood.

"And your sisters, Mr. Bingley," asked Mrs. Bennet, "are they still in London?"

"Indeed, they are," he answered. "Mr. Hurst owns a house there and I usually stay with him and Louisa and Caroline when I am in town. My youngest siblings are also in London, at boarding school."

"I had forgotten that your family was so large. And you are the only boy! Tell me, how many sisters do you have?"

"Five. Caroline is out, of course, but Louisa, my elder sister, is the only one to be married."

"And do Mr. and Mrs. Hurst have any children?"

"Not yet. I suppose it will come with time."

"Still, has it not been a few years since they were married?" insisted Mrs. Bennet.

"Indeed, it will soon be three years."

"Three years! How surprising... When I think back, I was expecting our dear Jane only a few months after my wedding with Mr. Bennet. Our family has certainly never experienced any difficulty in that regard!" she observed with a small laugh.

And while Jane blushed crimson at her mother's lack of modesty, her fiancé uncomfortably sought to bring the conversation back on track.

"I have no doubt that you will be blessed with the same happiness," continued Mrs. Bennet. "I do not think there is anything more joyful in a house, don't you think, girls?"

"Caroline and Louisa will soon be back, along with Mr. Hurst," said Bingley, extending a plate of cakes to Mrs. Bennet in an effort to distract her. "I am eager to see them again. I am so used to always being in their company that I miss them awfully whenever we are separated! Although, with Jane joining our small group, and my good friend Darcy, whom I will not fail to visit often, I think life will be wonderful..."

"When are they arriving?" asked Jane.

"Two days before the wedding, my darling," answered the young man. "They will return with Darcy who actually is off to London tomorrow."

"Tomorrow? Just before the wedding? I was not aware." Jane remarked, startled, with a glance at Elizabeth. "Is it not a bit late?"

"Of course not! What could happen? When Darcy is in charge, everything always goes according to plan, believe me!"

Elizabeth listened to this conversation, eyes focussed on her tea cup as she stirred, and felt all the emotions she had been trying to quell for an hour rising up in her throat.

Knowing that her fiancé was going so far and for so long brought back old fears that she thought she had tamed. She remembered Lady Catherine's abrupt visit to Longbourn and her anger that such a match had been made. Then there were Caroline Bingley's sly comments, the various remarks on the suitability of their union, and also, the simple fear that her fiancé would come around and realise that marrying her was madness. All these thoughts raced through her mind so quickly that she was unable to keep a clear head.

"Well, it might not be such a bad thing," mused Mrs. Bennet with a shrug. "This way, Elizabeth need not worry about her fiancé while she tends to the wedding preparations. I am sorry to inform you, Mr. Bingley," she added mischievously, "but we have so much to do sometimes, that being occasionally relieved of our husbands makes life easier!"

Jane let out an indignant cry:

"Mamma!"

A few painful moments ensued whereby Mrs. Bennet defended her comments while Kitty tittered, and Mr. Bennet awkwardly joined the conversation in an effort to understand what had transpired. During all this Elizabeth felt tears well up in her eyes. Trembling, she set her cup of tea down on a table and stood up.

"Excuse me," she stammered.

Then, under Jane and Bingley's compassionate gaze, she fled the room.

~

Darcy cursed himself inwardly for his clumsiness. It seemed obvious that Elizabeth would not appreciate his disappearance less than two weeks before their wedding. It was his fault if she was upset and he should have taken greater care when announcing the news to her.

Engaged in a discussion with his future father-in-law, he had not followed the conversation as it unfolded next to him. He had only heard the last part of Mrs. Bennet's reply and had immediately understood the reason for Elizabeth's sudden departure. He then also apologised to the group and followed her.

The young woman had started running and he saw her disappear around the corner. He only caught up with her a little further away. Half hidden behind a nook in the wall, Elizabeth wiped her face and was preparing to face him, a fierce look on her face.

They did not exchange a single word. Taken aback by her large, beautiful black eyes that stared at him in defiance, Darcy allowed his instincts to take over. Taking the young woman's hand, he dragged her through the nearest door, into a small music room that was plunged in darkness.

There, he took her in his arms and embraced her tenderly. He felt her tremble as her tears started falling again.

"There, there, my darling," he whispered comfortingly.

Thankfully she did not cry for long. Shaken and awkward as he was, he would not have known how to proceed.

"Forgive me," whispered Elizabeth, breathing in short breaths to choke back her tears. "I am just a little worn out by everything that has happened. I was not expecting to see you go, but all is well now. I am fine."

Yet she made no move to leave his arms. Instead, she slipped her arms behind his back and tightened her grip, wiping her cheek on the collar of his coat.

"I am sorry to have troubled you so, Lizzy," he whispered. "I have no control over my commitments."

"Do not apologise, I understand," she sniffed again.

Without thinking, and because it seemed like the most natural thing to do, Darcy took the young woman's face in his hands, observing her for a moment in the faint glow that filtered through the window, before kissing her.

He felt Elizabeth gasp and was not sure if it was a sob or a reaction to the kiss. Nevertheless, she did not push him away or turn away blushing. Her lips were not pinched in unconscious defence or even passive. Quite the contrary, she returned his kiss as best she could, somewhat awkwardly but with tenderness, curiosity and – dare he say – certain delight.

When they finally stepped back from the embrace, both dazed by the sudden intimacy, they dared not look each other in the eye. Elizabeth smiled again. Then, to dispel their embarrassment, she whispered:

"Good heavens... is this your way of ensuring that I will wait for you, Mr. Darcy?"

He stifled a laugh and hugged her again.

CHAPTER 2

Huddled on her bed and bundled up in her shawl, Elizabeth was struggling to focus on *The Odyssey*. She was approaching the end of the book but her mind was elsewhere, her eyes constantly drifting towards the window and the view outside. Unfortunately, the rainy weather did nothing to cheer her up.

It had been six long days since Darcy had left and almost as long since he had written to her.

It felt like an eternity.

As promised, Elizabeth had received a letter from her fiancé the day following his arrival in London. He wrote that the journey had gone well and that he had made arrangements with his servants for the house to be ready to welcome her. He hoped she would find it to her satisfaction. He asked her to make sure that her trunks were ready on the eve of their wedding so they could be sent earlier, allowing the newlyweds to travel lightly the next day. He also mentioned that the Hursts would be hosting a dinner soon with other acquaintances and spoke about a painting exhibition making headlines in the city. He concluded with much civility, writing that while London could not compare with the fresh air of the country it nevertheless had its advantages, and he looked forward to sharing them with her soon.

These were rather fine words but they were cruelly lacking in emotion. Nowhere did Darcy make any mention of missing his fiancée and finding London charmless without her beside him, nor did it include a postscript containing some further proof of his attachment – in short, it was devoid of the delightful things a lover might write and which Elizabeth would have been most happy to read.

Knowing how reserved he was, she might not have minded as much had he simply written to her again. But this was not the case. Yesterday, she had rushed over to collect the post and had done the same again today. Her father did not hesitate to tease her.

"Well, my dear! I knew you loved reading but such impatience for a simple letter! Let the poor man breathe!"

To save face she had retorted with the first quip that crossed her mind, but deep down she was anxious. Darcy's silence worried her.

Now that he was far away, once again in his element and surrounded by London society, who knew what they were going to tell him? What sort of welcome would he receive now that his questionable betrothal was known? Elizabeth was not naive. She knew that as respectable as Darcy was, his peers would consider him a fool. How could he not be after choosing a wife so far below him in social standing, who offered neither dowry nor connections, and who could not even claim dazzling beauty?

On her bed, the young woman sighed. At the moment, her mental state was as bleak as the weather outside. Without Darcy's penetrating gaze upon her, she was losing confidence in her powers of seduction and was beginning to ask herself what he had found so attractive about her in the first place. Would he ever come back? What if, under pressure from his acquaintances, he changed his mind? Sometimes, engagements ended... Going back on his word would certainly be a disgrace to Darcy, but he was rich enough to eventually be forgiven.

"Don't worry," he had told her. And yet, the young woman could not help feeling anxious.

She was roused from her unpleasant thoughts by her older sister.

"Oh, there you are!" Jane cried out. "The trunks have arrived. Hill will bring them here in a moment. The two large ones are for you, the smaller one is mine. Netherfield is not so far so I shall make several trips."

Jane opened the wardrobe inspecting the clothes stored in it while she talked.

"I will ask Betty to wash the shifts that we gave her. It is not laundry day, but we may make an exception. There are also a few pairs of shoes that were left in the antechamber. And Mamma said that we could take anything we fancied in the house. I have always been fond of the little porcelain shepherdess – you know, the one in her parlour? I always wanted to play with it when we were young, do you remember? I shall ask her if she will let me have it. Charles told me that I will have my own parlour once we are settled, so I may keep it there. How about you? Is there anything in particular that you want? Apart from books, of course!"

She then noticed that her sister was not listening.

"Lizzy? You do not look well. Is everything alright?" she asked. "Ah... he has not written, has he?"

Elizabeth nodded.

"I miss him," she replied, looking forlorn. "I can no longer bear this engagement. It makes no sense to spend it without him."

"My dear..." her sister murmured, sitting down next to her and hugging her.

"I am so impatient for him to return, Jane. There are days when I fear I shall never see him again and it terrifies me!"

"Don't be ridiculous. You know he will be back in just a few days. The wedding is on Friday! All this will soon pass, you will see... Do you want to start packing your trunks? It will keep your mind occupied."

Elizabeth was about to point out that Darcy had only written once since his departure, which was a bad sign. In all likelihood, his friends in London had brought him to his senses. However, she pressed her lips together and fell silent. There were certain things she could not share with her older sister.

Gentle, loving, and kind, Jane had unshakeable trust in human nature and in the future, which sometimes made her a little unaware of what was truly happening around her. Filled to the brim with joy for her upcoming wedding, she did not realise that the anxieties Elizabeth now had were acutely similar to those she had herself endured last year, when Charles Bingley had suddenly departed Netherfield without warning. The distance had proven fatal to their budding romance. Far from Jane, Bingley's feelings, although sincere, had not been able to resist the pressure exerted by his sisters and Darcy, who had convinced him to forget all about his beloved. Moreover, he would never have returned to her if Darcy had not intervened again to rectify the situation.

It was easier for the innocent Jane to believe in a misunderstanding rather than to admit that her suitor had given up, and this was why she was unable to take Elizabeth's concerns seriously. Darcy had declared his love so why fear a change of heart? With the wedding quickly approaching surely nothing unfortunate could happen.

And so, Elizabeth kept her fears to herself.

~

Mrs. Philips and the residents of Lucas Lodge came to admire and to swoon over the blue silk taffeta dress. Talk of it had even echoed all the way to the Meryton market. Shortly thereafter, Elizabeth's dress was also delivered.

The dressmaker made a few personal calls to Longbourn for the various fittings – a privilege she only granted to her best customers. The Bennet girls were, of course, not used to such preferential treatment, and could hardly conceal their excitement at each visit, crying out and clapping their hands in childlike delight. Although the dressmaker spoke to them with a civility she usually reserved for her most dignified clients, the Bennet girls were not in the habit of giving themselves airs and graces. How could they enjoy themselves if they had to imitate the jaded affectations of rich Londoners? Elizabeth had scoffed at Caroline and Louisa's beautiful clothes and their haughtiness far too often to emulate them. She had no intention of trading her joy for pretentiousness.

However, when she tried her dress on for the final time so the dressmaker could verify that nothing was amiss, the young woman remained strangely silent as she stared at herself in the mirror.

She was enchanted by what she saw.

The dress was stitched with the green percale that she had chosen. It was overlaid with immaculate tulle, soft and fine, on which delicate embroidery had been sewn here and there in silver thread. A square neckline displayed her neck and the sleeves were puffed at her shoulders and fell down over the tops of her hands, stitched with silvery patterns. The dressmaker had seen to it that they could be removed so that the dress could easily become a ball gown if desired. On the front, the bodice was made of small, complicated folds where the tulle and the percale played with one another to produce an almost transparent effect. In the centre under the chest, embroidered in silver, the overlay parted in two to reveal the pale green dress underneath which fell, without a crease, to the ground. On her back, between her shoulder blades, more folds wove the tulle and the percale together to create a short train. The dress was complimented by a lovely white straw bonnet, the inside of which was lined with the same pale green material, that knotted under her chin with a long ribbon. There were also satin shoes Elizabeth could have only dreamt of owning even a short while ago.

As with Jane's dress, the dressmaker had exceeded herself. The lines were meticulous and perfectly adjusted. The ensemble conveyed an impression of delicacy and sobriety as well as obvious luxury.

Mrs. Bennet herself was speechless when she saw her daughter, while Jane and Kitty clapped their hands together in excitement. Mary, who had also pushed open the drawing-room door to see what was happening, was the first to react.

"You look really beautiful, Lizzy. How lucky you are," she acknowledged, with a hint of envy.

Elizabeth, touched by Mary's uncharacteristic tone of admiration, embraced her. Then, when the others continued with a steady shower of compliments, she blushed a little.

"You are truly breathtaking, my dear!" her mother uttered. "Don't you agree that your sister is lovely, girls? Look at her! A real duchess!"

Not used to being referred to as beautiful nor lovely by anyone, let alone her mother, who usually reserved such praises for her eldest daughter, Elizabeth looked at Jane for a verdict she could rely on. It became clear that her sister also approved.

The young woman looked at her reflection once again and smiled to herself.

For once, she felt as beautiful as Jane.

~

The next day, while the two sisters returned from Meryton where they had eaten with their aunt, they were surprised to see a familiar silhouette among the children playing on the lawn in front of Lucas Lodge.

"It's Charlotte!"

They quickened their pace and were greeted with effusion by the young Mrs. Collins and her sister Maria.

"My friends, you could not have arrived at a better time!" Charlotte cried out. "I was just telling Maria that I wanted to visit Longbourn today."

"When did you arrive? You never sent a letter to let us know you were visiting!" said Elizabeth.

"Indeed, Mr. Collins and I made the decision rather swiftly and would most likely have arrived before the post."

"Are you staying for the wedding?" asked Jane.

"Of course! Is it not going to be the event of the year? I would not miss it for the world!"

As the Bennet sisters had just finished eating, they declined the tea that was offered inside. Maria volunteered to look after the children whilst her sister enjoyed their company. The three friends headed out to the garden where they could talk in peace.

"Was Mr. Collins able to take leave from his parish without too much trouble?" Elizabeth asked, politely. "I seem to recall that when he last came to Longbourn this matter was most distressing for him."

"Poor William is always so anxious to do well, but he often just makes a fuss out of nothing," explained Charlotte. "In fact, Lady Catherine does not oppose it as long as the church services continue as planned. He called upon the town pastor to replace him in Hunsford, and as long as he does not abuse this favour, it works rather well. Although, I must confess, I had to put up a bit of a fight to convince him to come to Lucas Lodge."

"Will you be staying long?" asked Jane.

"Three weeks at least. Perhaps a month."

"That long! You must have led quite a campaign to convince him!" Elizabeth joked.

"Not as much as you might think, Lizzy," her friend responded. "I had the advantage of a strong argument."

Charlotte deliberately let her words hang, delighting in the confused looks her visitors gave her.

"Whatever do you mean?" asked Jane.

"What argument?" added her sister.

Charlotte did not answer immediately, instead heading to a small bench. She invited them to sit down next to her. Then, in a secretive tone, she finally revealed:

"I must inform you that there will soon be a third Collins at Hunsford..."

And while Elizabeth's eyes widened, Jane, who did not understand, asked in earnest:

"Which Collins?"

"Jane, I am with child," explained Charlotte patiently with a smile.

"Good heavens!"

"We are expecting the baby in May. Oh, my dear friends, if only you knew how happy I am!" she continued, bursting with joy. "It happened so fast! Some days I can scarcely believe it but it is starting to become more visible and it will soon be very obvious to everyone – including myself!"

Elizabeth was less astonished by this news than her sister. Both offered their congratulations to the future mother and, for quite a while, all wedding talk was cast aside in favour of the upcoming birth.

"Mr. Collins is highly pleased, as you might have guessed," said Charlotte. "I have never seen him so happy! He wants to refurbish the entire house and I am doing my utmost to convince him that arranging the nursery upstairs is enough for now. He also wants to hire an additional servant to help me."

"How kind of him to worry about your well-being, Charlotte," said Elizabeth.

"It is! I know he is not always very refined, but he has a good heart. I could not have found a better husband!"

Elizabeth refrained from commenting. Even in jest, it would have been inconsiderate.

At that moment, Maria hurried towards the three young women, pulling one of the boys by the hand. Having fallen, he hobbled and cried behind her. In the absence of Lady Lucas, she turned to her sister for help.

"Poor dear!" Jane cried out, seeing them approach. "No, do not move Charlotte. In your state you should rest. It looks like nothing more than a scraped knee. I shall tend to it."

Mrs. Collins thanked Jane and called after Maria, asking her to show the eldest Bennet where the cloths were so she could clean the wound. The two friends then continued their conversation.

"Soon it will be your turn to look after scraped knees, my dear," Elizabeth told her, smiling warmly. "Should I wish you to have as many children as your mother?"

"I shall have as many as the Lord is willing to bless us with. Mr. Collins is certainly in favour of having a large family."

"Leading by example, as usual."

Elizabeth immediately bit her lip. The comment had escaped her, but she did not want to laugh at Charlotte. She gave her friend an apologetic look.

"I know what you think of him, Lizzy," replied Charlotte without taking offense. "I also know that he would likely have been a terrible husband for you. You are far too spirited to tolerate someone so staid. But he suits me. I disregard the small annoyances and, instead, concentrate on the good things he brings me."

"This is why you are wiser than I, Charlotte, and have always been so. Your ability to always see the good side of things is a great strength."

"Indeed, I am satisfied with what the good Lord has given me. That said, I must confess that I am most excited at the prospect of having a small child whom I can dote upon..."

The two women spoke enthusiastically of the joy it was to look after children. It was clear that Charlotte, committed to a stable yet loveless marriage, would bestow all her affection upon her progeny. As she listened, Elizabeth had a strange premonition that, instead of uniting the Collins, the arrival of children would further alienate them from one another. Charlotte, who was too sharp for her husband, would keep him at arm's length in order to devote herself entirely to her children.

A rather dull life from Elizabeth's perspective, but to her friend, it seemed marvellous. After all, Charlotte had dreaded spending her life alone for so long that she rejoiced more than ever at having escaped that fate. Married and soon to be a mother, she had found her place.

"How is he by the way, your Mr. Darcy?" asked Charlotte.

Elizabeth was startled back into reality. The conversation had shifted.

"Fine," she replied. "He is in town at the moment, finishing the final preparations."

"You wrote in one of your letters that Lady Catherine was categorically opposed to the wedding. You must be happy that your fiancé ignored her instructions."

"Yes, I am actually still surprised! You know better than I do that one does not defy Lady Catherine so easily," replied Elizabeth with a nervous chuckle, trying to ignore the apprehensions that resurfaced.

"It is true... In fact, I will not deny that it is one of the reasons why I wanted to spend some time here. I would prefer that Mr. Collins and myself stayed out of sight until the storm passes."

"Oh, Charlotte, I am so sorry!" Elizabeth said, apologetically. "I hope my situation will not cause you any problems and that I may still come visit you in Hunsford occasionally!"

"Time heals all wounds, Lizzy. Lady Catherine's indignance will eventually subside and everything will fall into place, I am convinced of it..."

Once more, Elizabeth admired her friend's ability to take everything in her stride, with great philosophy. While they spoke, Charlotte had let her hand fall to her belly and the former sensed that all her wishes converged in her unborn child.

The rest of the world could readily fall apart around her, but in this moment, Charlotte was getting ready to experience unbridled happiness.

~

Finally, Darcy wrote again.

Elizabeth was both relieved by the contents of the letter and deeply disappointed that it was not longer. Writing concisely and paying less attention to his words than usual, Darcy informed her that he would be returning to Netherfield the next day as planned, and that he would be accompanied by Mr. and Mrs. Hurst, as well as Colonel Fitzwilliam. He had asked Bingley to invite the Bennets for tea so that everyone could convene. A more formal invitation would no doubt arrive soon, if it had not done so already.

Apart from the appropriate civilities expressing his eagerness to see her again, there was nothing else.

36

Puzzled, she read the letter over a few more times, searching for any hidden meaning between the lines. She found nothing. Darcy's writing was clear, efficient and contained no embellishments of any kind.

Jane, reading the letter when her sister handed it to her, found nothing to give alarm.

"Just imagine! He is in London and must make travel plans for people who live at different ends of the city. Poor soul, he must not have a minute to himself! You should be pleased that he found some time to write to you."

"Really? I'm not sure. His first letter was much warmer."

"Your fiancé is a pragmatic man who has always adapted to his circumstances. He must have come to the conclusion that a shorter message would suffice, considering that you are to see each other tomorrow. He knows that he will have ample time to show you just how much he loves and thinks about you," Jane reassured her.

"I suppose you are right..."

"Charles says that Darcy is very organised and that when his mind is set, everything goes off without a hitch."

"Which is not the case for Charles," replied Elizabeth amused, pushing her concerns aside. "Your Bingley is not renowned for being the most meticulous of men!"

"And it suits me perfectly, as I love him for his spontaneity," Jane retorted, undaunted. "In the meantime, it appears that it is you who needs to be better prepared. Have you not yet finished packing your trunks?"

Sufficiently chastened, Elizabeth eventually put the letter away and went back to work.

~

That night, lying in the bed they had shared since childhood, the two sisters spoke at length and fell asleep late. Aware that these were their last moments together, they were overcome with nostalgia: their childhood games, Elizabeth's night time escapades to see the fox cubs under the barn, swimming with their sisters in the pond, the imaginary ghosts in the house which had terrified them for so long, their trip to the seaside, the many young men who had gravitated towards Jane without her ever taking any notice, the sprain Elizabeth had suffered when she had gone running in a field which had left her limping for a month, the unforgettable fireworks in Meryton celebrating the turn of the century, their father's particular sense of humour, their mother's silliness, sometimes upsetting but often amusing, Christmas celebrations with their little cousins...

They also looked to the future and spoke of the new life that awaited them. Their concerns were similar. First, they wondered how they would take on the management of their new and eminently larger households, and secondly, they reflected upon the intimacy that they would soon share with their respective husbands. They often compared the two men, both in looks and temperaments, describing what they liked in one or the other. In hushed tones and in the strictest of confidences, they revealed the amorous moments they had shared thus far. Jane, ever trusting, approached it all with great serenity, relying on Bingley to take care of everything. Elizabeth, on the other hand, felt her emotions vibrating within her and she wanted nothing more than to fall into Darcy's arms, whether it was deemed proper or not. It made her seem mad to Jane but both of them laughed a great deal at the thought.

"I must say, you were singing a different tune when you spoke about that boy who kissed you at the Meryton ball two or three years ago," Jane reminded her, mischievously.

"Oh, do not speak of him! What awful memories!"

"If I remember correctly, he was rather pleasant..."

"Then you are a better judge than I. I don't even remember what he looks like!" retorted Elizabeth. "However, I do remember that he smelled strongly of port and was abrupt in his manner. What a scoundrel!"

"Indeed! And after that you judged all men to be utterly foul!"

Elizabeth laughed heartily at the recollection. A young man had indeed kissed her in a corridor of the Meryton hall, during a public ball. It had been her first kiss, but she had not enjoyed the experience in the slightest. The boy, a seasonal harvest worker with whom she had danced a few times and found quite charming, had revealed himself to be rather boorish after a few drinks. He had not really asked for her consent before kissing her and had felt entitled enough to let his hands roam where they were definitely not welcome. She had put up a struggle before the young man finally left her alone.

That incident had nothing in common with what she had discovered in Darcy's arms, tucked out of sight in the small music room. She found his embrace so pleasant and exciting that she wondered what their first night together would be like.

"Only three more days, Jane, can you believe it..."

Jane, who was not thinking about their wedding night, thought she was referring to the actual wedding.

"Charles tells me that everything is just about ready. Tomorrow we may not enter Netherfield's dining room, lest we ruin the surprise. Apparently everything is beautifully decorated. In the absence of his sisters, he relies entirely on his housekeeper to run the house and has said that she is excellent."

Elizabeth laughed heartily.

"How fortunate that Caroline is not here to take the lead! Last year she did not want a ball, imagine her reaction to a wedding, especially ours."

"Poor thing... She certainly would have preferred to stay in London."

"Jane! What are you saying? Are you finally growing cautious of your future sister-in-law?" teased Elizabeth.

Jane blushed and immediately defended herself:

"Caroline has always shown me kindness – and Louisa too. It would be petty of me to speak ill of them for no reason!"

"Be that as it may, it is my hope that they behave appropriately at their brother's wedding and that they will be excellent sisters to you. And if it isn't so, I assure you that I shall make them toe the line by any means necessary!" Elizabeth cried out, laughingly threatening.

Then, seeing that her sister wanted to add something:

"Yes? What did you want to say?"

Jane fidgeted under the sheets. She was never comfortable when she had to announce something that might prove harmful to someone.

"Well, Charles read me one of the letters that she sent him. It was shortly after he informed her that you and Darcy were also engaged."

Elizabeth tensed slightly, her eyes suddenly wide with curiosity.

"And what did she say?"

"Charles only read me a portion. Caroline implied that Darcy could have opened his eyes sooner and realised that he would have had no difficulty finding the perfect wife in his own circles. There was no need to mingle with rustic provincial society."

"'Rustic provincial society'... That does sound like our dear Miss Bingley, indeed."

"She is not as disagreeable as you believe, Lizzy. I think that she is just miserable to see the man she desired so, slip through her fingers."

"What can I say? Men are often too slow-witted to see the ways in which some women attempt to draw them in."

"I am sorry but I can hardly imagine Darcy being slow-witted," Jane objected. "On the contrary, he must have been very aware of the fact that his fortune would attract all the young women around him. You truly are the only one to have scorned him!"

"It is entirely his fault!" Elizabeth defended herself. "He scorned me first!"

The two women laughed.

"It is true that he was not particularly adroit, but neither were you," Jane continued. "Thank God you were both astute enough to recognise your errors. But imagine how poor Caroline must feel, cast aside after having nurtured so much hope..."

"She must certainly be miserable and jealous, but she is not foolish," Elizabeth answered, feeling very little compassion for the lady in question. "She has a significant dowry and is also very pretty. She should be able to acknowledge that a little more restraint on her part would go a long way towards making her even more appealing. It would multiply her prospects from the most promising parties."

Exchanging a knowing look with her sister she then added, "Thank heavens she will now have your example to follow. Both your kindness and your beauty have placed the entire county at your feet, well before Bingley fell under your spell!"

~

As they left the table that morning, Mary and Kitty quarrelled over a misplaced music book. The incident quickly escalated to cries and wails. The house was turned upside down while Kitty maintained that she had not touched a thing and Mary earnestly swore that she would never lend her sister a single one of her possessions again.

Over the last few weeks, the two younger sisters had observed their older siblings preparing to leave the house with growing apprehension. The prospect of finding themselves alone in the family home had increased tensions. Kitty was particularly affected: after losing Lydia, her constant companion, she would be losing both Jane and Elizabeth and left with the tedious Mary with whom she had little in common.

And so there were tears. They raced up and down staircases, flung things about, and slammed doors. Once the book was found, however, a relative calm was restored.

Mr. Bennet had long since disappeared into his library so as not to take part in a domestic quarrel that never failed to annoy him. As for Mrs. Bennet, after participating quite thoroughly in the commotion, she withdrew to her room, claiming she had a headache. Mary returned to her music and Jane, to distract Kitty, who was still outraged that she had been falsely accused, went with her to visit the Lucases.

Finally finding peace, Elizabeth settled down in the drawing-room. The young woman was in a fine mood: today marked the day that Darcy would be returning to Netherfield. Bingley had, as agreed, invited the Bennets to join them for tea that afternoon. In the meantime, as there were still a few long hours left with which to occupy herself, she brought out her writing box to draft a response to Mrs. Gardiner's latest letter.

Since the engagement had been announced, aunt and niece had kept up a regular correspondence. Margaret Gardiner confessed that she felt partly responsible for Darcy and Elizabeth's happy romance, for it was she who had insisted on visiting Lambton and Pemberley the previous summer, enabling the two young people to reunite. She greatly rejoiced in the upcoming marriage. First and foremost because she loved her niece and wished her all the happiness in the world, and also because it would be an opportunity for her to visit them in Derbyshire, a place full of charming memories that she treasured fondly.

In reply, Elizabeth assured her once more that the Gardiners would always be welcome at Pemberley and that she would be most happy to receive advice about the region. She added that even though she was settling down in an unfamiliar place, far from Hertfordshire, she was incredibly lucky, thanks to her aunt, to have a relation there: a friend of Mrs. Gardiner's who still lived in Lambton and whom Elizabeth had already met twice during their stay there. The young woman promised to call upon this relation as soon as she had settled down in Pemberley. In the meantime, she prayed that her aunt kindly convey her salutations. Lastly, she explained that she would be in London for a fortnight and hoped to receive them at the earliest opportunity so as to reciprocate the generosity they had shown her. She also wished to have them at her side in Pemberley for Christmas so they could celebrate together as a family.

Elizabeth was interrupted by a noise in the house. Jane and Kitty had returned from their visit. She listened closely: amidst her sisters' voices she suddenly recognised a much lower voice.

She leapt up, rushed to the door and flung it open, only to find herself face to face with Darcy. The young man, a smile on his lips, had not yet removed his coat and held his hat in his hand.

Behind him, Jane was cheerful, "Lizzy, look who we met along the way!"

"Pardon the intrusion, Miss Elizabeth, I know you were not expecting me..." began Darcy, bowing slightly.

Elizabeth stifled a cry of joy, not believing her eyes. She forgot all propriety and flew into his arms.

He was finally back! He was here! He was hers! For a moment she thought of nothing else, letting the intense emotions and sensations wash over her. The damp overcoat, the wool coat underneath, the warmth of his neck, the feeling of his arms embracing her, the scent of rain, horses, and dead leaves, which clung to him – all of it left her elated.

She was unable to find her words. When she met his eyes again, she could only burst out in nervous laughter.

"It is a pleasure to see you again, Lizzy. I see you are doing well," he whispered, visibly enchanted by his fiancée's reaction.

"Much better now," she replied, unable to weaken her embrace. "You are here! I thought I would not see you for hours still!"

"I could not resist the urge to come find you as soon as possible. When I arrived at Netherfield earlier, I stayed only long enough for my horse to be saddled."

Above them, Mrs. Bennet realised that an unexpected guest had arrived and she was in a state of agitation in her room.

"Jane? Girls? What is happening?" she called out.

"Nothing, mamma!" Jane shouted from the stairs. "It is Mr. Darcy who has come to greet Lizzy!"

In a minute there would be a fuss, compelling the young couple to join the rest of the household for the usual civilities. Knowing she would soon lose the comforting sensation of her fiancé's arms around her waist, Elizabeth was overcome by a sudden sense of urgency. She rose on her toes and placed a kiss on his lips, which he immediately returned after just a fleeting moment of surprise.

"Oh!"

Kitty, who had been giggling whilst observing the reunion, was stunned by her older sister's audacity.

"Leave them be!" Jane whispered, pulling her away to give the couple some intimacy.

They heard the girls climb up the stairs to speak in hushed tones with Mrs. Bennet.

Darcy, who still held his hat, showed no intention of ending their embrace. Elizabeth lowered her eyes, flustered. Little by little, she regained her senses and suddenly found it peculiar, and rather exciting, to be thus embraced in the passage.

"Perhaps we should go into the drawing-room," she whispered.

"Give your mother some time to come downstairs, there is no sense in pressing her..." Darcy replied, with a smile.

He kissed her again.

In the hour that followed, Jane revealed herself to be a godsend to the young couple. She managed to convince Mrs. Bennet to stay in her room in order to tend to her headache, sent Kitty and Mary about their business, and ordered sandwiches and tea for Darcy who had not yet had time to eat. While he wolfed down the contents of his plate on a hastily prepared corner of the table, she engaged him in conversation.

The young man quickly recovered his manners. He enquired after the family's health, asked if the trunks were ready, and whether the ladies were satisfied with the dresses they had received. Elizabeth was at his side, mumbling a few words here and there, too busy taking him in.

Now that he was back, she felt as though he had never left. The infrequent and impersonal letters, the never-ending days, the fears and doubts that had tortured her, all of it had disappeared in the blink of an eye. Once again, she soaked in his voice, his gaze, his presence, the gentle smile he had when he looked at her. He was there, next to her, and that was enough.

~

The day had long since fallen into night, but tea continued, much to Caroline Bingley's displeasure. She had tried to communicate with her brother several times, attempting to convey that it was time to send the guests home, but to no avail.

In the drawing-room at Netherfield, the Bingleys and the Bennets socialised, although some did so more than others. Caroline and the Hursts hid their disdain rather poorly behind rigid smiles and trite formalities, and avoided addressing the Bennets as much as possible – except for Jane, who was the only one to have found favour in their eyes. Conversely, Charles, along with Jane who always followed his example, worked hard to foster unity and spread cheer.

Between the two families, representing the Darcys, was Colonel Fitzwilliam who had come to attend his cousin's wedding. Elizabeth, who really appreciated his company, had been even more delighted to see him when she saw how genuinely happy he was to see her again. With the arrival of the Bennets and the general commotion that followed, he had only been able to greet her and congratulate her formally. It was only later, once the guests were dispersed in the drawing-room, that he was able to approach her privately.

"Miss Elizabeth, allow me to tell you once again how delighted I am that you shall soon be joining the family. When my cousin told me that he planned to marry, I was extremely surprised. But when he informed me that you were the chosen lady, I was less so. You are, beyond a doubt, the only woman capable of making him give up his single state."

"Upon my word! You give me far too much credit, Colonel," Elizabeth laughed, flattered nonetheless.

"No, I do not think so. I would never have dared to ask, of course, but I did notice the looks he gave you," the young man continued. "I don't believe that I overstate anything when I say that he had you in mind for quite some time."

Caroline, who was passing by, could not help cutting in.

"It must be that the air here in Hertfordshire makes young people giddy," she said, with biting pleasantry. "Beware, Mr. Bachelor, lest you find yourself engaged to one of the Bennet girls. There are two left, if I am not mistaken…"

Colonel Fitzwilliam, obviously accustomed to the young woman's sharp remarks, refrained from responding and only greeted her pleasantly, which forced her to greet him in turn and continue on.

"You will encounter much jealousy," he continued as they were alone once more, "but your detractors will quickly fall silent."

"I wish I could be so sure," sighed Elizabeth. "Unfortunately, I am well aware that for many, this wedding is not... shall we say... satisfactory."

As the colonel began to protest, she continued with the utmost sincerity:

"I am sorry, Colonel, but I am not one to shy away from unpleasant matters. Mr. Darcy reassures me as much as possible but I know that we are exposing ourselves to some difficulty. Incidentally, you are the only one in your family who has shown me friendship, and I am very grateful to you."

Fitzwilliam was silent for a moment.

"I am not sure what my cousin has told you regarding his visit to Rosings," he continued, and then lowered his voice until he was almost whispering, "but I am certain that with time, things will calm down. Words were uttered, to be sure, and Darcy will no doubt have to make an apology, but my aunt is not as stubborn as you might think. I am convinced that a reconciliation is still possible."

Upon hearing this, Elizabeth froze. Her cheeks reddened.

"What visit, Colonel?"

"The one we just made, of course."

The Colonel paused. He understood now that he had just committed a faux pas.

"Forgive me, Miss Elizabeth, I thought... I was under the impression..." he stammered awkwardly. "I mean... Did Darcy not tell you?"

"Indeed, he did not. He was at Rosings?"

"Two days ago, yes. Which is why I am here today. I was at Rosings myself these last few weeks and I then accompanied him here."

"I thought you were in London, with the others."

There was another silence. Embarrassed, Colonel Fitzwilliam searched for a way out of the situation. He threw several glances at his cousin who conversed with Mr. Bennet and Mr. Hurst on the other side of the room. Darcy, meeting his gaze, immediately understood that he had been exposed.

Meanwhile, Elizabeth sought to keep up appearances. She took on a reassuring tone and said:

"Don't worry, my friend, I shall speak of all this to Mr. Darcy in person. If there was any conflict, believe me, I shall ensure that it is rectified as soon as possible."

She curtsied lightly and was even able to give him a smile. But deep down, she barely contained the anger and apprehension that washed over her. She sat next to her mother, knowing that her incessant chatter would distract her thoughts. As for her fiancé, he watched her closely, but she made a fine show of ignoring him.

~

On the eve of the wedding, the Netherfield party paid a visit to the Longbourn ladies and they all headed out for a final walk.

Colonel Fitzwilliam accompanied Darcy and Bingley. In order to give the couples some room, he took it upon himself to distract Mary and Kitty, soliciting their help to discover the region, as he was not familiar with it. And so, they headed to a tiny chapel not too far away, where they placed small bouquets of flowers they had picked along the way. They then headed towards a forest path that led to the top of a hill.

Darcy walked alongside his future wife, his face tight. With a certain amount of bitterness he noted that the intimacy they had managed to establish in recent weeks had faded. Although Elizabeth kept up appearances and was as cheerful and lively as ever with their companions, she remained fairly impervious to his graces and small gestures. She had taken on a cool demeanour that was new to him and he felt somewhat undone. Everything about her behaviour defied him to explain himself. 'Well? I'm waiting!' she seemed to say with every step.

He had sought to speak to the young woman the previous evening, having seen Colonel Fitzwilliam grow pale at his exchange with

Elizabeth and understanding that his secret had been uncovered. But she did not leave her mother's side. Since she stubbornly refused to meet his gaze and he had also met Caroline and Louisa's inquisitive glances, he eventually refrained from making any comment. Then, tea had ended and the Bennet family had returned to Longbourn, leaving him without the opportunity to explain himself privately.

His opportunity came at last when they reached the top of the hill and admired the landscape, which was unfortunately cloaked in a dense mist. The ladies sat on a fallen tree trunk to catch their breath but as there was nothing much to see, the little party quickly prepared to go back down.

"Miss Elizabeth's ankle hurts a bit," Darcy announced. "Go ahead, we will join you."

Everyone, apart from Kitty, understood that he sought a moment of privacy, and left them behind without asking further questions.

When the last silhouette had disappeared behind the bushes, Darcy also sat down on the tree trunk. Next to him, Elizabeth, who was hot from the climb, removed her hat slowly, indicating that she expected to have a long conversation and that she was on the defensive.

The young man took the plunge.

"Please forgive me, Lizzy. I only sought to protect you by not telling you where I was going."

"You were supposed to go to town on business," she replied calmly, setting her bonnet on her lap.

"I did, to prepare the house. I suppose I could have done it in two or three days, but I had actually received a letter from my aunt summoning me at once to Rosings."

"Why? Was she not previously aware of our engagement?"

"Of course. As you know, she was one of the first people I informed. She had already sent me an initial response. But I suppose you were right: the publication of the banns made things more tangible. In a last attempt to change my mind she summoned me to her. She wished to speak with me in person."

He clenched his teeth for a moment in an attempt to banish the memory.

"Lord knows I am too old to be lectured at like a little boy, yet that was to be my fate when I arrived," he grumbled darkly.

Elizabeth fiddled with the ribbons on her hat.

"Colonel Fitzwilliam told me yesterday that you exchanged words with her? Were they... harsh?" she asked.

Darcy sighed. He would have preferred his cousin to have held his tongue on the subject.

"Indeed," he admitted. "Truth be told, she was insulting and I responded in kind."

As Elizabeth's eyes widened in alarm, he took her hand and squeezed it comfortingly before continuing:

"Please understand, Lizzy. Despite the respect I possess for my aunt, I could not overlook her comments about you. So, I left Rosings at once, stating that she would only be invited to Pemberley once she respected you as my wife. As of now, I am determined not to ask after her until she has accepted my decision."

"How awful!" Elizabeth cried out, mortified.

"It is not as bad as you think," said the young man, trying to temper the situation, "but I had to draw limits somewhere, or else my aunt and a few others would be tempted to believe that they are entitled to meddle in our lives. Which is not the case."

"And how did Miss de Bourgh react?"

"Anne? What could the poor child say?"

"Was she not terribly disappointed, since she was destined to be yours?"

Darcy gave a small, sardonic laugh.

Although Anne de Bourgh was almost his age, she was so frail that he still considered her to be a young girl. Insipid and living in her mother's shadow, she was incapable of speaking for herself, to the point that Darcy could not remember ever having engaged her in a conversation worthy of interest. What a wonderful wife she would have been for him, indeed!

"It was not my idea and certainly not hers either," he answered. "Our mothers had their ambitions, but I like to believe that I am the master of my own destiny."

To help ease the tension and calm the anxiety he could still see in Elizabeth's eyes, he continued in a tone of jest:

"Or at least I will be until tonight, for tomorrow I shall be entirely at your mercy..."

It did not have the desired effect. His fiancée only winced.

After a moment of silence where she seemed to collect her thoughts, she turned towards him and looked at him directly.

"Mr. Darcy," she began, "I once reproached you for having an unfortunate opinion about my origins. An opinion that, at the time, was far from courteous, although perfectly true. Indeed, I have never frequented the same circles as you, I have no fortune, no connections, nor anything that might serve your interests or embellish Pemberley. Even though she proved injurious, your aunt is merely expressing all the things that society will think when they see me at your side."

Darcy tried to interrupt but she silenced him with a gesture.

"I did not choose my situation any more than you did. I do what I can to limit the appalling damage that my mother is capable of causing, along with my aunt Philips or, worse, poor Lydia, whose behaviour is quite disgraceful. I understand our situation clearly. I know that I bring a fair share of embarrassments with me that you certainly did not wish for, least of all deserve. And I apologise, sincerely. But I promise you, I will do everything in my power to remain exemplary so that you will never, ever be ashamed of me."

Her voice trembled slightly as she finished her sentence.

"So, I beg of you," she concluded, pleading, "will you please write to your aunt and apologise? You should not have troubled relations with your family because of me..."

Darcy was momentarily taken aback. He had not expected such frankness, and Elizabeth's misgivings were moving. He would have liked to take her in his arms to reassure her, but he dared not. He merely squeezed her hand.

"Don't worry about the challenges that await us. It is true that we will face difficulties in the beginning, but I am here to take care of you," he answered gently. "We will live at Pemberley where we shall be at peace."

"But... your aunt?"

The young man tensed. All emotion disappeared from his features only to be replaced by a harsh expression indicating that he had reached his limits.

"Leave her be, Lizzy," he said in a brittle tone. "I shall only speak to her once she is prepared to accept you."

Elizabeth was silent. Seeing her harden in response to his attitude, Darcy reprimanded himself. He made an effort to calm down and stood in order to put an end to this painful conversation.

"We should head back. The others will be waiting."

Because she complied in silence, he pulled her against him and lightly kissed her temple. Only then did she smile at him, and they headed back down.

~

At Netherfield, once his valet had taken his leave, Darcy paced in his room for a long time. He had even lain in bed, unable to do anything except toss and turn in his sheets, eyes wide open. He eventually left his room in an attempt to take in the sleeping house's calm atmosphere. Without much thought, he let his footsteps guide him to the small music room where he had kissed Elizabeth for the first time. The place seemed appropriate.

It was not frequented often but its small size, single window, and drape-covered walls, made it so that it was not too cold despite the empty hearth. He set his candle down on a small table along with a glass of Madeira, which he had not yet touched, and sat down on the comfortable sofa.

The conversation that afternoon had left him feeling bittersweet.

On the one hand he was heartened to see that, once more, Elizabeth was not naive. She was firmly grounded and ready to face the criticisms that would inevitably come her way. It was not difficult for Darcy to imagine that there would be some disapproving eyes in London, and he suspected that they would not be much kinder in Derbyshire. He even had a clear idea of who they might belong to and was convinced that, eventually, these people would deliver small quips designed to hurt her deeply all while appearing insignificant. Elizabeth was indeed strong, and she would not let herself be defeated, but she would also be fairly isolated amongst people she did not know. He would be her only line of defence.

His social circle could be unfair. If things went wrong, Elizabeth was the one who would be ostracised and gossiped about. Darcy, protected by his family's prestige, had nothing to fear. He would merely be seen as having an unfortunate weakness, so excusable in a man, for the charms of a young lady. She, on the other hand, would be taken for a manipulator and a parvenue.

And yet... Did he not also have the right, like everyone else, to aspire to domestic happiness with a loving wife whose company he cherished? Was this incompatible with the status he had inherited, one he had hitherto never challenged?

He had followed conventions his entire life without knowing anything else. He had been raised in the strictest of ways, with moral principles he was proud of to-day, but they did not leave much room for fantasy and freedom. He had tried to free himself from the constraints that were imposed upon him, but he was always disciplined, at times rather harshly. Family honour always came first. And so, in order to meet expectations, he had learned to soften the edges and to curb his passions. With time, he had moulded himself to perfection into the role that was always demanded of him: a gentleman with impeccable manners.

While his mother's death had left him greatly distraught, his father's had resulted in a myriad of stifling responsibilities. Darcy found himself at the head of the family and master of a vast estate, which monopolised all his attention. The transition had not been easy. The change of status had also altered his relationships within his social circle. Suddenly, people sought to win his favour and he had lost count of the number of young, eligible ladies he had been presented. Since he was young, rich and single with no parents to watch his conduct, he had quickly become the ideal friend or fiancé.

Ladies, in particular, had always disappointed him. Some, quite beautiful, could have tempted him, but sooner or later he discovered their true natures: boring, obedient, resolved to making every effort to satisfy him while concealing their actual thoughts. In the face of such apathy and hypocrisy, the young man had reacted by hiding behind a certain aloofness. He had passively waited for fate to decide his future, in a slow stupor, dividing his time between London, Pemberley and sojourns with various friends. Not unhappy, but not very happy either.

And then he met Elizabeth. If at first he had not found her beautiful, she succeeded in capturing his attention by the way she spoke. Feisty, vivacious, brazen at times without ever being malicious, she had a pert smile and large dark eyes that sparkled with intelligence. For Darcy, she had been like a breath of fresh air. She shone in this tepid society with her liveliness and wit, which might on occasion have passed for impertinence, but which she applied lightly and skilfully, laughing at herself as much as others.

Darcy suddenly had an example of what he wished he had become, right under his nose. Indeed, she had called him out, jostled with him, and even shocked him at times. She knew how to provoke him, and would no doubt continue to do so in future. But he was realising that she had merely awakened that which had been dormant all these years. An appetite for life, which he thought he had lost, had suddenly been ignited again.

Life would be remarkably sweet alongside such a companion. He expected he would often be surprised, even completely destabilised. If he were honest with himself, he knew that he would probably not always enjoy having his habits disturbed. But in return, she brought him a liveliness he did not possess, an open-mindedness he greatly benefitted from, and, above all, a profound and sincere love, the likes of which he could not have dreamt of.

His father's advice urging him to always aim higher and never settling for his rank seemed so far away now! For while his mother, Lady Anne, had wished for a union between Pemberley and Rosings,

George Darcy had always wished for his son to marry a young lady of nobility, just as he had done.

"You are blessed, my son," he often told him. "Learn to use your assets and perhaps you shall be the first in the family to acquire a title!"

A title... A long-established hope kept alive by a man who wanted for nothing else. In his wildest dreams, the late Mr. Darcy had wished for nothing else than a seat in the House of Lords, the ultimate consecration that would crown the combined efforts of several generations in building a considerable fortune. An unattainable dream, of course, but one that had nevertheless motivated him his whole life.

However, the man had failed to pass his thirst for grandeur on to his son.

Darcy knew he formed part of an elite. Very young, he had been taught to distinguish himself from the people beneath him and to value the education he had received and the privilege of an enlightened mind that had resulted from it. Although he had also been taught to show kindness to the poor, the young man had developed a certain disdain for those who had not had access to the same education, and he was unable to recognise any great intelligence in people less privileged. With the exception of Elizabeth, who had charmed him with her vivacity. It was indeed for this reason that her unexpected response, declining his first proposal, had been so painful. Darcy could not comprehend how such an insightful young lady could refuse to rise up with him, both on a social and an intellectual level. Not only had she dared to reject him, but she had also treated him like a person of no great consequence. The humiliation he had felt had been bitter...

He was thus forced to call himself into question and had realised that while he did not have high regard for people beneath his rank, he also did not have much for those equal to or above him. He had loved his mother dearly because she had been a wonderful woman, full of insight and elegance, but that had little to do with the fact that she was the daughter of an earl. In comparison, her sister, despite receiving the same education, was extremely self-centred and behaved like a tyrant. Her insults against Elizabeth proved that regardless of her noble birth, Lady Catherine could behave like the most ill-mannered fishwife when sufficiently provoked. Their brother, the sitting earl, Fitzwilliam, was not much better. Darcy saw shine in neither him nor in his two eldest sons. For this reason, Darcy chose to socialise mainly with the Colonel, the only one in the family to possess genuine distinction in his eyes.

So, Darcy did not hold any real ambition to rise up in society, he found that his position was already lofty enough. He had only hoped to find an intelligent wife, who shared his values, and whom he admired enough to tolerate the occasional reprimand for his shortcomings. Now that he had found her, everything else – her birth, her non-existent dowry, even her awkward family – seemed incidental. After all, it was Elizabeth he was marrying, not the Longbourn estate.

People could entertain all the notions they wanted about this union. He knew that he prepared for his happiness to come. God would decide the rest.

Tomorrow was the wedding, then London and later, Pemberley.

For Darcy, life seemed to be opening up with bright possibilities.

~

His valet found him in the early hours of the morning, while the servants rushed to light the hearths and wake the household. Alarmed at not finding his master in his room, he had searched all the rooms on the floor, before heading downstairs. He searched several places without any luck before pushing open the door to the small music room.

The candle had long since died out and the glass of wine on the table was still full. Nestled in the sofa, Darcy was fast asleep.

CHAPTER 3

The wedding was celebrated on a Friday morning, in early November. The whole affair created quite a stir and, despite the freezing rain, many curious onlookers strolled past the church, just as the carriages from Netherfield and Longbourn arrived. Yet, if prying eyes had hoped to glimpse something remarkable, they were soon disappointed, for the wedding was celebrated privately by the families and remained quite conventional. Friends and honoured guests were invited to attend the wedding breakfast to be held at Netherfield after the service, so there was no crowd gathered in front of the church and therefore not much for the public to see.

The ceremony was longer than usual. Besides having two blessings to bestow instead of one, the rector of Meryton delivered his speech with meticulous care and it was only after an interminable sermon regarding the sanctity of marriage and the duties of a husband and wife, that the young couples were finally able to take their vows. Hearing Bingley, followed by Jane, her voice tense with emotion, Elizabeth could not help clasping her fiancé's hand tightly. Behind them, Mrs. Bennet began to cry, followed closely by Louisa Hurst, who, in spite of herself, was touched to see her brother so happy.

Then it was Darcy and Elizabeth's turn and both were affected in their own way. The young woman struggled to control the nervous laugh threatening to burst forth. As for her new husband, despite his efforts to maintain a solemn and dignified expression, his hands shook when he slid the ring on her finger. His eyes could not lie: deep down he was just as shaken as she was and he gave a sigh of relief once the ceremony was over.

The bell ringer had been handsomely paid and so the bells chimed heartily when the families left the church. As for the brides and grooms, they headed to the sacristy to sign the parish marriage register under the ceremonial gaze of the rector and his clerk, and Mr. Bennet and Colonel Fitzwilliam who were there to bear witness.

"... and this one is yours, Mrs. Darcy," said the rector, handing her a copy of the marriage certificate.

Elizabeth was momentarily dazed by two small details. The first was the 'Mrs. Darcy', which felt as unfamiliar as it was pleasant. The second was the certificate itself, which now proved that on this day in November, she had married Fitzwilliam Darcy, son of George Darcy and Lady Anne Darcy of Pemberley in Derbyshire, and that she could assert this status before God and man.

It was done. She was married.

Beside her, Jane was just as bewildered, turning the certificate she had received over in her hands, not quite knowing what to do with it. The two sisters finally slid the papers into their small reticules and everyone took their leave.

Outside the church, the rest of the family waited, engaged in cheerful conversation while the bells continued to ring. Thankfully, the morning's unpleasant weather had subsided and a small ray of light accompanied the applause that welcomed the four young people as they made their entry into the world as husbands and wives.

~

At eleven, Netherfield's butler promptly opened the doors to the dining room where a large, sumptuous table had been set.

There, in vast quantities, lay all the dishes needed for the perfect wedding breakfast: breads, scones, cakes with various fillings and an abundance of brioches, savoury pies, eggs served in a myriad of different ways, a giant glistening ham, tongue and other cold meats, exotically fragranced jams, puddings, honey tarts... All presented in a variety of silver and soft-paste china platters, complemented by overflowing fruit bowls, many of which seemed entirely unseasonable and had to have come from quite a distance. Also arranged here and there were baskets lined with freshly picked leaves and filled with delicate sugar flowers, along with candelabra decorated with ribbons, which had been lit to attenuate the gloom from outside. Arranged all around the table were plates and cups painted with colourful flowers or animals, with rims outlined in gold leaf matching the glint of the silver cutlery. In fact, the table was so laden with food that one could barely distinguish the tablecloth beneath it at all.

The drinks could be found at the back, on a long console flanked by a dozen footmen. Tea and coffee were ready to flow by the gallon, along with warm spiced milk and bitter chocolate. A few bottles of brandy were kept available to liven up the cups of those who desired it.

Finally, to crown the whole, an enormous, immaculately white wedding cake covered by a layer of sugar, was displayed in a corner of the room in such a manner that all could admire it.

The beautiful spread elicited a cry of delight from the guests. This feast promised to be memorable.

The newly married couples seated themselves at the centre of the table on four chairs decorated with ribbons. The forty or so guests then also took their places, their movements punctuated by the involvement of servants who ensured the comfort of all. Even Mr. Bennet, although quite impervious to such ostentatious displays, was impressed. Seated in front of his daughters and their husbands, he was about to start on a copiously laden plate when he leaned towards Charles and declared humorously:

"Well, son, I will admit that you know how to host a fine party indeed! What a pity that one only marries once, don't you think?"

His wife, seated nearby, her mouth already full of tart, retorted:

"Save your breath for the food, Mr. Bennet. I challenge you to taste every one of these dishes!"

The guests burst out laughing. Darcy surprisingly also laughed heartily along, which surprised his young wife.

"Come now Lizzy, do you really believe me incapable of appreciating your mother's remarks?" he whispered softly, eyes sparkling. "She does sometimes manage to deliver a witty turn of phrase, although I doubt she does it on purpose..."

Elizabeth chuckled and lovingly clasped her husband's arm. He even allowed himself to plant a furtive kiss on her neck, causing her to blush deeply as she crossed eyes with Mr. Collins who appeared rather piqued.

Within a short period of time, she felt all the knots in her stomach gradually loosen up, the agitation of the morning melting away the more she ate and drank her fill of exquisite foods and warm tea. She held a place of honour at the table along with her sister and with Darcy at her side who was much more at ease than usual, she felt wonderfully relaxed.

She could have dispensed with Caroline Bingley's affected smiles of course, along with the incessant nonsense her aunt Philips still managed to spout at every occasion. Thank heavens the latter was seated at the far end of the table and Elizabeth was able to ignore her quite easily. Apart from that, the young woman was delighted to spend this precious day surrounded only by those dearest to her.

The looks she met with above the decorated candelabra and high fruit bowls were happy and warm-hearted. Those who sat far from her and who were unable to converse with her directly, nodded and raised their tea or chocolate-filled cups mouthing their good wishes. Sir Lucas and Colonel Fitzwilliam were all kindness and affability, along with Charlotte, who wore such an expression of contentment that Elizabeth had rarely seen on her before. As for Jane, seated next to a euphoric Charles Bingley who laughed and spoke so loudly he appeared slightly inebriated, she radiated happiness and conversed in an ardent tone so unlike her, that it was a clear testament to the happiness she felt. She was a sight to behold.

Among the sea of delighted faces illuminated by the glow of candlelight, only a few were regrettably absent. Georgiana Darcy remained in Derbyshire, her brother finding the trip too long for such a short stay. Elizabeth would also have liked to have had the Gardiners present at her wedding but she found comfort in the fact that she would see them shortly in London. As for Lydia and Wickham, they did not turn up, much to the great relief of all.

A quartet of musicians had been summoned to entertain the gathering during the banquet, but there was such a din around the table that one could barely make out the music. There was much feasting, congratulating, exclaiming, laughing and animated exchanges about everything and nothing. The rector of Meryton, who had been invited to partake of the wedding breakfast following his performance, spun in his chair from the blessings he bestowed in all directions. From one end of the table to the other, people rejoiced over the excellent wedding and lavish spread.

"Lizzy? Would you like to taste the cake?" Darcy asked, lightly touching her hand to draw her attention.

"Pardon? Oh! Yes, of course, thank you..."

Immersed in her own thoughts, Elizabeth had not noticed the footman waiting nearby. He placed an enormous slice of wedding cake in front of her. Under the pristine layer of sugar, the aromas of candied fruit and rum brought her back to reality.

"Good Lord!" she exclaimed, amazed. "There is so much alcohol in this cake that it will keep for years! I wager that we shall still have some when we baptise our children!"

Darcy smiled in amusement. "Indeed, although, with the number of guests here today, we may succeed in eating a good portion of it."

"Do you think so? Look at them, it looks like they are all so full that no one will finish their plate."

"Your father has risen to the challenge and, as far as I can see, he is unwaveringly dedicated. As for Mr. Hurst, I believe he challenges only himself..."

Elizabeth laughed and leaned forward to observe Louisa's husband, seated a little further off. His self-indulgence was well known. He was an unremarkable man, without much wit, who spent the better part of his days waiting for his next meal. It was, however, the first time that she heard Darcy directly laughing at someone of his entourage. No doubt a result of their status as a married couple.

She gave her new husband a long, affectionate look.

"Mr. Darcy?"

"Yes, dearest?"

"I believe I love you."

Darcy, not expecting such a declaration, almost choked on the mouthful of cake. He looked at his bride. She wore a glowing smile on her face.

Darcy kept quiet in an effort not to ruin the charm of the moment. He swallowed his mouthful of cake, then, returning her smile, he took her hand and brought it to his lips, kissing it lovingly.

~

After such a hearty meal, the guests were called upon to proceed to the large drawing-room where chairs had been arranged to accommodate everyone.

A few people lingered at the table in order to glean one last treat, but most of the guests were relieved at the prospect of stretching their legs. Now free to move as they pleased, they went to enquire after one another, forming small groups according to their affinities. Several sat down to talk – or even doze –, others started a game of cards, while some of the men gathered in a corner to discuss politics.

The musicians were sent away as no one was inclined to do anything other than rest and digest their meal. They were, however, ordered not to leave the house immediately, in case the younger crowd decided to initiate a few dances. Meanwhile, Kitty, Mary and Maria Lucas sat at the pianoforte after receiving permission to play but were expressly forbidden to sing. The servants continued to come and go, serving digestives.

Leaving Darcy with a group of men, Elizabeth spent a moment with her mother who loudly requested that she describe the splendours of Pemberley in detail to her aunt Phillips, Lady Lucas, and the other women. Aware that it was an opportunity for her mother to shine amongst her neighbours, she consented with good grace and described what she had seen during her visit there in the summer. Her audience's dazzled exclamations left her slightly perplexed – she was still uncomfortable at the idea of boasting about the superiority of the Darcy's house –, but there was such pride in her mother's eyes that Elizabeth conceded and added humorous anecdotes to her story, leaving nothing out that might demonstrate the magnitude of the estate.

Then, leaving the ladies to freely comment on everything she had described, she slipped away to freshen up and take a moment for herself. This gathering, along with the laughter and celebration, was all a bit bewildering. The calm in the rest of the house made her feel better, if only for a few minutes.

She was retracing her steps when she met Charlotte, who was looking for her. The two friends had not seen each other since their last conversation in the garden at Lucas Lodge and happily lingered together in the passage. Elizabeth immediately asked how the baby was doing.

"He is doing very well, however I think he is protesting the lack of space now that I have eaten so much!" Charlotte replied in a cheerful tone. "But today is not about me. Let's talk about you, Lizzy: how does it feel to be married? Is it not exciting?"

"To tell you the truth, I am not entirely sure yet... I'm delighted to see that the celebration is so successful and that everyone is having so much fun. I don't believe I have ever seen Mr. Darcy smile so much! For my part, I feel as though I were living in a dream and I don't realise that tomorrow, my life will have changed."

"And in the most wonderful way! Your husband has reason to smile today. He is clearly besotted."

"Who could have foreseen such a thing a year ago?" said Elizabeth, laughing.

"Indeed! I watched you at the table earlier, and there is no doubt in my mind: you complete each other very well. You make an exemplary couple."

"Be that as it may, our dear Lizzy has yet to prove that she will measure up to Pemberley," Caroline Bingley interjected as she approached, her words falsely sweet.

Accompanied, as always, by her sister Louisa, Charles Bingley's youngest sister had shamelessly intruded upon a conversation that did not concern her. Elizabeth and Charlotte kept an air of composure and welcomed the two women with courteous resignation.

"The task won't be easy," Caroline continued, "heaven knows the estate is vast and very intimidating, wouldn't you agree, Louisa? Believe me, Mrs. Collins, compassion is what we should feel for the new bride."

"Compassion?" repeated Charlotte. "Goodness! What a Cassandra you are, Miss Bingley. I am quite certain Mrs. Darcy will be a remarkable mistress, whether it be at Pemberley or elsewhere."

"Don't be so sure, madam," insisted Caroline in a pedantic tone. "You don't know, as we do, the great prestige associated with this estate. Generation after generation of Darcys have built and expanded the lands over the years, you see, and I fear our friend has shown herself overly presumptuous in thinking she could so easily enter into such a family."

She then turned to Elizabeth.

"Don't underestimate the obstacles that await you, dear Lizzy," she added with an air of concern. "I would be most unhappy to see you distressed in your new life. One must have an excellent education, coupled with an unusually strong character, to properly manage such a property."

"I am not as convinced as you are about the disadvantages of leading a large house," the latter responded, undeterred. "Either way, I do not fear what awaits me for I shall be accompanied in this by my husband."

She hesitated a moment, debating whether it would be wise to openly attack Caroline, but the woman had been so offensive that Elizabeth felt no qualms responding in kind. So, before Miss Bingley could answer, she lowered her voice.

"I shall count on your guidance," she added conspiratorially, "for you have long kept house for your brother, have you not? And you will undoubtedly be looking for some occupation now that this role is to be filled by my own sister."

At these words, Charlotte and Louisa looked at one another, aghast. Caroline remained composed, a smile frozen on her face, but everyone felt her anger rising.

"You shall count on it, of course," she answered, "I would hate for you to find yourself at a disadvantage before your husband. Admittedly, we have known him for a very long time, and we know how firm and demanding he can be, do we not, Louisa?"

Elizabeth followed Colonel Fitzwilliam's example and said nothing further. The two women silently measured each other up before Caroline, who was incapable of holding her tongue, added coldly:

"I must admit, however, that you managed to enchant a handsome partner. You have ensured that your place in this world is more than comfortable. Most young women would not dream of it. Knowing your family, I admit that I am a little surprised that you could even lay claim to such a husband! But, as I was saying earlier to Louisa, I suppose it is in your nature to be this determined. I confess that I know not if I should congratulate you…"

"Mr. Darcy has always been free to choose as he pleases," retorted Elizabeth.

"Do you have the audacity to claim that you did not fervently wish for him, setting your traps along the way to secure your ambitions?" hissed Caroline, relentless.

"Not quite, no. I will even admit that I struggled to discern his qualities for quite some time. Though I am happy to have been proved wrong."

"Was that before or after you visited Pemberley?" said Caroline, throwing her sister a meaningful look.

To which Elizabeth replied with a mischievous grin.

"I have never judged the quality of a man according to his possessions."

"Oh, come now, enough with the hypocrisy!" Caroline interjected. "You know as well as I that one cannot refuse such worldly goods!"

"And yet, that is exactly what she did," replied another voice.

Caroline froze and the blood drained from her face. Neither the adversaries nor the witnesses of this verbal spar had noticed that Darcy and Colonel Fitzwilliam had approached. The groom held two glasses of liqueur. He held one out to Elizabeth.

"I was just looking for you, my dear. I could not find you in the drawing-room," he said, kindly.

He then turned to the rest of the group and continued with the characteristic coldness which he embraced most of the time when he was in company: "You can take my word for it, ladies, when I say that Mrs. Darcy, whom I am blessed to have at my side today, was difficult to persuade. In fact, I asked for her hand last April and she rejected me rather bluntly. Can you believe it?"

Caroline, Louisa, and Charlotte were all wide-eyed. Colonel Fitzwilliam, on the other hand, seemed to be familiar with his cousin's story and gave Elizabeth a knowing look. As for the latter, charmed to be thus rescued by her husband, she fell silent. She already revelled in what was about to follow.

"She rejected you?" Caroline's voice betrayed her shock.

"Precisely," replied Darcy, with his usual dignity. "Believe me, my surprise was far greater than yours. It was also, dare I say, an excellent lesson. I was truly humbled. You see, Miss Bingley, I did not expect to be rejected in the slightest. And so I made my advances, convinced that the answer was a foregone conclusion. My vain conviction served only to make her refusal that much harder to bear. After such a rejection, I believed for a long time that all was lost. I was very lucky that the matter eventually worked to my advantage, and that I was able to approach her a second time. I assure you that, since then, I have made amends."

He turned towards Elizabeth and lifted his glass in a toast.

"Today," he continued as he addressed the group, "it is with pride that I can say that I am one of those rare men who are loved for themselves rather than for their fortune."

"Well said, Darcy!" Colonel Fitzwilliam cried out, clapping his hands to dissipate the dramatic atmosphere that had befallen the group of young women. "Let us wish that many more may follow your example, my friends!"

Darcy nodded approvingly at his cousin and then turned to Elizabeth and offered her his arm.

"Shall we return to the drawing-room, my dear? Our guests want to see you and you are hidden here in the corridors. For are you not queen today?"

The men bowed and then returned to the other room with the bride, followed closely by Charlotte. As for the Bingley sisters, they stayed behind, silenced and more than a little mollified.

~

Elizabeth, who had stifled her laughter by biting the inside of her cheeks, let herself go as they entered the drawing-room.

"Such chivalry, Mr. Darcy! I do believe that as of tomorrow, all of Meryton will know that I had the audacity to reject you! I will be famous!" she burst out laughing.

Charlotte and Colonel Fitzwilliam joined in the laughter, although a little ashamed to be mocking Caroline and Louisa's defeat so openly. As for Darcy, he had regained his seriousness.

"I neither enjoy, nor have any talent for this type of tirade. In normal circumstances, I would have let it be, but today is our wedding and I shall not tolerate any insinuations that your motives were self-serving when I know this to be false, Lizzy," he declared calmly.

"You claim a lack of talent, Mr. Darcy, but what I just heard was worthy of the stage," Charlotte intervened. "And Elizabeth is right: rest assured that this will spread like wildfire throughout the neighbourhood."

"In that case, it is lucky that we are leaving the region tonight," answered the young man, still stoic.

"Poor Caroline... She must be very cross," said Elizabeth, who was more than a little pleased at how their latest exchange had ended. "Surely, you must have known where her motivations and affections lie, Mr. Darcy?"

He frowned, embarrassed by the question, especially in front of his cousin and Mrs. Collins.

66

"I suppose so. But she was never of any interest to me."

"I imagine that there have been a few admirers of this kind," his wife continued, mischievously.

"I suppose they never interested me either. Lizzy, must we really speak of all this?" he protested.

Upon seeing that Darcy had only limited patience for such teasing, Elizabeth did not insist.

"You are right, forgive me," she said, before creating a diversion. "Charlotte, I see that Kitty and Maria are quite without employment – it would seem that Mary has once again taken over the pianoforte. Shall we go fetch the musicians for a few dances? I am certain that Jane and Charles would happily join in. And you, Colonel Fitzwilliam, what do you think? Do you feel well enough to dance with some ladies?"

~

After having recruited the required number of dancers, the musicians were called back to improvise a ball in the dining room. The large table, on which there was still a vast amount of food, was pushed back against the wall and servants were asked to do away with the chairs. A large number of the younger guests participated under the indulgent gaze of their parents.

The brides and grooms took the lead. Darcy, feeling well disposed, danced with his wife three times and even granted Jane a quadrille before withdrawing, judging that he had fulfilled his duty. Elizabeth internally rejoiced at seeing him make that effort for her, especially since she easily recalled his moroseness on the night they had first met at the Meryton assembly. At present, Darcy was familiar with most of the people surrounding him. He was visibly more relaxed and it showed in his whole demeanour. She suspected him of deriving even more pleasure from dancing than he was willing to admit.

Deprived of the only partner with whom she wished to dance, Elizabeth moved away from the dancing and returned to the drawing-room. Along the way, she almost collided with Mr. Collins, who was coming from the opposite direction.

"Oh! Mr. Collins!" she greeted him.

"Mrs. Darcy," he replied, bowing with the utmost regard.

"Are you joining the dance?" she asked. "I have not seen Charlotte in a while, but if you seek a partner, I am sure your sister-in-law, Miss Lucas, would be delighted to have you."

"Thank you, madam, but I only wish to enjoy the music. What a delight, is it not? One should always have such music at home. It is a blessing that I might even venture to describe as divine to the heart and soul..."

A 'blessing divine to the heart and soul' was not how Elizabeth would have described the wild and popular Scottish dance the musicians were just now playing. Judging by the sounds emanating from the room, the dancers were laughing heartily as they muddled through the steps in an attempt to keep up with the rhythm. However, she responded to his ceremonious civility without derision. Mr. Collins had not lost his particular gift for delicate compliments of the sort no one wished to hear.

But as they exchanged a few words, Elizabeth noticed that her cousin would not meet her eye and that his way of addressing her was somewhat unnatural. She had not had the opportunity to speak with him since his arrival at Lucas Lodge with Charlotte, and she was now convinced that he was avoiding her.

The young pastor seemed very uncomfortable. He was the only one to have not fully enjoyed the meal, and since they had all moved to the drawing-room, he had not left the Reverend of Meryton's side, with whom he had tried, without much success, to start a theological debate. Everything about his behaviour made it apparent that he was aware of the quarrel between Darcy and his aunt. His presence at the wedding must have seemed to him an unforgivable act of betrayal against his benefactress. He would, of course, have sided against Elizabeth if he could have, but it was impossible, for as rightful heir to Longbourn, he found himself forever tied against his will to the Bennet family – and to Elizabeth and Darcy by extension.

For once, the young woman sincerely pitied her cousin. She would not wish to be conflicted likewise for anything in the world, especially knowing Lady Catherine's terrible temper. In order to put an end to his growing embarrassment, she preferred to address this delicate issue head on.

"Tell me, how is Lady Catherine?" she asked, with all the kindness and candour she could muster.

"She is well, thank you," answered the young clergyman, cheeks going red. "She showed great kindness in allowing me this leave of absence to spend a few weeks here in Hertfordshire. I acted upon Mrs. Collins' urging, of course, who went to great lengths to convince me, but I must say that I feel terribly guilty leaving my patroness and my parish without a shepherd. I do look forward to returning soon so I may resume my functions."

"Of course, it is only natural," sympathised Elizabeth. "Lady Catherine is very kind to you, she certainly is a generous and exemplary woman. Might I prevail upon you to convey my regards when next you see her?"

Upon hearing this, Mr. Collins looked at her cautiously. She gave him an apologetic smile.

"Forgive me for being frank," she continued, "but I am aware that my husband has quarrelled with his aunt and, believe me, I deeply regret it. There is nothing more sacred than family and I would regret it all my life if this disagreement were to persist. I would be infinitely grateful if you could assure Lady Catherine that I shall do everything in my power to ensure that the matter is swiftly forgotten..."

This time, Mr. Collin's expression softened. Elizabeth had gained her point. By ignoring the fact that she herself was the subject of the dispute and by demonstrating humility with regard to Rosings' authoritarian mistress, she was more likely to secure her cousin's help in easing tensions.

"You are right, madam, there is nothing more sacred than family," he responded.

With these words, a joyous thought crossed his mind, altering his demeanour completely. He now looked at Elizabeth straight in the eyes and said in a cheerful tone:

"On this subject, I do believe Mrs. Collins has conveyed the news, has she not?"

"Yes, she has indeed!" confirmed the young woman. "Allow me to congratulate you, dear cousin. May you have a large and beautiful family!"

Appeased, Collins began a long and animated description of all the arrangements they planned to undertake at the Hunsford rectory for the baby's arrival as well as projects he had planned if, good fortune permitting, the child was to be a boy.

While he spoke, Elizabeth could not help thinking that what he described was the life they would have had together had they married. For a brief moment she asked herself whether she might have been fulfilled.

She had always been aware of the precariousness of her situation. In the absence of a dowry, the Bennet girls had very little chance of finding suitable husbands, and Jane herself was the perfect example: in spite of her great beauty, which easily attracted men, she still had to wait until she was twenty-three to receive her first and only marriage proposal. Elizabeth's common sense should have led her to accept her cousin, whose social standing was very respectable. Maybe she would have, if the proposal had come from a less preposterous man. But Collins? Never. While not inherently bad, his unbearable obsequiousness towards people of higher rank, his pompous manner, and his affected airs made him the exact opposite of what Elizabeth hoped for in a companion.

Upon hearing him describe the paradise that his house would be for his unborn son, she sighed inwardly. It all made her head spin. Rejecting her cousin had allowed her to exchange an insignificant life alongside a hypocritical man whose grandiloquence rang hollow, in favour of a radiant future with Darcy, who, as she had discovered, was infinitely more noble. Comparing the two men made her shiver and only served to heighten the repulsion she felt when imagining herself married to Reverend Collins.

The latter continued his monologue and eventually the young woman excused herself under the pretence that she was being called away.

~

70

Light was just starting to fade when Darcy leaned over to his young bride and whispered:

"We should leave soon, my dear."

Engaged in an animated conversation with Colonel Fitzwilliam, Elizabeth felt a thrill of excitement and apprehension run through her. The knot she had felt that morning which had disappeared during the meal, suddenly reappeared.

She promptly informed Jane and they went upstairs together to one of the rooms in order to change. The elegant wedding gown was neatly packed away and she put on her travel clothes, plain, warm, and comfortable.

"Oh, Lizzy, I wish this day would never end!" exclaimed Jane, also struggling with a sudden rush of anxiety. "I don't quite realise that you are going to leave. Everything will be so different now!"

"Are you not looking forward to this evening?" laughed her sister. "Think of your handsome husband's kisses..."

Jane made no answer. Her lips trembled.

As for Elizabeth, she was not much calmer, but she tried to quiet her emotions. She held her sister in a long embrace.

"It is true that nothing will be as before, but you'll see: it will be even better!" she said, to give them both courage. "We are immensely fortunate that we married two good friends. In all likelihood we will spend the rest of our lives with one another!"

"But you are going to Derbyshire! It is so far!" Jane exclaimed, her eyes filling up with tears.

"I am going to London first. It is not so far removed, you know. I will see our uncle and our aunt Gardiner and we will have such a splendid time. And then I shall write to tell you all about it. And in the meantime, you will be here with your adorable Bingley, preventing Mamma from visiting you three times a day, and you will be happier than you ever could have imagined."

She hugged and kissed her sister.

"We will see each other very soon, my dear. I am already excited at the prospect of showing you Pemberley!"

Comforting Jane had enabled some of her boldness to return, but Elizabeth preferred to leave as soon as possible to prevent her own tears from falling. Downstairs she would be distracted by the crowd and it would be easier to smile and pretend.

She gave instructions to a servant she encountered in the passage to close her small travel trunk and take it outside to the carriage, and then raced down the stairs feeling reinvigorated.

At the bottom, her father awaited her.

"Mrs. Darcy," he greeted her ceremoniously.

His mischief was unmistakable. Elizabeth laughed and kissed him. She then clasped his arm and they walked a few steps together, in the calm of the hall.

"You are bound for a mighty journey, my dear," started Mr. Bennet. "In good company, thank heavens."

"You saw to that, papa. I have nothing to fear," Elizabeth answered tenderly. The knots in her stomach twisted again.

"I did nothing, you were an excellent judge in deciding who might possibly deserve your attention. And I must say, he who has shown himself to be worthy in your eyes, has proven to be even more so in mine. Your Mr. Darcy is a most surprising man..."

Elizabeth was delighted. She had so much affection for her father that, above all else, she wished for his understanding and approval of the choice she had made. The growing respect burgeoning between him and Darcy warmed her heart.

"I am so pleased you were able to spend some time together," she said. "I even had the feeling that you took pleasure in his company!"

Mr. Bennet's eyes narrowed and he took on a playfully affected air.

"All I shall say is that I was able to detect some sensitivity in him."

"'Some sensitivity'!" Elizabeth began to laugh, and her father soon joined. But he then sighed.

"Ah, Lizzy, the house will seem quite empty without you... Who will laugh with me now?"

"Do not underestimate Mary. If she were to gain some levity from time to time, she would understand your wit." his daughter comforted him. "Besides, nothing stands in your way of coming to see me in Pemberley at the very first opportunity!"

"The famous Pemberley... I look forward to seeing whether this house is as impressive as I have been told. I suppose that you will be there quite soon?"

"Not for a fortnight, as you know. I have already explained it all."

"I am afraid I do not recall. All this planning and upheaval... During the engagement I felt you slip away day by day, and today I feel I have already lost you."

Mr. Bennet's voice trembled. Elizabeth felt her tears well up.

"You have not lost me, papa. I shall write often and come see you," she replied, kissing him tenderly. "After all, someone has to take it upon themselves to provide you with news of the world, since you never leave your library!"

~

The farewell on the front steps of Netherfield was emotional. The Bennets knew that despite all her promises they would not be seeing their Elizabeth for some time. Jane, who was crying, was lectured by her mother – 'My dear! One does not shed tears at a wedding!' –, but soon, she too gave way to her emotions.

The moment she saw the young bride climb into the carriage was for her the hardest. As foolish and maladroit as she was, Mrs. Bennet was no less of a loving mother and in that moment, she suffered a great deal. Indeed, she did not always operate with subtlety, but she loved her children deeply, and their departure distressed her tremendously. She forgot all about Pemberley's splendour along with the pride she felt when she saw the envious looks of her neighbours who were jealous that she had secured such a desirable match for her daughter. She also ceased to think of the ten thousand a year that would make Elizabeth a fine lady. The moment the carriage door closed, Mrs. Bennet was not interested in the new Mrs. Darcy: all she saw was her little Lizzy, who was to live far away, her little girl who had always been so tender as a child and who, growing up, had brought so much joy into the house. As the carriage departed, she burst into tears on her husband's shoulder.

Handkerchiefs were waved and farewells uttered long after the horses had turned the corner. Then, once the commotion was over, the guests went back inside to take solace over a cup of tea, congratulating one another once more on a most beautiful wedding. It would be spoken of with enthusiasm and described in the smallest detail to the rest of the neighbourhood. The saddened parents were in good company and a cheerful mood gradually reappeared.

For Elizabeth, on the other hand, the first few miles taking her away from Netherfield, Meryton, and Longbourn were not very cheerful. She had bravely kept up appearances, smiled, embraced, waved, and pretended not to notice the emotion on her family's faces, but as she watched the familiar landscape of her childhood race by, she realised that she was leaving it all behind for good. In a few months, when she returned to visit, the little Longbourn girl who had run in these fields, roamed these woods, strolled down the streets and guided horses down the roads and paths, would no longer be the same. She would experience new things, learn to love other places, discover other hills and other landscapes. Miss Elizabeth Bennet was fading to make room for Mrs. Darcy, and it was such a profound upheaval that she quickly stopped trying to fight it: when the Meryton rooftops disappeared behind a grove of trees, she also began to sob with a heavy heart.

Darcy, meanwhile, said nothing. Sensible of what his young wife was feeling, he respected her grief and silently took her hand, stroking it gently. He could easily imagine the anguish felt by all newly wedded brides when they, like Elizabeth, were forced to suddenly leave their childhood homes, knowing scarcely anything else. Sitting in silence and moved every time he heard a sob escape from her, he soundlessly vowed over and over, like a prayer, to make her so happy that she would forget this heartbreaking moment forever.

~

The journey to London should not have taken more than three hours, but it seemed to go on endlessly. After a brief respite during the day, the rain had resumed with a vengeance. Despite the fact that the carriage was rather light and unencumbered by heavy trunks, the muddy roads and cloud-darkened sky forced the coachman to slow down the pace.

The young couple stopped halfway at an inn for a light meal, but neither one was able to eat much. Facing each other, alone in the midst of strangers, they had not spoken much.

Now, exhausted by this long, emotional day, Elizabeth had fallen asleep on her husband's shoulder, their hands entwined. Darcy dozed too, only opening his eyes from time to time in order to locate where they were and to ensure the comfort of the young woman leaning against him. It took him some time to realise that the ambient noise had changed and that the glow that filtered from outside came from gas streetlights that had already been lit. They were approaching Mayfair, the capital's elegant neighbourhood.

"Lizzy?" he said gently, stroking his wife's hand to wake her.

She started.

"Have we arrived?" she asked, sleepily.

"Not yet, but soon. We are in town."

Elizabeth sat up, stretched a bit, and then glanced outside. She could not see the beautiful houses plunged in darkness very well, only barely making out some gates, a few steps, and lacquered doors occasionally guarded by servants with lanterns, awaiting their masters.

This early in the evening there were still quite a few people walking about and carriages circulating in the streets. The horses moved slowly and the coachman could be heard exclaiming loudly to clear the road before them.

Shivering, Elizabeth removed her gloves and rubbed her hands to warm them up. She had slept so deeply that her body temperature had plummeted and she was now quite cold. She could not help letting out a few yawns.

"My darling, you are exhausted..." remarked Darcy.

Not wishing to appear so, Elizabeth shook her head vigorously.

"Oh no, I am quite well. I could still dance all night if I so wished!"

"But you are cold." he said, taking her hands to rub them between his own.

"Yes, I will admit to that..."

"Fret not, we shall arrive in a minute," he repeated. "You will soon be able to warm up."

Darcy smiled but his gaze quickly turned blank as he disappeared into his own thoughts. Elizabeth thought she detected some agitation. She put her gloves back on and leaned against him again, both for warmth and to attract his attention.

"Is something the matter, my dear?" she asked.

Brought back to reality, Darcy looked at her and shook his head.

"No... No, nothing. Just that..."

The young woman waited patiently for him to finish his sentence.

"I am uncertain as to how I should approach this, Lizzy. I would really like to avoid any kind of misunderstanding."

Still silent, with a look of encouragement on her face, Elizabeth waited. Her husband sighed deeply, searching for his words with difficulty, then lowered his voice and continued:

"As you are well aware, tonight is our wedding night."

Once again he stopped. Elizabeth eventually raised an eyebrow and replied with a smile:

"Indeed."

"Well, I..."

Darcy suddenly felt rather ridiculous. His young wife's openness made him wonder if the fears he had been harbouring these past few days were really rational. However, he resolved to finish his train of thought and finally explained himself.

"I only wished to say that once we have arrived, you might sleep in peace. I shall not come to see you tonight."

Nestled against him, Elizabeth did not immediately react.

She failed to understand. For weeks, she and Jane had pictured their wedding nights, giving each other mutual reassurance, offering advice, and sharing whatever whispers they had gleaned from other women. She felt as ready as one could be, and the few embraces she had shared with her husband had only served to strengthen her curiosity. She had some misgivings, but since it was Darcy, she felt comfortable enough.

What she had not expected, however, was having to face a husband who seemed to rebuff her on their very first night together.

Unable to prevent the anxiety rising up in her voice, she sat up:

"Why?" she began somewhat tremulously.

Darcy, feeling exceedingly embarrassed, squirmed in the seat. He realised that she might misinterpret what he was attempting to tell her.

"It is by no means a lack of... desire on my part," he said, his voice low, thankful that the darkness hid the blush that was creeping up his cheeks. "Quite the contrary. I simply do not wish to rush you. We have our lives ahead of us and nothing whatsoever compels us to do anything tonight. For this reason if... if you do not..."

At the sight of the young woman's bewildered look, he faltered, took some time to gather his thoughts and, in a clearer voice, finally added:

"Please understand, Lizzy, more than anything I wish to share my bed with you, but I don't want it to be out of a sense of duty or courtesy, that is all. I would like you to decide when you wish to be with me."

Elizabeth now saw just how delicate her husband was trying to be. A small, emotional smile blossomed on her lips.

But she did not have a chance to respond. The carriage had come to a halt in front of a flight of stairs and the front door of the house opened to make way for a young footman, lamp hanging from his outstretched arm.

Darcy, relieved to finally escape this agonising conversation, jumped out of the carriage. In an attempt to appear composed, he addressed his servant.

"Good evening, Everett. You shall find Mrs. Darcy's trunk in the back. It is the smaller of the two. Would you please take it up to her room immediately?"

"Of course, sir," the man replied, bowing deeply. "Ah... congratulations, sir."

"Thank you, Everett."

While Elizabeth, still distracted over the exchange that had taken place in the carriage, took her husband's hand to climb down, she met the servant's gaze. He seemed very curious to see what the new bride looked like and he cast a few quick glances in her direction. She responded by giving him a small nod.

"Come, my dear, this way," Darcy guided her.

~

The Darcys had purchased Charlton House, named after its previous owner, nearly twenty-five years prior, at a time when George Darcy already sought to build his young son a future. It was a beautiful, opulent townhouse, wider than its neighbours and at least as tall, with five stories. The kitchen was in the basement, the reception rooms could be found on the first floor, followed by two floors for the bedrooms, antechambers, parlours and various cabinets. The servants resided in the attic. The staff was rather small, barely a dozen people, but suitable enough to take care of the family.

Elizabeth, following her husband, was welcomed at the door by an old gentleman with sideburns and a venerable air.

"Mrs. Darcy," he greeted her, bowing low, "on behalf of us all I bid you welcome. Rest assured that we are delighted to receive you here. Sir, Madam, we offer our sincerest congratulations."

"Thank you, Hallcot," Darcy replied. "Elizabeth, may I introduce Mr. Hallcot, our butler. If you need anything, be sure to let him know."

"It would be my pleasure, madam," the old man bowed again.

"Thank you for your welcome, Mr. Hallcot," answered Elizabeth. "May I, too, say that I am equally delighted to be here today."

A footman approached to take their coats.

"You shall meet the rest of the house tomorrow morning," said Darcy. "It is a bit late now and we are tired. Could you bring us some tea in the drawing-room, Hallcot? I suppose the bedrooms are already prepared?"

"Of course, sir," the butler replied, respectfully. "The fires were lit almost an hour ago."

"Wonderful. Mrs. Darcy was a little cold in the carriage."

"Shall I serve supper?"

"No need, we ate on the road. Just some tea will be fine."

After which the young man turned to Elizabeth.

"Come with me, Lizzy, we shall get you warmed up."

~

The drawing-room was elegant and covered in a pale yellow and cream damask wallpaper. Most of the furniture faced a majestic sculpted white stone fireplace where a fire was burning brightly. The two large windows were covered with thick silk curtains to prevent the cold from penetrating inside. There was enough gilt to add shine without being too ostentatious, and the sofas seemed incredibly soft and comfortable. In the few minutes it had taken for the young couple to walk through the hall, a servant had already hurried to light the candles, so that when Elizabeth entered the room, she felt as though swathed in a golden cocoon.

"Oh, this is so elegant!" she exclaimed.

"It was my mother's favourite room," Darcy explained, delighted to see that his wife approved. "And mine too. I will show you the rest of the house tomorrow Lizzy, I do hope it will be equally pleasing."

Feeling more at ease now that he had resumed a more commanding manner, the young man saw fit to tell Elizabeth about the house's general history along with a handful of noteworthy features that distinguished it from the other houses in the neighbourhood. They were interrupted by Hallcot, who brought in a tea tray with fruit and biscuits.

Then, as Hallcot left as quietly as he came in, there was a long silence, punctuated by a few oddly shy smiles.

Settled in a chair facing Elizabeth, Darcy became restless. He picked up his teacup only to set it down again, before picking it up once more. He rose for a brief moment to examine something through the window, then sat down again. He glanced at the little clock on the fireplace and checked the arrangement of his cravat before rising again to reposition a burning log, for reasons more aesthetic than functional..

Elizabeth had no difficulty deciphering his gestures and in a different context, she would have laughed. If her husband became increasingly nervous as the minutes went by, it was because the inevitable would soon be upon them: sooner or later they would have to retire to bed and that meant facing the delicate subject that had been broached earlier in the carriage.

But the young woman was just as embarrassed. Seated straight as a pin on the sofa, she periodically took sips of her tea, swallowing only the tiniest mouthfuls, in such a way that the liquid in her cup cooled faster than it diminished.

She could not fathom what to do in a situation like this.

And so the silence prevailed.

~

Someone had unfolded the beautiful green dress that Elizabeth had worn all day and laid it out on a chair in an effort to smooth out the creases. The fire had been burning for a while and the room was warm, but as she sat on the rug in front of the fireplace, her bare feet pointed towards the flames, she felt cold inside.

Darcy had told her, as he accompanied her to her door, that she could ring for someone if she needed help undressing, but she had not done so. Left alone in an unfamiliar place after a chaste kiss that had done nothing to calm her heightened anxiety, she had undressed, undone her hair, freshened up with a jug of clear water, then had donned her shift and bed jacket.

The two large trunks that had arrived from Longbourn the day before were still in a corner of the room. They were empty. Invisible hands had already arranged her belongings in the wardrobes and on the dressing table. Even the books and small personal items she had brought with her were carefully aligned on the dresser. It was a very modest trousseau, but it was everything she owned, and gave her the feeling that she had brought her home along with her. Now, scattered in this large room, all these objects seemed a little absurd. Not in their rightful place.

Just as she felt, in a way.

It had only been a few hours since she had left Hertfordshire, and yet the memories of this extraordinary day seemed far away. She tried to push them aside, for fear of bursting into tears. She thought of Jane, who was undoubtedly experiencing a more peaceful wedding night, for she had stayed in the familiar comfort of Netherfield and had a considerate and affectionate husband who would certainly not have left her alone. She wondered what was transpiring between them at that precise moment, and smiled.

But her smile quickly turned into a grimace. She sighed deeply. Everything was too new, too formal, in this beautiful, unfamiliar house.

Flustered by the events of the day, she had not known how to react and had let herself be separated from the only person she wanted by her side. Of course, Darcy had only attempted to be tactful when he explained that he would not impose himself upon her that night, but he had, without meaning to, created a rift between them. A rift that neither had subsequently been able to bridge.

Elizabeth looked at her wedding dress, laid out on the chair. She had found herself so pretty in it and had been convinced that Darcy would inevitably have been seduced by it.

She felt disillusioned.

~

In the next room, Darcy stared out from his window into the London night, his head pensively resting against the wall, his hand pushing back the heavy drapes that hung over the windowpanes. Outside, the rain had stopped again. The moon, thinly veiled by wispy clouds, cast a cold light upon the wet rooftops and traced a pale triangle on the carpet in the room.

He felt miserable for having abandoned his wife.

During their three-week engagement, he had tried to create an atmosphere of trust so that their married life could begin on a solid foundation. But in wanting to do too much, he had lost his way. He now found himself alone and foolish, so close to her and yet incapable of joining her.

Stupid.

Maladroit.

Pitiful.

He sighed. His breath left a fine fog on the cool windowpane, but as he stared out into the distance, Darcy paid no attention. He tried to think of ways he could salvage the situation from disaster and attempted to convince himself that the next day everything would be easier.

Tomorrow, he would feel more in control.

Tomorrow he would have the courage to enter his wife's room. Just to see if she would accept him. He would at least risk it.

He already imagined her sitting amidst the sheets, blushing, perhaps surprised to see him and hesitant as to how she should conduct herself. If she sent him away, he would not insist, but she might also be more welcoming.

The thought sent a wave of desire coursing through him. Long-repressed feelings resurfaced at last, as if they had been simmering below the surface all this time, just waiting for the first opportunity to bloom again.

He had already had a few escapades some years prior and while not all that numerous, they had awoken in him an appreciation for pleasure. It was a sharp contrast to his education, which had only taught him responsibility and modesty. Darcy had never forgotten the advances made by a beautiful, sophisticated, and educated woman one night at the theatre. In hindsight, and with some regret, he realised he had been too young at the time to fully enjoy such company. He had preferred to be distracted by two or three attractive and enterprising housemaids who had made short work of the young man, foolish as he still was then. One of them, in particular, had enchanted him. She was a petite, intrepid girl whom he saw regularly over an entire summer at Pemberley, until his father became suspicious and abruptly sent the servant away, putting a dramatic end to their tryst. First furious and then resigned, Darcy had set aside feminine charms and had replaced the stifled laughter of secret meetings with the fresh air of hunting excursions.

His impulses had only resurfaced when Elizabeth had entered his life. He had observed her from a distance a few times, imagining the softness of her hair under his fingers or the warmth of her breath on his skin. Their recent, and fleeting kisses, only served to further pique his interest.

Despite this, he had come up with the absurd idea of giving her the choice not to share his bed if she so wished, even though their marriage gave him every right to do so.

He had been concerned to learn, via chance conversations held privately amongst friends, that some young women took a keen dislike to conjugal intimacy after being pushed too hard during their wedding night. After that, they did not consider it much more than a chore for the rest of their lives. Instead, Darcy's greatest wish was for Elizabeth to feel liberated and playful, like his lovers had been so long ago. As such he wished to avoid rushing her to avoid compromising their future intimacy.

All this was much easier said than done. He had prided himself on being more skilled than most but he now found himself in a rather pitiful state of mind.

Stupid.

Maladroit.

Pitiful...

"Mr. Darcy?"

Startled, he let go of the heavy drape, suddenly obscuring the pale light coming from outside. His eyes took some time to adjust to the sudden darkness but he could see a figure illuminated by the irregular flames of the fireplace.

Elizabeth was there, standing a few feet away, her hair falling in waves around her shoulders, looking hesitant.

She wore her wedding dress.

All at once he wanted to say something, to move towards her, but it was as if his senses had abandoned him. He said nothing, motionless. Without realising it, his gaze was drawn by the glow that the flames cast upon the young woman. A beautifully outlined cheekbone, those lips – oh! those lips! – gleaming faintly, her delicate neck that tapered at the shoulder, the rounded curve of her breast, the plunge of her arm down to her wrist and the nervous fingers of her hand, followed by the endless flow of her dress down to a titillating bare toe that poked out from under the fabric.

Under his fiery gaze, Elizabeth blushed exquisitely.

"I am not so tired, it seems," she whispered, biting her lips.

At the sound of her voice, Darcy came to his senses. Yes, she was there, of her own volition. So this time he swiftly bridged the gap between them and kissed her passionately, wrapping his arms firmly around her as if to persuade her not to change her mind and flee.

Elizabeth, surprised at first by his eagerness, realised that she had made the right decision.

She had felt a little foolish when, in the passage, she had heard servants whispering downstairs. For fear of being caught in a ridiculous position if one of them were to climb the stairs, she had hurried to her husband's room and entered without knocking, hoping wholeheartedly that it was the right door. Heart pounding in her chest she had glanced at the bed, thinking he might already be asleep, before spotting him motionless next to the window, his face bathed in moonlight. Darcy had not even heard her approaching.

The young woman relaxed. The misunderstanding was rectified and she was where she had intended to be: in her husband's arms.

"I didn't want to frighten you, Lizzy," he whispered in her ear as he buried his face in her neck.

"I know," she replied. "I'm not afraid. If anything, I am cold."

They both laughed. As the tension evaporated, Darcy took it upon himself to humbly recognise his wrongdoings.

"I promised you earlier that I would warm you up and instead I abandoned you," he sighed, holding his wife tightly against him. "What a sad husband I am, wouldn't you say?"

"You did not abandon me: you gave me a choice without affording me the chance to answer," she corrected him with a gentle smile. "And here is my answer…"

She lifted her chin and kissed him. He let her do so without protest.

"You ought to know," she whispered in his ear, "that I did not manage to tie my dress…"

Darcy stifled another laugh and buried his head in her neck. In spite of her weariness, Elizabeth still managed to adorably and humorously provoke him.

The young woman was in actual fact not as innocent as he believed her to be. She knew more or less what to expect. However, she still tried to differentiate between what her husband expected of her and the uncontrollable and fleeting sensations she felt when he held her against him. Especially now that the young man had traded his travel clothes for a simple cotton shirt and linen trousers. Elizabeth felt the heat of his body radiating through the fabric and was entirely captivated.

Sliding her hands against his back and without quite meaning to, she had pulled his shirt from his trousers, as if testing just how readily the fabric could be extricated. This did not escape Darcy's attention. With a rakish smile he also began pulling on his shirt to remove it, but as soon as the young woman tried to help him, he let her do it unaided. An encouraging look and a hand on her waist sufficed to let her know that the initiative was welcome.

Once the shirt was pulled out, Elizabeth daringly slipped her hands underneath to run trembling fingers along his sides. His skin was even warmer than she had anticipated, and the young woman felt bolder than ever as she faintly caressed him. She bit her lip. From the corner of her eye, she scrutinised the effects inspired by her boldness. Darcy's answering kiss was evidence enough that her actions were entirely appreciated.

In return, the young man's fingers slowly traced their way up his bride's back, grazing along the nape of her neck, exploring the soft hollow of her collarbone, before continuing along her shoulder. Elizabeth trembled. Darcy quickly understood that planting small kisses underneath her ear elicited the sweetest response.

Soon, his fingers ventured towards the laces of her dress that had indeed been left untied. He only had to pull slightly on the garment before it gently fell open, revealing her shoulders and the curve of her breast. She was unmistakably naked beneath her dress.

His excitement doubled. He suddenly felt markedly hot and pulled his shirt over his head. Elizabeth, who did not realise the effect she had just produced, stared in astonishment.

"Come," he whispered.

He took her hand and led her to the bed. It was a little cooler there than it had been next to the fireplace, and in that moment it was exactly what Darcy needed.

Looking into her eyes, he suddenly felt incredibly vulnerable. He saw in them a desire he had not expected – at least not so early – and, for a second, they stared at each other, Darcy half naked and Elizabeth still holding up her partially removed dress with one arm.

It was then that the young woman blushed and dealt him one final blow. In a gesture that was unpractised and therefore all the more engaging, she let her dress fall to the ground.

Both were left breathless. Hypnotised, Darcy pulled her towards him. For the first time, when he wrapped her in his arms, he felt the heat of her breasts and stomach pressing against him. Everywhere his hands alighted, he encountered only softness, warmth and skin pebbled with goosebumps. He could not tell if they were from the cold or the thrill of his caresses.

He did not resist the impulse to lay her down on the bed, amongst the soft blankets and pillows that the two lovers soon discarded on the floor.

That night, there was only space for them in the bed.

CHAPTER 4

Elizabeth was awakened by a sudden flood of light in the room. Someone had just opened the curtains.

The woman in question turned around and curtsied. She was of middling age and wore a pale grey attire that might have been mistaken for a half-mourning dress had Elizabeth not realised, in that instant, that it was actually a discreet servant's dress.

"Good morning, madam," said the woman. "I beg your pardon for my waking you, I was sent up by Mr. Darcy. I am Mrs. Vaughan. I am to be your lady's maid."

She picked up a tray from the dresser next to the door and placed it upon the bedside table.

"There is tea, if you so wish. I don't know if you prefer to have it as soon as you wake up, but I do hope this will do. Later, we shall have time to make the necessary arrangements so that my services are adapted to your needs."

The woman bowed again and then began to tidy the room. She retrieved the wedding dress, which had been discarded on the floor, and quickly smoothed it out before setting it down neatly on the back of a chair. She also collected the fallen pillows and Darcy's shirt, which lay on the carpet in front of the fireplace where someone – perhaps Darcy himself – had piled on a few new logs.

As she watched her, Elizabeth had the initial urge to hide beneath the sheets. All around her lay the obvious signs of the night she and Darcy had spent together and she was not particularly comfortable with the idea of anyone intruding upon it all. She was reassured when she saw that Mrs. Vaughan's gestures were entirely professional, cold and distant, and that nothing in her countenance or her demeanour betrayed any opinion she might have on what had transpired in the room. The servant had even had the foresight to bring a shift and a dressing gown so that Elizabeth, naked beneath the sheets, could leave the bed.

"I will leave you to wake up in peace, madam," said Mrs. Vaughan, in a kindly voice. "Mr. Darcy awaits you downstairs for breakfast but has indicated that he will wait as long as is necessary. Take all the time you need. You shall find me in your room when you are ready to get dressed."

After which, she withdrew, gently closing the door behind her.

Elizabeth gave a sigh. The day had begun.

~

"Would you like anything, sir?"

"No, thank you, Hallcot. I'm waiting for Mrs. Darcy. I will just have tea."

The butler poured the scalding tea he had just brought in, placed the teapot down, and quickly ensured that there was nothing missing on the table. Then, like a shadow, he left the dining room.

Seated at his usual place, Darcy set aside the newspaper he had been trying to read, albeit unsuccessfully. He was struggling to concentrate. A small smile appeared on his lips.

'I'm waiting for Mrs. Darcy', he had said. The phrase had materialised quite naturally and he was surprised to realise how little effort it had taken him.

For so long, the prospect of having a Mrs. Darcy at his table had seemed quite tedious to him. Meals were, in his opinion, part of the foundations of a happy marriage, but he could not imagine himself having to endure empty conversations with a flirtatious young woman, who spoke only of dresses, curtains, and dinners with acquaintances. The insipidity of this noise annoyed him to the highest degree and since he could not escape it in public, he had always sworn he would avoid it in his private life.

As he waited for the woman he had ultimately chosen, he realised that her company would be immensely welcome at each meal.

For the first time, he was really waiting for her. Hoping for her presence at his side. Anticipating subjects they might discuss. Wondering if she would prefer to sit next to the fireplace or else the window, and whether she liked plum jam or not. He realised that looking after someone other than himself would be a sweet distraction from his daily routine.

The butler entered once more.

"Mrs. Darcy," he announced in his most solemn voice, before disappearing to make way for the young woman.

Darcy rose to greet her and, in his haste, his heels collided together a little too hard. Seeing the amused look she gave him, he pursed his lips but managed to stay dignified as he sat down next to her.

Since they were alone, he had arranged for her to be seated at his right rather than opposite him, at the far end of the table. Elizabeth seemed to notice but she made no comment. Besides, her attention soon returned to Hallcot, who brought in their meal.

Apart from their quick dinner at the inn the night before, this was the first time that the young couple were eating alone together and Darcy did not immediately know what to say. Memories of their night together did nothing to help his concentration, now that he saw his wife again, fully dressed and in the light of day. He had to compose himself a few times to not let his thoughts wander. He eventually settled on blindly asking whether she had slept well and had everything she needed.

"Everything is quite perfect, thank you," she replied.

Elizabeth's tone was light, which indicated she was willing to talk, but she seemed equally too embarrassed to initiate any conversation. Thankfully, the butler intervened to courteously enquire after her culinary tastes, which led to a few exchanges that did not require Darcy's participation. The conversation then moved on to the different servant arrangements that she would benefit from, including the lady's maid who had been assigned to her.

"I hope that Mrs. Vaughan will meet all your expectations, madam. If you have the slightest grievance, do not hesitate to tell her directly or to let me know. I am at your disposal."

"That is very kind of you, Mr. Hallcot. Mrs. Vaughan was perfectly kind this morning. I don't doubt her excellence and I am sure I shall have nothing to complain about," the young woman reassured him.

"We brought her from Pemberley especially for you, madam, so that she may return with you when the time comes."

"Is that not the case for everyone here?"

"Oh no, Madam. The personnel here are intended solely for Chalton House. We attend to the house in your absence, so it is always ready to welcome you. Mrs. Vaughan, like Mr. Grove, who is Mr Darcy's valet, is part of Pemberley's staff, which, of course, significantly outnumbers us. She is also married to a footman there."

"I see. I was unaware of all this."

The butler cut her a slice of ham and placed it gently on her plate. She gave him a sweet smile.

"Thank you, Mr. Hallcot. For this and for your explanation."

"You are welcome, madam," he replied, bowing once again with great ceremony.

He beckoned to the servant who accompanied him. They both withdrew to the opposite side of the room, standing along the wall, waiting in case their masters needed them again.

Darcy, who had keenly observed the exchange and was hoping for Elizabeth's approval, relaxed. His personnel seemed to have made a good impression on his wife and that was all that mattered to him at the moment.

They ate in silence for a few minutes, and then Elizabeth asked:

"Do you have any plans for this afternoon, Mr. Darcy?"

"None. Like Mr. Hallcot, I'm entirely at your disposal," he replied. "It is important that we introduce you to the servants and that we visit the house, but after that, you are free to do as you please, as am I."

"In that case, would you also show me around the neighbourhood? I confess I have never stayed in Mayfair long enough to consider myself well-acquainted with it."

It was a graceful approach to the situation. Darcy guessed that she had probably never set foot in this part of town, especially if her visits to London were confined to visiting her uncle, Mr. Gardiner, who was settled in the business district, on the opposite side of the city.

"It would be my pleasure," he replied. "We could visit the Saint-James and Buckingham palaces as they are not too far from here and are quite beautiful. We are also very close to Hyde Park, since you enjoy walking in the forest. I cannot guarantee that you will find the same wilderness there as in Hertfordshire, but strolling down the paths is quite enjoyable. There are beautiful trees, and enough space that we may encounter other people without feeling obliged to greet them all."

"A great advantage in your eyes, I should imagine..." teased his wife.

"And a disservice in yours, since you so enjoy observing your peers," he retorted.

Elizabeth stifled a small laugh and took a sip of tea.

"I have noticed that you are learning to defend yourself, my dear," she said. "I can only commend you. It is a most sensible thing to do as a means of ensuring our future happiness..."

Darcy smiled.

"What would become of me if I were to become vexed whenever you laughed at me?" he countered. "I know that you will often take great delight in it, but I accept to bear this burden since it will allow me to enjoy your affection and attention in return. I know the difference between affectionate teasing and spitefulness, and I know you are mischievous rather than malicious. However, Lizzy, perhaps you should not call me 'Mr. Darcy' when we are alone."

"And how shall I address you, then? 'Fitzwilliam'?"

"Indeed, that is my name. Although, 'William' is what my mother and sister always called me."

"Not your father?"

"No, he did not wish to distort the name. As for myself, I don't mind altering it. The point is that it should be short and practical enough that it may be used in everyday life."

"Very well. In that case, William," Elizabeth concluded, looking at him affectionately before biting into a rather large piece of toast.

Darcy could not help but observe that she did indeed like plum jam.

~

Not long after, the new bride was introduced to the household, each person lined up in hierarchical order in the large hall. They were presented to her by the butler, one by one, and each bowed deeply, adding a word of congratulation or welcome.

In addition to Hallcot, Chalton was permanently staffed by two footmen, three housemaids, a cook, a fourteen-year-old scullery maid, a laundry maid, and a boy who ran various errands. It had not been deemed necessary to hire a housekeeper for such a small group. As for the coachman, like Darcy's valet and Mrs. Vaughan, he was officially part of the Pemberley staff and followed his master wherever he went.

Welcoming a new mistress to the house was no common affair, so the servants were exceptionally permitted to address her directly. Elizabeth would quickly realise that in everyday life, they never spoke to her, except to respond to an instruction. Only the higher-ranking servants who looked after her more intimately, such as Mr.

Hallcot or Mrs. Vaughan, had privileges that their counterparts did not. It was a far cry from the Hills and the people of Longbourn who, despite showing the basic respect required of their status, still displayed a certain amount of familiarity towards the Bennets. Their lack of ceremony had never shocked Elizabeth. She would have to get used to greater decorum, as life at Pemberley appeared more ceremonial.

Darcy then spent the rest of the morning showing her the house, aiming to share information and interesting facts about each room that would make the visit more engaging. He put in a great deal of effort and Elizabeth proved to be an enthusiastic visitor who, in return, asked many pertinent questions. Unlike the majority of the guests he had received before, she showed little interest in the value, provenance or age of the objects and furniture. She was more interested in hearing the family anecdotes related to them. It was not the house's luxury that made her eyes shine, but the stories of those who had lived there before, or still lived there.

As an unpleasant drizzle fell upon the city early in the afternoon, Darcy thought of abandoning their trip to visit the neighbourhood. But the young woman insisted.

"I will not be put off by the inclement weather and promise not to melt in the rain. There is too much I wish to see to justify staying indoors..."

And thus, dressed warmly, they left on foot along the pavement, Elizabeth holding on to her husband's arm.

Admiring the impressive façades of their square, the young woman could not help but stare at each well-shod person who crossed their paths. They greeted her a few times and she returned the courtesy. Did these people know Darcy personally? Did they know she was now his wife? Were they not curious? She felt herself blush a little, once or twice, sensing that perhaps their glances had lingered a little longer than necessary.

She thought of the ring that Darcy had slipped on her finger the day before and it felt like so long ago. So many things had happened since then! The gloves she had donned on her way out hid the ring, which meant that no one would know whether she was indeed married to the handsome gentleman by her side.

"What is it, my dear?" asked Darcy as he felt Elizabeth quivering with a small laugh.

Caught red-handed, she burst out laughing.

"Forgive me, dear Lord, for I have just had a rather conceited thought!"

"What do you mean?"

"I was just thinking that if I took my glove off, all these people would see that I am your wife. And then I remembered that this is exactly what poor little Lydia did after her wedding, and at the time I had found it most unbearable. She would not stop parading her ring about, ostentatiously showing it off in the streets, as though everyone around should be made aware of the news."

"And according to you, this would be vanity?"

"Well, yes, wouldn't it? I don't believe everyone ought to know that we are married. They have their own concerns and wanting to put myself on display at all costs only serves my own frivolity."

"But I am proud to have you by my side!"

The look that Elizabeth gave her husband was as surprised as it was flattered.

"We were married just yesterday, Lizzy, my dear. Do we not have the right to rejoice and to wish for everyone to rejoice with us? There is nothing frivolous about that."

And to illustrate his point, he took her hand and kissed it.

They soon arrived in front of the St James Palace and stood for a moment on the opposite pavement, where they could see the imposing building in its entirety.

"Does the King live here?" asked Elizabeth.

"I do not believe he does. I know he stayed there for quite a long time while convalescing, but I seem to recall that he is now in Windsor."

"So the palace is empty, then?"

"The Prince Regent stayed there last summer. Look, do you see that little window? The one on the top floor, just under the clock?" he asked, pointing at the façade. "That is his private office where he only entertains his closest acquaintances. I went there once..."

"Mr. Darcy!" Elizabeth cried out, falsely offended. She slapped his arm lightly. "I would be most grateful if you refrained from considering me foolish enough to believe such a tale. I have perhaps never set foot inside the palace, contrary to our dear Sir William Lucas who takes great pleasure in endlessly flaunting it, but I am quite certain that you have never been at home there."

Darcy laughed heartily.

"It is true, I must confess that I only visited the place once in my entire life," he said, lowering his voice to avoid being overheard, "and I can assure you that their receptions are somewhat tedious..."

He then pointed in another direction.

"Now that we have seen how the King and the Prince are doing, shall we go see the Queen? Buckingham Palace is just over there."

~

Darcy had been right. Many strollers ambled down Hyde Park's wide paths, either on foot, on horseback, or by carriage, but there was so much space that they all seemed fairly dispersed. It was easy to avoid engaging in usual civilities, if one wanted to. On warmer days, there would probably be more visitors out, but today, Darcy and Elizabeth only glimpsed anonymous silhouettes scattered far and wide.

Although the air was rather cold and wet, it was merely drizzling, and as long as the young couple continued to walk, they kept warm enough to enjoy their outing. Elizabeth certainly enjoyed herself immensely. The majestic, mist-shrouded trees had a somewhat ghostly feel to them that delighted her. It was the type of eerie landscape where she could easily imagine little elves hiding behind tree roots, sprites emerging from under rocks, and where marvellous adventures could unfold just like the ones she had read about in books.

She was utterly delighted when they reached the edge of a beautiful lake, which Darcy informed her was called 'The Serpentine' as it meandered over a rather long distance.

"How beautiful Mr. Darcy! One could swear we were lost in the wilderness, and yet it has been dug out and filled for our enjoyment."

"'William'," he corrected her.

"Yes, pardon me: William."

"It used to be a river made of several small ponds, I believe. They were then connected together. During the summer we can go out boating on the water."

They walked a few moments, and then the young woman changed the subject and forgot about the surrounding poetry:

"Tell me, you were baptised with your mother's surname, is that not quite uncommon? I don't believe I have heard of such a thing before. Should you not have been named 'George', like your father? It would have been expected for the eldest son, would it not?"

"It is not as surprising an idea as you might think. If you had known my father, you would know that on the contrary, it was quite like him to do such a thing."

"Oh, was it?"

"Yes, indeed. The nobility fascinated my father. He was thus immensely proud to have wedded the daughter of an earl. Naming me as such was a way to ensure that no one forgot it."

This amused Elizabeth.

"I see. Two great and noble lines joined together, personified by a wonderful heir who would, in turn, sire worthy children... All this is quite enchanting, indeed! All your life, you must have been the pride and joy of your parents!"

"It would be for them to judge, I cannot speak for them," Darcy replied, with usual solemnity. "But it is true that I have sought to always honour them in my deeds."

"Except, perhaps, in your choice of bride. They would have very likely found it regrettable."

The young man flinched before realising that her tone was one of jest and that she was not offended. He relaxed.

"My father would have had a great deal of affection for you, Lizzy. He was not as wary as I am and acknowledged that there was kindness in everyone he met. He would not have failed to appreciate your wit and your cheerfulness."

"Your description reminds me of my sister, Jane, who is compassionate with everyone, without exception."

"Their temperaments are quite similar, it is true, if you disregard the fact that my father had to contend with the responsibilities imposed upon him as master of a large estate, which gave rise to certain difficulties. In those moments he could be difficult, but thank heavens it never lasted too long. It is fortunate that your sister will never know such challenges. She will always remain virtuous and caring."

"I hope that these challenges, which are yours to bear now, do not have the same effect on you. But since you are irritable and taciturn by nature, you must have a far superior degree of resistance to adversity..."

Darcy let her tease him.

"I manage my affairs differently from my father," he replied, undeterred, "and so far I have never been confronted with a problem so terrible that it affected my mood, which has always remained rather steady."

He then went on the defensive:

"As for my character, you may call me taciturn all you want, but I do not think I am irritable. On the contrary, I have often been criticised for my composure when confronted with distressing news. You are perhaps the only person who has made me lose my temper, and I haven't yet decided whether this is good or bad."

Having no desire to return to old conflicts, Elizabeth cautiously chose to redirect the conversation.

"What about your mother, William? Tell me about her... What kind of woman was she? Was she much like your aunt?"

The young man's lips twitched into a half smile. Elizabeth often approached such matters indirectly, but he knew her well enough to guess how wholeheartedly she hoped that Lady Anne bore absolutely no resemblance to the authoritarian Lady Catherine.

"Not really," he reassured her. "Of the Fitzwilliam siblings, my uncle was the eldest, then my mother, and finally my aunt. There were also four other children, but they all died young. Unlike you and Jane, my mother and my aunt were not close in age – I think there were six years between them –, which meant they were not playmates. It was only later, once married, that they found each other again and spent a great deal of time together. We lived half the year in London at that time, and the journey to Rosings was easily manageable. We used to go there quite often, as my father and Sir Lewis would frequently hunt together."

Darcy seemed to lose himself in his memories.

"No, my mother definitely did not have the same temperament as Lady Catherine," he insisted. "I remember an incident in the park at Rosings. I must have been six. Georgiana was not yet born. It was summer and the group decided to hold a picnic next to the pond to enjoy the fresh air. My parents and my aunt and Sir Lewis were there, along with a few friends and neighbours. There were no children at Rosings and my poor cousin Anne was always so sickly that she would rarely accompany us on such outings. We invited the neighbour's children that day for the company."

Elizabeth, who could already picture the scene, listened to her husband with growing interest.

"We set up the tablecloths on the grass and ate a meal prepared with what I thought was the most delicious food in the world. I was young and being invited to eat with the adults was a rare privilege that I revelled in. I had a wonderful day, especially since the two boys were of similar age to me, and the three of us got along famously. You may doubt my word, but I was not always as reticent to make new friends as I am now..."

The young woman bit her lip to keep herself from reacting to his gentle provocation. The last thing she wanted to do was interrupt Darcy's story, so she merely squeezed his arm in encouragement.

"After the picnic, all three of us went looking for crayfish a little farther off. When I think back to that place on the lake shore, I can see now that our chances of finding any were slim. The shoreline was full of muddy pond scum and reeds, much better suited to frogs... Nevertheless, we were looking for crayfish. We had been allowed to roll up our pants to dip our feet, and you can guess where my story is headed: before long I tripped on a slippery rock and fell headfirst into the water."

This time, Elizabeth could not hold back a laugh. Solemn as a clergyman, Darcy continued his story, but she could tell that the memory also moved him.

"I tumbled in the reeds and, standing up, I tore my sleeve and scratched my arm. My companions immediately brought me back, rather sheepishly, to our parents. I was unbelievably ashamed and I still remember my aunt's shocked expression as she saw me approach. I was convinced that I would receive a thorough punishment. If I could have disappeared I would have swiftly done so."

"But it was not your fault!" Elizabeth exclaimed, bewildered. "Why should you be punished for what was clearly an accident? On account of your wet clothes and your torn shirt?"

Darcy paused. A gentle smile lit up his face as he turned to his wife.

"You seem surprised by such hard-heartedness. However, I had been punished for similar offences before."

"My poor darling! If that is how you were taught to fear ridicule, of others and yourself, I am very sorry for you," she said, looking dismayed. "In my opinion, there is nothing more innocent than a child playing in the water on a day filled with sunshine and celebration."

Darcy's smile widened.

"My mother must have thought the same, for when she saw me, she laughed heartily. You can imagine my relief. My aunt and one of her acquaintances, on the other hand, were horrified. They demanded that I be taken back to Rosings to change, and that I stay alone in a room for the rest of the afternoon to reflect on my conduct, which was deemed wholly inappropriate for a young gentleman. But my mother, loving as always, paid no heed. She ordered me to come closer so that she could judge the severity of my scrapes. Seeing that it was nothing too serious, she sent me back to my crayfish, telling me that since I was already wet I might as well enjoy a swim to cool down."

"Brava!" Elizabeth cried out, clapping. "What a wonderful response!"

"Indeed! I wholeheartedly applauded my mother's approach to discipline in this instance. To me, her actions were truly heroic. I admired her more than ever. Especially since I subsequently attracted the envy of my little group of peers. I could swim to my heart's content whilst my companions were not allowed to get wet past their knees. I enjoyed swimming until the end of the picnic and was then forced to sit behind the cabriolet so as not to drench the seats. Needless to say, I was a champion in the eyes of my companions for the rest of the day."

"How unfortunate! Did their parents not follow your mother's example?"

"I suppose not."

"And your father? What did he make of all this?"

"He shrugged his shoulders and nodded along, as he did for all matters that concerned my mother. I never saw him contradict her on anything, at least not publicly."

"A wise man..." said Elizabeth, mischievously. "Your aunt, on the other hand, must have been in quite a state!"

"Indeed, yes! You are quite familiar with her temper and her convictions. This tale is now a family memory that resurfaces when convenient. Even now, when she finds my behaviour contentious, she never fails to mention my actions as a young boy hunting for crayfish, reminding me how different things would have been if I had been her son."

"I am delighted that this is not the case! I can tolerate her becoming my aunt, but my poor mother is enough of a handful as it is. I cannot bear the idea of Lady Catherine taking on this role. On the other hand, I regret not having known yours, William. I would have dearly loved to have met her."

"I dare not imagine the complicity that might have grown between you," said Darcy, amused.

He was surprised to have shared the anecdote with Elizabeth. It was indeed the type of memory that one shared with one's wife, but the young man was, in general, not used to doing so with anyone. He was surprised to find how easy it was. He was also heartened to see how the unreasonable punishment he had almost received had prompted such a spirited response from her. It revealed that she possessed common sense and empathy, confirming what he already knew of her character. He continued his walk with her feeling invigorated.

~

When they returned, they were served tea in the yellow drawing-room, after which Elizabeth went up to her room to fetch the writing box she had brought with her from Longbourn. She proceeded to write a letter to her parents, and another, much longer one, to the new Mrs. Bingley.

Although her first day at Chalton House had not yet come to a close, there was so much to tell Jane that she had no difficulty filling up three pages. She described her new home in detail: the number and sizes of the rooms, the servants and the kind welcome she had received, as well as their stroll around the neighbourhood and Hyde Park. There was only enthusiasm and elation to convey. She reserved the last page for her husband, whom she praised, describing his exemplary conduct. She remained discreetly silent about the events of their wedding night, but nonetheless managed to slip in a few insinuations, to let Jane know that everything had gone well and that her new life as a married woman had begun auspiciously.

While she wrote, seated at the window to enjoy the little light left before night fell, Darcy read a book on the sofa, next to the flickering fireplace. He refrained from interrupting her, seeing how concentrated she was, lost in her thoughts. However, he took great pleasure in observing her.

He found her undeniably beautiful. Of course, she did not have Jane's perfect features. The latter was the paragon of beauty with her flawless complexion and large bright eyes. But Elizabeth was still a very pretty woman, and there was a natural elegance about her gestures that she seemed quite oblivious to. There was no faulting her slim silhouette, slender neck and beautiful hands, or the energetic gait, which reflected the obvious strength of her character. Elizabeth's vivacity was entirely different from the languid and exasperating affectations shown by most young women who thought themselves seductive. As for her mischievous smile and her piercing, intelligent gaze, they had both captivated him a long time ago.

The young woman's fingers were soon blackened by the ink and she uttered a small, discontented sigh that her husband found entirely charming. He could see her furrowed brow as she mused, her mouth pouting when she applied herself in her writing, and her eyes laughing silently as she thought of something amusing. Darcy had no trouble imagining her wit as she crafted her sentences and he smiled, quietly happy that she was beside him so he could witness it all.

After some time, she set her pen down, sighed, and stretched.

"Have you finished?" he asked.

"Yes, I have. I can no longer see very well, so I made haste. Look how the night has almost fallen... I will read over everything tomorrow, before sending it. I shall probably also rewrite it as I fear that it presently resembles nothing more than a few scribbles."

"Then leave it for now and rest by the fire."

Elizabeth obeyed. She put her quills and paper away, closed her writing box and stood. But while her husband expected her to sit on one of the chairs opposite him, she chose to nestle against him on the sofa instead, resting her head on his shoulder with her feet gathered beneath her.

The gesture was so unexpected that he stiffened.

He was unaccustomed to such familiarity. The young woman's hair tickled his cheek, but this sudden proximity was unfamiliar. He secretly hoped that she would shift into a different position, but she did not. On the contrary, she twisted her body to slip her arm under his and pressed even closer.

Increasingly uncomfortable, Darcy eventually made a sudden movement, as though to free himself. This time, Elizabeth straightened up and moved away.

"Forgive me, I am disturbing your reading," she said.

"No, not at all."

She then wedged herself against the back of the sofa, still turned towards him, but not touching him. They stayed like that for a minute, Darcy pretending to read again while she considered which attitude to adopt. But as neither situation was successful, the young man wound up closing his book.

"Forgive me, I did not mean to push you away, " he explained. "I am unused to such proximity."

"Because I rested my head on your shoulder?"

He nodded.

"I have no idea what it is like to have a wife, and no woman has ever had this kind of familiarity with me – nor me with her, actually. It is... surprising, that is all."

"Not even Georgiana?"

"Certainly not Georgiana!"

Elizabeth thought for a moment.

"In that case, I should probably explain that I am used to showing my sisters and my parents affection whenever we mutually feel like it," she explained. "If you don't like being touched, even when we are alone, please do let me know."

"I said it was surprising, not unpleasant."

His quick reply was more abrupt than he had intended. He was well aware that his attitude was too rigid, but he did not know how to behave otherwise.

Eating with her, holding her hand, accompanying her on walks, conversing with her... these were all familiar exercises he could indulge in without fear of embarrassment. He was even willing to do his best to make her laugh. However, being alone with her, without a specific activity allowing him to summon some composure, without even a table or a chair holding them at a respectable distance, proved to be an entirely new challenge. He had succeeded in establishing physical intimacy without too much difficulty the day before, aided by darkness and their mutual desire, but now, in the broad daylight of his mother's drawing-room, he felt vulnerable.

Let himself be embraced? Kissed and caressed? The thought had not crossed his mind. He was accustomed to maintaining a respectable image at all times, including within the privacy of his home. He had never been taught how to accept affection with grace and elegance.

He could not guess how intimate his wife expected him to be.

Nor could he fathom his own expectations.

Next to him on the sofa, Elizabeth moved slightly. She let her feet fall back to the floor, ready to get up.

"Forgive me, Lizzy. I sometimes express myself badly," acknowledged Darcy, gently. "I do apologise."

The young woman stilled. This time, she turned, scrutinising him for a few seconds, as if searching for something. He had the courage to hold her gaze.

Finally, apparently comforted by what she found, she smiled, took his face in her hands and kissed him with delightful tenderness.

"Is it not better this way, my dear?" she whispered.

Darcy smiled, more touched than he cared to admit. Determined to ease this moment of awkwardness, he took her in his arms and kissed her back passionately, which made the young woman laugh when she finally caught her breath.

"Mr. Dar... William! Could it be that I have only to make the slightest suggestion to provoke such a response? You were just saying that you were not accustomed to receiving such affection!"

Darcy relaxed.

"I also said that it was not unpleasant..."

He kissed her again and was delighted to feel her nestle up to him once more.

"You see? No need to be alarmed," she said, softly.

"I cannot guarantee that I shall be spontaneous at every turn," replied her husband, "but I do promise not to push you away and to learn to appreciate the importance of the gesture – which I do agree is significant. Please don't refrain from acting upon your impulses."

He hesitated, then softly confessed:

"Forgive me for being distant, it is just an appearance. It was instilled in me for so long that I don't even pay attention to it."

"There are some things that we shall learn to develop over time, I suppose," Elizabeth replied philosophically. "I have been married no more than you have, and I cannot pretend to know what pleases you. But I want to be a good wife to you, William."

"And I am grateful for it."

She paused, her eyes bright.

"In that case, know that my door will be open tonight," she added, biting her lip.

Darcy smiled, embarrassed. This type of exchange was a welcome departure from what he had imagined an evening spent with one's wife might sound like. Evenings similar to those spent in society, around games of tric-trac and accompanied by hollow conversations. Elizabeth unsettled him, but he had to admit that he enjoyed it.

"Shall I wait up for you?" she insisted, in a small voice.

He looked at her and saw a mixture of excitement and apprehension in her eyes.

"Of course," he replied, kissing her once more.

They then stayed entwined together, watching the flames in silence, until it was time to get dressed for dinner.

~

"Is it very cold in Pemberley during winter?" asked Elizabeth while they ate.

"Rather, yes. It is a large house. But we only use a few rooms and they are sufficiently heated, so you should be comfortable. Besides, nothing prevents us from coming to London should we fancy a trip. Why do you ask?"

"Mrs. Vaughan was telling me earlier that I would need to order warmer dresses."

"Indeed. You should ask her to accompany you to a dressmaker – I suppose that Mrs. Vaughan will know how best to advise you. Order all the clothes you need, my dear."

Darcy paused while the butler filled his glass with wine.

"We shall also need to see to your personal expenses," he continued. "I am not familiar with the amount a lady requires, but I believe that Mrs. Vaughan might be of service once again."

Elizabeth also had no idea what amount would be reasonable to ask of her husband.

"My father gave me two shillings a week," she replied, candidly. "It was not much, of course, but it was enough to buy myself a few books occasionally."

Darcy stiffened. He quickly glanced at the servants at the back of the room, and Elizabeth felt herself blush when she realised that she had committed a faux pas. It was wholly inappropriate to speak so crudely of money in the presence of servants who overheard everything, especially if it was to admit that you only possessed a pittance.

In an effort to rectify the situation, the young woman ensured that her voice did not betray any emotion and continued in a very natural tone:

"And it had the great advantage of enabling me to nurture a certain thriftiness."

"It is a very helpful talent for any young wife to possess and I am delighted that you have it," Darcy concluded, coming to her aid.

He took that opportunity to quickly change the subject.

"Mr. Bennet is a very good man," he said. "I greatly enjoyed furthering our acquaintance these last weeks. He is very well-read, and has considerable powers of conversation."

"Indeed, I love him very much," the young woman replied, softening at the mention of her father.

"By all accounts, he feels very much the same. I sometimes wondered what he must think of me."

Elizabeth's eyes crinkled with laughter. She thought of what her father had told her just before their departure to London.

"I think that he merely wondered what type of man you are," she replied.

"Me? Why is that?"

"I chose you."

Darcy took a bite and washed it down with a mouthful of wine. He then continued with a little smile:

"Is your taste in men that fastidious, Lizzy?"

"Well, if my father were to compare you to other suitors who may have presented themselves, then yes, I suppose I might have given him that impression. In truth, I was convinced that men were too self-important to merit my attention, much less my affection."

"Convinced?"

"Absolutely. Until I met you."

"You surprise me. I know how difficult it was for me to find favour in your eyes, but I can hardly believe that no one else proved worthy of your indulgence."

Elizabeth did not immediately reply. She thought of a few men of no great significance, then Wickham, the first handsome young man to have garnered her attention. She was very careful not to mention it, however. Darcy suspected that she had taken a liking to the handsome lieutenant at one time, but his true character had now been unmasked and it was better not to broach the subject.

She then thought of Colonel Fitzwilliam, whom she had found quite amiable. Was her husband capable of hearing this confidence?

"Well, your cousin might have been an interesting prospect," she ventured, her tone full of insinuation. "He has always been perfectly charming with me..."

"My dear, I regret to say that you won't manage to torment me on this subject," said Darcy, amused. "I was there when you both met in Rosings, remember, and I saw how his genuine curiosity about you quickly transformed into a solid friendship. I shall never fear leaving you alone with him."

"What a pity!" she countered. "How shall I make you jealous, then? The only proposal I ever received, apart from yours, came from a man you would never envy in the slightest!"

The confidence had escaped spontaneously, and Elizabeth clasped her hand over her mouth, but it was too late.

This time, however, she had succeeded in piquing his interest. He raised an eyebrow.

"I did not know that you had received another proposal, Lizzy. I am intrigued..."

The young woman then realised that she had unwittingly managed to elicit enough of a reaction that she could now have a little fun at his expense. Eyes sparkling, she laughed at her husband for a moment, leaving his questions unanswered, before finally consenting to explain.

"Mr. Collins made me an offer once."

Darcy looked appalled.

"Collins? Lord almighty!" he exclaimed, as he laughed heartily. "Collins! I thought that all the men who sojourned in Hertfordshire were attracted to your lovely sister, but it would appear that I was wrong: you truly are the queen of your county...! Collins! It never would have crossed my mind!"

"I wouldn't give my charms too much credit, for I doubt they influenced this matter much. You must realise that his only désire was to obtain Lady Catherine's approval. I am willing to admit, however, that he had the sense to seek a wife amongst his cousins. As he must inherit Longbourn in our stead, it would have been a rather agreeable way of allowing us to retain the estate after all."

"Indeed, it was an honourable proposal on his part," admitted Darcy, still astonished by the news. "And despite this, you rejected him?"

"Of course! What else was I to do? Can you imagine if I had become his wife? What a sad life it would have been!"

"Yet that is the life your friend Mrs. Collins chose, and she seems quite happy."

Elizabeth gradually stopped laughing. She reflected on what she knew of Charlotte's life. Her domestic pleasures and the invaluable relief she felt now that she was provided for at last were counterbalanced by a lack of strong feeling for her husband. This lack was already manifesting less than a year into their union and the imminent arrival of her child would be one of the rare joys to colour the life she had chosen.

"Even though Charlotte and I are excellent friends, we are not very similar. She has always been more sensible, and matters of the heart are no exception. You might say that I read too many novels and that they influenced my expectations, but I have known since I was a young girl that I would never marry unless I was deeply captivated by my husband. I would prefer to finish my life alone rather than having to marry a man such as Collins, as honourable as he may be."

As she spoke, she suddenly appeared determined, almost obstinate, which made her look beautiful and proud. Darcy could not take his eyes off her. While her words did not refer to him directly, they did amount to a formal confession of her feelings towards him. He found it very touching.

"How very like you," he replied tenderly, "to stay true to yourself and assert your opinion at all times..."

"You are one of the very few who appreciate this trait, my dear."

The young man reached over the table to take his wife's hand.

"Elizabeth, you can be certain of one thing: it is precisely for your character, your freedom of spirit, and your impertinence that I love you."

~

There was only one dressing room in Chalton House and it was reserved for the master of the house. Mr. Grove, Darcy's valet, considered it his realm and Mrs. Vaughan apologised for the inconvenience while she helped her mistress undress.

"When you are in Pemberley, you shall have your own dressing room, madam," she assured. "It is rather large and well furnished so you will be quite at ease. How fortunate that you did not bring all your gowns, for we would not have had enough space. I will ask Mr. Hallcot to arrange a real dressing room when you next visit. I cannot conceive that a woman in your position could be without one!"

The clothes that Elizabeth had brought in her two trunks were all that she owned, and the only one that was new and of very good quality was her wedding dress. She did not know what the servants had been told about her, but the maid, upon seeing how lacklustre her wardrobe was, could no longer doubt Mrs. Darcy's lack of fortune. She was, however, discreet enough not to make any comments, which Elizabeth appreciated.

In the morning, and before and after their walk, along with their time at home before supper, she had been repeatedly dressed and undressed by the expert hands of this woman who would now be part of her daily routine. Even if it was still very strange, she would have to get used to this discreet presence by her side seeing her bare, helping her wash, styling her hair, clothing her, repairing her dresses, and watching over her jewels. Mrs. Vaughan would curl or cut her hair as needed, mend her undergarments and stockings, brush her hats and shoes, rub her back as often as necessary, buy perfume if Elizabeth wished to wear any, order bonnets and clothes from milliners and dressmakers, cut her nails, and would very likely be the first to know when her mistress was with child, since she was also tasked with collecting her menstrual linen.

Forging a relationship with her was necessary, although Elizabeth would have preferred doing all these tasks herself.

Upon hearing that, the maid almost laughed.

"Oh, madam, once you become accustomed to holding receptions and making visits to the town, you will have a great deal more to think about than mending a petticoat or cleaning a stain! That is why I am employed in your service."

Thankfully, Mrs. Vaughan was of a similar age to her mother, which helped Elizabeth's trust. But it was only when Darcy entered the room a little earlier than planned, that she realised the woman had not been an arbitrary choice.

She was seated in her shift at her dressing table while her maid brushed her hair, when the young man peeked around the door that led to his own room.

"Lizzy?"

"I am here, William. You may come in."

Gone were the spotless cravat, the silk waistcoat, the perfectly fitted tailcoat and polished boots. Barefoot on the carpet, wearing only a nightshirt and banyan, Darcy had lost some of his refinement. He seemed self-conscious and looked somewhat embarrassed. Elizabeth, however, found him charming.

"I am disturbing you. Would you like me to come back later?"

"I shall be finished in a moment, sir," Mrs. Vaughan apologised.

The young man hesitated, and then walked towards the bed. He removed his robe and slipped under the sheets as quickly as possible. There at least, he felt a little less vulnerable than when he stood in the middle of the carpet.

"Forgive me, sir, but I have not warmed the bed yet," warned the maid. "Would you like me to call someone?"

"That won't be necessary. The sheets will be warm by the time Mrs. Darcy joins me."

"As you wish, sir."

Elizabeth observed this innocuous exchange with curiosity. Already embarrassed at having to undress in front of this woman, she found it quite incongruous to see Darcy lying thus in their bed, waiting for the servant to leave so they could be alone together.

It did not last long. Mrs. Vaughan was almost finished with her duties.

"There, madam. I bid you goodnight," she said softly, laying the brush down on the table.

Then, before Elizabeth could rise from her bench, the maid picked up her mistress's clothes, looked around to confirm that everything was in order, and left the room with utmost discretion.

"You seem lost in thought. You were expecting me, were you not?" worried her husband.

"Yes, of course!" she reacted, rising at last.

As she lay down next to him, Elizabeth understood that a woman old enough to be her mother would also be too old to appeal to Darcy. Thus she could freely go about her duties in the intimacy of their quarters, without any risk.

Clearly, Mrs. Vaughan had been chosen with a great deal of care.

"Forgive my intrusion, I thought you were finished," said the young man. "Perhaps next time we should agree on a specific time?"

Elizabeth burst out laughing.

"Are you perfectly serious? Are we to arrange a particular time to retire each night?"

Darcy frowned. He did not think he had said anything that warranted being laughed at.

"And why not? It seems sensible and we could thus avoid any uncomfortable encounters with servants."

"This is one of those things requiring a certain amount of spontaneity, my dear..."

"I am indeed not known for this particular quality," he said, gruffly.

"Rest assured, it has not stopped me from being very much in love with you," Elizabeth comforted him, turning to face him with a smile on her lips. "But we will not make appointments to see each other at night: it is bad enough that we have to arrange to see one another at all. Why not simply sleep in the same room?"

"What an odd thought! A husband and wife should always have their own rooms."

Elizabeth stared at him.

"In what world do you live in, William? Do you not find it natural for a couple to share a bed?"

"Are we not doing precisely that, right now?" he retorted with a smile intended to be playful, but that also came across as slightly annoyed.

Elizabeth sensed it was best not to insist, so she smiled somewhat forcibly in return, showing him that she granted him victory. Their conversation in the drawing-room before dinner had already been a big step for Darcy, she could not expect too much of him all at once. Their first day of marriage was coming to an end. They would have ample time to debate daily arrangements later.

She currently faced another challenge: how to bridge the remaining inches that separated them so that she could enjoy the feeling of his body against hers once more. While he had warmed up his side of the bed, her side was still cold. She discreetly slid her hand under the sheet, hoping to brush against him, in what she hoped would look unintentional. She could feel his body heat radiating through the cold bed linen.

By chance, Darcy's hand brushed against her leg in that same instant. She quivered, and perhaps he did too, but his hand continued and finally rested on her knee.

"How bold you have become, Mr. Darcy," she whispered, mischievously.

A smile lit his face.

"Will you approach me or shall I?" he asked, in the same tone.

"I cannot say. Are we to make arrangements to address these and similar concerns?"

Without waiting for a response, she slid up to him and put her arm around his neck to kiss him.

CHAPTER 5

While at Chalton House, Elizabeth was treated as an honoured guest. Over the first few days, she waited for the servants to come to her, not knowing whether, or how, she should assert herself as mistress. But the house ran with great precision and no one ever called upon her. Intimidated and fearful of committing a faux pas, the young woman settled in the yellow drawing-room, where she spent some of her time writing letters and the rest reading books that she borrowed from her husband's library.

Meanwhile, Darcy received a number of invitations from his London acquaintances, all of whom were anxious to meet his wife. But he declined each one in order to allow her time to adjust to her new life. He replied by giving them a few details about the ceremony and praising the grace with which Elizabeth was assuming her new role, but explained that they were both far too busy to find time to entertain or to visit anyone, and offered his apologies.

There were, however, two exceptions.

The first was a dinner suggested by Thomas Hawkins, a friend of Darcy's from university whom he never failed to visit when he was in town. Hawkins was a rather handsome young man, not very tall but with good features, laughing eyes and an easy wit. Having lived in London all his life, he had so many tales about the city that Elizabeth

116

liked him instantly. Together with his wife, Isobel, they had five children – the youngest of whom was only a few months old. Isabel, a plump woman who seemed worn out by her successive pregnancies, welcomed Elizabeth warm-heartedly, and all four of them spent a very pleasant evening together. The conversation revolved mainly around the new Mrs. Darcy, whom they were naturally curious about, and since they were close to Charles Bingley, Jane also featured prominently in the discussion. Having known about Bingley's numerous dalliances over the last few years, they were not surprised that he had found his match, especially if the lady in question was as sweet and as pretty as described. In comparison, Darcy proved much harder to please and Hawkins, having hounded him for years to find a wife, declared himself relieved for his friend. He raised his glass at every opportunity to honour the one who had finally managed to save him from remaining single.

The Gardiners were the second exception. Wanting to please Elizabeth, Darcy suggested they invite the couple to Chalton House. His efforts were rewarded and she positively glowed that afternoon, delighted at being able to introduce her aunt and uncle to her new life. She led them on an extensive tour of the most beautiful rooms in the house, enthusiastically describing everything she had discovered since her arrival. Later, while they drank tea and coffee, she offered them a variety of cakes and biscuits, eager to prove herself worthy as a hostess. Amused, the visitors kindly indulged her and were, as usual, most agreeable. Personable and engaging, Mr. Gardiner was unquestionably unlike his sister, the incorrigible Mrs. Bennet, to the point that one might even wonder at their being related. As for Mrs. Gardiner, she had such a cheerful manner that she was a most pleasant companion. She was even able to make Darcy laugh twice – an exploit that surprised even her.

Excepting those two visits, and relieved of all other social obligations, the newlyweds enjoyed each other's company. A wave of icy dampness had engulfed London but they ventured out whenever the rain stopped. They went for walks in Hyde Park, strolled down streets full of shops and entertainment, and meandering down big avenues lined with beautiful houses. They even had someone drive them to the Isle of Dogs to admire two majestic warships departing for Portugal, to continue the war against the French.

One afternoon, Darcy took his wife to see the painting exhibition he had mentioned in his letter. They stayed for two long hours, wandering through the large halls, arms linked, admiring the paintings and occasionally greeting the visitors they met. However, as soon as Elizabeth stifled a yawn with her hand, her husband quickened his step and set about finding her a place to rest.

Ever since their wedding, he seemed determined to give her his undivided attention and always made sure she never wanted for anything. A book, a shawl, a cup of tea, a stool to raise her feet, a little more heat in the fire, more wine in her cup, a quick rest on a bench... Elizabeth teased him for his solicitude. She was perfectly fine and not so fragile as to warrant such attention, reminding him that if she lacked something she would not hesitate to ask. To which Darcy stammered that since he had no idea how to be a worthy husband, she would have to patiently wait until he found the right balance.

Tables and chairs had been arranged in the large hall at the entrance of the exhibition, accommodating warm drinks, sandwiches and cakes. They sat down and ordered the fare on offer.

"I shall write to my aunt this evening to recommend that she come here," Elizabeth said. "All these paintings are exquisite!"

"Not all of them, surely." said her husband, one eyebrow raised enquiringly.

"What did you enjoy then?" asked Elizabeth.

"There were a few beautiful pieces but I found it, on the whole, a little disappointing. People spoke so highly of it that I expected something finer."

"Ah, you are perhaps too fastidious. Having little talent in this regard I am all admiration for those who do put paint to canvas."

Darcy smiled and did not respond. Elizabeth was about to continue when she saw a couple approaching, visibly intending to address them.

"My dear Darcy!" exclaimed the man. "There you are, at last! All of London wondered where you were!"

The young man who, a moment before, had been smiling and relaxed, instantly altered his face to show the solemn expression he usually wore in public. He rose to greet the newcomers.

118

"Sir Henry, madam... It is a pleasure to see you."

"As it is for us, my friend!" continued the man with a friendly smile, while glancing at Elizabeth with curiosity. "I now understand why you have been in hiding. You seek to keep this young lady to yourself..."

He bowed with grace in her direction. Elizabeth also rose and returned his greeting.

"Mrs. Darcy," declared her husband, "allow me to present Sir Henry Egerton and his wife. Sir Henry was a very good friend of my late father's."

"Madam, I am quite honoured to make your acquaintance," said the latter as he bowed his head to kiss her hand. "Allow me to offer you my most sincere congratulations."

"Thank you," replied the young woman, a little intimidated.

"Would you join us?" offered Darcy.

"No, no, it is very kind of you but we are just passing by," replied Sir Henry. "We are going to see the exhibition."

The man was in his early fifties. He had a strong presence and spoke with ease. As for his wife, she was much younger and the perfect example of a refined, fashionable Londoner. Dressed in particularly elegant clothes, she had a way of constantly readjusting her ribbons so as to draw attention to her dress.

In her simple blue dress and well-worn spencer, Elizabeth could scarcely bear comparison besides a woman of fashion. The look Lady Egerton gave her only served to confirm this impression. In spite of her amiable smile, Elizabeth could sense her scrutiny.

"My friend, you and your wife must certainly come dine with us this week," said Sir Henry. "We are entertaining a few friends tomorrow night, please join us!"

"That is very kind of you, but I am afraid that we are otherwise engaged."

"Ah, but you cannot refuse!" the man insisted. "You have been married ten days and no one has yet met your wife. You cannot keep her cloistered for so long, else poor Mrs. Darcy will perish from boredom! Am I right, madam?"

Wary, Elizabeth dared not refuse him and tried to tactfully navigate the interaction.

"Thank you for your concern, but please do not worry on my account," she replied. "London is a big city and there is so much to do and discover that I am certainly not bored!"

"Then you must take advantage of it and meet your neighbours and friends. Shall we say tomorrow at eight? There will be eight or nine of us..."

Darcy gave in and accepted the invitation.

A few more civilities were exchanged before they bid each other goodbye and parted ways. But as the newlyweds sat back down at their table, they struggled to pick up where they had left off. Elizabeth no longer thought about the paintings, focusing on the dinner instead. It would truly be a baptism of fire. She would meet people who were part of her husband's social circle and they would undoubtedly scrutinise her. She would have to be irreproachable.

"I shall ask Mrs. Vaughan to remove the sleeves from my wedding dress," she declared. "And to find long white gloves to replace them, of course."

"I beg your pardon?"

"My green percale dress with the tulle overlay. I shall have to wear it tomorrow, as it is the only suitable dress I own for the occasion. I hope we don't receive any more invitations like this one before I receive the other gowns I ordered."

Darcy, who did not understand why his wife was suddenly discussing her clothing with him – a subject he barely paid any attention to – did not answer.

"You seem puzzled, my dear," she said, examining him carefully. "I am no doubt tiring you with this talk of clothing..."

"I dare say that I would not have thought you thus preoccupied, Lizzy."

"Indeed. But you are aware that I cannot be introduced to these acquaintances of yours tomorrow night, clothed as I am today?"

"Why not? Your dress seems quite suitable."

"For an outing such as this, perhaps. But did you not notice the appraising glances Lady Egerton gave me just now?"

"No, I cannot say that I did."

Elizabeth raised an eyebrow. Darcy did not understand the point she was trying to make.

"My dear," she sighed, "you know that I am determined to make a good impression on your acquaintances. You told me that the Hawkins' were intimate friends and that we could call on them without 'dressing up like we are going to the theatre' – those were your own words, were they not? As for my aunt and uncle, they know me well enough and I knew that my attire would be of little consequence to them. However, if I understand correctly, tomorrow will be a formal social affair where my appearance will be scrutinised as much as my manners. So, I must make an effort to conform and that is why I shall ask Mrs. Vaughan to remove the sleeves. That is all."

She drank a sip of tea before concluding:

"And, until I have received my new gowns, I would be most grateful if you did not accept any more invitations."

Stunned by this speech, Darcy nodded obediently.

~

Despite the very short notice, Mrs. Vaughan worked wonders, showing Elizabeth off to her best advantage. By the following night, not only had the sleeves disappeared, changing the ensemble into an evening dress, but the maid had also given her mistress an intricate hairstyle in the latest London fashion, and offered her splendid jewellery which Darcy, understanding the message, had put at her disposal.

When the young woman came down the stairs to join her husband, his face lit up.

"I already thought you were the most beautiful bride I had ever seen," he whispered, giving her a quick kiss on the neck, "but tonight I am rather speechless."

His gallantry made Elizabeth blush and it soothed her apprehensions a little.

She usually had no trouble meeting strangers. She knew she was capable of tailoring her language to the people she met. Even the most ornery individuals did not frighten her. But the stakes were high tonight. She was more aware than ever of her humble origins and the gulf that separated her from this elegant society. She had to call upon all her courage to convince herself that the evening would go well. As they arrived in front of their hosts' residence, she took a few deep breaths to compose herself, and squeezed Darcy's hand tightly, until the large door opened and they were invited inside.

Her attire was impeccable, which was a great help. Now she had merely to remain deferential, amiable, and cheerful with all those presented to her, and hope to make a favourable impression.

Sir Henry Egerton, a baronet who had made his fortune importing sugar from Jamaica, had been married before and had several children, now grown. A widower, he had left his business to his eldest son. He then moved to London, where he remarried an heiress twenty-five years his junior and she had given him four more children. Now, he lived off his income.

That evening, the baronet was entertaining a few more guests than had initially been announced. In addition to the Darcys, there were three couples: the Reverend of the parish and his wife, a young clergyman whom Sir Henry had taken under his wing, and his unmarried sister.

All these guests had known each other for a long time, which meant that Elizabeth, the only newcomer to this little party, caused quite a stir upon her arrival.

"Mrs. Darcy!" she was greeted with applause when she entered the drawing-room. "Finally, we can put a face on the charming woman who took our friend from us!"

"How pretty she is! Do you not think, my dear, that she is handsome?"

"Truly, I know of nothing more joyful than newlyweds. Look at Mr. Darcy! He seems twenty again!"

"My friend, we must congratulate you, your wife is quite delightful."

"May God bless you, my children. May God bless you..."

Elizabeth was seated between two ladies, while Lady Egerton handed her a glass of port and shortbread biscuits.

"Here, my dear," she said, "while we wait for dinner to be served. And allow me to congratulate you, your dress is simply exquisite!"

There was much talk around the newcomer for quite a while, in the midst of which, various congratulations and exclamations were sent from all sides. As people took the opportunity to introduce themselves to her, Elizabeth tried to rapidly memorise their faces and names.

"Where do you come from, dear?" asked her neighbour, a Mrs. Redford.

"From Meryton, Hertfordshire," the young woman replied.

The party immediately praised Hertfordshire. Some, having been there before, declared that it was a charming county, while the others came to the conclusion that it was surely the most delightful region in the country if it was home to such beautiful ladies.

"Who are your parents?"

"Is this your first time in London?"

"Do you have family here? Acquaintances?"

"How did you meet our Mr. Darcy?"

"Are you planning to move to Derbyshire soon?"

"Who made your gown? I truly must have your dressmaker's address!"

"How do you find this port? It is excellent, is it not? It is quite hard to find these days..."

With each answer that Elizabeth provided, her new companions made little comments, before one of them asked another question. Darcy even tried to intervene a few times in an attempt to calm the incessant flow, but Elizabeth put on a brave face and did rather well, even though she deliberately evaded some of the more indiscreet questions by pretending she did not hear them.

Finally, once the essential information had been communicated and repeated a few times, the enthusiasm subsided. Lady Egerton demanded the attention of her guests, as she wished to introduce her children, who were ready to say goodnight before going to bed.

"Come here, children. Come, come, let us see you!" she said, addressing the toddlers who were waiting in the doorway with their governess and wet nurse.

There were three little girls, sweet as dolls, and a baby, barely a year old, who was on the verge of crying before so many strange faces, and hid in his nurse's lap.

"Come along, show us your face, young man," insisted Lady Egerton, teasing the child.

Watching her, Elizabeth noticed how intimidated the children were, not only by the guests, which was quite understandable, but also by their own mother. The baby held on to his nurse as though his life depended on it, and Lady Egerton made no move to touch him or take him into her arms. As for the little girls, they let themselves be coddled by the women in silence, but their eyes were huge and it was clear that they were only obeying the instructions they had been given. They even performed clumsy bows, immediately cheered on by the adults, who laughed and clapped in delight.

Elizabeth thought of her young cousins in the Gardiner and Phillips families, the Lucases and all the children she knew in Meryton, who behaved so differently. Seeing the Egertons, who were put on display in the drawing-room like circus performers, she felt a pang. They evidently did not have a very intimate relationship with their parents. The children never made any move to embrace them, nor were they invited to do so by Sir Henry and his wife. When his eldest daughter approached him, the baronet returned her curtsey with a formal greeting while his youngest, teased a little too forcefully by his mother, began to cry in his nurse's arms.

"Now, now, the little darling is crying!" she said, laughing. "He must be tired. Ladies, take the children, we have seen them enough for tonight."

The youngsters swiftly disappeared and the butler announced that dinner was ready to be served. The guests stood, and everyone left the drawing-room in lively conversation.

Darcy slid up to Elizabeth to present her with his arm. In a low voice he asked her:

"How do you feel, my dear? I am sorry you had to endure all those questions earlier. They were merciless."

"Oh, it was to be expected," she answered. "I can only hope that it went well."

"You were perfect," he whispered with an encouraging smile.

They were separated once again during the meal. Elizabeth sat between Sir Henry and the rector, whilst Darcy was seated two chairs down, next to Mrs. Redford. There were three courses, each comprising half a dozen different dishes, including a delicious seafood soup, pies, poultry, veal stew, along with delightful little partridge pies. Each person was served one, something Elizabeth had never experienced before. She found the idea as charming as it was elegant. Receptions held in elegant London houses were decidedly different from those in Hertfordshire.

Her two dining partners were very attentive throughout the meal. They made sure she never ran out of wine, and discussed the pleasures of dining and hunting, concluding that a partridge was never so good as when you shot it yourself. Having often accompanied her father on his hunting excursions so she could enjoy the fresh air, Elizabeth delighted the two gentlemen by providing relevant answers to their questions.

"Do you ride, Mrs. Darcy?" asked Sir Henry.

"No, I'm afraid I do not. The idea of being precariously perched upon such a large animal has never inspired me."

"You surprise me. Hearing you speak of your father like that, and evoke the beautiful woods in your county, I assumed that you would be an accomplished rider."

"I'm terribly sorry to disappoint you. However, should my husband find it necessary, I will gladly learn how to ride."

"You will find that he is an excellent teacher. I have often observed him on a horse and Darcy is an outstanding rider. His father was very proud indeed."

"Have you known the family for a long time?"

Sir Henry nodded.

"Miss Georgiana was not yet born. At the time, I had just returned from Jamaica and permanently settled in London, and I met my friend Darcy through common acquaintances," he explained. "I have since stayed at Pemberley a few times."

"And indeed you shall be invited again," Elizabeth responded graciously.

"You are most kind, madam."

At the other end of the table, Lady Egerton was engaged in an animated discussion with her neighbour about the painting exhibition she had seen the day before. The subject soon drew the attention of the other guests and so the mistress of the house explained how she and her husband had chanced upon the Darcys, which prompted the invitation.

"Much like everyone else in the city, we were left to imagine what the new bride might look like, since Mr. Darcy declined all the invitations we sent him," she told her guests.

"Hardly surprising. We all know how reserved our friend is," replied Mrs. Redford. "Who could possibly have guessed the real reason for all his visits to Hertfordshire? How sly! In fact, we were only informed of the wedding two days prior to the event – were we not, Mr. Redford? It was an incredible surprise!"

As her husband nodded, she continued, turning towards Darcy himself:

"I do not find your attempt to remain discreet very surprising, Mr. Darcy, but please, understand that we are curious! For so long we saw how indifferent you were to the women around you. We were simply eager to meet the lady who had finally caught your eye."

"And the choice could not have been more surprising," Lady Egerton retorted. "I assure you, Mrs. Redford, when we saw him yesterday, it took us a moment to realise that the woman who accompanied him was actually his wife. Mrs. Darcy is dazzling tonight, but I shall wager that the rest of the time, she is even more discreet than her husband. Had I not known that Mr. Darcy was married, I would likely have mistaken her for a simple governess!"

She concluded her speech with a laugh, joined immediately by a few people around the table.

Upon hearing this, Elizabeth looked down, flushing red. She tried smiling to show that she took no umbrage, but, unbidden, her mouth twisted into a grimace and she hurriedly took a sip of wine in an attempt to appear composed.

Darcy, sorely offended, came to her rescue.

"You speak of discretion, madam... Well it so happens that it is precisely for her decency and thoughtfulness that I appreciate my wife. These are rare qualities amongst young women today," he retorted, his tone icy.

Lady Egerton's laugh caught in her throat and, around the table, a few disconcerted looks were exchanged. But before any real sense of unease could set in, the baronet gave Elizabeth an amiable smile and went on to raise his glass:

"My friend, I could not agree with you more! I would like to propose a toast to Mrs. Darcy, to her discretion, her decency, and her thoughtfulness!"

All the guests lifted their glasses. Smiles and congratulations were bestowed upon the bride before they moved on to other matters.

~

In the carriage, on the way back to Chalton House, Elizabeth found it hard to relax. She sat rigidly in her seat, still feeling the tension that had simmered within her all evening. She was tired and no longer smiled.

"Dinner went rather well, don't you think?" her husband asked softly. "I would have preferred fewer guests. I found them rather intrusive with all their questions, but you made an excellent impression."

"Do you think so?"

"Of course! After dinner, when I spoke with the other gentlemen, they had nothing but praise for you. Sir Henry and the rector told me you were a most engaging dinner partner. It would seem that you greatly impressed them with your hunting knowledge."

Elizabeth remained thoughtful. She eventually removed her hat and massaged her neck a little. She then finally let herself lean against the back of the seat. She sighed and Darcy put his hand on her knee in a gesture of comfort.

"Ladies judge a person's character more harshly than men do, and they usually conceal their opinions with agreeable smiles..." she noted. "I fear I may have uttered a few foolish remarks that are now permanently lodged in their memories only to be called upon when they want to have a little fun at my expense."

"They found you quite amiable, Lizzy, I assure you. Do not give way to such gloomy thoughts."

"They found me as I am: a country girl who is unfamiliar with the ways of the city. You should have seen Mrs. Redford's face when I had the misfortune of reaching for my own cup before Lady Egerton could offer it to me! And you can imagine *my* face when I was subsequently taken to task like a child..."

"These are trifles, Lizzy, dear. They know you come from Hertfordshire. They cannot expect you to behave like a perfect Londoner. Besides, I don't think they even expect it of you."

"I suppose we cannot tell, can we?" sighed Elizabeth looking dejected as she wrapped an arm around her husband's and rested her head on his shoulder.

"If there's one thing I do know it is that you were beautiful tonight, and I was proud to present you at the party," Darcy added as he kissed her lightly on the hair. "And, if it may be of any consolation, know that Derbyshire society will not be as... stringent. If you get the impression that people here are disdainful, you will find them a great deal more affable over there."

"You, of all people, would know, I suppose. Was it not you, freshly arrived in Meryton last year, who regarded us in distaste and found us far too boorish for your liking?"

Darcy smiled. If his wife's wit had returned then he had succeeded in calming her fears.

"I had just arrived from London and, indeed, I found Hertfordshire society limited in many respects. I still hold that opinion but I have learned to appreciate its charms..."

Elizabeth immediately slapped his arm, scolding him for his jest, and then laughed.

~

"Forgive me, sir... Mrs. Vaughan is asking whether she should wake madam. It appears she is still sleeping."

"Let her rest. Mrs. Darcy will summon her should she require any assistance."

"Very well, sir."

Hallcot bowed and withdrew to carry the message.

And so, the day after their evening with the Egertons, Darcy ate alone. Elizabeth was still in bed, worn out by all the emotion, and he did not want to disturb her.

As always when he ate alone, the young man made quick work of his breakfast, then sat sipping his tea while his butler cleared the table. The scene might have resembled any number of other meals he had eaten there over the years, except for the fact that the chair to his right, while empty in that moment, had taken on new significance.

They were leaving for Pemberley in a few days where their one-on-one meals would be over. Elizabeth would sit opposite him, separated by Georgiana and Mrs. Annesley, and he would no longer feel his wife's dress brushing against his leg under the table, nor take her hand whenever he saw fit. The proximity of their chairs at Chalton House might seem a paltry detail, yet it was one of those little things that made their stay in London all the more enjoyable. He was not quite ready to share his wife with the rest of the family yet.

His thoughts drifted to the reception the day before. In hindsight, he should have been firmer with Sir Henry and refused the invitation. Granted, he felt incredibly proud to present the woman who now shared his name with the rest of his social circle: Elizabeth was an elegant, intelligent, and educated young woman. She was everything he could have hoped for, both for himself and for the honour of his family. Which explained why Lady Egerton's treachery was so hard to accept. What nerve she had, criticising her own guest so publicly – a perfect stranger, no less! Even though he recognised her for what she was: frivolous and volatile, Darcy had been just as surprised as Elizabeth by the gratuitousness of her comments.

What was this mysterious competition some women seemed to indulge in, with petty remarks and meanness masquerading as wit? He thought it was to be expected – albeit deplorable – that a young woman like Caroline Bingley would have fun playing such a game. She was on the prowl for a husband and, as a consequence, also probed for any weaknesses in those likely to compete with her. But Lady Egerton? She had been settled for years and was known and respected by all. She had nothing to gain. Could her conduct be blamed on a natural jealousy towards her own sex? Unless she sought to destabilise Elizabeth because of the latter's social standing. Darcy would not be surprised if someone like Lady Egerton already possessed that information, since Louisa and Caroline, who were in London when he had announced the engagement, did not refrain from speaking ill of his wife. If some, like the Hawkins, had simply shrugged, amused by the fact that Darcy would finally break free from all the mothers seeking to marry their daughters, how many more had frowned upon hearing the news?

Elizabeth had been received with the greatest respect at the reception. In response to their polite smiles and the curious eyes gazing upon her, she had responded with angelic patience, always amiable, smiling, and attentive. But throughout the evening, and although everyone had not always been looking at her, Darcy had felt that his wife was being subjected to intense scrutiny. In the end, he was not sure whether she had made as good an impression as he had led her to believe.

The young man sighed, gulping down the rest of his drink. Upstairs, he heard movement and guessed that Elizabeth had just risen.

A new day was beginning and it was best to forget all about the previous night's vexations. Only time would tell if she would be able to carve a place for herself, and perhaps even make some friends within this demanding society.

~

The six new dresses that Elizabeth eagerly awaited were finally delivered to Chalton House. Mrs. Vaughan had shown impeccable taste, guiding her to several renowned dressmakers in London and suggesting the fabrics and cuts that would best suit her needs. She had also recommended that two very warm coats be made along with a few pairs of shoes and boots and several hats.

"Pemberley is a beautiful place during the winter, madam, but it is also challenging. Especially since your husband informs me that despite the cold, you might like to spend some time outdoors to enjoy the fresh air. If that is the case, you had best be adequately prepared, at least for the first few weeks. We shall then see what, if anything, needs to be added."

Elizabeth, who was used to wearing her older sister's dresses after they were altered for her, had never received so many clothes at once, much less such pretty ones. She opened the boxes and unwrapped the tissue paper with evident pleasure, while Mrs. Vaughan watched with a kindly eye.

She soon had the opportunity to wear one of her new outfits when Thomas Hawkins spontaneously appeared at Chalton House one morning. He was one of those rare friends who could simply knock on Darcy's door without any prior announcement, or fear that the latter would take offence.

"Madam, you told me the other day that you had not had the opportunity to visit London very often. As your departure to

Derbyshire is fast approaching, I feel that it is my duty to show you all the beautiful sights your neighbourhood has to offer, so that you shall want to return as soon as possible. Allow me to make a true townswoman out of you!"

Before such enthusiasm, the Darcys gladly allowed their friend to whisk them through the streets. His efforts were honourable and would no doubt have been charming had Hawkins not led them primarily into fashionable shops. Already surprised that Elizabeth had refrained from bringing a footman with them, his astonishment grew when he noticed that she admired everything yet bought nothing.

"Come now Darcy, are your wife's desires so well satisfied that she does not even succumb to the urge of buying new gloves or a pretty necklace? If Isabel were here, I guarantee that she would not have left empty-handed."

Darcy gave a small smile.

"Elizabeth is quite capable of emptying my wallet, Hawkins, but if that is your purpose today, I suggest you take her to a book shop instead. I don't think I have ever met a young woman who reads so voraciously!"

"If that is the case, we should applaud the fact that you have finally met your match, at least in this respect..."

Darcy was about to graciously respond that his wife was indeed the ideal partner for him, when she turned to him and smirked.

"Are you really afraid that I will rob you, my dear?" she said, teasing him in turn.

"Certainly not," he replied at once, in a very serious tone. "Besides, did you not tell me, not so long ago, that your father had imparted a certain thriftiness upon you?"

This remark confirmed to Hawkins that shopping was not an ideal way to please his new friend. And so, he changed his tactics and suggested they stroll through quieter streets, to admire the architecture without colliding into passersby.

The weather was splendid but quite cold, so the three of them found themselves in a coffeehouse afterwards to warm up. The place was rather elegant and full of visibly wealthy patrons. For once, Elizabeth found that she did not have to compare herself unfavourably to the other ladies. With her new dress, her lustrous fur-lined pelisse, and her new hat, she displayed all the requisite finery. No one paid any unwelcome attention to her: she was greeted kindly, but not scrutinised. As for her two companions, they held themselves with such ease that she soon followed suit and forgot that this was not a place she would have ever frequented before. Well-versed in the London codes of elegance, Darcy and Hawkins were entirely attentive to her needs. For proper etiquette, she merely had to copy their gestures.

Once seated around a little table laden with sandwiches and fragrant, piping hot drinks, Hawkins continued his role as a guide.

"You may not know this madam, but the Mayfair district is thus named because of a real May fair that was held there for centuries," he explained. "Unfortunately, it was banned fifty or sixty years ago, otherwise I would have shown it to you. People came from all over the country to see it! There were shows, competitions and exhibitions that would have pleased you, if I am to understand your temperament."

"Your understanding is correct, Mr. Hawkins. I am, without a doubt, more sociable than my husband. Unlike him, I like places filled with a great variety of people. I never tire of observing my fellowmen! And... I must admit, I feel somewhat ignorant for having travelled so little. My parents always loved their quiet life in the country, but I find that there are so many fantastic and curious things to see in the world. It is a shame to limit ourselves to our homes."

"Well, now that you are married to our friend Darcy, you will certainly have the opportunity to travel as you desire. He is unable to stay still for long! These last few years he travelled far and wide, rarely spending more than two consecutive months in the same place. It has been a headache writing to him!"

Hawkins and Elizabeth began to laugh while Darcy looked at them with mixed emotions. He tolerated being teased, but wished to prevent them from joining forces in the future to deride him, and so counter-attacked wickedly:

"I do enjoy a change of pace, and tend to travel often. It is true, Elizabeth, that your way of life will be somewhat different with me than it might have been with Mr. Collins..."

She almost choked on her coffee and her eyes widened. She was amazed to hear her husband's unabashed revelation of what she considered to be quite an intimate detail. He would never have done so in normal circumstances, and the fact that he was so transparent before his friend was proof of how much he trusted him.

Hawkins immediately grasped the opportunity presented to him.

"Mr. Collins? Who is he?" he asked, innocently.

"My wife's cousin, as well as one of her suitors," replied Darcy with utmost calm.

Upon hearing this, Hawkins laughed heartily before trying to contain himself. Seeing his friend's impenetrable look, he was not sure whether the matter was serious or not.

Elizabeth, on the other hand, clearly saw the teasing glint in her husband's eyes as he looked at her.

"Mr. Darcy seeks to mislead you by implying that all the Hertfordshire men were at my feet. Please know that this is untrue. He mistakes me for my sister, Jane," she explained.

"Mr. Collins must have been a cherished relative whom our friend had to challenge tenaciously to win your affection, I suppose?" Hawkins continued, understanding the tone was one of jest.

"Oh, not at all!" Elizabeth exclaimed, all the more amused as a grimace appeared on Darcy's face while he held back a laugh. "Mr. Collins is rather – how shall I say... He is a cousin whom I met less than a year ago. I found him to be very courteous and... attentive..."

She stammered slightly, not knowing how to tastefully answer Hawkins' question without putting anyone at a disadvantage. Darcy watched as she became increasingly tangled up in her words, making no attempt to help her.

"He eventually found favour with a dear friend. They are now settled in Kent and perfectly happy," she concluded, somewhat weakly.

Hawkins, seeing her discomfort, refrained from asking any more questions. With polite formality, he concluded the subject and quickly moved on.

Elizabeth, a little nonplussed, halfheartedly engaged in the conversation.

Of course, Darcy could tease her about Mr. Collins' marriage proposal. He was an easy target, a caricature that was easy to laugh at. Besides, he knew that Elizabeth had never seriously considered the proposal. However, discussing this in the presence of Hawkins, who was an amiable, eloquent and attractive gentleman, reminded her of the vivacity and striking presence of another young man, whom she had found quite to her liking, unlike Collins.

Elizabeth could not forget how she had once fervently hoped for a proposal from Wickham. Admittedly, she had been quick to change her mind once she had discovered his true nature, but for many weeks she had thought him handsome and his manners pleasing. She would never be able to share this secret with Darcy. Certainly not in affectionate jest like they had just done.

Younger, she had been convinced that when she had a husband, she would share her most intimate thoughts with him. It would be tender, wonderful and uncomplicated. She realised now that there were matters that were best kept in confidence, for both their sakes.

~

Elizabeth guessed from the weak light that barely filtered through the thick bedroom curtains that dawn was breaking. The city was stirring and the sound of horses tramping outside resonated a few times. Within the calm of Chalton House, she detected the muffled sound of servants heading down the service staircase from their attic accommodations.

Though it was early, she was far too excited to go back to sleep. Today they would depart for Derbyshire.

Her recollection of Pemberley was quite vivid, but having thought about the place so often in recent weeks, she wondered if her memories were now distorted. Her visit with her aunt and uncle had been such a whirlwind of corridors and drawing-rooms that the images flitted bewilderingly in her mind. Only Darcy's portrait in the gallery, which she had so admired, emerged clearly. She remembered the drawing-room, of course, a vast space exuding luxury and elegance, where she had seen Bingley and his sisters in the company of a shy Georgiana. She also remembered the large, majestic park, with its century-old trees, well-maintained paths and beautiful views of the valley and river.

Would she be disappointed when she saw it all again? Or would it remain faithful to the idyllic vision that her chaotic memories conjured?

She had been staring at the brocade drapes above her bed for some time, lost in thought, when she noticed a change in the quiet and steady breathing next to her. She turned her head. Darcy, who until now had been sleeping with his back to her, was on the verge of waking. He stirred a little, then turned and lay on his stomach, his face buried in his arm. With a deep sigh, he settled down again.

They had made love the night before, like every night since their wedding, and, unlike her, he had not put his shirt back on. Elizabeth pulled on the sheet, covering his shoulders to ward off the cold, and gently touched the nape of his neck with her fingertips. She watched him for a moment, smiling.

Since their conversation in the yellow drawing-room, Darcy had made a concerted effort not to spurn her advances. In public, Elizabeth attempted no affectionate gestures so as not to make him uncomfortable, preferring to let him come to her if he so wished. At home, the matter was more delicate. She did not know him well enough yet to recognise his mood. He was always so indecipherable! She had nevertheless noticed that if she made her intentions clear in advance, he would gladly embrace her in response, but it was best to avoid taking him by surprise, especially if there were servants nearby.

By contrast, once night had fallen and they were alone in Elizabeth's room, everything was easier. Her husband abandoned his inscrutable mask and adopted a more natural demeanour. If he was in a playful mood, he knew how to be tender and affectionate, not hesitating to caress her body. Elizabeth found that she did not hesitate either, for that matter. She still could not bring herself to see him bare, but as soon as they both lay beneath the sheets, she took great pleasure in curling up against him and letting her hands roam over his torso and his back, something he seemed to greatly enjoy.

As for their lovemaking, she had no complaints. She preferred to let him take the lead, as she did not know what initiatives to take. She accepted what he had to offer her and found it to be more than satisfying. She loved his caresses, his kisses, she liked to feel the weight of his body upon hers, the way he entered her and, above all, she loved watching him find pleasure. In those moments, she saw him surrender himself and it gave her the exhilarating feeling that she was all-powerful. Was it possible for a woman to make a man lose himself so utterly? It would appear so.

"Did you sleep well?" Darcy asked her, his voice sluggish.

He opened his eyes and smiled at her. She nodded, a little shy of having been caught in the middle of such daydreams.

He hoisted himself up on an elbow and passed an arm around her waist to draw her to him. She immediately turned around so that their bodies could fit snugly together, she on her side while he nestled behind her. She loved being with him like this and he would often stroke her back or kiss her neck, making her flutter in delight.

"Ready to undertake the journey?" he murmured against her shoulder.

"I was ready the day I married you, William," answered Elizabeth peacefully, wriggling slightly to free her shift from under her. "We are not heading into uncharted waters."

"Truly, I have found a fantastic, beautiful wife, ready to follow me to the ends of the earth without fear..."

"Your teasing begins awfully early, my love, for someone who was fast asleep but a minute ago," scoffed Elizabeth.

She wriggled again and finally managed to free the pleat that bothered her.

"I was asleep. But if you insist on writhing like this, I will soon be fully awake and I cannot be held accountable for what may happen," whispered Darcy in a languid tone, kissing her behind her ear.

The young woman laughed as she realised that her movements were, indeed, quite suggestive. And as his kisses spread along her shoulder and his hands slid towards her thigh, she understood that she had unwittingly stoked the fire.

"William! What are you doing?" she whispered, equal parts shocked and thrilled.

"I would have thought it quite obvious, no..." he replied, still whispering, his face buried in her hair.

"But, it is morning!"

"What of it?"

The young woman had little time to enjoy his advances, for just a few minutes later, as she reclined on her back and surrendered to his touch, the two lovers heard someone knocking on the door.

"Later!" Darcy called out.

Elizabeth stifled an embarrassed laugh. Her fears had materialised, but her husband did not seem bothered in the slightest.

"Forgive me, I asked Mr. Grove to wake me up early this morning," he explained, resuming his kisses.

"How absurd! Making love in broad daylight while the servants are up and about!"

Darcy paused. He straightened on one arm to look at her.

"Come now, Lizzy, you don't believe that this is something done solely under the cover of night, do you?"

Yet that was exactly what the young woman had always naively imagined. Stung by the faintly ironic look her husband was giving her, she scowled. For once no scathing reply came to mind, so she freed herself from his embrace and curled up on her side of the bed, hiding her head in her pillow.

She hated feeling so silly.

"Forgive me, my love, I meant no offence!" exclaimed Darcy.

He could see that he had offended her, but he could not quite refrain from laughing. It took him a moment to school his expression, while Elizabeth glowered.

"I'm not comfortable with the idea of servants, or indeed anyone else, knowing what goes on in this room," she grumbled. "I do apologise for giving you the impression that I was too rigid."

To win her back, Darcy embraced her gently and rested his chin on her shoulder.

"In that case, I should tell you that there is no obligation or rule of any kind," he replied, stroking her side. "And the servants do not particularly care what we do, they have other things on their minds. You and I are free to... say... meet at any time of the day or night, as long as it is done discreetly. It may be several times a night, a day, or even not at all for a while. There are no rules."

When Elizabeth did not respond, he kissed her close to her ear and added:

"Well actually, there is one simple rule: we must both desire it. Now shall we forget all this and continue where we left off?"

Soothed by his words as well as by his sudden submissiveness as he tried to get back in her good graces, Elizabeth eventually turned to face him and wrapped her arms around his neck, drawing him towards her.

A few minutes later, her shift was gently tugged over her head.

~

They left Chalton House that morning. Elizabeth did not know when she would see this beautiful house again, but she was so excited to see the Pemberley estate that her attention soon turned to the road and the slow-moving landscape.

It took a full twenty hours of travel to arrive at the estate. The journey could be accomplished in under three days, provided the carriage was fairly light and the roads were good. Luck was on their side as the first frosts had hardened the roads and lessened the ruts.

The Darcys travelled in a carriage with limited baggage, while Mr. Grove and Mrs. Vaughan followed in a bigger coach. Once again the heavy trunks had been sent a few days prior, so that the masters would find their belongings once they were at their destination.

They made a stop at Northampton for the night and then went onwards to Derby.

In the early afternoon on the third day, the small town of Lambton finally appeared on the horizon.

CHAPTER 6

The entrance to the estate lay just after Lambton, marked by two stone pillars decorated with bas-reliefs. Once crossed, there was still half an hour of travel left before the house would come into view.

If Elizabeth had envisioned finding herself in familiar territory on the very first day, she was soon disappointed. She did not remember the journey from the entrance being so long, and even the grounds seemed unfamiliar. The road snaked through meadows, overtaking a succession of wooded areas, without a single distinctive feature to help her navigate the country. At every turn she held her breath, convinced they had arrived, but each time she was disappointed: more trees, rocks, mounds, and an obstructed view that prevented her from seeing further than thirty steps ahead of the horses.

"Good Lord! Will we ever arrive?" she cried out in exasperation, much to her husband's amusement.

The path continued a little further, until the carriage reached the top of a hill. It was here that Elizabeth uttered a small yet exalted cry: at last the landscape was familiar.

A wide valley sprawled out before her, flanked on either side by forested mountains. A river flowed at the bottom, with hilly terrain on either side forming a multitude of small hills arranged closely to one another, like the rounded backs of sheep. Despite the foggy weather, spindly branches and faded colours, Elizabeth found the scenery wonderful. Everywhere, groves, meadows, trees and bushes were arranged in such harmony that it seemed as though a painter had been hired there to render an ideal English country scene. Neither the sheep, scattered here and there, nor the herd of deer in the distance, had been left out. Even the river, which had taken on an iron-grey hue that day, reflected enough light from the sky to brighten the landscape.

On the other side of the valley, perched on the slope of the highest hill, lay the soul of the place: the elegant façade of Pemberley House.

The carriage began its journey down into the valley, crossed the bridge over the stream, then made its way up a road that bypassed the house and led them around the back to the main entrance. The coachman slowed down the horses.

The servants must have seen them coming from a mile away as a few of them were already waiting to greet them on the porch with all the pomp warranted by such a prestigious manor. Elizabeth felt her stomach tighten. She was not arriving at Pemberley as a mere visitor, nor a friend, but as mistress of the house. As such, she knew that she would be welcomed as befitted this new station . She was used to Longbourn's simple manners and consequently far more intimidated than she dared to admit.

The carriage finally came to a halt in front of the stairs. One of the footmen opened the door and positioned the footboard. As Darcy climbed out and turned to his wife to help her, Georgiana and her companion appeared at the door.

"Elizabeth!" the girl cried out, rushing towards her new sister-in-law to kiss her. "Oh, Elizabeth, I am so happy to see you again! Welcome to Pemberley!"

"I am also delighted to see you again, Georgiana," she replied, greeting her warmly.

"I was so looking forward to your arrival! Especially since you are here to stay! Is it not wonderful?"

"Indeed, it is" replied Elizabeth, smiling. "But, do my eyes deceive me? You are even prettier than when we saw each other last!"

Flustered by the compliment, the adolescent blushed with pleasure, struggling to find the right words to formulate a reply. Darcy took the opportunity to interject.

"Where is my welcome?" he asked.

"Oh! Forgive me!" his sister apologised, blushing even more as she turned towards him to kiss him.

They then climbed the porch stairs, where Mrs. Annesley, Georgiana's companion, curtsied and greeted them politely. A few steps behind her stood the housekeeper along with a man who appeared to be the butler.

"This is Mr. Weston, our butler," confirmed Darcy, making introductions. "And I believe that you have already met Mrs. Reynolds."

The two servants greeted her warmly.

"Mrs. Darcy, it is a great joy to welcome you to Pemberley," began the man. "We hope that you will feel at ease in your new home."

"It is a pleasure to see you again, madam," added the housekeeper, with a kind smile. "I hope that you find the house to your liking and that it brings you much happiness."

"Thank you very much, Mrs. Reynolds, Mr. Weston," Elizabeth replied. "May I, too, say that I am equally glad to be here today."

"As am I!" Darcy exclaimed with a broad smile.

He then addressed the butler:

"Are they all here?"

"Yes, sir. We can present Mrs. Darcy shortly, if she is not too tired."

"Not at all," the latter was quick to reply. "I would be delighted to meet everyone, if you would lead the way."

"It would be my honour, madam. Please follow me..."

With much bowing, as if to apologise for having to pass in front of her, the butler headed inside, followed by Elizabeth and everyone else. A few minutes were needed to remove their coats, then they walked through the vestibule and entered the main hall.

The young woman held her breath.

She had already visited this majestic hall, with its marble floor, gilded consoles, its busts and paintings, along with the commanding central staircase that led upstairs to the main bedrooms. But during her visit she had only been in the company of the Gardiners, all three of them guided by the housekeeper, and the hall had seemed as vast as it was empty.

Today, however, a small army awaited her.

The forty servants who made up the house staff had been lined up in order of importance. On the left were the men who all fell under the direction of Mr. Weston. There were at least eight footmen, four second footmen, two coachmen, the third being the one who had driven them from London, two stable boys and a master gardener with his three sons. On the right were the people under Mrs. Reynolds' charge: the head housemaid and the six housemaids she supervised, three laundry maids, one cook along with his four assistants and two scullery maids. All were at their best: the footmen were in livery, the maids wore starched bonnets and immaculate aprons, and those who did not wear uniforms had put on their best clothes.

Weston took the time to introduce each one of them to the new mistress and, as had been the case at Chalton House, he allowed them to address her with a word of welcome. It was not long before Elizabeth completely lost track of all the names, positions, and faces, so she merely smiled, sometimes shaking a hand that was offered to her and paying particular attention to each person. Behind her, Darcy followed without intervening in her exchanges. His people had not seen him for many weeks, so he took the opportunity, after, to exchange a few words with some and to enquire about the health of others.

Once the last kitchen maid had been introduced, the ceremonial presentation ended. The servants disappeared in perfect alignment under the great arches of the hall that led to the servants' quarters, and Darcy offered his wife his arm in order to lead her up the main staircase.

They were finally home.

~

The Darcy family, whose most distant distinguished ancestor dated back to the 11th century, had purchased the lands of Pemberley during the reign of the Virgin Queen. Originally, it was a comfortable residence, built in the purest Tudor style, but as time passed, the house became impractical and began to deteriorate. As a result, there was nothing left of it today. Another, certainly richer Darcy, had knocked it down to rebuild it all again, making it a great deal larger. The project, which had begun a century before, had lasted more than thirty years.

Pemberley House was composed of four wings, arranged in a square around a central courtyard and rose three stories high.

The east wing flanked the mountainside and was reached by following the road from Lambton. A large vestibule, furnished with a cloakroom, led to the majestic hall, which had clearly been designed to impress visitors. From there, one could access the inner courtyard and the servants' quarters or use the grand staircase to go upstairs where a vast gallery of paintings, sketches, models and sculptures could be found. It was open to the public and attested to both the genealogy of the family – each Darcy was represented at least once – and their appreciation of the arts.

The reception rooms occupied the south wing. Beyond the gallery was a majestic dining room capable of seating a few dozen guests, followed by two sitting rooms, one slightly smaller than the other. And finally, one last sparsely furnished and versatile area that could serve as a ballroom or theatre. A long corridor whose windows overlooked the inner courtyard connected all the rooms. They also led into one another via double doors, which could be opened or closed as needed. When Pemberley hosted parties and all the rooms were open and illuminated, the effect was spectacular.

Much like the south wing, the west wing enjoyed beautiful sunshine for the better part of the day. This was where the family's personal quarters were located and since the rooms were used on a daily basis they were not open to visitors. A small dining room was used for family meals, and either the drawing or music rooms were used for evening gatherings. The master also had a study while his wife had a personal parlour.

And, finally, the north wing was mostly reserved for servants. Indeed there was an elegant library, shelves brimming with books, along with a cabinet of curiosities, but half the floor was taken up by the kitchen located below, whose high ceilings and large chimneys rose up through the entire building, up to the roof. Most of the activity therefore took place on the ground floor, which was accessible from the outside via a private path. Carts were stationed in front of the suppliers' entrance to unload all the merchandise needed for the household. From there, the outbuildings were accessible, with multiple work rooms or storage areas.

Along with the ground and first floors there was also a second floor with sixteen bedrooms of various sizes, as well as cabinets and antechambers. Of course, the masters' quarters far exceeded all the others, both in size and in the luxurious amenities they contained: the master's room faced south, the mistress's faced west, and both had their own dressing room. Here, too, a corridor stretched all around the inner courtyard, connecting each room. As for the servants, they slept in the attic. Their windows faced the courtyard, so that they were not noticeable from the outside.

While Pemberley House was the crown jewel of the estate, its park and the rest of the valley were just as spectacular. The view could be admired from each window as well as from the big garden which was either accessible through the large sitting room via a double stone staircase, or on the western side via a large terrace. Unlike the buildings, which had remained unchanged for a hundred years, the green spaces evolved with the seasons and the renovations. They required constant maintenance, but because the gardener's touch was in such harmony with nature, one never felt as though the environment was artificial. Much like their masters, the gardeners preferred the poetry of an English garden, where plants seemed to have grown wild and free, as opposed to the rigid geometry of a French garden.

At the back of the house, on the mountainside, were the outhouses. The stables had intentionally been built far enough from the main house so that neither the noise nor the smell would inconvenience its occupants. The building was surrounded by several fenced meadows and had stone arches as high as they were wide, organised around a paved courtyard. The Darcys usually only used a dozen or so animals, but there was enough space to house up to fifty horses and a large number of carriages, which meant that a considerable number of guests could be accommodated without difficulty.

Further on, beyond the coachmen's quarters, a large vegetable garden and a farmyard supplied the residents with fresh produce. This was where the gardener's family lived. While the man and his sons worked throughout the estate, his wife was responsible for maintaining the vegetable garden and feeding pigs, chickens, ducks, geese and rabbits. The task was considerable and quite a few of her children helped her every day. During the sowing and harvesting periods, footmen were sent to help her as needed. There was also a pretty greenhouse where tangerines, lemon trees and delicate greens grew. Lastly, an ice house had been dug deep into the hillside, allowing for ice to be stored throughout the summer to be used in refreshments throughout hot days or during lively balls.

Around Pemberley House, the estate's land stretched for nearly thirty miles. It contained many farms and houses, but they were all situated quite far. As a result, the only neighbours in the vicinity were the residents of Maesbury, a hamlet located on the way to Lambton, and those of Woolbert, another hamlet two miles northwest of the house, where Mr. Moore, the steward, lived.

Finally, on the other side of the hill, a beautiful chapel could be found. Built at the same time as the first Tudor house, it was the only remnant of that period, bearing witness to most of the Darcys who had lived there. It had known a few weddings, along with several baptisms, as well as funerals as the small cemetery grew with each successive generation.

This was where Darcy brought his wife, on the day of their arrival.

After they had been presented to the servants, they were served tea in the music room. Georgiana, who was delighted at finally having companions other than the austere Mrs. Annesley, had spent a moment showing Elizabeth her music books and her instruments, including her pianoforte of course, but also her harp and a few flutes. She chattered happily about the fantastic evenings they would be able to spend playing together. However, her brother soon interrupted to ask Elizabeth if she was too tired from their journey and whether they might consider going to the chapel before nightfall. Following her acquiescence, a carriage was hitched.

As they arrived, Elizabeth realised that Darcy wished to introduce her to his parents. With the light fading, the wind rising, and the black sky foreshadowing the rain that would fall later that night, the scene seemed worthy of a gothic novel.

Darcy pushed the door of the chapel open and ushered her inside. The place was well looked after. It still vaguely smelled of wood wax and the flowers on the altar, although wilted, were not completely dried up.

"We attend the Sunday service in Lambton with the rest of the parish," the young man explained, "but this chapel has always been used by the family for baptisms and funerals. And, of course, we come here from time to time to pay our respects. Although, I shall admit, Georgiana is more diligent than I am in this matter."

"Were your parents married here?"

"No, the ceremony took place at my grandfather's home. He was the former Lord Fitzwilliam," he answered. "As you see, my father, too, went to his fiancée's home to get married," he added with a smile.

"... before bringing her to Pemberley, where she must have been very happy," Elizabeth finished, smiling in return.

"I suppose, yes, but to find out you shall have to ask her yourself. Would you like to go see them?"

Closing the chapel door, the couple headed to the cemetery.

Most of the tombstones bore the Darcy name, with a few bearing the name of kin who had lived out their days on the estate. Some were so old that the inscriptions were too faded to read. Among them, two stood out with their polished surface and the beauty of their bas-reliefs: those of George Darcy and his wife, Lady Anne.

Standing in front of the graves, Elizabeth suddenly felt her husband become unusually emotional. Silently, she took his hand and squeezed it. They stayed like that for a few minutes, sombre and contemplative.

Reading the names of all the people she was now connected to but would never have the chance to meet felt peculiar. She thought back to the stories Darcy had told her about his mother: her impulsive laugh as she saw her little boy drenched from his fall in the lake, her husband's ambition to obtain a hypothetical title that would bring his family ever closer to the Crown... She thought of Darcy and Georgiana who had lost their mother so young, and who, after the death of their father had been forced to care for themselves. In Hertfordshire, Elizabeth had grown up alongside both large families, and people who remarried and had children with their new spouses. The Darcy siblings, however, were alone, forced to look after one another along with the estate. It was a heavy responsibility for her husband, and she now understood why his approach to life was always so serious. He had not had the opportunity to be carefree very often.

Darcy eventually signalled that it was time to go. He remained silent on the way home as the first drops of rain began to fall.

~

Georgiana became increasingly emboldened as the evening progressed. Being in the presence of Elizabeth gave her newfound confidence and she uttered everything that came to her mind. It was a stark change from her usual shyness and surprised her brother a great deal. He nearly asked her to temper her impulse but paused when he saw that Elizabeth had no difficulty responding kindly to her repeated requests for attention. While he deemed her eagerness somewhat intrusive, it must have appeared quite ordinary to his wife, who had been raised with four sisters. He was well aware, for having witnessed it, how exasperating Lydia or Kitty could be. Georgiana, by comparison, was nothing more than a delightful child who had been secluded from the world for too long.

They spent the evening in the music room. Elizabeth and her new sister took to the piano to play a few pieces, while Mrs. Annesley worked on her embroidery and Darcy simply sat, enjoying the performance. Now that his wife had joined them, it was his first glimpse at his new family life, and he was curious to see how it would unfold.

"William," Elizabeth called out cheerfully, seated at the piano, "Won't you come sing along with us?"

"I prefer to enjoy your talents, which are far greater than mine."

"Don't be silly! I am certain you have a lovely voice. I seem to recall hearing you sing a few airs, when you thought no one could hear you. Come sit next to me!"

Darcy allowed himself to be cajoled a little longer, and to Georgiana's astonishment, he eventually acquiesced. Although he felt slightly uncomfortable, Elizabeth was in a joyful mood and her enthusiasm was contagious.

"Heavens!" she said, gleefully moving over to make some space for him. "If the look on your sister's face is anything to go by, I suspect this will be the first time she has heard you sing!"

"That may well be the case."

"You cannot be serious! You have an outstanding musician under your roof and you have never taken the opportunity to sing with her?"

"No, I do not believe I have."

The adolescent shook her head vigorously, increasingly bewildered by this turn of events. Her brother's presence had made her shy once more.

"Well, we shall remedy this dire situation at once. How about... Let me see..."

Elizabeth rifled through a few pages before pausing on a popular Italian aria.

"Shall we try this one? Georgiana, if you want me to keep playing, I implore you to sing along with me. As for you, my dear, I also wish to hear your voice. You are familiar with this piece?"

"I believe I am."

"Well then, follow my lead. Are you ready?"

And before her two partners could change their minds, Elizabeth began to play.

Feeling rather out of place, Darcy was left wondering how he had been drawn into this scheme but nevertheless made an effort to please his wife. Unable to feel at ease and truly sing – especially since he did not know the melody well enough and was incapable of deciphering anything more than the lyrics under the staves –, he followed Elizabeth's example and managed to hum along to the chorus. He had a beautiful baritone voice, which stood out clearly against the other two and there was no need for him to be embarrassed of his performance as he could carry a tune quite well.

Delighted, Elizabeth laid a kiss upon his cheek to thank him for the effort he had made. She was, however, unable to convince him to commit to another aria.

"I believe I am distracting you from an otherwise impeccable performance," he said, regretfully. "That being said, I am happy to stay next to you and turn the pages, so long as you tell me when I should do so."

To his great relief, she did not insist, satisfied that he would at least stay next to her. As for Georgiana, she was captivated and occasionally cast bemused glances at her brother.

He had chosen a remarkable wife indeed. The new Mrs. Darcy had only been there for a few hours but her presence had already unsettled the somewhat dull balance that had previously existed between him, Georgiana and the nearly invisible Mrs. Annesley. It seemed like everyone would now have to find their place within this new dynamic.

The coming weeks promised to be full of surprises.

~

"You cannot imagine what a pleasure this is, madam. It is always so quiet around these parts... I must say, we are rather far from town, and it is not very convenient for our acquaintances to visit us, nor is it easy for us to go to them."

"Come now, Fanny, I do believe you are exaggerating. Did you not go to Lambton less than a week ago?"

"Indeed, my dear, but don't you think that three or four outings a month is quite insufficient? Speaking of which, I should remind you that the Aldens still await an invitation in return. Truly, we are fortunate to have the Sunday services, otherwise I would never see anyone! You see, Mrs. Darcy, my husband is often on the road and does not seem to realise that I am quite alone. Thankfully, I have my dear children to keep me busy!"

"You forget that this house is by far the most comfortable we have ever had. Living in Woolbert is a great opportunity, Fanny, as you well know! Mr. Darcy has always been incredibly generous to us and we are forever indebted to him..." Mr. Moore retorted stiffly, visibly worried that his employer would be offended at such bold criticism of the house that had been made available to his family.

And as Darcy assured them that he had merely done what was necessary, Elizabeth kindly replied to her hostess:

"I shall gladly visit you. I, too, grew up in a little hamlet. It was not as remote, but I do understand the importance of maintaining good relationships with one's neighbours."

Satisfied, the woman gave her a smile of relief and the conversation moved on to other matters.

The Darcys' first visit was with the Moores. The steward, who had been absent on the day of their arrival to Pemberley, had invited them at the very first opportunity, eager, as he described it, to meet the new bride. Elizabeth realised with amusement that his wife, who was sorely lacking in distractions, must have actually berated him to do so.

Woolbert was a pretty hamlet which clung to the hillside. It consisted of three farms along with the Moores' cottage, which was a good-sized house where the steward lived with his wife, their seven children, a housekeeper and three servants.

Upon entering her hosts' house, Elizabeth realised, not without some curiosity, that this was where Wickham had grown up, in the days when his father had himself been steward. It was a strange feeling for the young woman, to imagine the little boy laughing and running through the garden, or tumbling down the hill to attend lessons with Darcy. Who would have thought that this undoubtedly angelic-looking child, who had been promised a bright future under the protection of his influential godfather, the late Mr. Darcy, would become the deceitful officer in the red uniform that she had since come to know: a self-indulgent profligate with fondness for gambling and pretty women, and who had run away with her sister Lydia on a whim. One really had no way of knowing how people would change as they grew up and it was a lesson Elizabeth would never forget.

Edward Moore was a gentleman from a neighbouring county who, like so many others, had the misfortune of being the second-born son. Since the eldest had inherited the family land, he had been forced to seek out a career as a lawyer. Based in Derby, the capital of the county, he met Darcy during a financial litigation over the purchase of a farm and had made a good impression on him. So much so that the young man had offered to make him steward of Pemberley. Consequently, Woolbert's cottage was at his disposal, along with two horses and a light cart which allowed him to travel around the estate, collecting rent, verifying the production and sales of goods, and resolving the problems that arose. He had now been working for Darcy for five years.

Elizabeth had observed the steward since arriving. She could already see that he was a meticulous man, attentive to his duties, albeit slightly maladroit when addressing guests. He was rather informal with Darcy, who treated him as an equal, but a great deal more ingratiating towards her, in an attempt, no doubt, to make a good impression. It was apparent that he meant well but was more comfortable with his books than society.

His wife, who was initially quite reserved, became less anxious when she understood, during the conversation, that Elizabeth was a receptive conversation partner. The poor woman was isolated in her little hamlet and had no neighbours – the farmers were not a social group she could frequent. Her entire life revolved around her children, the oldest of whom was not yet fifteen. With her husband often absent, the responsibility of running the household fell on her shoulders and with nothing and no one to distract her from her daily tasks, she found that her days were long. Elizabeth promised to come see her and to invite her regularly.

"Will you be paying Mrs. Langhold a visit?" the steward asked Darcy.

"We have not planned anything yet, but I suppose we soon shall," he confirmed. "It would seem she greatly anticipated our return for I found several letters from her upon my arrival."

"She is not the only one," returned Mrs. Moore. "All of Lambton has been in turmoil since we heard about the wedding!"

She let out a little laugh and leaned in towards Elizabeth.

"My dear Mrs. Darcy," she said, lightly patting the young woman's knee, "you will be scrutinised from head to toe! You have captured the most eligible bachelor in the county, and many young ladies now despair at having to search for other prospects. Everyone will wonder how you succeeded where everyone else failed!"

"In that case, I fear that everyone will be quite disappointed for I don't believe I possess anything extraordinary," Elizabeth responded with unfeigned modesty.

"I would not be so sure!" countered Mrs. Moore, kindly. "You have the great benefit of coming from an unknown county. It will make you seem very mysterious indeed..."

"Unless they simply think of me as a stranger. Which is the case, isn't it?"

"Not for much longer," Darcy interjected with a smile. "I know you are able to adapt to all circumstances and I believe that in just a few weeks you will start to feel quite at home here, as in the rest of Derbyshire."

"Well, you are certainly no longer a stranger in my house, Mrs. Darcy. I hope that we shall see each other often and become good friends!"

At that moment, Mrs. Moore was interrupted by a growing noise from outside.

"Heaven help us..." she sighed, annoyed. "Stevens was bound to choose this precise moment to bring the animals in!"

"Sheep?" asked Elizabeth, recognising the bleating.

"Yes. Each farm has its own herd. Would you like me to show you?"

The two women approached the window. In the distance, several heads appeared, followed by an entire herd, bleating and jostling, winding up the path in front of the cottage.

"Stevens passes through every morning and evening, taking the animals out to graze. Derbyshire produces a fair amount of wool, you know, and you will find sheep wherever there is a little grass to eat," Mrs. Moore explained, before sighing again. "I have grown accustomed to it now, but when my husband first moved us here, I can assure you that it was a significant change from my life in Derby. I am from the city, I never imagined I would one day settle in the country. Ah! What I would not give to see London again one day!"

Elizabeth tried to comfort her, sensing that her hostess sought to project more elegance than she actually possessed.

"Life holds many surprises for us," she replied. "As for myself, I was born in the countryside and I do hope to spend most of my life there. It is such a pleasure to enjoy the fresh air and beautiful landscapes that I would not trade it for all the cities in the world!"

~

Following the death of her father, Georgiana spent several years in a boarding school for girls in London. It did not elicit very fond memories. Life there was rigidly governed, and her shy nature prevented her from making many friends. As an adolescent, her peers proved to be rather cruel towards her, shamelessly taking advantage of her inability to defend herself. These incidents were painful enough that Georgiana eventually found the courage to ask her brother to remove her from the school. Darcy first moved her to Chalton House under the care of a lady's maid. Then, in the summer, he sent her to Ramsgate for a few weeks, convinced that the fresh ocean air would bring colour back to her cheeks and banish any unfortunate memories that remained.

Naive and dazzled by a world she knew nothing about and where everything seemed so wonderful, the adolescent was caught by surprise when George Wickham suddenly declared his love for her. Of him, she recalled only charming memories and the games they played together in the gardens of Pemberley when she was younger. Fond of romantic stories, overwhelmed that such a handsome young man was interested in her, the girl had unwittingly followed him without hesitation and it would only have been a matter of time before she fled with him.

As a result of this unpleasant saga, she was immediately brought back to the family estate, escorted by a matronly woman who was far less indulgent than the first. Mrs. Annesley was an educated lady who spoke with ease, yet she remained aware of her rank and stood back when she was in society. She was entirely intransigent towards her pupil. She constantly reprimanded her, correcting her posture and her manners, questioning her at every turn to test her general knowledge or practise her Italian and her French, all with great courtesy but very little flexibility.

At seventeen, Georgiana was still largely unaware of the real world and took refuge in music and books to relieve her boredom. Elizabeth's arrival was a breath of fresh air and suddenly gave her many ideas for outings of all kinds.

"Would you like to go to the lake today, Lizzy?" the adolescent asked one morning over breakfast. "There is a fishermen's lodge there, with a stove to warm us up. We could have a picnic there this afternoon, what do you think?"

Darcy, who was immersed in his newspaper, nodded.

"If Elizabeth agrees, I have no objections. But I must meet Mr. Moore today, so if you don't mind, I will let you both go with Mrs. Annesley. You could take one or two footmen along to drive you and light the fire."

"Oh, yes! What do you think, Elizabeth? Say yes, please!" added Georgiana, pleading.

"It is a wonderful idea," she replied, smiling broadly at her young sister-in-law. "I would love to see the lake."

"Fantastic! I shall speak with Mrs. Reynolds immediately!"

The girl was about to get up from the table when she was called to order with a glance from Mrs. Annesley.

"May I be excused?"

Her brother acquiesced and Georgiana left the room fluttering like a bird, soon followed by her companion. Calm returned.

Elizabeth was quite fond of these peaceful moments, at the end of meals, where neither she nor her husband were in any hurry to leave the table. While she took her time to finish her tea, staring off through one of the windows, Darcy abandoned his newspaper and picked up a letter that Weston had just brought him. She would not have noticed his troubled look had she not turned her gaze towards him at the exact moment he unsealed the letter. He grew slightly pale.

"Is everything all right?" she asked.

Darcy recovered, his expression changing into something that was meant to be more engaging.

"Why, yes, everything is fine," he answered.

However, his slight frown as he read the page seemed to indicate otherwise. Elizabeth did not insist. She waited for him to finish.

After about a minute, Darcy realised that his casual manner did not fool his wife and finally conceded:

"Wickham has written to me."

This time, it was Elizabeth who paled. Neither of them had spoken about the ensign or Lydia since their wedding. The young woman, believing the issue to be buried, for now at least, had not expected him to suddenly make an appearance in their conversation.

"What does he say?" she asked.

"He sends us his congratulations."

"Oh..."

As Darcy did not seem willing to say more, she added:

"Is that all?"

"Yes, that is all. His letter is formal, to say the least. I imagine that for now he seeks only to ensure that the doors to Pemberley are not entirely closed to him. I expect I shall receive more urgent letters once he requires help again."

The new kinship that now united Darcy and Wickham via their respective wives offered the latter enticing possibilities. The handsome officer was not one to pass up an opportunity to take advantage of others. Since his first approach had not worked – Elizabeth recalled the letter sent by Lydia just before the wedding –, he now had the gall to write directly to Darcy.

"Will you answer?" she enquired.

"Certainly not. Your sister is welcome to visit as long as she comes alone. I agree to watch over her out of affection for you, but as far as Wickham is concerned, he can go to hell. Which may yet happen..."

"What do you mean?"

"With that infernal Bonaparte, there is no end in sight for the war and Wickham is no longer part of the militia. Now that he is a member of the regular army, he may well find himself in the heart of battle one day, especially with such a low rank. I do not wish for his death – good Lord, no! – but it is a possibility that should not be omitted."

Then, as if to exonerate himself from having uttered such words, Darcy immediately added, with a grimace full of irony:

"Although, knowing him, I would not be surprised if he found a way to evade his duties once again... Either way, I should not like to stand in his place. I pity him."

Elizabeth looked surprised.

"Have I shocked you?" he asked, amused.

"To say the least! I was certain you despised him more than I did!"

"Rest assured, I do! His shameful conduct has barred him from this house forever. But I also do recall that he was once a pleasant childhood companion, even if our paths diverged later in life."

Darcy seemed on the verge of revealing a precious confidence, but the subject was delicate. He was suddenly silent.

Although discretion dictated that she not press the issue, Elizabeth's curiosity got the better of her. After making sure that the servants had left the room, and waiting just long enough in silence to demonstrate that she respected the seriousness of what her husband might reveal to her, she insisted with all the tact she could muster:

"Mr. Wickham once told me that your father preferred him to you," she said softly, "but I have since realised that he always distorted reality to his advantage. So now I am unsure whether this is true."

"It is, to a certain extent. Wickham is almost the same age as I and we were once the only two boys from around these parts. We spent all our time together. I long considered him to be my brother so I would not be surprised if my father considered him a second son."

"How, then, did you come to dislike each other thus?"

"Growing up, we began to fight for his affection and a pattern of favoured treatment became evident. Papa indulged his whims whilst relentlessly refusing mine."

Elizabeth's lips formed an indignant 'Oh!'. But although Darcy's tone had hardened a moment before, the mere mention of his father softened it and a tender look appeared on his face.

"I imagine that this happens in all families," he continued. "Wickham was, in a sense, the second child while I was the eldest. My father was a good man, but given that I was his heir, he had to ensure that once I was a man, I would be able to take over the estate. I suppose it was a great deal of responsibility to instil in a young boy and he believed there was no time to waste on childishness. Wickham would never bear the same responsibility so there was a more emotional connection between them. Papa could afford to be more tolerant with him."

"And yet he was merely his godson. He was not even family, was he?"

"That bears no relevance when you love someone, Lizzy, and Lord knows that Wickham has the talent to endear himself to all who know him. As godfather and protector, my father offered him a gentleman's education. But the more he gave, the more Wickham became temperamental. I have only recently begun to understand why he went down such a bad path, despite his good fortune. To tell

159

you the truth, I realised certain things by observing you and your sisters."

"Really?"

"Yes. I saw all five of you evolve, each with a distinct identity. Despite the fact that you are all closely knit, it seemed to me that you all sought to distinguish yourselves from one another, and strive to be appreciated for yourselves rather than in comparison to another sister – which is quite natural, come to think of it. With your personality, you are without a doubt the first to shine in society, but we know that Lydia is not to be outdone when it comes to seeking attention. I also think of your sister Mary, who seeks to impress with her intellect, or Kitty, whose outbursts are intended to draw attention. Out of all of you, Jane is perhaps the most withdrawn, and I suspect she is so less out of modesty than out of a sincere selfless dedication to you all."

Elizabeth listened in amazement. It was the first time she had heard her husband give his opinion about her family with so little inhibition.

The young man continued:

"If I apply this to the only brother I have ever had, I realise that we, too, sought to prove to my father how worthy we were of his affection, and how both of us wished to be acknowledged for who we truly were. But that dear man was more concerned about our future. He was engrossed in the task of finding us our place in the world and did not care to mediate our childish fights, which, to us at least, were crucial. I believe that is how the gulf slowly widened between Wickham and I."

"I am surprised to hear you say such things, William. You forget that this man also has a strong penchant for gambling. Why did he squander the money offered to him when he could have put it to good use and make an honest life for himself? Searching for paternal approval does not explain such conduct!"

"You are right."

Darcy paused to reorganise his thoughts, before continuing.

"You have identified a deeper problem," he acknowledged. "If you want my honest opinion, I believe the favours bestowed upon

Wickham when he was young spoilt him far more than they benefited him. We were raised together, participated in the same games and education, and yet we do not belong to the same world. The fortune to which I was entitled was inaccessible to him. He was unable to come to terms with the fact that he would have to work his whole life for his own success. And since my father always provided for him, it was a discipline he never acquired."

"He must have been terribly envious of you..."

"He was careful not to utter it openly, but his behaviour did indicate this to be the case. I was by no means the only one, however. At Cambridge, he envied anyone who had better ranking – that is to say, everyone. His fine manners, presence and handsome countenance secured him access to the highest society but he rapidly reached its limits: even if his father was an exemplary man, he was not a gentleman, which made it harder for Wickham to rise to the same rank as you and I. He certainly would have succeeded through sheer perseverance but, as I have just mentioned, that was not a skill he had acquired. He preferred easy money and tried to make his fortune at the gambling tables."

"Or by marrying an heiress."

Elizabeth refrained from mentioning Georgiana, but Darcy clearly understood to whom she was referring. His face hardened.

"I dare not imagine what might have happened had he succeeded," he said, jaw clenched. Married to such an individual, my poor sister would no doubt have been utterly miserable. It took her months to recover from the disappointment, poor child, and I am convinced that she never wholly grasped how severe it might have been, nor how much she had been manipulated. She is still convinced that Wickham loved her dearly, but that another had turned his head. I even wonder if she blames me for having prevented their union."

"I am quite certain she does not. She loves you and respects you too much," Elizabeth reassured him.

Her husband gave her a weak smile.

"I regret that he wound up preying upon your sister, Lizzy. I still have not forgiven myself for staying silent when I saw him again in Hertfordshire."

"We have already discussed all this, my dear," she replied, taking his hand in comfort. "And you forget that while Wickham was guilty of indulging his dreadful whims, Lydia is just as guilty of improper conduct. She, too, was spoilt as a child, unfortunately..."

The conversation ended there, and the ensign's letter concluded its journey in the fireplace. Both of them knew that it was just a matter of time before the subject cropped up again.

~

"Mr. and Mrs. Darcy," announced the butler in a deep voice, once they appeared in the drawing-room.

"Mr. Darcy! There you are, finally! And this is your lovely wife!"

The lady who had risen to meet them was mistress of the house, Mrs. Langhold herself. She appeared to be between forty and fifty years old and was adorned with large quantities of jewels that twinkled on her grey silk dress. A widow, she lived with her two unmarried sons in Langhold hall, a beautiful home, which Elizabeth immediately compared to Netherfield. She made it a point of honour to host the finest society of the region in her drawing-room, several times a month.

The room in question was richly decorated and lit by a plethora of candles. To mark the beginnings of Mrs. Darcy's time amongst them, the wealthy widow had invited the Clarksons, Sir Andrew Norton, accompanied by his sister and their young cousin, a certain Mr. Blackmore and his wife, along with the Viscount Hastings and his wife, both proudly representing the nobility of the region.

Langhold Hall was located quite far from Lambton, but all had braved the cold night and the distance to be present that evening. Elizabeth did not know whether she should take pride in having piqued their curiosity, or whether their attendance was solely the result of their hostess's influence.

The ritual was the same as in London. Everyone praised the newcomer for several minutes, exchanging bows and civilities, after which the young woman was invited to sit down with the ladies while Darcy joined the men. Once again, Elizabeth tried to memorise the names, faces and various relationships that connected them as quickly as she could, so as to answer their questions in the most courteous way.

"Dear Mrs. Darcy, we were most eager to meet you!" began Mrs. Langhold. "Are you happily settled at Pemberley?"

"Indeed, I am, thank you," replied Elizabeth.

"You had already visited once before, I believe, had you not? Tell us everything!"

"That is correct. I was visiting Derbyshire with my aunt and uncle when I crossed paths with Mr. Darcy, with whom I was already acquainted. He very kindly invited us to join him and a few acquaintances and I had the pleasure of meeting Miss Darcy."

"Ah, that dear child! I cannot wait for her brother to allow her to be presented. She is simply delightful. She would make a fantastic addition to our card games! I know of a few players for whom she would make for very pleasant company!"

Elizabeth wondered for a moment whether Mrs. Langhold was suggesting that Georgiana would thus be introduced to her sons. But as no other guest seemed to respond to the allusion, she did not react either.

A servant came to serve Madeira and the rest of the conversation was lost amidst gallantries.

"Darcy," said Sir Norton, "I am delighted that you have finally joined the club of married men! Lord knows that my dear wife has referenced your unfortunate single life far too often. We were beginning to despair for you, my friend..."

"I suspect that my being single was harder on my acquaintances than it was on me," he replied. "Before, I could not imagine that one's partner in life could bring me so much happiness and I now realise how sorely I was missing it."

"Although, one must meet a young lady who knows how to awaken such feelings," Clarkson interjected. "The unmarried state can be very pleasant. It only becomes painful when one begins nurturing certain hopes..."

"Or, if you no longer nurse them!" replied Mrs. Langhold, bringing the women into the men's conversation. "Since my husband's death, the house has never seemed so empty. I would not know what to do if my dear sons were not here to ease the burden!"

"You are quite right," said Darcy. "The single state can only be more burdensome once we have met and appreciated the object of our desires only to lose it again."

He glanced at Elizabeth, who, for a second, was plunged back into that disastrous moment in Hunsford, when Darcy had first asked for her hand. She felt herself blush.

Her discomfort might have gone unnoticed had there not been so many eyes on her since her arrival.

"Mr. Darcy, contain yourself! You are flustering your wife!" Lady Hastings chuckled.

Darcy glanced at his wife again and gave her a tender smile. Mrs. Clarkson stepped into the conversation.

"Can you believe they knew each other for a year before their engagement! You must have caused poor Mr. Darcy much suffering!" she burst out laughing.

"Please do not believe that I did so voluntarily," Elizabeth defended herself. "I knew nothing of Mr. Darcy's feelings for me."

"It is true that our friend is very discreet... Let this be a lesson to you, Darcy! One gains nothing without plainly asking for it," retorted Mrs. Langhold.

"Patience is a virtue," he replied. "It took some time indeed, but as you will have noticed, I did succeed eventually..."

~

As in London, Elizabeth was beset with questions for the better part of dinner. Everyone wanted to know about her family, how she met Darcy, their wedding and how she was settling down at Pemberley. Were they expecting to stay all winter? Did they plan to return to London in February for the season? What did she think of the charming Georgiana? Did she often go to Lambton? Did she have relatives or acquaintances that would soon visit her? Did she not miss her family too much, now that she lived so far away?

She answered patiently and was most amiable to everyone and felt much less intimidated than she had been at the Egertons'. Not only was she beginning to grow accustomed to her new circumstances, but also Derbyshire possessed a familiar quality that reminded her of home. This was the country, and all these people, although very elegant in their evening clothes, did not have much in common with the proud Londoners who had sneered at her. Even Lord and Lady Hastings, although titled and slightly condescending, did not intimidate her as much.

The small party concerned itself with the same ordinary matters as the people of Meryton. They spoke of the weather, the latest harvest, hunting and the arrival of winter, which would confine everyone next to the fire, limiting activities such as card games and balls. The most remarkable conversation was about a cousin of Mr. Blackmore's, a rector who was about to leave for India to spread the Word of God amongst the heathens. Everyone knew of the enterprise, which he had prepared for months, and commented on which clothes he should bring, the best route to take by boat and their fears of landing in such a barbarian country. The man had not yet departed but everyone already prayed for his safe return.

Derbyshire was quite remote. For its inhabitants, a simple journey to the capital was already such an undertaking, that travelling to India seemed nothing short of torture... With the exception of the Darcys, the Langholds and the Hastings, all of whom were wealthy enough to travel to London, Bath or any fashionable destination whenever they wished, the other guests did not leave the county very often. It was noticeable in their conversations, which inevitably went around in circles. Elizabeth was amused to find that although she had always considered herself lacking in culture, she had no reason to fear that she might appear uneducated to them. On the contrary, she refrained from making literary references when the conversation turned to travelling, so as not to draw attention to their limitations.

Mrs. Langhold had seated Elizabeth to her right in honour of her arrival amongst them and was a very pleasant hostess. It was no surprise that she was the centre of social activity in the area: she had a real talent for putting people at ease. Her sons, on the other hand, were much less chatty. The eldest, James, a young man in his

165

twenties, seemed utterly bored and made no effort to take part in the conversation. His brother, Jacob, would have gladly participated, but he spoke so softly that no one heard him, for there was always someone who spoke with more animation, drawing their attention away from the retiring young gentleman.

Miss Russell, the Nortons' younger cousin, was one such guest. Elizabeth observed her from the corner of her eye, for they were nearest in age and she wondered if they might become friends. She quickly changed her mind as Sophie Russell proved to be somewhat overbearing. She often interrupted, jested without restraint about everything and everyone, was impertinent and simpered a great deal. She was seated near Darcy, whom she addressed repeatedly, so much so that Elizabeth raised an eyebrow, astonished by the display. Darcy answered, as always, with polite indifference. The other guests also seemed accustomed to her intrusive temperament: no one paid her any mind and neither Sir Norton nor his sister intervened to mitigate their cousin's behaviour.

Elizabeth eventually began to enjoy the evening, but she promised herself that she would invite Miss Russell as little as possible.

~

After settling in the drawing-room following dinner, a game of cards was suggested, but most of the men withdrew. They preferred to go to the library for a glass of cognac and serious conversation. Jacob Langhold sat down with Mr. Blackmore around a game of tric-trac, while the ladies, disappointed by the lack of male players, resigned themselves to sitting next to the fireplace and chatting.

Leaving them to their conversation, Mrs. Langhold took care of her new guest, offering to show her the neighbouring rooms and the gallery. Elizabeth was thus able to view paintings of excellent craftsmanship along with wonderful bronze statues that the Langhold family had been collecting for several generations. She gave the hostess her sincerest compliments.

While the two women were still in the gallery, the butler appeared. He apologised for interrupting his mistress but needed her attention regarding an important matter that could not wait. Mrs. Langhold apologised in turn.

"Forgive me, madam, I must leave you for a moment. Can you find your way back to the drawing room?"

"Of course."

"Thank you. I shall return as soon as possible."

After the mistress had left, Elizabeth spent another moment admiring the paintings before finally deciding to return to the others. Her footsteps were light and made very little noise on the wooden floors. She arrived at the door unnoticed and overheard the conversation occurring on the other side.

Curious, she listened.

"...and really," said Lady Hastings, "I struggle to comprehend how Mr. Darcy could have made such a decision. With his fortune, he could have attracted the finest matches!"

"He is not an impulsive man," added Mrs. Blackmore. "He has always been very conscious of his rank and, as we know, he would never have married a penniless woman."

Elizabeth felt her heart stop. She had only recently arrived in Pemberley: how did they know about her lack of fortune already, and that Darcy had married beneath him? The servants must have said something. There could be no other explanation.

"It would appear that his aunt, Lady Catherine, is furious with him," said Miss Norton with an affected air.

"Understandably so," responded the Viscountess. "Our poor friend no longer had his parents to advise him. Lady Catherine took that role very seriously and wished a most advantageous union for him. What a disappointment for her!"

"And for us, too!" exclaimed Miss Russell. "Why did he feel the need to find a wife so far from Derbyshire, when he might have found all the happiness in the world here, amongst his equals? Were we not good enough for him?"

Motionless against the wall behind the door, Elizabeth thought, not without some irony, that those utterances were almost identical to those made by Caroline Bingley.

167

Miss Norton tried to appease her cousin:

"It is true, my dear, that you possess everything that might please such a gentleman. Lord knows what came over him when he became infatuated with this 'stranger'."

"She is hardly pretty," Sophie continued with disdain.

"It is true, she has neither your blonde hair nor your beautiful bright eyes, both of which are so widely admired," Mrs. Clarkson chimed in, "but I do find her quite lovely. There is something rather distinguished about her features, would you not agree?"

"Not at all!" countered Sophie, vehemently. "Her nose is too thick and she is as dark skinned as a Moor!"

At these words, Lady Hastings finally decided to intervene in an effort to check the young woman.

"I would ask you to watch your words, my dear," she declared with authority. "You forget yourself."

This was followed by an uneasy silence. Behind the door, Elizabeth bit her lip.

"Be that as it may, there is no denying that Mrs. Darcy has very good conversation," continued Mrs. Clarkson. "Knowing our friend, I would not be surprised if he was charmed by her wit and vivacity. Perhaps he needed a woman like her."

"It is possible, but still, her personal strengths are not the only thing to consider," objected Miss Norton. Mr. Darcy is no fool, and yet he has taken a great gamble: surely he is aware that a person of such modest means cannot possibly be ready to look after a house as prestigious as Pemberley."

"That is quite true," Mrs. Blackmore replied. "Indeed, one would hope that he will not allow her to ruin everything. After so many generations spent growing the estate, it would be a disgrace to the family!"

Exasperated, Elizabeth sighed inwardly.

Why in heaven's name were all these people so preoccupied with the way she intended to run her house? Did they really fear that she would squander her husband's fortune and ruin Pemberley? And even if she did, what did it matter to them? They were not even family.

"I find you rather harsh, ladies. I think we should give her the benefit of the doubt before judging whether she will fail or not," Mrs. Clarkson tempered once again. "It always takes time for a young wife to find her bearings. We can all attest to that."

"In the meantime, one of the most eligible bachelors of the country has been taken from us by a vulgar stranger!" hissed Sophie, undeterred.

This time, Elizabeth decided that she had heard quite enough and quietly moved away.

She had been prepared to face criticism, both here and elsewhere. She was also not surprised, after what she had seen at the table, that Sophie Russell employed no restraint in expressing her disappointment at not having succeeded in seducing Darcy. She would undoubtedly not be the last to do so: if Derbyshire mothers were as eager to marry their daughters as Mrs. Bennet had been, and if the ladies were as coquettish as Lydia or as interested as Caroline Bingley, Elizabeth could well grasp the resentment she now faced.

Nevertheless, she was surprised that it was all happening so fast and with so little discretion. These women spoke unabashedly, while she was in the house, ready to appear at any time. Did they have no decency? Or was it simply the anger at having 'their' Mr. Darcy taken from them that rendered them so careless?

Elizabeth knew she would have to prove herself. It was up to her to make an effort to earn their acceptance, to adapt to their way of life, to learn to appreciate them. But she hated the idea that they were so unfavourable to her already, without knowing her true character.

Hearing this sort of malice only served to strengthen her resolve to show them who she was and to prove that she had her place at Pemberley, and amongst them.

CHAPTER 7

While Elizabeth was too proud to admit it, she was nevertheless incredibly impressed by Pemberley.

The house was as vast as it was elegant. The interior was tastefully decorated and yet somewhat less ostentatious than the gilded rooms found in Rosings or even at Langhold Hall. There were, however, signs of great wealth everywhere: furniture made of fine wood, wood floors inlaid with complicated patterns, crystal chandeliers, oriental carpets, silks, embroidery and satin. On walls covered in delicately coloured wallpaper, hung large, beautiful paintings, sparsely arranged so as not to be overwhelming. On every table, console or mantelpiece, there were fine bronze pieces, ornate mirrors, delicate vases, or even adorable little clocks, exquisitely tying everything in the room together to harmonious effect.

Nevertheless, Elizabeth did not feel at ease. It was all incredibly beautiful, but also quite frozen in time, and she dared not move anything for fear of being reprimanded. Already, in her room, she could barely discard a piece of clothing or lay a book down on the sofa without Mrs. Vaughan cleaning up after her. So much so that the young woman sometimes struggled to find her belongings. The living area on the first floor was worse. She never saw the servants but felt their presence everywhere, which gave her the unfortunate impression of being an intruder on their territory. They had been instructed not to disturb her with day-to-day problems until she had settled into her new home, which meant that, much like at Chalton House, they treated her with a distance usually reserved for guests. Weston, the butler, for instance, only spoke to her when he had no other choice. The rest of the time, he addressed Darcy, giving Elizabeth the unpleasant sensation of being invisible. As for Mrs. Reynolds, who was always mild-mannered and kept her hands folded in her apron, she kept her head lowered in front of her mistress and Elizabeth was unable to determine whether it was out of defiance or as a result of a meek disposition.

To make matters worse, the meals were as ceremonial as formal dinners even though their group was small and intimate. While civility was essential in society, Elizabeth had hoped that within the privacy of their domestic circle they would allow themselves to be more casual. Yet light-heartedness was precisely what Pemberley sorely lacked. Mrs. Annesley's austere presence at the table and her constant efforts to correct her pupil's manners whilst silently observing Elizabeth's, did nothing to assuage the situation.

The house was too quiet. There were neither children, nor birds chirping in cages, nor dogs barking and scampering cheerfully down the corridors. Georgiana was the only one who brought some life into the house through her music. Thankfully, she was always very happy to perform, or else Elizabeth might have perished from boredom.

To escape this atmosphere, which she found entirely too rigid for her liking, the young woman had found respite in the parlour situated on the first floor, once reserved exclusively for Lady Anne. No one entered without her permission – even her husband always knocked on the door. She kept a fire burning there all day and since the servants only entered at night to empty the ashes and clean the room, she could scatter her personal items about the room as she wished or lie down on the sofas to read at her leisure. Unlike Darcy, she was not used to holding herself straight as a board at all times, and she relished in these idle moments with an almost guilty pleasure. Here, at least, no one could scrutinise or judge her behaviour.

The room had not changed since the days of Lady Anne and, at first, Elizabeth dared not touch anything. Then, realising that she was free to alter the layout as she pleased, she brought the sofa closer to the fireplace, stacked a pile of books she intended to read next to it, drew a table to the window to set up her writing box, and took down the paintings that were not to her linking. One of the key features of the room, a tightly locked, magnificent mahogany secretary, intrigued her and so she asked Mrs. Reynolds for the key which the latter promised to find.

"Lizzy?" called Darcy, knocking gently at the door.

Elizabeth had retired to the parlour that afternoon, after a long walk leading her far into the valley, along the river. It had rained the previous days and she had taken advantage of a lull in the downpour to enjoy some fresh air, but the muddy paths had frozen her feet. She was curled up on her sofa, under a blanket, her legs pointed towards the chimney where a fire was burning, when her husband came to join her.

"How was your walk earlier?" he sat next to her. "Poor darling, you look frozen stiff!"

"The view was beautiful and well worth the effort," she replied, smiling with pleasure at the memory. "I am not to be pitied: I have a roof over my head, a fire burning at my feet, blankets and now a lovely husband here to comfort me!"

Darcy laughed and kissed her.

"I am quite happy to comfort you, but I actually came to give you this," he said, taking a small golden key out from his waistcoat pocket. "I believe you asked Mrs. Reynolds to find it for you."

"Oh! Is it the key to the secretary?"

"Yes, I had it. But as you are now mistress of Pemberley, it belongs to you. If I'm not mistaken, you shall find quite a few papers and letters belonging to my mother. This secretary has not been opened since she passed away – at least not by me. I leave it to your discretion to burn anything you deem necessary."

"Of course," Elizabeth replied, looking at the little key with an eager interest. "Would you like us to have a look together?"

Darcy frowned. The thought of going through his mother's belongings did not appeal to him.

"No, I trust you. She certainly would have approved of my giving you this key and I suppose you shall find old ledgers there that might be of use to you."

He then kissed her once more and got up.

"Would you like me to ask for tea to be brought up?"

"With pleasure, thank you! Would you and Georgiana like to join me for a cup?"

"Why not?"

With a smile, Darcy withdrew, leaving his wife alone with the little key in her hands.

~

Although her curiosity was piqued, Elizabeth had to wait until the following morning before she could finally open the secretary. It was an imposing piece of furniture, as high as a wardrobe, and divided into three parts. At the bottom there were large drawers, all closed. In the middle, also locked, was a hinged desktop that could be unfolded to serve as a writing table. The little key that Darcy had given his wife unlocked the two doors above.

As she opened them, Elizabeth's eyes widened.

While the exterior was made of rich mahogany, the interior was overlaid with a light chestnut veneer that gave it a startling, almost golden luminosity. In the centre, a small, mirrored panel opened up to reveal a storage box, while above lay compartments filled with rolls of paper and small objects. On the sides were shelves for books and notebooks and, below that, were eight tiny drawers. There, she found a set of keys, which opened the desktop. Covered in beautiful red leather, it provided a very comfortable workspace, also adorned with storage nooks of various sizes that allowed for any number of items to be stowed away.

Elizabeth pulled out a chair and sat down in front of this little wonder of carpentry. She was struck by the ingenuity of the piece. Everywhere, tiny handles or locks could be used to operate drawers and panels. With such fine craftsmanship, she would not be surprised to learn that the secretary also contained a few secret compartments. She was eager to discover them all in time.

Darcy had been right: there were many books, letters and objects belonging to his mother, and Elizabeth had the very clear and somewhat unpleasant feeling that she was intruding upon her privacy.

A ring, which Lady Anne had forgotten. Her nibs and her ink, whose drops had dried on the edges of the bottle. Her letters, bundled up with ribbon or string, broken lead pencils and a seal with its wax. An ink-stained glove which she had forgotten to give to the servants to clean. A box of sand, part of which had spilt out into the compartment. A painted miniature of Darcy from when he was about ten years old, candles, a bouquet of dried flowers, two old fans and a small ivory-handled knife. A medallion containing what looked like a lock of Georgiana's hair when she was a baby. A damaged peacock feather. A silver vinaigrette from which a few whiffs of perfume still emanated. An amethyst geode...

Elizabeth paused, flooded by all these details that suddenly made Lady Anne's presence almost palpable. If the new Mrs. Darcy were to use this secretary to carry out her duties as mistress, she would have no choice but to sort through her predecessor's belongings. However, the emotions they elicited were too strong.

She rose and went to the window to compose herself.

The secretary's golden key was still in her hand and she began to stroke it absentmindedly. The object, as innocuous in appearance as it was, had just opened up a door to Lady Anne's world and ensured that Elizabeth would have to heed its contents.

She could easily visualise the woman's charming face, which she had so often admired in the portrait gallery. She also thought of her name, carved in the polished tombstone near the small chapel. Previously, when the young woman had tried to imagine what her mother-in-law looked like, both physically and in terms of personality, she had imagined a second Lady Catherine, imperious and authoritarian. But the figure that now emerged was entirely different. Could one be an esteemed lady yet still stain one's gloves? Or spill sand everywhere rather than sprinkling it over a freshly inked letter where it belonged?

Misplacing one's perfume box under a pile of papers? Or collecting pretty crystals and dried flowers?

Elizabeth stood at the window, lost in her thoughts. She now understood why her husband had not wished to be involved. What would he have said upon seeing his miniature portrait? Or Georgiana's lock of hair? Unlike his sister, he had spent many years at their mother's side and would almost certainly have been affected by all these memories, as tender and painful as they were.

The young woman finally composed herself.

"Lady Anne," she said under her breath, addressing the sky above the valley floor, "I will have to sort through and tidy up your belongings, but I assure you that I will do so with the greatest respect. I also promise that, even if it all were to disappear entirely, you will remain fixed in the memories of those who knew and loved you. I do regret not having had the privilege myself."

Heartened by this little prayer, she returned to the secretary and sat in her chair once more, pondering how best to sort through it all.

It took her the entire day. After refusing Mrs. Reynolds' help, Elizabeth spent hours alone in the parlour, emptying each compartment, drawer and cabinet. She set aside books, notebooks and anything else that might be reused or placed elsewhere. She kept the amethyst stone, placing it on the mantle above the chimney, and burnt the bundles of letters without untying the ribbons. She also burnt the stained glove, the quills, the old unused paper and anything else that no longer had any value. She then had rags brought up with furniture polish and cleaned every little cabinet from top to bottom. As for the miniature portrait and the lock of hair, she slipped them into her pocket to return them to their rightful owners.

When it was time to go upstairs to change for dinner, the secretary was entirely empty.

~

The greenhouse was a little structure made of glass and white metal, placed upon a stone wall, about three feet high. Inside, the warmth and humidity contrasted pleasantly with the cold air outside. It smelled like soil and citrus fruits.

Georgiana, who was delighted to act as a guide for her sister-in-law, chattered away sweetly. She showed her the lemon and mandarin trees, as well as the handful of lettuces still able to grow so late in the season. She also pointed to the gardener's tools, which, she said, were not to be trifled with.

"You know, Lizzy, a greenhouse exists in a very delicate balance. It only takes a small jump in temperature or change in humidity for all of this to perish," the adolescent explained with an affected air, as if reciting a lesson.

Elizabeth went along indulgently, amused to see Georgiana share her knowledge in such a spirited fashion.

In reality, the poor child did not know much. Although she had now been at Pemberley for two years, she lived in seclusion, and when Elizabeth had asked her to show her the less frequented parts of the house, she realised that the young girl had never set foot in some of the rooms. Her life was limited to the west wing, her own bedroom and a few other places like the library and the greenhouse, where she was bold enough – by her own account – to venture alone.

"But this is your home, my dear, isn't it? Have you never felt inclined to explore its mysterious nooks and crannies?" Elizabeth had asked, surprised, for she had no trouble imagining that her own curiosity would have prompted her to explore the entire house.

Alas, the adolescent had a rather different disposition. Her peaceful life in the shadow of Mrs. Annesley was good enough for her and, as Elizabeth listened to her speak, she thought to herself that someone ought to take it upon themselves to animate this overly demure girl.

The two sisters had just finished their tour of the greenhouse.

"I shall always remember the first time I came here," said Georgiana, stopping next to a mandarin tree. "At the time, there were two orange trees, and George brought me here to smell the flowers. He often took care of me, when I was younger... He was so kind!"

It took Elizabeth a moment to realise that the younger girl was referring to Wickham.

"I shall take your word for it," she answered. "He is indeed a charming young man."

"Did you know him well?"

"Not as well as you, but I did meet him on a few occasions in Meryton."

"You must be delighted to have him as a brother now!"

Flustered, Elizabeth sought an appropriate response.

"I believe I love having you as a sister even more," she replied with an affectionate smile.

Georgiana had never been told about the scandal surrounding Lydia and Wickham's marriage. She was far too innocent. It would have been cruel to reveal a truth that she was not yet ready to hear. So Elizabeth remained silent about the details, but since the adolescent had broached the subject with an obvious desire to confide in someone, she encouraged the girl gently.

"William told me that you also held Mr. Wickham in high regard at one time. You must be very upset with him for having chosen to marry Lydia..."

Georgiana blushed.

"I suppose your sister must be an extraordinary young lady," she stammered.

"I have only agreeable things to say about her since she is my sister," Elizabeth answered, tactfully, "but I would quite understand if you felt even the slightest amount of scorn for a man who left you for another. Indeed, it would be entirely natural. I hope you won't hold it against me now that I am connected to him."

"Not at all, rest assured!"

But a heavy silence settled between the young women. To create a diversion, Elizabeth spoke up in a cheerful tone:

"Do you know what, Georgiana? I cannot wait for you to be brought into society. You will see that this country is full of amiable young men. And the parties and outings keep the mind so busy that there is no room for such regrets. We simply cannot keep you here all your life: you must come out soon!"

"My brother says I am too young still."

"He is simply trying to protect you, but you seem to be perfectly ready to take this step. I shall have a word with him."

"Really?"

"Yes! Why not? I cannot always go out to dinner or attend balls with my friends knowing that you are alone in your room. I am certain that within a few months, we shall be able to do something about it!"

Georgiana seemed to forget about her disheartening infatuation, and her eyes began to shine. The prospect of coming out was rather charming, indeed.

For her part, Elizabeth silently congratulated herself on having succeeded in livening her up, and, looking to banish all traces of Wickham once and for all, she took her by the arm and led her outside, requesting a tour of the vegetable garden.

~

"... But, if that is the case, I don't understand where all this poultry comes from. They seem rather young to me."

"Mrs. Reynolds orders them from the town, madam. The Lambton market is excellent and it is more convenient than bringing them in from the estate farms, which are too far away."

"But if you were to keep a few eggs to hatch, would that not solve the problem?"

"Yes, certainly, madam."

"So why not do it?"

"You would have to ask Mr. Hewitt. He is the one who collects the eggs."

"All of them?"

"I suppose he needs them in the kitchen."

During her visit, Elizabeth had found that the gardener's cottage was well kept and that his wife, Mrs. Cox, also took good care of the vegetable garden and farmyard. She was a welcoming woman who did her best to answer her new mistress's questions, but Elizabeth noticed that she appeared a little uncomfortable. She gave her a reassuring smile.

"Forgive me, I am troubling you with all my questions."

"Not at all, madam."

"I seek only to understand the ways of this house. Everything here is so new to me!"

"Of course, madam."

The two women stood at the fence that enclosed the farmyard. Georgiana, quickly overwhelmed by logistical considerations that she did not understand, had lingered next to the hutches to pet the rabbits while two young boys of about five or six pulled at her skirts. Seeing that the visit was over, she returned to Elizabeth. Mrs. Cox immediately called her children to order.

"Stop pestering Miss Darcy!" she lectured them, before sending them back into the house.

"Don't scold them, please! They behaved so sweetly with me," she apologised on their behalf.

"I hope so miss, I would hate for them to have soiled your pretty dress..."

They all wished each other a good day, and Elizabeth and her sister made their way back to the house. Georgiana was cheerful, as if they were returning from a big party.

"It was such a lovely visit, was it not?" she exclaimed.

"Yes, it was. And very interesting too."

"Indeed, you showed considerable interest in kitchen matters," the adolescent laughed, throwing her companion a teasing look. "You almost reminded me of my aunt, Lady Catherine, who is always full of advice on all matters. I am quite certain that if she had been here, she would have found something to improve in the farmyard!"

"She would not have been wrong. There is always room for improvement. As for me, I am more in a position to receive advice than to give some. But I do find it odd... Why bother to buy poultry when you could so easily raise some yourself?"

"I suppose that the idea is to have them at hand when you need them. The means do not matter."

Puzzled, Elizabeth turned to Georgiana.

"They do, if they cost money, my dear. Why spend more when there are alternatives? I imagine you are aware that your family did not expand the estate through indiscriminate spending."

Georgiana shrugged, more interested in the small bunch of wildflowers that the Cox children had picked for her than such vulgar topics as money or poultry.

Elizabeth changed the subject.

"You spoke of your aunt earlier. Do you write to her often?"

"Not so much, no." In fact, my brother is better acquainted with her than I as he often stays at Rosings."

"If that is so, perhaps it would be a good idea to invite your aunt for a visit. It would be an opportunity to see her again. Or perhaps you might wish to stay at Rosings a few weeks yourself?"

Unaware of her sister's ploy, Georgiana replied, looking forlorn:

"I would love to, but William tells me they are not on the best of terms these days. He did not specify why."

"He has informed you that there has been a disagreement in the family yet did not explain why?"

"To spare me any worry, I suppose. He has always done so."

Elizabeth rolled her eyes. Despite all the love she had for her husband, she found his habit of concealing hardship quite ridiculous. How could he keep a girl as naive as Georgiana away from everything that was happening in the family? Did he really think that she would obediently put the matter aside and no longer pay it any mind? A quarrel between Rosings and Pemberley was no small thing

180

and the adolescent, with her head full of tales and dramas, must have imagined the worst reasons possible.

Elizabeth made an effort to contain her annoyance and continued gently:

"I have no doubt that William is the best of brothers to you, just as he is the best of husbands to me, nevertheless he is wrong to keep you in the dark like this. You should know that it is my fault that he and your aunt are currently at odds."

"You? How so?"

"Because I was not the excellent match that your aunt had hoped for William. I was unable to provide a dowry or connections."

"But he loves you!" exclaimed Georgiana, candidly. "Is that not all that matters?"

"It is true, he loves me, and I love him. Unfortunately, this is of little consequence to your aunt. She seeks to avoid me, and the bad influence I represent, not your brother. Forgive me for such frankness, Georgiana, but you are no longer a child and I believe you should be made aware of such things."

The front of the house appeared from behind the line of trees. They were getting close.

"Would you be willing to talk to William?" Elizabeth insisted. "I have attempted to convince him to apologise a few times, but he is obstinate – and I fear that your aunt is worse in that regard. I have sown discord in spite of myself, and I wish for the Darcy and de Bourgh families to be as united as before."

Embarrassed, Georgiana tried to evade the question by not answering. Her sister-in-law, however, stared at her unwaveringly until she finally stammered a response.

"I will try..."

~

The next day, Elizabeth was reading undisturbed in her parlour when the housekeeper asked to speak with her.

"I heard that you went up to the Cox's cottage, madam. I wished to make sure that everything was satisfactory."

"Indeed. Miss Georgiana showed me the greenhouse, so I took the opportunity to visit the grounds. I found Mrs. Cox very kind. It is daunting labour, but she does a remarkable job: I have rarely seen a barnyard so clean!"

"Yes, we are very happy with her. Her children help her a great deal and we provide her with extra sets of arms as soon as the need arises."

Elizabeth suspected that Mrs. Reynolds had not taken the uncharacteristic initiative of coming to speak with her just to praise the gardener's wife. She thus decided to address the core of the matter directly.

"I did find it curious, however, that with the amount of poultry we own, we do not have enough eggs to raise a few clutches. Mrs. Cox tells me that you buy the birds at the Lambton market?"

"Indeed, madam," replied the housekeeper, lowering her eyes as if she were being rebuked. "We have always done so."

"Really?"

"Yes. I have been at Pemberley House for twenty-five years and it has been a long time since we have raised our own hens on the estate. Whenever possible, Mr. Darcy's farmers provide them to us, but the estate is big and it is not always easy to travel around. The Lambton Market is much closer. I assure you, madam, the products there are of excellent quality!"

"I do not doubt that. I am in no way questioning your management, Mrs. Reynolds, I simply found it surprising for my family did things differently."

"I understand, madam. In that case, rest assured: everything is perfectly under control and you need not worry about such details."

The conversation appeared to be over, but the housekeeper, who had curtsied, stood in the middle of the rug as if waiting for something. Elizabeth realised that she awaited a formal dismissal. She made a brief gesture and Mrs. Reynolds left.

Alone again, she put her book aside. She mindlessly stroked Lady Anne's little golden secretary key, now tied by a cord to her belt.

This matter of eggs and poultry seemed quite trivial, and she might not have given it much more thought had the housekeeper's attitude not intrigued her. Mrs. Reynolds was an honest and competent woman, but she clearly feared any kind of disruption within the household. This was precisely what Elizabeth would have to do should she deem it necessary. She was now at the head of the Darcy fortune along with her husband, and it was her responsibility to ensure that money was not spent needlessly especially if there was a way to produce a number of things directly at Pemberley House. Raising a few clutches to increase the number of birds available in the farmyard instead of paying full price for them at the market was a simple project that Elizabeth felt quite capable of undertaking. After a full year, and given the daily consumption of poultry at Pemberley to feed masters and servants, it would save a substantial amount of money.

For the rest on the other hand...

The young woman had no idea where to begin. Darcy had told her that she would probably come across his mother's old ledgers in the secretary, but she had found nothing of the sort. However, she did remember having seen a handbook dedicated to teaching new wives how to successfully manage their households. This manual suddenly seemed of the utmost importance.

Abandoning the novel she had on her lap, she retrieved the manual and opened it. In the margins, Lady Anne had added personal comments in the margins.

Elizabeth sat comfortably on her sofa and immersed herself in the pages.

~

"Excuse me, Miss Darcy, *non ho sentito quello che ha detto?*" asked Mrs. Annesley.

"*Dicevo che Elizabeth balla, oltre che cantare,*" answered Georgiana.

Elizabeth and Georgiana danced together in the drawing-room, practising a complicated cotillion. There was much laughter, for they had to imagine that other couples danced all around them, which both complicated the task and amused them greatly. Mrs. Annesley accompanied them on the piano. Meanwhile, Darcy commented on their steps while sipping tea.

"I told her that your dancing is as good as your singing," the younger girl translated for her dance partner, as she continued twirling.

"Do you not speak Italian, Mrs. Darcy?" the companion asked, surprised.

"Not a word, no."

"How surprising. You sing so well in Italian that I was convinced you were fluent!"

"That is because she is as talented at singing as Georgiana is at playing the piano," Darcy replied. "With such an ear for music, you need not understand a foreign language to perform it with the right inflections."

"And you, William, do you speak Italian?" challenged his wife, winking at him.

"A smattering. I studied Latin at university which has helped me a great deal," he replied with great seriousness. "Though evidently Georgiana far surpasses us all."

"What use is it?" the girl sighed. "When Mrs. Annesley is no longer here, I will have no one with whom to converse. I shall rapidly forget it all."

"Nothing could be further from the truth," countered Elizabeth, twirling her partner. "We never quite forget something that we have strived to acquire – is that not why we are working so hard to learn this cotillion? And Georgiana, the day you meet a young, handsome Italian minister visiting London, you shall no doubt be very happy to address him in his own language..."

The young girl giggled under the stern gaze of Mrs. Annesley, who dared not say anything and continued playing the piano. Darcy, too, did not seem to find the jest very amusing.

"Come now, William, don't look so sombre!" teased Elizabeth. "You know that your sister will one day leave you to forge her own path!"

"If that is to be the case I wish for it to be as late as possible. And certainly not alone."

"Oh, poor darling," his wife went on, laughing again while she continued dancing, her steps becoming increasingly tangled. "You see how your brother dotes upon you, Georgiana... However shall we convince him to let you come out into society?"

The adolescent's eyes opened wide, half shocked, half amused, and Darcy stiffened on the sofa.

"What do you mean, Lizzy?"

"That Georgiana will soon be eighteen years old which is certainly something to consider. How much longer is she to remain hidden away in this house, do you think?"

"I cannot say, I had not given it much thought until now. Pemberley is hardly a prison, I might add."

His face had tightened. Elizabeth realised that she had pushed him a little too far. Letting go of Georgiana's arm, she went to him and placed a tender kiss on his cheek as a sign of apology.

"Please forgive me, my dear, you are right. I spoke too quickly. Let us speak no more of it!"

His eyes softened, reassuring her that all was forgiven.

But as the two young women resumed their cotillion, Darcy interrupted them again.

"Speaking of society, my dear, is it not time we returned Mrs. Langhold's invitation? What say you to organising your first reception?"

"Already? But I have barely been here for a fortnight!"

"Our friends have been quite gracious, not calling upon you too often to give you time to settle into your new home. It seems to me that it is up to us, or rather you, in this case, to take the first step."

At this Elizabeth stopped laughing and dancing. Organising one's first reception was an important step in every married woman's life and, with such a prestigious house to represent, it would be quite the challenge. Had Darcy been inspired by the fact that she had requested the key to his mother's secretary? Did he think she was now ready to fully embrace the responsibilities of a wife?

"How many guests did you have in mind?"

"I would say mostly those you are acquainted with already. Mrs. Langhold and her sons, Lord and Lady Hastings, the Clarksons, the Blackmores, the Nortons and Miss Russell – along with the Moores, of course. Reverend Smith would be delighted to be in attendance, I'm sure. And you could invite your aunt's friend, the one you called upon yesterday. I would thus have the pleasure of making her acquaintance along with her husband, of course. Remind me of her name?"

"Mrs. Munroe."

Elizabeth silently tallied up the numbers.

"Seventeen guests, along with the two of us – a large number of people to feed and entertain!"

"Does it seem excessive?"

"It seems fully in accordance with what people might expect of an invitation from Pemberley."

"So it is settled. You will just have to decide on a date at your convenience."

When he saw that his wife remained lost in thought, he tried to reassure her:

"Ask Mrs. Reynolds to help you, Lizzy. She is accustomed to these types of receptions."

~

Whether she liked it or not, Elizabeth set to work in the days that followed.

First and foremost, she began to fill her secretary with all the supplies she would need to run her household. In the upper part of the secretary, behind the mirrored door of the central cabinet, she locked away all her most precious belongings: her birth and marriage certificates, along with an antique brooch her mother had given her on the day she had turned twenty-one. It was the only valuable object that had followed her from Longbourn. She then put the handbook, annotated by Lady Anne, on one of the shelves along with a few other books on the same subject she had found in the library. She kept her old writing box next to the window, intending to use it for her personal correspondence, and had paper, quills and ink brought to her, which she put in the central part of the secretary. And, as it began to recover some of its former functionality, she took up the habit of always locking it with a set of keys, which she then placed inside the locked desktop, keeping only the little golden key with her.

She now felt a little more prepared to face her responsibilities.

Her first task was to balance out the number of guests. As they were one person away from being an equal number of men and women, Darcy suggested that she invite Mrs. Keen, a forthright and very pious widow, who was respected in the parish for both her bluntness and her involvement in charitable work. She knew the family well for she had been one of Darcy's teachers in his youth. Elizabeth took it upon herself to personally write to all the guests. One by one, they each confirmed their attendance. The easiest was done.

Next, the menu had to be decided. Here, matters became more complicated. Elizabeth, who had asked to go down to the servants' quarters in order to speak directly with Hewitt, the cook, was gaped at by a horrified Mrs. Reynolds who could not conceive that her mistress might set even so much as a foot in such a place. It was therefore agreed upon that Mr. Hewitt would instead go upstairs to meet her in her parlour.

It was the first time that Elizabeth was seeing the cook since she had met him on the day of her arrival at Pemberley. The man, red-faced and jovial in appearance, showed himself to be determined: he had a great deal of experience, had worked in the house for years and had strong opinions about how things should be done. Elizabeth sat him down at a table, accompanied by Mrs. Reynolds. She was about to brief them when he hurriedly embarked upon a detailed explanation of the menu he had devised since hearing of the reception: three courses, fish and crayfish in aspic, orange poached turkey, bouchées à la reine, rabbit fricassee, duck pie, cheeses and at least five desserts. This was followed by a list of small treats to be served after dinner, along with meats, breads and other cheeses for their supper at eleven.

Surprised, Elizabeth waited for the deluge of information to end before intervening.

"Do forgive me, but I'm afraid that I am not inclined to the idea of serving rabbit fricassee," she began.

"A veal stew, perhaps?" the cook promptly suggested.

"No, I don't..."

"Or perhaps some venison? At this time of year, it would not be difficult to procure a deer."

"Just a moment, Mr. Hewitt, you will not allow me to finish," she answered, slightly annoyed.

His mistress's rebuke did not appear to fluster him in the slightest, but he fell silent.

"I am not partial to saucy dishes which have simmered all day," she then explained. "Please do not misunderstand me, yours are delicious, but stews always resemble thick, fatty soups and I do not find them very elegant. For this dinner, I want the dishes to be as pleasant to look at as they are flavoursome. This is important. I would therefore ask you to take special care with the presentation."

Hewitt nodded, his countenance appearing to say that this was an obvious statement to make. She continued:

"I want to serve roasted lamb, which you will make on the spit. Mrs. Reynolds, you shall tell Mr. Weston to carve the meat upon the request of each guest. I do not want my guests to be inconvenienced by large cuts of meat. Each must be able to select the part they wish to eat. Oh! And make sure you also have some veal roast, in case some are not partial to the taste of lamb."

Mrs. Reynolds pulled out a small notebook from her pocket and began taking notes.

"I have written it all down, Mrs. Reynolds," added Elizabeth, pointing to a sheet of paper she had placed in front of her. "For the first course, your fish and jellied crayfish suit me very well, Mr. Hewitt, as well as your duck pâté – I had also thought of it. And you will add some vegetable soups, if you please. For the second course, the poached turkey should do nicely, with perhaps a few salads and, of course, a few sweet treats. For the third course, in addition to the roasts and the side dishes which I shall leave up to you, I propose that you replace your bouchées à la reine with something a little more daring that I once saw at a dinner in London: a partridge pie, with the usual decorated crust, but served in individual portions."

"Individual portions, madam?" the cook asked, surprised.

"Yes. I want one smaller pie per person. I suppose that half a partridge each will suffice."

The housekeeper and the cook glanced at each other wearily. Clearly their new mistress was asking for something quite out of the ordinary.

"I have never done such a thing before, madam. Shall I make use of moulds for the pastry?"

"I do not know, Mr. Hewitt. This is your area of expertise, not mine. But I plan to host the dinner next week, which leaves you with a few days to practise. In fact, I would very much like to taste it beforehand."

"Very well, madam," replied Mr. Hewitt with some hesitation

The discussion continued for a while longer. The rest of the dishes that were to accompany the meats were agreed upon, along with the time at which dinner and supper would be served. Once the two servants had left the parlour at last, Elizabeth collapsed on her sofa, both excited and exhausted.

She felt weary after having composed herself throughout the exchange. She had chosen her words carefully and said 'I want' instead of 'I would like,' used compliments so as not to hurt her cook's pride, watched her tone and the movements of her hands – which, as a result of her anxiety, had the unfortunate tendency to move in an agitated manner She had initially been shaken by Hewitt's self-importance, but felt that she had succeeded in gaining the upper hand and was pleased with herself.

Now that the kitchen was organised, she tackled the tableware. Accompanied by the butler, she reviewed the crystal, the silver and the porcelain, choosing one set amongst the seven that were available.

"You will have to hire additional help, Mr. Weston. I would not want there to be a shortage of footmen."

"It will be done, madam. And what about the wines?"

"I must confess that I know nothing about wine, but I have every confidence that you will serve whichever is most appropriate. Tonight I shall ask Mr. Darcy whether he has preferences or whether he knows if our guests have any themselves. And while we are seated at the table, you will close the doors to arrange the big sitting room. I wish for lotto and card tables to be set up."

"Are we to also open up the little sitting room?"

"No, leave the doors closed. However, light the fireplace and the candles, and make sure that everything is impeccable, for the gentlemen will no doubt wish to congregate there for a short time. Please also ensure that two or three footmen are available to serve the drinks throughout the evening. Shortly before eleven o'clock, you shall come to me: I will then decide, based on what our guests are doing, whether we are to serve supper or wait."

Elizabeth emerged from this exchange feeling a little more heartened. Unlike the cook, the butler had obediently approved everything his mistress had told him and she felt happy that she had not forgotten anything.

That evening, during the meal, Darcy was rather surprised to hear his wife tell him all about her preparations.

"Upon my word, Lizzy! I thought you would let Mrs. Reynolds take care of everything, but I see you have taken matters into hand with great confidence! I can only commend you, my dear."

He raised his glass of wine in her direction, in a sign of admiration. Elizabeth was flattered. She was putting a great deal of effort into ensuring that this reception would be perfect and she appreciated that her efforts were being properly recognised.

"I know of someone who will be pleased to hear that my wife is so competent in her role as hostess," he continued.

"Who would that be?"

"My uncle, Lord Fitzwilliam. He has written to say that he will be visiting with his wife just before Christmas. They will be journeying north for the holidays and will stop here. They plan to stay between eight and ten days."

"Heavens, William! This dinner is already quite a challenging task for me. Shall I be allowed a moment's rest before facing your uncle and aunt's scrutiny?"

Elizabeth laughed, but, in truth, she was most intimidated. Not only was she to welcome her first guests for a lengthy stay – a new challenge for her –, but also, it would be the Earl, whom she imagined to be just as dreadful as his sister, Lady Catherine. The man no doubt planned to investigate whether the little parvenu from Hertfordshire was causing any damage to the Darcy name.

Understanding that his news had shaken her, her husband immediately clarified:

"Colonel Fitzwilliam shall also be with them. You will not be entirely surrounded by strangers."

"Oh, what delight!" Georgiana cried out. "I do so love the Colonel, he is most kind!"

"In that case, I have more good news for you, Georgiana, for we shall have other visitors once the Earl and Countess have left us."

Elizabeth gave her husband an alarmed look, but he smiled at her tenderly.

"I promised you that we would invite the Gardiners for Christmas, my dear: it is done. But since I felt it might not be enough to make you truly feel at home in Derbyshire, I have also invited Bingley and your sister. They will all be here, and I dare say they might bring Kitty along with them."

Georgiana began to clap her hands like a child, delighted at the prospect of finally having people around to distract her.

As for Elizabeth, she was silent at first, before bursting into tears.

She was not sure whether it was apprehension over the upcoming dinner reception or else the terrifying prospect of the Earl's forthcoming visit, or even the happiness she felt at soon being able to hug Jane, but it required an intervention from both her husband and her sister-in-law to dry her tears.

~

The night in question came upon them quickly, both for Elizabeth, who feared that everything would go terribly wrong and that she would humiliate herself in front of Lambton society, and for the servants who had to double their efforts. Mrs. Reynolds had spent the last few days assembling the food supplies. After a few attempts, Hewitt had created a little partridge pie that was both charming, with little patterns cut into the golden pastry, and delicious, with its aromas of cognac, hazelnut, mushroom and squash. Elizabeth tasted the dish and was delighted by the result. She was excited to see the effect it would have on her guests. As for Weston, he had guided his footmen masterfully. They had polished the silver, starched the tablecloths and napkins, and spent an entire afternoon setting up a magnificent table in the dining room.

Mrs. Langhold and her sons were first to arrive. As the widow was always very pleasant, Elizabeth had no difficulty conversing amiably with her as they waited for the other guests. Lord and Lady Hastings arrived next, untiring in their praise for the house, regretting that Darcy did not entertain more often and hoping that Elizabeth's presence would finally change that. They were followed by the steward and his wife. Mrs. Moore, happy to enjoy an evening out, wore a cheerful smile.

Even more impressed were Mrs. Munroe and her husband. Elizabeth did not know them well. She had met them briefly the previous summer and, since her arrival at Pemberley, she had only visited Mrs. Munroe once. Nevertheless, she welcomed them with the utmost amiability. Even though it was not much, she was very proud of being able to present respectable people that belonged to her own social circle, and not her husband's. It allowed her to foresee the day she would be able to do the same with Jane, Kitty and the Gardiners. For his part, Darcy, who could be aloof with strangers, made an effort that evening and Elizabeth was grateful. He showed himself to be most considerate towards the Monroes, ensuring that they fit in well with the rest of the company.

The Clarksons arrived next, soon followed by the Norton siblings and their cousin. Thankfully, the young Sophie Russell was more civil, abashed perhaps by the impressive surroundings... She showed impeccable – if insincere – courtesy to Elizabeth.

Finally, the Blackmores arrived accompanied by Reverend Smith and Mrs. Keen, with whom they had shared their carriage. The infamous widow Keen, whom Elizabeth had heard all about from Darcy, Georgiana and even Mrs. Reynolds, advanced in age as she was, gave the impression of having lived long enough to no longer trouble herself with tedious details. She immediately made an excellent impression upon Elizabeth, despite her slightly sanctimonious discourse that invariably circled back to her charitable deeds.

Darcy sent for Georgiana so she could greet the guests. Accompanied by Mrs. Annesley, she only stayed with them for half an hour, just long enough to exchange a few words with the people she knew and receive a great many compliments on her complexion, her slim waist and her pretty curls. But as soon as the butler announced that dinner was to be served, opening the double doors wide, and as Elizabeth took Lord Hastings arm to show him the way, the young girl and her companion retired. Georgiana, not able to join them yet, could not help sneaking an envious look at the majestic, brightly lit dining room

~

During the meal, Elizabeth found herself at the center of attention. Sitting at one end of the table, opposite Darcy whom she could not even see, for he was hidden by a long row of candelabra, she sat like a queen, wearing the green wedding dress that made her feel so at ease. However, she could not really enjoy the company of her guests. She was used to keeping up appearances and so she smiled and engaged in charming pleasantry, but she was so anxious at the thought that something might not go according to plan that she constantly glanced at Weston to make sure that everything was going well.

The wide variety of fine dishes brought out by the footmen earned her abundant praise for her good taste. The carving table where

Weston cut the roasts at the request of each guest, as well as the duck pie and poached turkey, was universally acclaimed. But during the third course, as Elizabeth impatiently awaited the partridge pies to be served – which would undoubtedly be the highlight of the dinner due to their originality and delicate execution –, she saw with great dismay that the bouchées à la reine were served instead.

She could hardly believe her eyes. For a moment she remained still, shocked at the omission, and then her eyes started burning and her chin quivered uncontrollably, to the extent that she grabbed her serviette and pretended to wipe her mouth in an attempt to hide her tremors. Composing herself, she apologised to her guests and left the table.

In the passage, the servants who came and went gave her little privacy. She took refuge in the gallery, plunged in darkness. She sat down trembling on a bench at the foot of a marble statue and breathed, willing her heart to quieten.

Above all, she did not want to cry. Her red eyes would not go unnoticed. But she was both distraught and furious. Had Hewitt imposed his own initial choice, or had something unforeseen occurred in the kitchen? Regardless, she had lost an opportunity to put her own stamp on her first dinner party. Overwhelmed and stunned by this obstacle, which, at that moment, seemed like a disaster, she remained on the bench for several minutes.

A great laugh in the distance pulled her out of her thoughts. In the dining room, the guests continued to talk animatedly and the atmosphere was excellent.

Little by little, Elizabeth reasoned with herself. This was no great calamity. It was awfully disappointing for her but it would remain unnoticed in the eyes of her guests. There would be time tomorrow to request an explanation from the servants. For now, she had to go back to the dining room and resume her role as hostess.

Which she did. For the rest of the meal she continued to smile, drink and converse with her neighbours.

However, she did not eat a single bite of her bouchées à la reine.

~

It was very late when the reception finally ended. At the bottom of the porch, in the light of the lanterns, a procession of carriages transported their passengers away into the night in dribs and drabs. The footmen were hard at work handing out coats and hats. As for the hosts, they stood in the great hall bidding their guests goodnight one last time.

Thanks and praise were bestowed from all sides for this beautiful evening spent in such good company. Elizabeth was exhausted but she put on a brave face until the very end. Always beyond reproach, both in his posture and his speech, Darcy must have felt her exhaustion, for he discreetly offered her his arm to lean on. They had not spoken much to each other over the course of the evening, busy as they were entertaining their guests; feeling her husband's warmth against her had the most soothing effect.

At last, the trial was over, and apart from the bouchées à la reine and some innocent foolishness she may have uttered on occasion, there had been no major disturbance.

"I wish to congratulate you on a wonderful evening madam," said Mrs. Keen, who waited her turn to enter the vestibule with the reverend and the Nortons. "As I said earlier, having known Lady Anne, I can assure you that she would have been very proud of such a reception being held in her house."

The old lady kindly clasped her hand before turning to Darcy to congratulate him for not only having chosen such a pretty wife, but one who was also educated and sensible. After having noted throughout the evening that the widow's reputed candour was quite warranted, Elizabeth was all the more reassured that Mrs. Keen looked upon her favourably.

"I am the first to be amazed at my wife's talents," replied Darcy. "Believe me, madam, when I say that she surprises me every day!"

Mrs. Keen gave a small chuckle of amusement.

"Ah, the age of youth and love... Enjoy it, my dears! As for you, Mrs. Darcy, do not think that I will forget you. I have told you of my charities, but I did not perhaps mention that Lady Anne always had an active role in them? If you are capable of putting on such fine, elegant dinners, perhaps we could talk about charitable events to raise money? The poor shall be with us always, you see, and what would become of them if people like you and I did not take care of them?"

But before Elizabeth could answer, Miss Norton intervened.

"Oh, Mrs. Keen! Lady Anne's great charities were more than just dinner parties!" she exclaimed, putting on a somewhat theatrical tone. You should not be so hasty to ask our new friend for such a commitment. Mrs. Darcy has not yet acquired the experience to compare favourably with Lady Anne."

The widow gave the woman a sharp look but did not answer. She merely greeted the Darcys again and then entered the vestibule where the reverend and the Blackmores awaited her. Not in the least embarrassed at having been so critical, Miss Norton began to expand upon her argument, but her brother elbowed her, signalling that it would be better to stay silent.

As for Elizabeth, she just continued smiling.

~

It was with the greatest relief that the young couple finally climbed the stairs up to the second floor. Elizabeth increasingly leaned on her husband's arm.

"Lizzy, I am proud of you. You were an impeccable hostess from start to finish," he said, gently. The service was perfect, the meal was delicious and our guests seemed to greatly enjoy themselves."

His wife's annoyed little 'humph' did not escape his notice.

"What is it?" he asked.

"The bouchées à la reine..."

"Yes? They were delicious."

"They were supposed to be little partridge pies. Remember: the ones I requested from Hewitt. I even asked to taste them beforehand. I wished to reproduce the same thing we ate at Sir Egerton's, in London."

"And Hewitt did not follow your orders?"

"It would appear so. I do not know what happened, for I have not had the opportunity to speak with Weston and Mrs. Reynolds. But I will have a word with them tomorrow!"

"Would you like me to be present?"

Elizabeth hesitated. Then shook her head.

"No, I need to learn how to handle these types of matters."

They arrived at Elizabeth's door, in front of which Mrs. Vaughan had left a candle.

Darcy suddenly pressed his wife tightly to him.

"I am proud of you, Lizzy. Truly. I know that it is not so easy for you to arrive in this house and find your place in it, but please know that you may count on me if you need anything."

Comforted, Elizabeth put her cheek against his shoulder and heaved a deep sigh. They stood entwined for a few moments in the flickering glow of the candle. Then Darcy took her face in his hands and kissed her.

"You have worked so hard and I see that you are exhausted. Would you like me to leave you to sleep in peace?" he whispered.

"Yes, but do sleep next to me, please. Don't leave me alone."

"Very well. I shall come join you later."

He smiled at her, kissed her again, and let her join Mrs. Vaughan who waited to help her undress.

~

At Longbourn, the servants had never been very disciplined. The Bennets were rather lenient on the matter – like so many others. Mr. Bennet refused to involve himself, and when his wife wished to be obeyed, she had a tendency to shout and get angry. Eventually no one listened to her much. Failing to fully impose themselves they had both preferred to lower their standards. As long as the tasks were, for the most part, carried out, and the house was functional, they did not care to know whether the Hills took a little more than their designated daily pint, or whether Betty was a day or two late in washing the laundry.

One time, however, Elizabeth had seen her father fly into a rage when one of the farming families had attempted to cheat with their crops. Mr. Bennet had summoned the five people in question, one by one, and she had never forgotten their embarrassed looks as they sat on a bench outside the library, waiting their turn to be reprimanded.

The following day, Elizabeth paced in her parlour, preparing her speech. Then, when she felt ready, she summoned Hewitt, Weston and Mrs. Reynolds. To their great surprise, she used the same method as her father, letting them wait at the door and refusing to let them go back to work until she had addressed them.

She first called upon the cook. His case was the most complicated to handle, for not only was he responsible for the missing dish, but she had also not appreciated his general attitude towards her. Hewitt must have suspected it, for when he entered the room, he had lost some of his usual swagger.

Elizabeth was seated at her table, next to the window. She left him standing in the middle of the rug and promptly reminded him to kindly remove his hat in her presence. Flustered, the man immediately obeyed.

"I await your explanation, Mr. Hewitt," she began, her voice calm but cold. "I asked for partridge pies and I approved those that I tasted. Why were they not served last night?"

At first, the cook stumbled over his words, uncomfortable. He then came to his senses and explained that there had been a problem in the kitchen and he had run out of time, which had forced him to turn to the bouchées à la reine – a recipe he mastered perfectly and which, in the end, was very similar to the pies. In fact, his bouchées à la reine did contain partridge, which amounted to the same thing.

"No" Elizabeth countered, "they are not the same thing. I had a very clear idea of what I wanted to present to my guests. Let me remind you that I wished for the spread to be as pleasant to look at as it was flavoursome to eat and, even if your bouchées à la reine were very good, they were far from resembling the lovely little pies that you successfully made two days ago. Secondly, if there was a problem in the kitchen, it was not up to you to decide what changes to make, but up to me. You should have told Mrs. Reynolds to fetch me, instead of taking the initiative of making the bouchées à la reine. This would have saved me the very unpleasant surprise I had to endure last night in front of my friends."

And, as Hewitt hung his head pitifully, the young woman let a few moments of silence hang over them. She then added:

"I understand that you have all been affected by my arrival. Since there has not been a mistress for a long time, the house had been organised differently and I do not doubt that you have done a very good job over the years. But now that I am here, I am the one to whom you are accountable. You shall have to get used to it, Mr. Hewitt, for if I am not satisfied with your work, as talented as you are, you may have to ask yourself how permanent your place at Pemberley is. I would therefore ask that this type of situation not happen again in the future. Now, is there anything else you would like to share with me?"

The cook shook his head and Elizabeth thanked him. She then gave herself a few minutes to breathe in deeply, composing herself before summoning Mrs. Reynolds.

Her speech was a little different this time. When Elizabeth enquired about the mysterious reason it was deemed necessary to replace the pies with the bouchées à la reine, the housekeeper justified herself.

"There were not enough partridges, madam."

"How so? After all, you did order ten, so as to have half per person, did you not?"

"Indeed, madam, and they were perfect and fresh when they were delivered. But yesterday morning, three were missing."

"I beg your pardon?"

Embarrassed, Mrs. Reynolds did not answer.

"I suppose the meat is locked up downstairs?" Elizabeth continued.

"Of course, madam."

"Who has the key?"

"I do, along with Mr. Hewitt."

The housekeeper saw fit to clarify:

"The servants are not thieves, madam. The partridges were perhaps stored elsewhere and we were not able to find them in time to prepare them."

"Or, in the midst of all the preparations, you or Mr. Hewitt simply forgot that you used a few birds during the trials. The pies that Mr. Hewitt gave me two days ago contained partridge, as far as I know!"

From the housekeeper's expression, Elizabeth could tell that it was just dawning upon her. The poor woman had probably spent the night tossing and turning, wondering where the birds had gone, and now her mistress had found the explanation without even setting foot in the kitchen.

"Well," said Elizabeth, her voice softening, "this confirms one thing: the monitoring of provisions is not strict enough. To prevent this from ever happening again, I will have to take matters into my own hands, Mrs. Reynolds. I would ask you, therefore, to bring me the ledgers for the last three months tomorrow. We shall also plan a visit to the servant quarters: I wish to see exactly how you are organised and how you work. Do you maintain a regular inventory?"

"Yes. I mean, no... It is not always regular."

"We shall fix that. I would like for you and I to work together, so that nothing is overlooked and everyone can work under the right conditions. Are we in agreement on this?"

The housekeeper nodded and Elizabeth dismissed her.

Weston was the last to come in. The young woman explained to the butler that she was about to conduct a large inventory of the kitchens and provisions, in order to have an accurate idea of what the household consumed on a daily basis. She also announced her plans to do the same with all the objects in the house – furniture, linen, crockery, silver, art works, even the equipment used by the servants every day. Finally, she asked to see his own ledgers and insisted that no invoice should be paid until she had seen and approved it.

After the meetings, exhausted by the nervous stress of it all and the scope of the task ahead of her, she nestled into her sofa and slept for a couple of hours.

CHAPTER 8

As planned, Mrs. Darcy visited the servants' quarters. However, she could not have anticipated the scale of the world awaiting her.

Leading the tour, Mrs. Reynolds began with the suppliers' entrance, a large room where goods delivered on carts were piled against the walls before being dispatched to their final destination. On one side, there were several areas dedicated to storing wood for the various chimneys in the house. On the other side, a small hall could be found, connecting to the kitchen and the rest of the quarters.

The kitchen was certainly impressive. Its two-storey ceiling was curved to allow smoke to escape through the upper sections of large windows. There were three big chimneys that rose above a row of stoves of varying sizes. Large workstations were organised in the centre, and shelves laden with pots and pans lined the walls. Elizabeth visited these quarters early in the afternoon, when everything was quiet, but she had no trouble imagining the sweltering heat, the burning stoves and frantic servants rushing to prepare large, holiday meals.

The two big pantries next to the kitchen were filled with cupboards, crates and baskets laden with food, as well as a locked room for bacon and meat, and a scullery where cauldrons were cleaned. At the end of the corridor, past the entrance leading to the great hall, was the wine cellar, which was reserved exclusively for Weston's use. Just past it lay a flight of service stairs that climbed up to the first floor. It led to a vestibule adjacent to the dining room from which the footmen could enter and exit when waiting on distinguished guests. This staircase was very wide so as to ensure smooth passage for those going up and down, especially when arms were laden with trays.

The butler and housekeeper's private rooms were located under the south wing, but Elizabeth declined to enter when Mrs. Reynolds invited her in. The rooms were reserved for her two most eminent servants, and the new mistress of the house did not wish to impose upon their privacy. The housekeeper seemed to appreciate her thoughtfulness.

The silverware was stored next to Weston's room. As with the wine cellar, the butler was the only one in possession of the key and he regularly drew up an inventory to prevent thieving. A succession of work and cleaning rooms followed, culminating with the servants' dining room.

It was a large, bright room that could be found in the southwest corner of the house. It had a fireplace on each side and several tables arranged end-to-end, flanked by straw chairs. The servants were too numerous to eat at the same time, so food was served in two waves: the first one well before the masters' meal and the second one after. The rest of the time, everyone went about his or her business. A few padded chairs had been added around the fireplaces so that staff could unwind when they had a moment to themselves, or a day off. Mrs. Reynolds, however, thought it appropriate to mention that the windows were always closed during the day, so that their conversations would not disturb anyone who might be out for a stroll in the garden.

"Men are entitled to a pint of beer a day, half for women," she explained. "We did attempt to brew our own on a few occasions, with disappointing results, which is why we prefer to bring in good lager from Lambton."

"Is the staff satisfied with it?"

"Indeed, madam, they are. Mr. Weston hands out the pints in the evenings before dinner so that people don't take more than their share. It also encourages everyone to arrive at the table on time."

Next to their dining room, there was another staircase that led upstairs to the west wing where the family's private rooms could be found. Finally, at the very end of the servants' quarters, there was a large laundry room equipped with huge vats and an ironing room. Between the masters and servants' linen, along with all the tablecloths and sheets – which all had to be washed separately –, there was enough daily work to occupy three laundry maids who were also tasked with carrying out small sewing jobs. To dry all the laundry, they used a large, well ventilated and easily heated room under the attic. On sunny days, they hung it out to dry near the vegetable garden.

After this visit, Elizabeth began to think.

Back in her parlour, on the table beneath the window, she spread out the accounts and ledgers she had requested. The butler and the housekeeper had handed over all the documents, but the young woman sensed their caution. They understandably deemed her too inexperienced to intervene in the organisation of the house and feared she might bring chaos into a system they had already perfected.

Yet Elizabeth had no desire to interfere with their habits. It would be entirely unnecessary for her to change the entire household, particularly on the eve of Lord Fitzwilliam's arrival. She merely wished to identify any irregularities in order to suggest sensible solutions. Her goal was to assert her authority: since Pemberley House was under her supervision, she needed to acquire a good understanding of its intimate workings.

At first, the challenge had seemed daunting.. But she had devoured Lady Anne's handbook, and handled the partridge pie matter rather well, which had given her more confidence. In fact, Mrs. Reynolds came to tell her that Hewitt would henceforth be presenting his mistress with the menus he planned to make every week, so that she could approve them. While inwardly she exulted, Elizabeth struggled to keep her face emotionless as the housekeeper gave her the message. It appeared that she had succeeded, for now at least, to get her obstinate cook to comply.

For three days, she went through the various bills, comparing them with the accounts. It was a formidable task. Weston's script was difficult to decipher, and the invoices were arranged in chronological order rather than by commodity type. The same was true regarding the obsolete inventory she had been given for the servants' quarters: not only did the notebook date back to the year before George Darcy's death – it had therefore not been updated in over six years –, but the information had been carelessly organised.

Elizabeth was quick to identify a few omissions. Several bills failed to mention whether a payment had been made. At the fourth error, she left her parlour and went directly to her husband's study.

Darcy sat next to the fire in an armchair, reading. He was surprised to see his wife enter abruptly without so much as a knock.

"Do you know whether we have any outstanding accounts?" she asked.

The young man almost laughed at the incongruity of the question.

"Whatever do you mean, my dear?"

Elizabeth shook the papers she held in her hand.

"I have four bills here that have been poorly managed and there may well be more as I have not finished reviewing everything. Usually, Mr. Weston writes on each of them, indicating the date and whether payment has been made. But there are no notes on these. So, I ask you: do you know if we have any outstanding accounts? Are we to expect reminders from some of our suppliers?"

Amused by his wife's firm, scolding tone, Darcy was careful to keep a neutral countenance. He put his reading aside and stood up.

"Let me have a look," he said, heading to his desk.

One by one, Elizabeth laid out the invoices, all of which dated back to the previous month. Her husband studied them carefully, before declaring:

"I don't know whether these have been paid or not, for I was with you in Hertfordshire at the time they were issued. Mr. Moore pays the accounts when I am away. He and Weston work it out amongst themselves."

"So, you don't know?"

"I confess, I do not. But I can assure you that all the accounts are promptly paid here. I am not in the habit of leaving debts. Have a look with Weston, I am certain he will tell you that everything is in order."

"If that is the case, he shall have to be more diligent."

"Perhaps his attention was called upon by other matters. It does happen."

"Perhaps it was..."

Once again, Darcy held back a smile at the sight of Elizabeth's unimpressed look. These were ordinary details but they seemed to be an extraordinary source of concern for her.

"Did you know that the supplies that are delivered to us are never weighed?" she added suddenly.

"What do you mean?"

"I learnt this from Mrs. Reynolds, this morning. I pointed out that I had not seen a scale in the entrance hall where the goods are delivered."

Her husband had no idea what his wife was getting at.

"What of it?"

"What of it?" repeated Elizabeth, continuing her train of thoughts. "Do you not see how this has us at a disadvantage? I don't wish to imply that the Lambton merchants are ill-intentioned, but really, if, for instance, you were billed for thirty pounds of beef, would you not wish to ensure that there were indeed thirty pounds delivered and not, say, twenty-nine?"

"Well, yes..."

"This is why we must fit a scale in that entrance and weigh all incoming supplies that are paid for according to weight. I shall tell Mr. Weston to ensure that a footman is present at each delivery, to oversee the recount and the weighing. We will no longer be rounding off prices without first verifying that all is as it should be."

"That seems rather sound to me, indeed."

"Oh, and I will have to check the chickens, too..." Elizabeth continued, picking up the bills that were displayed on the desk, still lost in thought. "Were you aware, William, that most of the poultry we eat comes from the Lambton market? We have a well-equipped farmyard, but we use the hens only for their eggs. We do not allow them to brood. Can you believe it? It hardly makes sense! When I think back to when your friends almost mistook me for a common farm girl in London... Well, I can assure you that this country woman will be bringing some of her common sense to Pemberley's affairs!"

Upon which, elated by her project, she placed a kiss on her husband's cheek and flounced out of the room, in search of Mrs. Reynolds.

Bemused, Darcy watched her go, wondering what had come over her.

~

It was one of the maids, while cleaning a room, who first saw the carriages begin their descent into the valley. Word soon travelled. The carriages were just crossing the small bridge over the river when Darcy peeked his head around the door to the music room, where his wife and sister were.

"They are arriving!"

They both immediately dropped their books and their embroidery and rushed with him to the hall, where Weston had already gathered half a dozen footmen. Mrs. Reynolds arrived at the same time from the servants' quarters, followed by the head housemaid and five other maids.

"Do we really need all these people?" Elizabeth whispered to her husband. "To what purpose?"

"To impress," he replied with a small smile.

"In that case, you have succeeded. I think I am the most impressed of us all!"

Darcy took her hand and squeezed it. He then leaned towards her and placed a furtive kiss near her ear.

"Everything will be fine, Lizzy. I am here."

And, as the sound of the approaching horses could be heard, the young couple went out onto the porch.

~

The Fitzwilliams were not such an old lineage as Lady Catherine led people to believe.

It had all begun a little over a century ago with a certain Joseph Fitzwilliam, the son of a rector. After brilliantly completing his studies, he embarked upon a remarkable career in politics, which brought him in close proximity to those in power, leading to his eventual ennoblement. He became a baron and his title was passed down from one eldest son to the other. True prestige, however, was achieved through the lineage of his fourth son. One of the descendants, a lieutenant colonel, fought alongside the King during the battle of Dettingen. It was unclear what his exploits were, but he attracted enough attention to gain royal favour. The man returned with both a wounded leg that would handicap him for the rest of his life, and the title of Earl, which became his family's greatest pride.

He was thus the first Earl of the Fitzwilliam family. Darcy's uncle, who arrived that day at Pemberley, was only the third of his name.

Seated in the small drawing-room, the newcomers rested as they drank tea and coffee, recounting their journey. The road conditions were fair, but as they had broken a wheel on the way, they had been forced to board a mail coach that was passing by so as to stop in a nearby town.

"There were so many people in that poor coach!" said Lady Fitzwilliam. "I did not think we would be able to climb aboard. Luckily, two gentlemen offered us their seats and climbed up on the coachman's bench. Ah, one must truly be inspired to travel so far, this time of year!"

"I am certain you shall be rewarded for your efforts when you see your grandchildren," replied Elizabeth, kindly.

The comment had the desired effect. Lady Fitzwilliam's offended expression gave way to a soft smile.

"You are quite right. The children are indeed a blessing..."

Her husband, quite uninterested in the current conversation, changed the subject.

"I see that the house remains quite unchanged since the last time we saw each other, nephew. Remind me now, when was that?"

"Last year at summer's end," replied Darcy.

"Ah, yes, yes... Not long before you left to go gallivanting with your friend Bingley, I believe. If I had been told then that you would be bringing home this fine bride of yours..."

... I would have dissuaded you from leaving, Elizabeth finished silently.

Lord Fitzwilliam was in his fifties, dashing, tall and rather slender. He had a receding hairline and a head of greying hair that was cut short and brushed forward, with long, trimmed sideburns. He must have been handsome in his youth, but now, between his shifting, unfocussed gaze and his affected air, he looked like any other dull and pompous gentleman.

His wife was a plump woman of cheerful countenance, who wrapped herself up in significant amounts of lace and waved her hands about as soon as she opened her mouth, as if to make sure she had indeed captured her audience's attention. Unfortunately, her conversation was rarely engaging and she had a tendency to repeat herself. She looked older than her husband, even though she was in fact a few years younger, and she often placed her hand on her belly, a habit she had developed in the course of numerous, successive pregnancies, spanning most of her adult life. She had indeed given her husband no less than eleven children, only three of whom had died in infancy. They were all married now, except for the last of their daughters and, of course, the Colonel.

Elizabeth was relieved that he had accompanied his parents. The Earl's probing gaze made her uncomfortable and the thought of being able to rely on his son's friendship during their stay reassured her.

"I am told that one of your sisters had married Mr. Wickham, whom we know well," continued the man, turning towards her. "Such a pity, however, that you are now tied to that dreadful person!"

Darcy stiffened, while Georgiana blushed with confusion, as she often did every time her former suitor was mentioned.

Lord Fitzwilliam had barely arrived and he was already criticising his nephew's marriage. He succeeded, for Wickham – whose mere name in Pemberley House rang out as blasphemy – was indeed the worst connection the new Mrs. Darcy could have. The Earl could not have been aware of the events at Ramsgate, but he knew the character, and Lady Catherine would certainly not have omitted to tell him the shameful conditions under which Wickham and Lydia's union had taken place.

Elizabeth schooled her emotions. Showing no signs of distress, she replied with all the amiability she could muster:

"When Mr. Wickham became known in Hertfordshire, he appeared to be a very pleasant and decent young man. My father saw no objection to his marriage with my sister, and there is every reason to believe that they are very happy now."

"Nevertheless, heaven knows he is not the worthiest son-in-law that one might wish for," the Earl insisted, sternly. "Your sister should have exercised more caution. I believe that he has the unfortunate habit of leaving debts wherever he goes!"

"So I have heard, Your Grace, although I am unable to attest to this. If all this is true, then I am just as sorry as you are. But now that he is well situated in the army we can hope that he will settle down honourably."

Lord Fitzwilliam muttered something, showing that he did not believe a word of it.

"In that case he has chosen the wrong uniform. He should have joined the navy if he wanted to make a fortune, not the army," he said, contemptuously.

He did not seem to care that his own son wore an army uniform and might be offended by such a remark. Although his rank, purchased at great cost, was unlikely to lead him into enemy crossfire one day, the Colonel was nevertheless very proud to wear it.

He seemed accustomed to his father's incisive remarks for he did not appear offended. On the contrary, he took the opportunity to deflect the conversation by turning towards Elizabeth.

"Since we are on the subject of your family, madam, Darcy tells me that you are welcoming the Bingleys for the holidays?" he asked her, most courteously. "You must be very happy that you will soon be seeing your sister Jane again. You will not have been separated for too long."

An exchange ensued regarding the Bingleys, and then the Colonel related – to his mother, mostly – the magnificent double wedding that had taken place at Netherfield. This distraction was effective enough that Lord Fitzwilliam could find nothing other to say that evening than mundane pleasantries, much to everyone's relief.

~

The first few days went off without any difficulty.

Elizabeth spent most of her time with the ladies in the drawing-room in an effort to be as amiable as possible towards Lady Fitzwilliam. Her guest made a few surprised comments regarding her lack of interest in drawing and embroidery, but the young woman compensated by accompanying Georgiana often in her music, proving she was not entirely bereft of talent.

Exceptionally, she allowed Mrs. Reynolds to intrude upon her as often as necessary. She then addressed the minor domestic issues in a soft voice, while Lady Fitzwilliam, curious, listened with barely concealed interest. Managing a large family and a prestigious house were two things that the Countess had mastered perfectly, and she soon slipped her niece a few recommendations.

"You should instruct your housekeeper to send a scullery maid to empty the ashes upstairs instead of a maid," she advised. "Those girls are very useful, and since they are often without work outside of meal preparations, it is best to keep them occupied. Otherwise, before you know it, they start lingering around the footmen which leads to nothing but trouble!"

Each time, Elizabeth nodded in agreement and warmly thanked her aunt for her valuable information. She had no intention of heeding her advice, but at least she had achieved the desired effect of proving to Lady Fitzwilliam that she knew how to run her house. She had, in fact, shared some of the adjustments she planned to put in place and had received the strongest encouragement.

"One can never be too careful with tradesmen," the Countess declared upon hearing about the newly installed scale in the suppliers' entrance. "Most are thieves as far as I am concerned. As soon as they sense the slightest distraction, they take the opportunity to make you pay more than their due. I am convinced I could have bought my youngest daughter a lovely cottage with all the money that has been taken from us over the last thirty years! As for the servants... It is so hard these days to be satisfactorily waited upon! I am unable to remember the names of my footmen for they are always changing. As soon as they are the least bit unhappy with their situation, they leave you without notice to find better wages. Not to mention the maids! It is a rather difficult problem. It is impossible to employ married women, for they have their families and are no longer as readily available, yet the unmarried ones never seem to stay still. Did you know that just last year, I had to send two of mine away because they were with child? These people are brutes indeed, it is a real shame..."

Excepting these exchanges, the rest of their time together was spent in idle chatter around embroidery work, watercolours, or Georgiana's musical talents. This did nothing to help the adolescent. Since the guests' arrival she had retreated behind her natural shyness. Each time her aunt addressed her, she cast a distressed look in Elizabeth's direction before stammering a response. As for Mrs. Annesley, she held her rank and stood back. And thus, to avoid having to engage in conversation with the Countess all day, Elizabeth decided to invite Mrs. Moore to join their little gathering. The steward's wife was delighted at the prospect of an outing and, as she already knew Lady Fitzwilliam, the two women entertained each other most pleasantly.

The men spent their time outdoors. Darcy and his cousin often went to the stables, either to see the dogs, inspect the animals and carriages, or to have their mounts saddled up before braving the cold and galloping through the hills. The Earl, for his part, took advantage of being in Derbyshire to visit Lord Hastings and other gentlemen of his acquaintance. He was thus out all day.

The party would meet again at dinnertime. The meal was served in the large dining room and Elizabeth had given instructions to use the finest dinner service. There were to be six footmen instead of the usual two, and the chafing dishes were to be filled with embers so that the food was never lukewarm. The butler was free to choose the best wines he could find in the cellar. With Darcy's full approval, she spared no efforts, and neither Lord Fitzwilliam nor his wife could fault the manner in which they were received.

At the table, the Countess took it upon herself to tell her husband everything that she had discovered about their new niece during the day.

"Our Mrs. Darcy is managing her staff rather well," she declared one evening. "Just this morning she was very clear and firm with her housekeeper, as though she had done this all her life. Remind me, dear madam, did you not say that you had consulted an instruction manual?"

"That is correct, Your Grace," confirmed the young woman. "I suppose Lady Anne received it at her wedding, for I discovered a few annotations in her own hand."

"I do recall receiving such a manual myself, a long time ago. It is very much needed, for when we are young, we do not realise how complex managing a household can be and what difficulties may lie ahead. We must be firm from the start, or else the servants quickly take advantage of us."

"Well, it seems to me that adequately managing one's staff is the bare minimum one might expect from a wife," the Earl replied with indifference.

"Except for the fact that Pemberley is a large house and that the task may not be within everyone's reach," Darcy objected, "especially, I must admit, since my mother left us. The place had been somewhat abandoned, for neither my father nor myself were very present. But Mrs. Darcy has shown much diligence and intelligence in this regard. We have barely been here for a month and I am already seeing her positive influence everywhere."

Then, inviting his sister to witness, he continued:

"Georgiana, do you not find the general mood of this house to have pleasantly changed since her arrival?"

But as she opened her mouth, Lord Fitzwilliam interjected:

"It is true that a bride brings a certain energy wherever she goes, and I will admit, my nephew, that Mrs. Darcy has a good disposition and is handsome enough. All we can do is wait for her to give you a son."

Darcy's faint smile froze.

"My sister, Lady Catherine, has spoken of you in fairly disobliging terms, madam," continued the Earl, addressing Elizabeth, "but I do not share her opinion. In reality, I flatter myself for being more sensible, and your origins are not so important to me as long as I can see that you are a healthy young lady, able to produce heirs."

He then turned to his nephew:

"And to think that my sister wished you to marry her poor little Anne. What would you have done with an ailing wife, I ask you? In that respect, I do admit that you have chosen a far better filly. One who will bear you beautiful, strong and healthy children."

Upon hearing these words, which were both flattering and insulting, Elizabeth felt her heart miss a beat.

Darcy had grown pale. There was an embarrassed silence, during which only the Earl continued to eat, and then the young man took a sip of wine to regain his countenance, before replying coldly:

"Indeed, I have no regrets. Mrs. Darcy brings me great happiness in every way. Having said that, I would appreciate it if you did not compare her to a filly, however spirited she may be. It seems to me that a spouse provides many more joys than merely bearing heirs."

"That goes without saying! Forgive me, madam, if I have offended you," the Earl apologised absentmindedly, without seeming remorseful.

And, as the unease seemed to persist, Weston, who had witnessed the entire scene from the back of the room, had the good sense to distract them with more wine.

~

The Colonel undoubtedly suffered the most distress as a consequence of Lord Fitzwilliam's comments. As the group settled down in the music room, he found a moment to address Elizabeth privately.

"My dear cousin, I would like to apologise for my father's remarks earlier," he uttered, ruefully. "I am certain he meant no harm, but he sometimes does not realise how utterly inappropriate he can be. I am so sorry that you were the target of such careless remarks."

Grateful, the young woman tried to temper matters and put him at ease.

"At least your father's opinion of me is quite clear," she said with a mischievous smile. "Personally, I don't know him well enough to form an opinion and, in any case, the important thing for me is to maintain agreeable relations between my husband and the rest of his family. In this regard, as long as Lord Fitzwilliam does not turn his back on us, I am satisfied."

"How noble. My father does not deserve you as his niece."

"Of course he does, for it means I am now your cousin."

The Colonel smiled and bowed before her tact.

"Since we are talking about the family," added Elizabeth, "have you any news of Lady Catherine?"

"No, not since I went to Rosings a couple of months ago. But with the holiday season approaching, it will be an opportunity to exchange greetings."

"Would you send her my best wishes? I have desperately tried to convince Mr. Darcy to write to her, but he still refuses. You know how stubborn he can be!"

"Would you like me to speak with him?"

"Yes, please. I no longer dare to broach the subject for I can see that it angers him. I suppose I am the last person who could advise him on this."

"Pardon my impertinence, but if my aunt no longer wishes to see you, should you not rejoice that your husband seeks to protect you?"

"There is nothing joyful about a family torn apart by conflict, Colonel. Lady Catherine certainly bears me no great love, but she is nonetheless your aunt and, as such, she deserves our respect. Besides, I am foolish enough to believe that, with time, she and I might accommodate ourselves."

The Colonel bowed once more.

"That is an honourable sentiment and you have all my respect, dear Elizabeth. I shall try to speak with Darcy."

"Thank you. Oh! Look, he is watching us," said the young woman, amused as she realised that her husband watched them from the other side of the room. "Would you like to wager that he has already guessed what we are talking about? Laugh loudly, as though I have just told a good joke. That should confuse him a little..."

Surprised at first, the Colonel proved to be a good sport.

"Cousin, you are full of mischief! I would not want to be the target of one of your pranks!" he whispered.

And, with those words, he laughed heartily, immediately joined by Elizabeth.

Darcy, on the other side of the room, frowned, looking puzzled.

~

The Earl and Countess Fitzwilliam's presence at Pemberley did not fail to impress Derbyshire society. One did not often see such illustrious visitors passing through, and as such, it did not take long for invitations to start pouring in.

As they were only there for ten days, there was only enough time to invite them to two official dinners – one with the Hastings, the other at Mrs. Langhold's – but, very soon, Mrs. Moore was not the only one keeping Lady Fitzwilliam company in the afternoon. The Blackmores and the Nortons were more than happy to join the group, showing up on the doorstep even though Elizabeth had not been expecting them.

She knew that the crowds were only there because of her husband's aunt, but she enjoyed it nonetheless. However, at the Hastings' dinner, she learned that the ladies in the area regularly visited one another without her knowledge, which only added to her bitterness. Worse still, she learned of it indirectly, in a conversation addressed to Lady Fitzwilliam. No one thought that Elizabeth might wish to join them.

The only ladies she saw regularly were Mrs. Moore and Mrs. Munroe, both of whom always welcomed her with great pleasure. As for the others, she would simply have to be patient.

The day she would be invited for herself and not because of her association with her husband or – in this case – with his prestigious aunt and uncle, was not upon her yet.

~

One morning, while the men were in Lambton, the Countess kept to her room, claiming to suffer from a headache. Elizabeth went upstairs to make sure that her guest had everything she needed. Once she realised that her faintness just concealed the need for sleep and some quiet, she went back downstairs, happy to have some time to herself.

"Call Mrs. Vaughan," she said to a footman she passed in the passage. "I'm going out."

She then informed Georgiana, who was surprised:

"Outside? But it is far too cold!"

"So stay indoors, darling. I shall be back this afternoon."

Soon after, wrapped in a long pelisse and wearing her walking boots, she set out from the house. She had been so attentive towards her distinguished guests from morning to night that she was in much need of fresh air and solitude. The cold and damp surprised her a little, but she quickly warmed up as she set off at a good pace.

She took the path leading up to Woolbert, intending to turn off just before and head towards the summit on a path she had observed on a previous walk. On the way, she ran into Mr. Cox and one of his sons, who were busy cutting up a tree they had felled. She paused for a minute to greet them. Cox explained that the garden was ready for winter, all the fragile plants having been adequately protected. He was now busy removing the dead or diseased trees that would provide wood for subsequent winters. It was a task that would keep him and his sons busy throughout the cold season.

"Will you tell your wife that I will be speaking with her soon? I wish to raise our own broods next spring and it may add to her workload," Elizabeth announced, before continuing on her way. "But she need not worry about a thing. We shall see how the situation can be remedied."

As she arrived at Woolbert, she caught sight of the little path and quickened her pace, wishing to set out upon it as soon as possible. She did not want anyone from the Moores' cottage to see her, as she would not have been able to refuse their invitation to stay a while. Luckily, no one called out to her and once sheltered on the path, she felt herself ease up. The climb was hard, but the sound of leaves crunching beneath her feet was so pleasant that she felt greatly heartened. Her efforts were rewarded more than once by sudden openings, which gave her breathtaking views out across the valley. The stable roofs were clearly visible and somewhere below them, Pemberley House lay hidden beneath the canopy of trees.

It took her almost an hour to reach the top of the mountain, and a little longer to escape out of the woods on the other side. There, perched on a small bluff, she was able to admire the plains where the lake stretched out in the distance. She could even make out the fishermen's lodge she had visited with Georgiana. She thought of her uncle, Edward Gardiner, who had thoroughly enjoyed the fish-filled waters of the river last summer. He would surely love fishing in such a vast lake. She did not know if he liked to fish in winter, but she would be sure to ask him. She had seen how easy it was to cast lines along the pier and then return to the warmth of the lodge, waiting for a bite.

The cold suddenly brought her back to reality with a shiver. She was about to climb down when she remembered that she was not too far from the little chapel.

She might as well pay her respects to George and Anne Darcy while she was there.

She changed direction.

~

"Is Lizzy not with you?" asked Darcy, when Georgiana joined the rest of the company in the drawing-room where tea and cakes had been served.

"No, she went out for a walk," replied the girl. "I suppose she should be back soon, she told me she would return in the afternoon."

Colonel Fitzwilliam, who was standing near one of the windows, remarked:

"Well, she is not in the gardens. I don't see anyone there."

"Elizabeth is not one to settle for a garden," Darcy replied with a smile. "She loves open spaces and long walks in the woods."

"Your wife is a restless one," added Lord Fitzwilliam, impassive.

His nephew chose to ignore his comment and brought his lips to his cup. The Colonel came to join them.

"In that case I wish she would come home soon," he said, "for the weather has closed in and it won't be long before it rains."

~

"Which waistcoat would you prefer, sir? I have picked out the pearl grey one, or else there is the striped blue one that you like."

"The blue one, Grove, thank you."

In his dressing room, Darcy readied himself for dinner. He was worried.

His gaze rested on the little clock that lay on a pedestal table, and his frown deepened. Evading his valet's hands, he drew closer to the veiled window and opened the curtain. Outside, night had fallen. Worse still, the rain had begun to fall relentlessly.

"Sir?" called Grove.

His master was not listening and sighed in exasperation, leaving the valet standing there as he darted down the passage.

219

He was tumbling down the stairs when he saw the butler below.

"Weston! Has Mrs. Darcy returned?" he called out over the railing.

"Not yet, sir. Mrs. Reynolds has her eye on the gardens and the valley and will let us know if she catches sight of Mrs. Darcy. I have asked Aston and Oliver to take lanterns with them to the stables and down the path that leads up to the woods. One can barely see anything out there, sir."

"You did well. Send out another two or three men..."

For a second, Darcy was still. Then he turned around and ran up the stairs.

"...and saddle my horse, along with the Colonel's, Weston: I must find her!" he ordered. "Grove? Grove! My coat! Fitzwilliam, a word, if you please!"

Lord Fitzwilliam peeked around the door, but before he could utter a thing, his nephew addressed him in a reassuring tone:

"Don't worry, Uncle, Elizabeth has not gone far. I am merely going to spare her a difficult journey back under the rain. Fitzwilliam!" he called again.

His cousin came out into the passage with his shirt half buttoned up.

"Is she still not back?" he asked, worried.

"No, unfortunately not. I am leaving on horseback to fetch her. Do you wish to come with me?"

"Of course! But do you have any idea where she might have gone?"

"I have not the foggiest idea, that's the problem," Darcy grinded, before rushing away to find his valet so he could dress up warmly.

By the time the two cousins were at the stables, their horses were ready. Elizabeth was unlikely to have made it down into the valley as she would have been seen, so Colonel Fitzwilliam headed for Woolbert on the left and Darcy went towards the mountain on the right.

He threw his horse into a gallop but quickly had to slow down. The path was dark and the young man could not risk hurting his horse. There was no one in front of him. At every turn, he hoped to see a silhouette, but saw nothing. And when he called out his wife's name, only the scattered sound of rain answered.

He went quite far along the road, venturing down smaller paths and crossing clearings and groves. After a while, he felt that the distance he had travelled was too great and that Elizabeth could never have become lost so far. He knew that she was quite capable of orienting herself. As long as she could see the valley, there was no mistaking the way home, for it was only a matter of skirting the mountainside. His anxiety mounting, he decided to turn around.

Darcy knew the network of paths that stretched throughout the woods off by heart. In his head, a succession of possibilities presented themselves. It was unlikely that she had been attacked by an animal. There were only deer in the estate's woods as there had not been any wild boar in the region for years. However, she could have twisted an ankle, or simply sought out shelter somewhere while waiting for the rain to end. The young man's anxiety increased. He hated the idea of having to organise a search party in the middle of the night to find her.

He eventually took another route, which brought him further up the mountain, towards Woolbert. And finally, he glimpsed not one, but two silhouettes, accompanied by a dog, just ahead of him.

"Elizabeth!"

Jumping down from his horse, he rushed to hug her.

"Good Lord, Lizzy! Where did you go? Everyone is looking for you!"

"Forgive me... I lost my way coming down the mountain. Mr. Stevens is the one who found me. He was kind enough to accompany me."

The man was one of Woolbert's farmers. Having taken his sheep out countless times, he knew the woods and surrounding plains very well.

"Stevens..." Darcy said, shaking his hand vigorously. "You cannot imagine how comforting it is to know that you came to my wife's aid. I am indebted to you."

"Not at all, sir," the shepherd answered. "I must say, I was rather surprised when I saw her. The lady was a fair way away from home, especially in such weather."

"Indeed! But I'm sure that this is something that will not happen again. Would you help her mount the horse?"

While Darcy climbed back into the saddle, the farmer extended his hands to Elizabeth in order to create a step, allowing her to climb up behind her husband. After which, they greeted one another one last time. The shepherd whistled for his dog and headed back to Woolbert, whilst the couple descended towards the house.

~

Weston ran out when he heard his master's horse.

"Madam!" he exclaimed. "What a relief it is to see you!"

"Bring some hot tea to her room, Weston," ordered Darcy, "and inform Mrs. Vaughan. Mrs. Darcy will need to change out of these wet clothes. Has Colonel Fitzwilliam returned?"

"Not yet, sir, but he went to the stables again just now."

"In that case, send someone to tell him we have returned."

"Very well, sir. And when shall I serve dinner?"

"In an hour. Serve my uncle and aunt a glass of wine to alleviate their wait."

"As you wish, sir."

Two footmen reached out to Elizabeth to help her off the horse, while another went upstairs to inform her maid. Grasping his wife's hand, Darcy led her inside.

He had not said a word, nor looked at her since finding her in the woods. His distress had given way to anger and he was now glacial.

As for Elizabeth, she was most ashamed.

~

It had begun to rain when she reached the chapel. Thinking it was a mere downpour, she had not paid it any mind.

Kneeling at Lady Anne's grave for a long time had felt good. Having discovered the woman's personal effects and now using her notes and her secretary, she felt like she was learning to walk in her footsteps. Although she had never known her, she was forging a benevolent image of Lady Anne for herself and liked to believe that her mother-in-law approved of the little changes that were beginning to take place at Pemberley.

As the rain intensified, Elizabeth finally took refuge in the chapel, hoping the downfall would subside. That was when she realised that no one in the house knew where she was. Counting on Weston to send her a carriage was out of the question and, in such a secluded area, she had no chance of stumbling across a passing cart. Overwarm from the exertions of her walk and then wet from the rain which had fallen on her shoulders eventually penetrating her pelisse, she was now getting colder and colder. She could no longer wait.

She therefore resolved to go back down to the house through the woods. The road was winding and would have taken her on a long detour through Woolbert, while cutting through the wooded area would be faster, especially going downhill. She knew where she was, she simply needed to make haste.

But she had somewhat overestimated her knowledge of the terrain. After crossing over the ridge and sinking into the woods, she came across a myriad of small paths that frequently crossed one another. In essence, she knew she had to make her way down and to the right, but this was proving difficult.

She really began to worry as night fell.

It was Stevens' dog that found her. Emerging like a beast of the woods, the animal happily jumped all around her before dashing off in another direction, called away by a series of whistles. She followed him, calling out a few times until the shepherd answered, quite surprised to find a stranger alone in the middle of the woods in such awful weather. He had been even more surprised to learn that she was the new Mrs. Darcy.

They still had quite a long way to walk. Elizabeth was thoroughly tired, her feet hurt and she was parched but at least she was no longer lost. Once she heard the gallop of the horse and recognised its rider, she breathed a sigh of relief.

~

When they entered the room, Darcy led his wife to the freshly lit fireplace and tossed his coat on the bed.

"Let her be, Mrs. Vaughan, I shall take care of her," he coldly dismissed the servant as she approached to help her mistress.

She retreated.

"I shall fetch some hot water so that Mrs. Darcy may wash up," she said, before slipping away.

"And some tea! Bring some tea, for God's sake! Do you not see how she shivers?"

Darcy added two logs to the fire, grumbling about how no one had thought to light it sooner, then he turned to his wife and firmly removed her hat and soggy pelisse. He untied her dress, then her muddy boots. Frozen, Elizabeth allowed herself to be undressed.

"You have to change, or else you will catch your death. Look at the state you are in!"

The stockings were tossed onto a chair, followed by the dress and the petticoat, which, despite the pelisse, had soaked up so much water that they were wet halfway up her thigh. It was then that Darcy realised that the young woman's teeth were chattering.

"Lizzy... How foolish of you to go out in such weather!"

"It was not raining when I left," she stammered somewhat mournfully.

He glared at her. Then he grabbed the towels that Mrs. Vaughan had brought in and began rubbing her back and her arms.

"Must I really tell you that what you did was utterly absurd?" he said. "Why ever did you go so far out into the woods?"

"I wanted to climb to the top of the mountain to see the view. I almost went to the lake and then I thought I might go pay my respects to your parents."

"I beg your pardon?" said Darcy, taken aback.

"You went all the way to the chapel? On foot? Are you out of your senses? You should have asked for a carriage!"

"I did not think I would go so far, at first. I changed my mind along the way, and then..."

She was forced to pause and collect herself, for she began shaking uncontrollably.

"... and then the rain took me by surprise. I'm sorry, I never wished to cause you all this trouble."

"You are frozen," he grumbled in response. "Look at you: your bodice and shirt are drenched, too. And God only knows how long you have been in this state... Turn around."

Elizabeth meekly obeyed, and the last of her clothes were lifted over her head. Naked in front of the flames, she allowed herself to be massaged again. She felt like he was rubbing her down like a horse, but it proved very effective in bringing heat back to her limbs.

Mrs. Vaughan came back, her arms laden with a tea tray, but upon seeing the scene before her, she thought it best to set the tray down and leave. Her master seemed in no mood to be disturbed.

After a few minutes, satisfied that Elizabeth was no longer shivering, Darcy helped her put on a clean shift. He made her sit in a chair, put a cup of tea in her hands and, while she drank, he knelt down to rub her feet and legs.

"You are aware, I hope, that your behaviour today was beneath you," he growled.

Elizabeth pressed her lips together. Her husband continued:

"What will my uncle and aunt make of all this? It is the sort of incident that can ruin all the effort you are making to please them. And what will the others say? The servants? The people of Woolbert? You can be sure that all of Lambton will be made aware of your adventure at the next market!"

He rubbed her again.

"It is inconceivable that one should find Mrs. Darcy alone in the woods, at such an ungodly hour, covered in mud and in the company of a farmer," he concluded. "Do I make myself clear?"

Elizabeth nodded. She tried to hold back the tears that welled up in her eyes.

"I feel like I am your little crayfish catcher, today," she murmured.

Her husband sighed. His hands slowed down as he softened.

"With your temperament, I was expecting this kind of caper sooner or later. I simply wish you had not made it in the presence of the Earl, and above all, I would have liked to avoid the fright you gave me! I was about to assemble all the men in the area into a search party!"

"Please forgive me, William..."

He put the foot he had been rubbing down and got up. He was now tolerably composed.

"I suppose we should be pleased that nothing untoward happened. But you will do me the favour of never repeating this sort of escapade again. I shall leave you with Mrs. Vaughan. I must reassure our guests and make sure that Colonel Fitzwilliam is back."

Before going out, he turned one last time.

"Would you like me to ask for your dinner to be brought up?"

"No, I shall be down in a moment. I would rather face everyone's displeasure tonight."

Darcy gave her a look that was fraught with meaning. Then he left the room.

~

The next day, after breakfast, Elizabeth had the carriage readied. Accompanied by Georgiana and Lady Fitzwilliam, she went to the Stevens' farm to bring the shepherd a basket of pastries as a token of her gratitude.

As the man was not there, his wife welcomed them instead, both surprised and intimidated to receive such a visit. She hastened to welcome them in, offered them tea, sent her children away so they would not disturb the ladies and apologised several times for the state of her house. Upon seeing the treats she had been brought, she thanked them effusively.

"It is the least I can do," declared Elizabeth, with an amiable smile. "Your husband was most obliging, last night. Believe me, I was very pleased to find someone who could help me find my way!"

She took the opportunity to enquire after the family's health and whether the farm was doing well. She assured them that they should not hesitate to call upon her if they needed anything. She also promised to come back to see them around Christmas. The children she had seen earlier would certainly not say no to more treats. When Elizabeth left the farm soon after with Georgiana and the Countess, Mrs. Stevens had nothing but praise for her new mistress.

The ladies then stopped at the Moores' house. Everyone in Woolbert was already aware of Mrs. Darcy's misadventure and the steward was relieved to see that she was doing well. As for his wife, she was in a marvellous mood and it was not entirely clear whether she was relieved to see her neighbour safe and sound, or whether it was the pleasure of having their company. She managed to keep them far longer than was usually expected of a simple courtesy call.

Through it all, Lady Fitzwilliam nodded her approval. The disapproving look and pursed lips from the night before had disappeared. Elizabeth had quite a talent when it came to storytelling. She was able to relate her story so as to highlight the amusing anecdotes whilst minimising the regrettable aspects, and it had ultimately paid off. Her husband's aunt forgave this breach of conduct, when she learned of the harmless particulars. One could not fault Elizabeth for wishing to honour the family's ancestors.

Elizabeth went to great lengths to ensure the Countess's favour. More than ever, she relied on both her and the Colonel's influence to win the Earl over. As was to be expected, Lord Fitzwilliam had also not appreciated his niece's 'boldness', and made it very clear by uttering a few unpleasant remarks.

"Just imagine if the Earl and Lady Catherine decided to despise me together!" Elizabeth whispered to her husband. "What would happen then?"

"Nothing at all," he answered, his face impenetrable.

Fortunately, their guests' stay was coming to an end and Elizabeth even missed out on the last moments, her escapade in the cold having left her feeling unwell the following day. Her husband's energetic rubbing had undoubtedly helped her avoid the worst, but it did not save her from being struck by a high fever that left her miserable. Georgiana came in several times to keep her company, and the Countess sent her broths seasoned with a mix of spices she had used to treat her children. In her words they 'did wonders for colds, chills and all manner of painful ailments that may ruin a season'.

Darcy returned to his own room for a while. His wife was too feverish to bear his presence and was also restless in her slumber, which would also have prevented him from sleeping. A doctor was called in from Lambton, but he did not recommend much except keeping the patient warm, changing her sheets as often as necessary and making her drink plenty of broth and tea. At the very least, his visit had the merit of confirming that Elizabeth had nothing to fear, for she was of an excellent constitution. Lord Fitzwilliam, for once, refrained from saying that this proved his point.

The day of their departure, whilst Elizabeth was still bedridden, her guests came to bid her farewell. They thanked her for her welcome and wished her a prompt recovery.

The young woman longed for it too, for the Bingleys would be there in less than a month and missing such a reunion was simply out of the question.

CHAPTER 9

On the long-awaited day, Elizabeth paced relentlessly before the windows that overlooked the valley so that she would be the first to see the carriages arriving. When she finally caught sight of them, her heart gave a leap. She raced down the passage to rouse the rest of the household.

"William! Georgiana! They are arriving!"

Ever vigilant, Weston had made arrangements for a large number of servants to be present on the porch. There were eight adults and four children arriving and he wished to avoid any mayhem.

"Mrs. Reynolds? Mrs. Reynolds!" Elizabeth called out excitedly upon arriving in the vestibule. Would you please prepare some tea at once? It is rather cold outside, and I would like our guests to warm up quickly."

"Very well, madam."

"Have the fires been lit in the rooms?"

"I have just given the order."

"And you have made sure that the wood stores are full?"

"Indeed, madam. The rooms are as ready as can be."

Darcy appeared alongside his wife. "Such eagerness, Lizzy!" he quipped. "You were not so hasty when my aunt and uncle arrived."

"I confess that I do wish everything to be perfect," she retorted with utmost seriousness. "I do not seek to impress them, but, because they are my family, I want only the best for them. And Georgiana? Where is Georgiana? She must be here!"

"Do not fret, my dear. She will be here in a minute."

Despite what she had just said, Elizabeth did wish to enchant her guests. Jane and Kitty's first impression of Pemberley held a degree of importance to her.

"Weston? Are they arriving? Do you see them? Oliver, my coat, if you please! I should like to wait for them outside."

The young woman bundled up with care. She still had a cold, but aside from being slightly hoarse and using an abundance of handkerchiefs, she felt quite recovered from her recent bout of fever. She would have been quite miserable with herself if her recent misadventure in the woods had spoiled the time she could have spent with her sisters.

The minutes seemed endless, until the first carriage finally appeared around the corner of the house and started down the lane. It belonged to the Bingleys.

"Jane! Kitty! Finally, you are here!"

The three sisters shared a long embrace, punctuated by laughter and kisses. Shortly afterwards, a second carriage came to a stop on the drive and the Gardiners and their children stepped out. The little ones were indeed slightly intimidated, but upon recognising their cousin, they rushed into her arms.

To Weston's great dismay, joyful mayhem ensued on the porch and in the vestibule, where the footmen hurried to take the visitors' coats. They were tired from their journey, but the Gardiners were quick to offer warm thanks to their host: Darcy had sent a carriage from Pemberley to London to fetch the entire family, saving them from a far more arduous journey by coach, particularly for the children who were between the ages of four and nine years old. As for Jane and Kitty, their weariness did not dim the excitement that shone in their eyes and the pleasure of seeing their sister in her new surroundings. Already dazzled by the elegance of the facades, they were awed by the great hall that followed.

"Good Lord, Lizzy, how beautiful!"

"Follow me, let me show you the rest of the house... I cannot tell you how glad I am to see you all again!"

But, as she led her sisters and cousins towards the staircase, she was called back by Darcy. The Hursts' carriage was now approaching and it would be improper if the mistress of Pemberley were not there to offer them the same welcome.

Once everyone had arrived, the company gathered in the sitting room where drinks and sandwiches were served. A clamorous happiness persisted as news was exchanged, punctuated by the odd joyous exclamation. The Hursts and Caroline Bingley, who had not seen Georgiana in many months, surrounded the young woman and were profuse in their praises. Darcy and Bingley began exchanging with the Gardiners while the children took advantage of their mother's distraction to grab as many sandwiches as they possibly could. Kitty, intimidated by the splendour of the house, stared wide-eyed at everything and did not utter a word.

Seated next to one another, Jane had not let go of her sister's hand. She was far too happy to be reunited with her lifelong accomplice.

"So, my dear, how are you? Your voice is strange, have you been ill? How was London? This house is truly beautiful... It is much larger than Netherfield! Have you heard from Charlotte? Did you receive my latest letter? Oh, you must tell me everything! Do you know that Papa has a new obsession? He has developed a rather unexpected passion for antique medals."

It had barely been a month and a half since the two sisters had parted, but they had both experienced such exciting things that time seemed to have stretched. They felt as though they had not seen each other for years and had a thousand stories to tell one another.

Jane gave news of Hertfordshire. It was strange for Elizabeth to hear second-hand accounts of her parents, her uncle and aunt Philips, the

Lucases and the people of Meryton... She had written and received a handful of letters since her wedding, but they never described the details of ordinary life: the horse's lame foot, a coffee and cocoa shop replacing the old haberdashery, a neighbour leaving for the city, Betty's nasty fall down the stairs, a complicated embroidery that had been started at the beginning of summer finally coming to an end, the music lessons that Mary had been gifted, all the small details that were part of daily life in Longbourn and its surroundings.

"As for Netherfield... Charles and I are so happy with the place that we are thinking about settling down permanently, if the owner accepts to sell it. Charles has spoken about making him an offer, to gauge his reaction."

"Don't be so hasty, you have time enough to settle down permanently. That said, I suppose Mamma will be excited by this decision! Is she at your house every day as I predicted she would be?" Elizabeth asked, amused.

"Not every day, no. But it is true that she expects to have dinner with us at least once a week. On this subject, you may be surprised to learn that our parents receive a great deal more invitations than before! After the wedding, they went to an endless stream of receptions. I think they visited our entire circle of acquaintances in less than a fortnight. Papa could hardly take it anymore!"

"I have no doubt! Poor Papa... And you? And Charles? Do you go out often?"

"Sometimes, yes. I wrote to you, I believe, that we went dancing at the Meryton assembly, but I did not have time to add that we also spent a few days in London, with Louisa and Edmund."

Kitty, who had grown tired of being left out, interrupted the two women.

"You must have felt terribly daunted when you arrived, Lizzy," she said. "This house is so large! I do believe I could get quite lost in it!"

"I assure you that it is quite possible," Elizabeth replied, winking. "Would you like me to show you around later when you have had time to change? Unless you would prefer a visit tomorrow?"

"No! Tonight! Now, if possible!"

Elizabeth smiled at her younger sister's enthusiasm.

"Speaking of which... Mr. Darcy?" she called.

"Yes, dearest?"

"If you see Mr. Weston in the corridor, would you please send him to me?"

The young man bowed and headed towards the door. A moment later, the butler leaned respectfully over his mistress's shoulder.

"Would you kindly bring some hot water to the rooms?" she asked him. "I believe our guests will soon want to change."

"Of course, madam. Will dinner still be served at six o'clock?"

"Yes, as usual. The children's meal is already prepared, I suppose?"

"Quite right, it will be served in the nursery. Mrs. Reynolds has allocated two maids to look after them if your aunt so wishes."

"I shall ask her. Thank you, Weston."

The butler bowed with the utmost decorum and took his leave.

This little demonstration of domestic authority had two effects: first it made the young Kitty, who found her sister rather pompous, giggle, and second, it attracted the attention of Louisa and Caroline.

"You have made yourself quite at home, Mrs. Darcy," commented Caroline, in her usual sickly sweet voice.

"How fortunate for me then, since I live here now."

"Are you not exhausted? I warned you that it would be a considerable task, did I not? One must think of so many things..."

"I am very fortunate to have the guidance of someone best situated to give me advice," Elizabeth replied, serenely.

"Really? Pray, who is it? Not your husband, I hope! Men know nothing of such matters."

Darcy and Bingley, hearing the word 'husband', interrupted their conversation and strained their ears to hear the rest.

"No, I was referring to my mother-in-law, Lady Anne."

"Whatever do you mean?" asked Louisa, inanely.

"Only that I have found her notes, along with a few of her personal belongings, and they have proved useful in helping me manage my household."

Caroline shrugged.

"You mostly have the possibility of doing what you please, without anyone telling you otherwise, or criticising your decisions. What a blessing to no longer have your in-laws under your feet, truly!" she smirked. "Not everyone has this comfort, especially at such a young age!"

"Losing one's parents is certainly no comfort, Miss Bingley," Darcy declared, sharply. "You know that as well as I do."

The young woman blushed.

"Forgive me, Mr. Darcy, that is certainly not what I meant..."

"We all wish that the late Mr. Darcy and Lady Anne were still with us. They are indeed two people whom I would have been delighted to meet and appreciate in person," tempered Elizabeth. "Speaking of which, would you like to go up to change now?" she added, turning towards her sisters. "I could then show you their portraits, followed by a tour of the rest of the house whilst we wait for dinner. What do you think?"

And, as the group rose, Elizabeth noticed that Darcy still looked sharply in Caroline's direction. She touched his arm gently.

"Leave it, William..." she whispered.

~

Pemberley's mistress was delighted to show her sisters the first floor, starting with the painting gallery and the reception rooms, and ending with the drawing and music rooms, the cabinet of curiosities and the library. She now knew the house well enough to be a good guide. She was able to name most of the ancestral portraits and relayed, with her usual eloquence, the family anecdotes Darcy had shared with her.

As the visit progressed, she realised with some satisfaction that she was beginning to feel at home in the imposing house. She was rather surprised to see how a month spent in Derbyshire had changed her. Despite having everything in common with her sisters, she had the strange sensation of belonging a little less to the world of Meryton and a little more to that of Pemberley.

The large dining room impressed Jane a great deal and Elizabeth took the opportunity to recount the first dinner she had hosted.

"Twenty people at the table, you say? And you were not very familiar with most of them? What an ordeal it must have been for you!" Jane commiserated.

"Have you also given your first dinner at Netherfield?"

"Yes, but it was just Papa, Mamma, Mary, Kitty, the Lucases and the Philips. In truth, if any mistakes were made, they did not matter much. Whereas here... It cannot be easy to get to know all these acquaintances! Is Lambton society much like Meryton's?"

"More or less. We have a viscount, a baronet, a very wealthy widow and other families. But I do not know everyone yet, of course."

"Do you go to Lambton often?" asked Kitty. "We merely passed through, but it seems quite a pretty town. Are there many distractions?"

"I don't actually know, Kitty. I have only been there on a few occasions to shop with William or Mrs. Vaughan."

"Who is this Mrs. Vaughan?"

"My maid. She needed to have my measurements taken by a tailor so he could make me a riding habit. I am without, as you well know, clothes of this kind."

She had spoken blithely, but it did nothing to diminish the dazzling effect of her words on her younger sister. At Longbourn, one was hard pressed to find funds for a new ballgown, never mind a riding habit!

"So, you wish to go hunting? On horseback, I mean?" the younger girl pressed.

"I have no idea. I might have to learn one day and, if that is the case, I shall ask William to teach me how to ride properly. But if it were up to me, I would prefer to go about beating the thickets with my legs firmly planted on the ground!"

Although she had greatly admired the women in Hyde Park who rode side-saddle, Elizabeth did not feel very comfortable riding alone. None of the Bennet sisters had ever been taught how to ride a horse. Mr. Bennet's two horses were mostly used on the farm or to pull the carriage, and an extra mount would have cost far too much, especially if it was only used for leisure. So, in his daughters' eyes, horses remained large powerful creatures, unpredictable and difficult to control, and best left to the care of men.

"To return to Lambton," she continued, "now that you are here, we shall go there at the very first opportunity, as we shall need materials to assemble our Christmas decorations. Our aunt can guide us, she knows the town better than any of us!"

~

This visit was organised two days later, on market day. Margaret Gardiner sent a note to inform her friend Mrs. Munroe that they would pay her a visit once they were done with their shopping. Since the gentlemen did not wish to join them, and neither did Louisa and Caroline, who saw no point of going out in such cold weather, Elizabeth and the other ladies were accompanied only by a footman who was tasked with carrying their parcels.

With the festivities approaching, the market was teeming with activity. Mrs. Darcy was often recognised and was always greeted with the utmost respect. She stopped for a moment to chat with Stevens, who had come to sell his lambs, as well as with two other Maesbury farmers whom she did not yet know very well. Behind her, her sisters explored the market with curiosity, finding products they were not familiar with in Hertfordshire. They did not have to be asked twice when they were offered a piece of cheese or a bite of cake. The poultry were so loud that everyone was forced to raise their voices and there was a fair bit of jostling from people passing by in a hurry, but the general good humour meant that everyone was quite forgiving of these minor inconveniences.

After the market, Mrs. Gardiner guided her nieces towards some of the shops she remembered. The young women stocked up on ribbons, string, gold and coloured papers, as well as moulds to make small wax figurines. Kitty wanted to buy everything she saw and dragged Georgiana along with her. Not wanting to ruin their fun, Elizabeth decided not to deter them, which meant that the two girls emerged with their hands full, their eyes bright and laughter on their lips.

They stopped at an inn for lunch, allowing them to warm up and rest a little. But as the small party headed back to one last shop to buy cinnamon sticks and other spices for the decorations, Elizabeth recognised a silhouette in front of her.

"Mrs. Keen?"

The elderly woman turned around, a broad smile lighting up her face as she recognised Elizabeth.

"Mrs. Darcy! How delightful to see you!"

Elizabeth was quick to introduce her sisters and her aunt.

"Well, I see you are in excellent company!" the widow exclaimed.

"Indeed, and this is not even our entire party. We have a few friends who preferred to stay warm at home today, and we are expecting the Moores and the Munroes on Christmas day."

"Lady Anne would be most delighted to hear this. I fear there have not been many family celebrations at Pemberley House since she left us, dear soul. Is that not so, Miss Darcy?"

Georgiana acquiesced shyly.

"What about you, Mrs. Keen? Will you be spending Christmas with your relatives?"

"Alas, no! I no longer have much family left, dear madam. I would have spent Christmas Eve at the rectory, as usual, but this year the Reverend Smith is invited to his brother's house. So, no, I shall simply stay at home and visit those in need."

"In that case, would you like to join us?" offered Elizabeth. "I am certain that my husband would be delighted to have you."

Claiming she did not wish to intrude, Mrs. Keen was soon persuaded.

"How very kind of you, Mrs. Darcy. Oh, and since you are here, might I recommend a few people who are in need of a caring soul to help them during this festive season? I suppose you have already planned to visit your people, but if I could convince you to travel a little farther, there are three or four families that are quite destitute in the Lambton region..."

"You may count on me, madam. I would be most happy to visit them," Elizabeth replied, kindly. "Shall we discuss this further on Sunday after the service?"

Mrs. Keen gave her approval and they parted ways after wishing each other a good day.

~

At dinner that evening, the conversations were animated. There was a certain excitement in the air as the guests expressed their joy at being united once more and revealed their impatience as they awaited the approaching festivities.

Bingley proposed an outing to cut down the greenery, which would serve to decorate the house. He even offered to climb the trees himself to pick all the mistletoe the ladies might desire.

"Climbing up trees? Come now, Charles!" Louisa huffed.

But the young man gave a hearty laugh and confirmed that he would surrender to all whims, even the wildest ones. He attempted to encourage Darcy in this endeavour, but the latter replied that it was a task better suited to the Cox boys.

Elizabeth declared that the drawing-room would be requisitioned for a day and turned into a workshop to assemble all the decorations. Jane added that the children, who might be delighted to help, should participate. Mrs. Gardiner agreed.

"I do think we are going to have a marvellous Christmas!" exclaimed Georgiana, overjoyed. "Each project seems more exciting than the last. What a difference from last year!"

"You were in London last year, dear child," Caroline reminded her. "What better way to celebrate the festivities than by enjoying all the entertainment the city has to offer? Have you forgotten all the beautiful shops we visited?"

"And the charming pantomime show in Drury Lane!" said Louisa, from the other side of the table.

"And yet I much prefer being here," replied the young lady, undaunted. "I think there is nothing more joyful than a house filled with family and children on Christmas!"

Caroline made no answer. She looked puzzled, but it was difficult to say whether she was disconcerted by Georgiana's words, or whether it was because, for once, she had replied with aplomb.

Darcy smiled. His sister's newfound liveliness had not escaped him.

"I quite agree with you, Georgiana, and I promise you that from now on, we shall endeavour to be in good company every year," he said.

~

The greenery was collected amidst a lovely sprinkling of snow, which had fallen the previous night. They walked down towards Maesbury, guided by the Cox boys driving a small cart. They knew the estate off by heart and easily guided the group to the best spots.

Charles Bingley stubbornly followed through with his plan, much to his sisters' chagrin. He scaled the trees with remarkable ease and plucked several bouquets of mistletoe. Each time he climbed down he appeared increasingly dishevelled, dirty and covered in snow, but he laughed heartily and his good mood was contagious. Meanwhile, Elizabeth led her uncle along the river to fetch a few rushes for plaiting, and they both returned quite muddy from walking along the waterlogged banks.

Seeing them, Darcy sighed.

"Would you mind keeping your feet dry, Lizzy?" he exclaimed. "Did you not learn your lesson last time?"

"But look at what we have found!"

Bright-eyed and cheeks reddened from the cold, his wife smiled from ear to ear as she pointed to the large bundle that her uncle carried on his shoulders, as though it were the year's best catch. Darcy was unable to hold it against her: he found her far too beautiful.

Georgiana and Kitty waged a battle with the smaller Gardiners and eventually, the entire party was competing for snowiest coat. Only Jane and Mrs. Gardiner successfully maintained their dignity and elegance. As for Caroline and the Hursts seated in the cart, they were in no danger of getting dirty. However, numb with cold, they looked increasingly miserable.

Once the cart had been laden with large armfuls of ivy, mistletoe and holly, the expedition headed further into the woods in search of the best Yule log. The children were called upon to do their share.

"Spread out and search for the largest fallen tree trunk! The log must burn for a long time!"

"Could you not instruct your servants to take care of all this, Mr. Darcy?" asked Louisa, taking off her gloves to blow warm air on her fingers. "I cannot fathom why we have to walk so far."

"The pleasure is in the hunt, madam," the young man replied politely. "Look at the children now that we have given them this task. When they return, beaming with pride at having found what we are looking for, you will understand."

"You poor thing, you seem frozen," said Elizabeth. "You should move about to stay warm, my dear! But perhaps you would prefer to go home? I could ask one of the boys to take you. Or else, you could go to Maesbury. I am certain that a farmer there will be happy to welcome you into the warmth of his house."

"No, thank you!" replied Louisa with a disdainful look. "We shall wait for the 'hunt' – as you call it, Mr. Darcy – to come to an end."

In the end, it was Jane and the Gardiners' youngest child who found the most promising log: A fallen tree whose main branch was deemed ideal. The four-year-old had not quite grasped what he was being credited for, but upon seeing his mother's pride, he soon began to parade like a little peacock shouting: 'It is I! I found the log! I found it!'

The Cox brothers brought out a saw and Darcy and Bingley took turns finishing the chore. The log was then loaded up onto the cart, and the children, who were tired, clambered upon it and the party made its way back home.

~

With all her guests to look after, along with the children dashing down the corridors, and the preparations successfully under way, Elizabeth had no time to herself. She considered herself lucky if she had even half an hour to walk in the gardens, while waiting for breakfast.

Not only did she have to care for her guests this festive season, but she also had to take her servants and farmers into account as they all awaited a gesture on her part. Not to mention those in need, who now relied on her charity to ease their difficulties.

The little golden key was put to good use. The young mistress would refer to her list of names at all hours of the day, and she was very glad to have Jane and her aunt's help in sorting out the linen intended for the poor. Mrs. Keen had been rather overbearing when she had submitted her list of poor families needing help, and acquiring enough shawls, bonnets, blankets, baby clothes and flannel petticoats represented a great deal of work – not to mention the sickly, as they had very different needs. She solicited Mr. Grove to sort through Darcy's wardrobe and bring her the coats and boots he no longer wore. She did the same for the late Mr. Darcy and Lady Anne's clothes, which had been stored in the attic. The fabrics were of fine quality and those who received the items would be able to alter them into sturdy clothes.

As for the servants, she summoned Mrs. Reynolds into her parlour for advice. Elizabeth did not know her people well enough to decide upon personalised gifts herself. The box they were to receive the day after Christmas was an important occasion that could not be squandered if she truly wished to be appreciated by her staff.

Fortunately, the housekeeper knew exactly what to do and she even sent packages to Hallcot and his team at Chalton House.

Once the foliage from the woods had been sufficiently dried out in one of the rooms downstairs, large tables were set up in the drawing-room, and the ladies and children began to make the decorations: a delightful albeit delicate chore. Caroline and Louisa lent a helping hand at first for good measure, but they quickly grew tired and let the others continue whilst they happily commented on the constructions taking shape before them.

In the middle of the afternoon, back from the stables, Bingley, Darcy and Mr. Gardiner also made an appearance to check on progress.

"Mr. Bingley, Mr. Darcy, instead of both standing idle, why don't you lend us a hand?" asked Elizabeth. "We still have large amounts of paper to cut for the garlands. You too, Uncle, if you will! We need all the help we can get!"

Under the bewildered gaze of his friends, Darcy sat down in the chair she had gestured to and graciously began to cut strips of pink and green paper. The Gardiners' eldest daughter, a girl of nine who was busy with the same task, set about correcting him with much authority:

"You might want to cut it here and here. Look at mine!"

Whilst his friend unflinchingly carried out the order, Bingley laughed heartily.

"Well, well, Darcy! Here you are, a dutiful husband, and reprimanded by a little girl at that! I would scarcely believe it had I not seen it with my own eyes. Good heavens! What has come over you?"

"Laugh if you must, Bingley, but there is a vacant chair in front of me and something tells me that you shall soon be seated, too," Darcy retorted with a small smile. "Besides, were you not acting like a monkey climbing up trees yesterday, for the sole benefit of your beloved wife?"

"It is true!" Jane chimed in, amused. "And the mistletoe you cut is right here, my dear. Would you like to help me arrange them into bouquets?"

Bingley, beaten at his own game, sought a way out, but Darcy put on an affected air as he insisted:

"Come now, my friend! Since your wife asks so nicely… Show some gallantry!"

The young man had no choice but to comply and, amid great laughter, he finally sat down, laughing. .

"Gentlemen, this is what marriage truly is," Mr. Gardiner then declared. "Go hunting, riding and exploring, be as adventurous as you like, but you should also be prepared to cut little bits of pink paper when your lady so wishes!"

"This is a lesson you learned a long time ago, is that not right, dear Edward?" retorted his wife, looking at him with affection. "You better be grateful, gentlemen, that we do not ask you to change the baby's linen!"

And, as everyone laughed once again, Mr. Gardiner sat down with his two boys and also began crafting decorations.

The party spent the rest of the afternoon thus happily employed. Amidst the cups of tea and cocoa served by Elizabeth, they produced a lovely collection of paper garlands and flowers, woven reed crowns, and bouquets of mistletoe and holly tied together with ribbon. The candelabra were brought out, along with silver baskets intended for the feast, and covered in greenery, little stars cut out of brilliant paper and decorations made of metal thread or woven straw. Mrs. Gardiner took over the wax workshop: she showed one of her daughters how to cast beautiful angels that she then fixed upon the candles. Georgiana and Kitty cut the gingerbread into shapes and added lemon, dried tangerine slices, cinnamon sticks and star anise to the crowns and bouquets. Lastly, Mrs. Reynold made a sudden appearance from the kitchen with a large tray laden with sugar flowers, which delighted everyone.

"Georgiana, would you play for us? Your music is so pleasant!" Jane asked. "I am certain that Caroline can replace you."

The girl happily consented. She opened the doors leading to the music room and sat down at her pianoforte. Meanwhile, Caroline took a seat at the table once again and smiled in an attempt to conceal her reluctance. Edmund Hurst did not involve himself and

243

was forgotten in a corner while his wife, Louisa – no doubt in solidarity with her sister – eventually approached the table, showing vague interest in what unfolded there.

Darcy, still seated next to the little girl whose instructions he humbly followed, exchanged long glances with Elizabeth from time to time. He was not accustomed to being treated with such familiarity in front of others, but there was such a pleasant conviviality in the room that it was worth swallowing his pride a little.

Elizabeth set her woven crown down on the console next to the rest of the completed decorations and leaned over her husband to wrap her arms around his neck.

"So, my dear, what do you have to say about all this?" she whispered in his ear. "Did you not have great fun cutting out the garlands?"

He smiled and dipped his head. It was the closest admission that Elizabeth could hope to obtain from him. With a little laugh she kissed his cheek. She then motioned to the rest of the room where adults and children alike worked together in good cheer.

"Do you remember the little Egertons in London?" she whispered again. "Those poor children were put on display as though they were at a county fair and seemed intimidated by their parents. Well, when I think of the family we shall have one day, I hope it will bear closer resemblance to this..."

Then, without waiting for a reply, she stood up and offered to help her uncle, who had become tangled in ribbons.

~

The twenty-fifth of December was a memorable day, the likes of which had not been seen at Pemberley for a long time.

It had snowed once again, which made the journey to the church a little more complicated than usual. Once there, the bench reserved for the Darcys was not big enough to accommodate all their guests. Since Elizabeth's family were naturally given priority, the Hursts and Caroline Bingley found themselves seated with ordinary parishioners, which prompted a disdainful sneer on the latter's lips.

After the service, they lingered to greet all their acquaintances, along with the merchants and the farmers. Many took the opportunity to introduce themselves to Elizabeth, who did not yet know all the residents. She, on the other hand, was well known to them. They then fetched Mrs. Keen, and everyone climbed back into the carriage to head home and warm up.

The twelve days of celebrations could now begin.

~

Christmas day was a rather casual affair. The servants had been discharged for the day and only Weston and Mrs. Reynolds remained, along with two maids and a footman whose families lived too far away for them to afford a visit. The meals and drinks had been prepared in advance, and the wood supplies overflowed in each room so that the family would not want for anything until the following morning.

To further widen their social circle, Darcy and Elizabeth also invited the Moore and Munroe families, who arrived at about eleven o'clock. This added quite a few children to the group: sixteen altogether, including the little Gardiners. Weston winced at the sight of so many potential rascals intent upon bringing chaos to his ordered household. However, the older ones ultimately watched over the younger children, which allowed the butler and the parents to enjoy their day relatively undisturbed. Jane was overjoyed at the prospect of coddling such a lovely bunch of little faces, and to that end she had a great number of treats at her disposal. Following her lead, Georgiana also leant her attention to the youngest ones.

The decorations had been set up throughout both the dining room and the big sitting room and the doors were opened wide so that they could enjoy having additional space all day long. The little sitting room next door was reserved for the children and their games. The Yule log, lined with ribbons and woven straw ornaments, was prominently on display, waiting to be set on fire. The consoles along the walls were laden with items of confectionery, sandwiches and all the necessary items needed for the guests to brew their own tea, coffee or bitter cocoa. But they were quickly replaced by bottles of Bordeaux wine, then Madeira wine, Marsala and sherry. After all, there were plenty of toasts to be made. The party raised their glasses to their hosts, and to Elizabeth's health in particular, as they all wished her to be blessed with a large family soon. It was followed by a toast to the Infant Jesus and to the festive season, which promised to be full of good cheer, starting with Lord and Lady Hastings' New Year's Eve ball. Part of the fun was wagering on who would make an appearance or not.

Georgiana began to play the pianoforte, and Elizabeth, who was not yet light-headed from the wine, sang a few graceful airs. Kitty recited a poem her sisters recognised straight away as being one of Mary's favourites. This inspired a few of the children, who, having listened to her, slipped away to prepare a few recitations and a play of their own. But, as the afternoon had only just begun and there were still several hours to go before dinner, Elizabeth called upon Weston.

"I suppose the luncheon is ready downstairs?"

"Of course, madam." Mr. Hewitt has spread everything upon the kitchen tables. The guests need only help themselves to eat. Aston and I shall do the service."

"Do not trouble yourself! Enjoy the day and rest a little. We shall help ourselves."

"In that case I shall tell the others to start bringing out the plates."

"Don't fret, I have a better idea!"

She slipped into the room where the children played and gathered them around her.

"We are going to make our way to the kitchen and bring the dishes up to the sitting room," she explained. "Follow me!"

The stream of children of all ages that poured out into the corridor in a most disorderly fashion did not go unnoticed. Jane joined them.

"What are you up to?"

"We are heading downstairs to fetch the food. I am calling it 'The Hungry Bellies Expedition'!" replied her sister, playfully.

"Wait, I will help you!"

The troop invaded the entire kitchen downstairs before the horrified eyes of the butler and the housekeeper. The younger children attempted to pilfer food from the plates, but they were quickly called to order by the older ones whilst Elizabeth and Jane made their way to the tables. In the midst of all the chaos, they began to distribute dishes or bowls to each child.

"Go up the stairs and await the signal before entering the sitting room, all right?"

"And be careful not to knock anything over!"

This instruction, however, did not prevent the contents of two plates from landing on the vestibule stairs. At five or six years old, concentrating on both the precious cargo they carried and the stairs they had to climb was difficult.

"Leave it be, we shall clean it all up," Mrs. Reynolds reassured the embarrassed children. She softened at the sight of their angelic faces, each one more adorable than the next, dressed in their Sunday best.

At the top of the stairs, Weston lent a hand. As the children arrived with their hands full, he draped a few serviettes over one of their arms and inserted a handful of teaspoons into a few of their pockets so that they would make quite an impression on the adults when they finally entered the large sitting room.

"Heavens, how adorable!"

"They are simply charming!"

"Would you look at him! Watch your plate my child, or else there will soon be nothing left in it!"

"Biscuits! Would you mind if I helped myself to one, young lady?"

"Oh! Look, he has spoons and forks in his waistcoat! Are they all not simply enchanting!"

"But how many are there? There is no end to it!"

At first surprised like everyone else by this unexpected parade, Darcy had the presence of mind to take over from Elizabeth and Jane, who were still busy downstairs. He showed the children where to set their consignments down, after which the youngest of them proudly ran into their parents' laps, to be embraced and congratulated. The guests were delighted. Mrs. Keen gave the little ones a kiss when they passed by, and even Louisa and Hurst were moved by the sight.

When Elizabeth, last to arrive, entered the room, her husband grabbed her by the waist. He slipped her a kiss on the neck.

"What an exquisite idea you had, my dear. I must congratulate you..." he whispered lovingly.

"Good Lord, William, how extravagant of you to show me so much affection in front of your friends. Have you been drinking?" she whispered in response, before discreetly returning his kiss and then laughing heartily, quite pleased with herself.

The platters emptied as the guests ate their fill. Since it was Christmas, the children were allowed to eat seated on the carpet or on their parents' lap. A few clothes were stained but Mrs. Reynolds had the foresight to put cleaning items at their disposal. Besides, the adults had started drinking well before eating. The alcohol was taking effect and no one paid much attention. Even Mr. Moore, usually so distinguished, drew attention to himself when he knocked some of the contents of his glass onto his lap, but he was already slightly drunk and laughed it off.

After the meal, overpowered by the heat of the roaring fireplaces, the guests were rather tempted to have a nap. But they had not considered Bingley who was always the liveliest one in the group. He managed to organise a few games, which lasted most of the afternoon. He never ran out of ideas to make both the old and the young play together. There were card games, of course. For once, Hurst was in his element and diligently took on the role of president at the card table. There were also a few rounds of blind man's bluff and all sorts of other chasing games. The furniture in the small living room was even pushed aside to organise a round of Hunt The Slipper.

"I am surprised that you find enjoyment in such a game, Mr. Darcy," said Louisa as he passed by on his way to join the others.

The young man pretended not to hear. He had been persuaded to join by Georgiana, just before she dashed to her room to fetch the little slipper, and he was determined to please her.

248

Over a dozen players sat down on the drawing-room carpet, to the amusement of the other guests who had come to observe the game. The silliness of the adults joining the children made it all rather delightful. There were the three Bennet sisters, Mrs. Gardiner and her husband, Mrs. Moore, Mr. Munroe and a few children of all ages. Bingley stayed on his feet, for he intended to be the first hunter.

"Here it is! Here I come! Wait for me!" shouted Georgiana as she ran down the passage, a shoe in her hand.

"Of course we will wait for you, my dear. We cannot play without the slipper!" Elizabeth returned.

The adolescent let herself fall to the floor, out of breath and excited, between her brother and one of the Moores' daughters. Seeing that Bingley was already rushing towards her with a chuckle, she reacted by throwing the slipper to Kitty seated a little further away.

"Oh!" the latter protested, with fright and laughter. "The game had not yet started!"

"Well, I do declare that it has now begun!" announced Bingley as he moved about the circle with a fierce look on his face that made the children giggle. "Woe betide you if I catch you!"

"If you are as agile on the ground as you are in the trees, my friend, we are done for!" replied Mrs. Gardiner.

Those who had participated in the mistletoe expedition began to chuckle.

"So? Has the game begun?" asked Kitty, who had hidden the slipper under her skirt.

Bingley rushed towards her and touched her on the shoulder.

"You talk too much, Kitty! Catching you was far too easy! Come now, up you get! It is your turn to go hunting!"

But the girl shook her head and showed him her empty hands.

"Whatever do you mean, Charles? I do not have the slipper," she protested, looking falsely angelic.

"What? But where..." Bingley fussed, surprised that his sister-in-law had managed to make a fool of him.

Kitty laughed cheerfully, pleased with herself. The slipper had passed from player to player, sliding under their laps until it was on the other side of the circle, in the possession of Mrs. Moore.

The hunter began running again to catch it and the game began.

~

At nightfall, Darcy and Bingley placed the Yule log in the fire as the guests applauded. It seemed enormous, filling the entire fireplace, and promised to burn until morning.

A group of children took advantage of the freedom they had been given before bedtime to put on a play. They had rehearsed all afternoon and presented their show using the double doors that separated the big sitting room from the smaller one as a stage. After the performance, sleeping arrangements had to be made, as it had been decided that the guests would stay overnight to spare them from travelling home in the snow at night. The two remaining maids were selected to watch over the rooms that had been converted into overnight dormitories.

If there were any disturbance upstairs – which was more than likely to be the case, for the children were all very excited –, the adults were none the wiser. For them, it was time to feast.

During the play, Weston and Mrs. Reynolds had discreetly closed the doors to the large dining room and brought up all the dishes. When the guests entered the room, they discovered a well-laden table bathed in candlelight.

Hewitt had spent a few days in the kitchen with his cooks preparing either cold or easy to heat dishes worthy of a feast. The pièces de résistance consisted of roast goose, two ducks and a haunch of venison with rosemary, accompanied by a frumenty with almonds and currants. He had also made a Christmas pudding, a large tureen of white soup, beef porridge with dried fruit mixed with an almost unreasonable amount of port, breads and cheeses, as well as a pig's head terrine. Since Elizabeth did not enjoy meals composed solely of meat, she had asked for both an asparagus and a cabbage soup, to which Hewitt had added honey glazed carrots and pumpkin. But it was the dozens of mincemeat pies, precariously balanced one on top of the other at the centre of the table, which drew the most attention. The cook had varied the fruit and mutton fillings in each pie to keep the guests guessing right up to their first bite. The pies contained apples, prunes, raisins, or apricots, and were flavoured with lemon or orange and spiced with cloves, ginger, nutmeg, or saffron. They had one thing in common: they were all generously soaked in brandy.

The guests had eaten well throughout the afternoon, some gladly helping themselves more than once to the food set out for them on the consoles, but this did not prevent anyone from feasting once more. Everyone sat down on the first available chair and passed around the dishes, their laughter increasing as the wine flowed. With the alcohol and the log producing a vast amount of heat, the ladies quickly took out their fans and the men removed their tailcoats, remaining in shirtsleeves. Bingley even went so far as to remove his tie, closely followed by Darcy, but it was still not enough and several of the windows had to be opened for some fresh air.

Georgiana was unrecognisable. She had played music part of the afternoon with Kitty and Mrs. Annesley, and had eaten a great deal and participated in almost all of Bingley's games. Then, she had rested for a moment whilst conversing with the other ladies, an infant on her lap, before allowing Kitty to drag her off for a final catch game that she found so silly she had not thought herself capable of laughing so hard. At dinner, she told everyone who would listen that she had never spent a more joyful Christmas. Her cheeks were so red that Darcy eventually removed her wine glass, resulting in the adolescent vigorously protesting that she was no longer a child. In vain, for her brother coldly instructed her to drink nothing else but tea. Mrs. Annesley was unsuccessful in her attempts to impress greater restraint and civility upon her pupil. So mortified was she that Darcy eventually came to find her, assuring her that she was permitted to lower her vigilance and he would not hold it against her.

Instead, he took on the responsibility himself. After the enormous dinner, her excitement seemingly subsided all at once and Georgiana collapsed exhausted in a chair, listening absentmindedly to Kitty's conversation. Seeing this, Darcy leaned over to Elizabeth:

"Look at her: she has had too much to drink and she is falling asleep. Should we not take her up to her room?"

"Certainly not!" his wife protested. "She will resent you for depriving her once more of the pleasure of our company. Give her freer rein, William, so she may finish the evening like the rest of us. After all, it is not Christmas every day... By the way, since the children are in bed, Charles has suggested we move over to the small sitting room to dance a little. Would you come with us? Mrs. Munroe will play for us."

Darcy declined in the moment but when he heard Jane, Bingley, Elizabeth and Mr. Munroe's joyful laughter as they engaged in a frenzied quadrille, he could not resist joining them to watch.

"Well, Mr. Darcy, what a startling party!" said Caroline from behind his shoulder. "And to think that this is merely the first day!"

"I have indeed been told so by a good number of guests this evening," he replied with usual calm.

"All the same, I dare say that I no longer recognise Pemberley," she insisted. "I feared that in the servants' absence things might be more chaotic, but I did not expect this level of revelry! Knowing your taste for calm and decency, I am surprised that you have not yet restored order."

"Far be it from me to contradict your notions of my preferences, Caroline, but please know that, like Georgiana, this Christmas day has been the most joyful one I have experienced in years."

"Ah, Georgiana, I must admit that I do worry about her..."

"Really?"

"Do you not find that her temperament has changed somewhat? I find her rather sharper-tongued these days. We are not quite accustomed to it."

"Admittedly, Georgiana has always been quite reserved. But I am pleased to see her so emboldened, it can only do her good."

"Do you really think so? I was speaking with Mrs. Annesley earlier, and I am given to understand that she worries about her little protégée."

"If Mrs. Annesley has anything to say, she knows she can come to me at any time."

"From what I could gather it would seem she fears a certain influence over Georgiana..."

Darcy refrained from sighing in exasperation.

"What do you mean, Caroline?" he asked dryly. "Do speak on your own behalf, please, there is no need to involve Mrs. Annesley in this."

The young woman was momentarily disconcerted. She had not expected to be confronted thus. Nevertheless, she ploughed on, determined to finish her thought.

"I shall only say that since we have arrived, Mr. Hurst, Mrs. Hurst and myself have observed that much has changed in the way of life here. Pemberley was rather peaceful last summer. Everything was quite respectable."

"And?"

"Well, we find that, among other things, Georgiana has become – dare I say – somewhat bold. You know how naive and easily impressed one is at that age, and I believe it is my duty to warn you so you may correct the situation if necessary."

Darcy did not flinch. With his most impenetrable expression, he bowed to her.

"It is most kind of you to worry about my sister's well-being, Caroline, but I assure you that you need not concern yourself. I am best suited to attend to it."

"But do you not think that..."

"Forgive me," he interrupted. "What you call boldness is nothing more than a charming spontaneity the likes of which she has never shown before and I approve of it wholeheartedly. My sister is happier now than she has ever been. I would therefore be most grateful if you refrained from sharing your reservations about the manner in which I run my house."

"But, I..."

"I believe I have been abundantly clear, Miss Bingley."

This time he gave her an icy stare. Caroline blushed crimson and finally held her tongue. He continued to stare at her, until she eventually made a small curtsy, turned around and went to sit next to her sister, attempting to appear casual.

As for Darcy, he breathed a deep sigh and turned his attention to the dancers who were still enjoying themselves. Elizabeth danced with Mr. Munroe. As always, she was laughing and vivacious, even if the alcohol made her slightly more clumsy than usual.

The young man approached Mr. Gardiner, who was also observing the dancers, foot tapping along to the tempo.

"I believe we have two drowsy young ladies we should revive, dear friend," he said, motioning towards Kitty and Georgiana, slumped on a sofa. "Shall we go fetch them and join this merry quartet?"

Mr. Gardiner enthusiastically accepted and the group of dancers soon doubled as the party continued.

~

It was very late when the last guests went to bed. Weston and Mrs. Reynolds had watched over them for part of the evening in case their masters needed anything, but Elizabeth had long since sent them away.

Mrs. Keen had been the first to head to her room, citing her advanced age. She was soon followed by the Moores, then the Hursts and Caroline. The dancers, tired out, had then gathered in the large sitting room around the fireplace where the log was now a mound of burning embers. They sang Christmas carols and told each other stories while drinking hot tea. When Georgiana fell asleep on Elizabeth's shoulder, who was herself leaning against Darcy, the signal was clear and it was time to end the evening. It was past three in the morning.

After having wished everyone a good night, the Darcys lingered a little while longer. Around them, a beautiful mess bore witness to the celebration: glasses, tea cups and plates were lying everywhere, forgotten shawls, sunken cushions, abandoned sheets of music, a chair that had tipped over, torn garlands, scarves and accessories that had been used in the games...

"I had a wonderful Christmas," whispered Elizabeth, sighing in delight and hugging her husband as they stood before the fireplace.

"Me too," he replied. "I was a little reluctant at the idea of having so many children in the house, but I admit that, without them, today would not have borne the same significance."

"And Mrs. Keen! What a pleasure it was to have her with us! I knew she was full of humour and wit, but tonight she was delightful. She made Mr. Hurst laugh more than once, which is quite something!"

With a smile, Darcy tightened his embrace and placed a kiss on her hair.

"Did I satisfy your dancing requirements, my dear Lizzy?" he asked.

"I think I was one or two dances short of being fully satisfied, but I dared not abuse your goodwill..."

"You should have asked Bingley. I don't know what he ate or drank, but he had boundless energy this evening. I do think he was most disappointed when we stopped dancing."

Elizabeth chuckled. The food, the wine, the conviviality and the heat of the fireplace had all been enjoyed in abundance since the morning, and she felt satiated. She snuggled closer to Darcy.

"While we are on the subject, I wish you to know that I found you particularly handsome tonight. You cannot imagine the effect a scarcely open shirt sans cravat can have on a wife," she whispered, slipping her fingers through the gap of his collar.

"Really?" he replied, as his hands travelled down her back. "Do you still have a little energy left, my dear?"

She evidently did.

For the young couple it was time to go to bed, but sleep was the furthest thing from their minds.

CHAPTER 10

There could be no prestige at Pemberley if not for its strict respect for traditions and social conventions. Accordingly, the staff's gifts were handed out the day after Christmas with the utmost decorum.

The process was simple, but solemn. All the servants lined up hierarchically in the great hall. In front of them, standing beside a table laden with identical cardboard boxes, the Darcys called upon each person by name and personally handed them their gift, along with thanks for their service to the house and well wishes for the coming year. The servant then gravely bowed or curtsied before returning to his or her place, awaiting the end of the ceremony to unwrap the box in the servants' quarters. Depending on their rank and seniority in the house, it contained a new cap, leather gloves, a stole, a small box of sewing necessities, or a pretty lace scarf. All the gifts came with a more or less significant sum of money.

Weston and Mrs. Reynolds were not included as the young masters preferred to see them afterwards in private. They were thus summoned to the study where they were commended for their loyalty and excellent work. The butler received a beautiful chain for his pocket watch, and his colleague received a china tea service to replace the rather ordinary one she had in her personal room.

"Mr. Weston, Mrs. Reynolds, I am very grateful for the patience you have shown me since my arrival," added Elizabeth, shaking their hands. "I am aware that it has not been easy for you to adapt to a new mistress. I may have upset a few of your habits, and will no doubt continue to do so, but know that I am extremely pleased with you."

Of course, the two servants adamantly denied this, thanking and praising her profusely. But the young woman was not fooled: they were perhaps very attached to Darcy, to whom they showed total devotion and clear admiration, but that was still far from being the case for her. Their service was utterly beyond reproach, but they kept a distance from her that she hoped would disappear over time. Unlike Lady Fitzwilliam, who treated her servants with a certain amount of contempt, Elizabeth wished to make herself both loved and respected.

She was granted a more heartfelt compliment when the time came for the two servants to leave the cabinet. Mrs. Reynolds curtsied shyly to her mistress.

"If I may say, madam," she asserted, "your presence breathes great cheerfulness into Pemberley and is proving to be a real joy. Yesterday was a testament to that. It was so joyous to see all these people and children in the sitting rooms! We had not seen such a thing in so long!"

Then, without adding another word or waiting for an answer, the housekeeper curtsied again and disappeared.

~

The following days were spent visiting the farmers of Maesbury and Woolbert, as well as the poor whom widow Keen had recommended in Lambton.

It was quite the expedition each time. Elizabeth's sister, or her aunt sometimes accompanied her, or else Georgiana and Kitty, for she preferred not to be accompanied by all the ladies at once so as not to intimidate the people she visited. She brought along a coachman for the carriage, two footmen to carry the baskets filled with warm clothes and treats, which she handed out in generous amounts. She even sought out Mr. Moore's assistance to present her to the farmers she did not know. These excursions proved to be rather trying, but it was an opportunity to put faces to the names Darcy occasionally mentioned and to see for herself how they lived.

Compared to what Elizabeth had known in Hertfordshire, her husband's farmers were significantly more privileged. The interiors were comfortable and the children were decently clothed. Moore explained that Darcy provided for his people so that they were able to work in good conditions. He knew how to be generous when he had to, tolerated lower production in the event of illness, paid the doctor's bills, as well as provided basic education for the younger boys. He also shouldered the loss when livestock died of infection or got lost in the mountains, without holding the shepherds responsible – after all, there were a few situations that were out of their control. Lastly, when a problem presented itself, he first sought to work with tenants to resolve the issue instead of letting them fend for themselves.

In exchange, he insisted on good harvests and healthy livestock, and did not tolerate unjustified excuses or duplicity. For instance, he once parted with a family without any hesitation because they had led him to believe that their harvest was less fruitful than usual and had then proceeded to sell the undeclared surplus outside the estate. As for those who rented his cottages and houses, they were assured to have a well-maintained property, but in exchange, he expected all payments to be made on time. Darcy was an understanding master, provided one did not attempt to take advantage of his generosity. This subtle balance between firmness and benevolence made him a respected landlord.

"Your husband is firmer with his people than his late father was," said Mr. Moore. "To tell you the truth madam, I am convinced that his approach is best, even if I know he sometimes has doubts. When one is at the head of a large estate such as Pemberley, one cannot afford to be indulgent..."

These conversations with the steward taught Elizabeth a number of things, giving her greater clarity as to how the estate functioned. She only visited the nearest farmers of course, for it was not feasible for her to travel too far, but she realised that Charlotte had not lied when she had presented her to Darcy: Pemberley's territory was indeed almost half the size of Derbyshire. It also had the incredible advantage of being relatively unparcelled. For two centuries, the Darcys had worked hard to buy neighbouring lands and now, large quantities of merchandise could be circulated without ever having to leave the family estate. In other words, they were far less exposed to taxes and tolls.

The atmosphere was quite different in the Lambton families aided by Mrs. Keen's charitable work. From the bedridden elderly, to the small and sickly children, including the tired mothers and the men worn out by hard work or alcohol, there was indeed much to be done to ease their daily life. Elizabeth was welcomed as the Virgin Mary, both queen and saviour, and the gifts she brought were greatly appreciated, especially the clothes. She rather regretted having brought only sweet fare, as the children looked as though they needed a big slice of bread topped with a large piece of ham instead, but she promised them all that she would have more baskets brought to them.

It was not an empty promise. Once back at Pemberley, she summoned Mrs. Reynolds in order to agree upon a new arrangement: once a month, basic food items would be provided to those who needed them most.

The housekeeper was not surprised by this request.

"In her day, Lady Anne did the same," she explained, "but I admit that these charitable acts have been somewhat lost over time. Mr. Darcy has always made generous donations to support the good works of the parish, but it goes without saying that nothing can compare to a personal visit from the lady of the house to help the poor."

~

Of all the receptions that made the holiday season a daily celebration, the great New Year's ball, hosted by Lord and Lady Hastings, was a firm fixture. Certainly, the viscount was not as rich as Darcy or Mrs. Langhold, but his title won him great respect, not to mention an array of interesting acquaintances. One was always sure to meet auspicious company at his home, and since nothing inspires interest more than the allure of novelty, the New Year's ball was often an occasion for young ladies to come out.

Unfortunately for Georgiana, her brother persisted in denying her this pleasure. He was still stung by the dreadful Ramsgate mishap and refused to let her meet gentlemen who were unacquainted with the family. Elizabeth, briefly joined by Jane and Bingley, attempted to convince him otherwise but her appeals were made in vain

"Since we shall both be present to watch over her during the dances, let her join! I shall gladly chaperon her."

But Darcy remained resolute and that night, with tears in her eyes, Georgiana watched the little party depart for the ball. Even Kitty felt guilty. She solemnly swore that she would have no fun with the Hastings without her companion by her side.

Once there, of course, her convictions faded: the Bennet girl enjoyed herself tremendously, just as much as her sisters, for that matter. There were close to a hundred and fifty people, a feat, which required all the rooms on the ground floor to be rearranged in order to have both the space to dance and to serve dinner.

The Moores and the Munroes were there and Margaret Gardiner spent most of the evening with her friend, reminiscing about the other Lambton balls they had attended together in the past when they were not much older than Kitty herself. The widow Langhold and her sons were also present, along with Sir Norton, who had come with his cousin Sophie Russel, but without his sister who had stayed with the children. Elizabeth was delighted to present Jane to this little society, who was unanimously declared very beautiful and quite amiable and distinguished. All marvelled that Hertfordshire could create such a lovely creature. Jane proved to be a fantastic asset to the new Mrs. Darcy, who was anxious to show her best side to Derbyshire society.

"Your sister is quite delightful," Elizabeth was told a few times.

"Such elegance! What grace! Look how prettily she dances!"

"She has a natural modesty in all her gestures, doesn't she?"

"She is a beauty, that much is certain. Mr. Bingley must be very happy to have such a wife."

"He himself is quite handsome too: just imagine the children they will have! Little angels, indeed!"

Darcy danced in the beginning of the evening, a few times with Elizabeth, once with Jane, another time with Kitty and lastly with Caroline. After which, considering himself relieved of his duties, he disappeared into another room to talk with a few neighbours. Elizabeth was then invited to dance by Lord Hastings himself, then by Reverend Smith and then by a handful of worthy gentlemen, whom she then presented to Jane and Bingley's sisters. Within a short time five or six new families had been introduced, along with a handful of eligible men from London.

This was perhaps why Caroline and Louisa were very pleasant that evening. They felt perfectly at ease amongst these rich and titled guests who all lived in town for the most part and were only present that evening due to family visits. Caroline, who was in a splendid mood, was charming towards Elizabeth, whom she recognised as a helpful intermediary in her quest to meet amiable young men. It was a change that even Jane noticed.

"Caroline is so pleasant this evening!" she whispered to her sister as they rested between a couple of contredanses, sipping a cool glass of punch à la romaine. "Is this the beginnings of a great friendship between the two of you?"

"Are you jealous, dearest Jane?" Elizabeth teased her.

"Not at all! But do you not find her attitude greatly changed?"

"Believe it or not, I have never doubted that Caroline could be most amiable when she wished to be. I suppose that the presence of several baronets, the cousin of a duke, or the sons of a very rich widow must give her great joy. Not to mention that handsome marine captain who, it is said, has seized two French ships and accumulated just over thirty thousand pounds in prize money. Much good may it do her! At least she is not speaking ill of me to my new neighbours..."

"What could she possibly say about you? She would never dare to say that you stole the man she coveted, it would make her look far too ridiculous!"

Elizabeth looked at her companion magnanimously. The lovely Mrs. Bingley had lost nothing of her innocence. Protected by the sheltered life of Hertfordshire where she had lived all her life, she did not yet possess enough hindsight to accurately gauge the degrading way in which some higher born individuals sometimes perceived the Bennet girls.

"Do you fear that she might disclose the conflict that has arisen between Mr. Darcy and his aunt due to your union?" Jane continued.

"Well! On that score, I'm afraid the damage has already been done," retorted her sister with a shrug. "I had barely been settled at Pemberley for a fortnight before everyone knew that I had no dowry and that Lady Catherine did not look upon the match with a friendly eye."

"But how did they come to know this?"

"I have not the faintest idea! The servants, no doubt... As you know, it is the sort of information that one finds hard to keep to oneself."

Jane had a horrified look on her face, which prompted a laugh from her sister.

"Come now, don't make that face!"

"All the same... since I have arrived, I have only seen charming greetings and much affection for you."

"Affection? My dear Jane, you are far too good. I may be mistress of Pemberley, but I remain a stranger in their eyes."

Elizabeth thought about all those afternoon receptions the ladies attended together, to which she had yet to receive an invitation. She also thought of the visits made by Mrs. Blackmore and Miss Norton, which had not been repeated since they had first come to greet Lady Fitzwilliam during her stay. Even Judith Clarkson, who seemed to find her quite amiable, had never travelled to Pemberley to see her. Of course, the Christmas season meant that most of the festivities were spent amongst family, and the presence of the Bingleys and the Gardiners may have been intimidating for potential visitors who did not wish to impose upon them. Nevertheless, Elizabeth sensed that she was not part of the Lambton circle yet. At least, not without her husband.

"I suppose it will take some time before they accept me as one of their own, but I shall keep trying until I succeed," she concluded with a broad smile. "You know how stubborn I can be!"

"In that case, you should begin by easing relations between your husband and his aunt. If Lady Catherine eventually gives you her blessing, people will no longer be able to take exception."

And while Jane scraped the bottom of her glass with her spoon to collect the remaining meringue and half-melted ice, Elizabeth sat disconcerted.

Innocent as she was, her sister had just had one of those sparks of foresight that could, on occasion, strike a marvellous idea. She was right. If the new Mrs. Darcy wanted society to forget about her inferior birth, she would have no greater ally than Lady Catherine.

~

Four horsemen with torches had been made available by the Hastings to light the way to Lambton. The carriages, filled with occupants who had climbed aboard in a most orderly fashion, now stretched forth in a long convoy lit by lanterns which made them look like fireflies lost in the dark night.

Bundled up in his coat, his knees covered with a thick blanket and his feet resting on heated bricks, Darcy sighed in contentment. After the dizzying fuss of the evening, he enjoyed a moment of peace, a rare thing in recent days.

Elizabeth had nestled in next to him. They had been driving along in silence for a while and he thought her asleep. He was surprised when he felt her hand slide over his and her voice utter gently, as if an afterthought:

"My love, you should write to your aunt to wish her well."

The young man's face darkened. The mere mention of Lady Catherine had instantly broken the spell.

"Not again!" he said, annoyed.

"It would be a good way to renew relations, don't you think?"

"Perhaps, had that been my intention, but you know that is not the case."

"Indeed. However, I believe that having spent so much time with you has made me as obstinate as you are."

She had attempted a joke, but Darcy had no heart to laugh and did not respond. She insisted:

"With all the guests we are hosting at the moment, do you not see how wonderful it is to have a beautiful, large family that is unified and loving?"

"So many adjectives for a single family..." retorted her husband, somewhat sharply. "Lizzy, as you well know, I do this to protect you from my aunt's criticism. Why do you insist on my writing to her thus? Don't tell me that you ardently wish to also have her as a guest here at Pemberley!"

"Truth be told, that is exactly what I do hope for."

"You cannot be serious!" he said with a shrug.

Elizabeth had a talent for surprising him with her responses and, in different circumstances, he might have laughed. That night, however, he would have preferred not to revisit the disagreement and he was determined to remain steadfast in his decision. Colonel Fitzwilliam had already tried to convince him otherwise, not to mention the Earl. Even Georgiana had timidly broached the subject. Would he ever be left alone on the matter?

Cries could be heard outside. They had arrived at Lambton and the torch-wielding horsemen had stopped and were greeting the carriages as each went on their separate way home.

Elizabeth took the opportunity to straighten up under the blanket that covered them both. This was the signal that she was setting aside her affectionate approach as he had come to know it in favour of a more serious discussion. Darcy muffled an annoyed sigh.

"I know that you don't like this subject, my dear, and I am truly sorry to put so much emphasis upon it. I would not do so if it were not important."

In the shadows, he saw her worry at her lip while she searched for the right words.

"I understand that you wish to protect me from your aunt," she began, "but by doing so, you are doing me more of a disservice than you realise. I don't know if you are aware, but our neighbours and friends know full well that Lady Catherine opposed our marriage, and why. They also know that this dispute persists between the two of you, and I am considered primarily responsible for it."

"Nonsense! I would defy anyone to lay the slightest blame upon you! I shall happily offer an explanation if needed," said Darcy, stubbornly.

"No one will ever ask you to do so. You are as well aware of this as I. For now, you must choose between the following actions: either you flatter your pride by standing up to your aunt, or you work towards my acceptance into Derbyshire society. You cannot accomplish them both at once."

"What do you mean? Who does not accept you here? Are you not greeted everywhere with the utmost respect?"

Elizabeth took another second to gather her thoughts. At her silence, Darcy felt the anger that had welled up in him transform into an unpleasant feeling of apprehension.

"Should I be worried, Lizzy?" he asked, this time more gently.

"Not at all. It is up to me to prove myself worthy of the esteem of our neighbours, and time will help. Having said that, I assure you that, by reconnecting with your aunt, you would be greatly aiding my situation in the county. I know how much you resent her, and I love and admire you for taking a stand on my behalf, but in view of what I have heard, this dispute only hurts my efforts to be accepted. It cannot go on like this. And as you are even more acquainted with her than I am, you know that we cannot expect a peace offering from her. So, I implore you, put aside your pride and your anger, and write to her. You would be doing me a most welcome favour."

This time, Darcy remained silent.

It was not easy for him to understand what she was experiencing, having been so suddenly immersed in an entirely strange place. He was also quite convinced that it was just a matter of time before Elizabeth found her place within Pemberley and in the region, but he had to admit that at the moment, her situation was rather uncomfortable. She struggled on all fronts to show just how capable she was, and it was a great deal to ask of such a young woman, even one with such a strong a character as hers.

"Must I really invite her to stay with us?" he finally asked.

"It would bring me the utmost joy..." Elizabeth murmured softly, curling up against him once more.

"In that case, I shall think on it."

~

After twelve days of visits, receptions, balls and gaieties of all kinds, the festivities came to an end with Twelfth Night.

Pemberley's dining table increased in size, for the household was preparing to receive almost fifty people for dinner. Elizabeth was exhausted. She had a great deal to do with just the Bingleys and the Gardiners under her roof, not to mention the courtesy calls and charity visits, and she would have gladly foregone the responsibility of having to organise such a reception, but it was her husband's idea. Darcy had always limited his social gatherings, preferring to entertain a small party of close friends, but he suddenly seemed to have taken a liking to presiding over large tables. It was as if, now that a new lady was present, the house could finally reopen its doors to all of Derbyshire society.

It was a heavy burden for Elizabeth's small shoulders. Luckily, she was learning fast and had gained confidence. She knew the house better and felt more at ease with the servants and their daily routine. She no longer hesitated to go down to the servants' quarters when she needed to, even though Weston and Mrs. Reynolds still grimaced when they saw her do so. It was Hewitt who first understood that it was in their best interest to let their mistress meddle in their chores, for she was prepared to labour with them to find solutions that would alleviate the burden of their daily tasks. Informed of the imposing task that awaited her servants, Elizabeth had no qualms about hiring kitchen help along with a dozen additional footmen to help with the service. She may have been willing to cut back on daily expenses she considered unnecessary, but she spared no expense when it came to her house's reputation. Pemberley had to shine in the eyes of the guests.

266

Following the New Year's ball, the Darcys' reception became the most talked about event in the environs. There had not been so many guests present all at once since the days of Lady Anne. Those who had been invited paraded, proud as peacocks, and those who had not hid their deception behind tight-lipped smiles. The Bingleys, Hursts and Gardiners were naturally front and centre, joined by the Hastings, Langholds, Clarksons, Munroes, Blackmores, Nortons, the Reverend and his usual companion, Mrs. Keen. In addition to these familiar faces, four other families joined the party, along with other relatives who were visiting their loved ones: cousins of the Blackmores and the Langholds, Mrs. Moore's recently bereaved sister-in-law, one of Clarkson's brothers accompanied by his wife and – to Caroline Bingley's great delight – the rich, dashing captain from the New Year's ball.

Even though children had no place at this reception, Georgiana was invited to join them. Her brother did not have the heart to deny her this pleasure, but he made it clear that it was an exception and that she was not to consider herself out. Docile, the adolescent acquiesced without making a fuss, happy to enjoy another festive evening in the company of Kitty, even if it had to be done under Mrs. Annesley's close supervision.

"You would be wise to remember your education, Miss Darcy," the lady warned, sternly, "for tonight, there will be no question of laughing too loudly nor drinking too much. You are a lady of the house and, as such, you owe it to yourself to behave in an exemplary fashion."

In truth, Mrs. Annesley was more concerned about Kitty, for it was the young Bennet's fiery temperament, which was often the cause of Georgiana's misbehaviour.

However, Darcy fully approved of this growing friendship. He had not forgotten what his sister had said about her horrid classmates in boarding school and he was pleased to see her finally enjoying the company of a girl her age. Kitty may have been cruelly lacking in manners but she was not yet preoccupied with rank and fortune: she was without prejudice against Georgiana and approached her without inhibition and was full of sincerity, quickly putting the latter at ease. Now inseparable, they were both having a delightful time and Darcy looked upon them kindly, comforted to see his sister finally behaving more freely.

~

To Elizabeth's relief, the evening was a great success.

In the dining area, the Christmas wreaths had somewhat dried up, but the shimmering dresses and jewels that glittered under the almost audacious amount of candlelight more than revived the room's festive air. With so many guests it was quite a challenge for the young mistress to exchange pleasantries with everyone, but she endeavoured to do so as best she could, and since most of the guests knew each other already, the spirit was quite friendly. The dinner, composed of four courses, each more gargantuan than the next, delighted everyone. Once more, she was congratulated for her wonderful spread.

"Mrs. Darcy," said Lord Hastings, seated at her right, "I must confess that we have not seen such splendour at Pemberley since the days of our late beloved Lady Anne. It is becoming apparent that we have you to thank for this. Your husband must be very happy to have you, and we are honoured to be amongst your guests."

"Very true, your Lordship," added Mrs. Langhold, seated just across the table. "I am impressed, madam, your talents as a hostess seem to come so naturally. It seems as though you have been a hostess your entire life and I am well placed to know what a struggle it is for a lady to plan such a reception... Lady Anne could not have done better tonight!"

Elizabeth was touched. Not only was the praise considerable – such a flattering comparison with Darcy's mother could only delight her –, but also it came from two of the most influential people in the area. If they finally recognised her legitimacy as the mistress of Pemberley, the rest of society would soon follow.

"What you are unaware of, is that our dear Mrs. Darcy loves to burden herself unnecessarily!" added Louisa, who had followed the conversation and wished to contribute "In fact, she worries about her servants so much that she organised a large festive dinner for them, too! As if there was not already enough work to do!"

She punctuated her comment with a small, sour laugh, but stopped suddenly under Mrs. Langhold's patient look.

"If that is so, then this added kindness is all to Mrs. Darcy's credit," the widow replied. "I don't know if you have a large house to manage, Mrs. Hurst, but it seems to me that one is never served better than by people who are satisfied and devoted, and to that end one must grant them certain privileges. It was an excellent initiative."

Realising that she was being admonished, Louisa abruptly ceased to posture. With an embarrassed chuckle and a shrug, she cautiously uttered that the widow's speech was full of wisdom before hurrying to engage her neighbour in conversation.

She had spoken truthfully. Since it was the last day of festivities, Elizabeth had wanted to mark the occasion by offering her servants a lavish meal. The planning had been more complicated, but she was able to exchange a few words with Weston just before dinner and she knew that the gesture had been most appreciated.

"How was the dinner downstairs? Was everyone happy?"

"Absolutely, madam, the suckling pigs were a great success and everyone received a double ration of beer. They all thank you."

"Did you serve the punch?"

"Yes, madam, to everyone except the footmen. They shall receive their share after the guest's dinner."

"Very well. I shall try to dismiss them as soon as possible. They deserve to celebrate!"

Despite her good intentions, the footmen serving the fifty guests remained on duty far longer than anticipated, as the meal wore on. Between the endless bottles of wine, the incredible amount of dishes at each course, the conversations and the laughter, the feast was so delightful that no one was in a hurry to get up.

Finally, as the guests gradually sank further into their chairs to make room for their ever extending midriffs, the dish everyone awaited was brought in: the triumphant Twelfth Night cake. It was at least two feet in diameter, six inches tall, and was covered in white sugar icing beautifully dotted with holly leaves, candied orange slices and small coloured sugar paste figures. Inside, a mixture of raisins, candied fruit and almonds, flavoured as always with a great deal of alcohol.

Despite being full, the guests were still able to praise the dessert, and Darcy had to stand up to draw their attention.

"Let us proceed with the utmost respect for tradition," he said. "I would like to invite a few representatives of our household to join our party so that they may share this cake with us."

Weston, Mrs. Reynolds, Grove and Mrs. Vaughan then entered the room, slightly stiff in their fancy clothes, and intimidated at being thus presented to the company.

As head of the household, Darcy distributed the helpings. The four servants ate standing in a corner of the room, while the guests gently sifted through their portions. No one wanted to risk swallowing the coveted object by mistake.

"Ah! I believe that Mr. Moore has found something!" exclaimed Mrs. Blackmore, pointing at an object resembling a dry bean in her neighbour's plate. Come now, my friend, were you going to come forward or did you believe you would go unnoticed? There is no escape: you are now king!"

And as Mr. Moore, who was now king for the night, was being congratulated, Darcy's valet leant over his master's shoulder and whispered something in his ear.

"And we now have the pea!" the latter exclaimed to the crowd. "Mr. Moore, greet your queen: Mr. Grove!"

Everyone chuckled. Kitty pouted a little at not having found the pea or the bean herself, but she quickly stifled the emotion and regained her good humour. As for Bingley, he rushed to the next room to fetch two chairs in which he seated the king and the queen, while everyone applauded. Neither Moore nor Grove seemed very comfortable about being exposed to such scrutiny, which amused the guests and prompted new toasts.

This distraction gave everyone the signal: while some finished their plates, others headed to the sitting rooms to settle down in the sofas with sighs of satisfaction. Elizabeth had hired musicians. It was too early to dance, but in the meantime, she had set them up in one of the rooms to entertain the guests while they digested their food.

No one would have heard what transpired beyond the walls of the house in the midst of the evening, if Weston had not come to alert his master. The music stopped.

"My friends," Darcy declared loudly in an attempt to get everyone's attention, "it would appear that we have visitors at our door... If my wife would kindly join me, we invite you to follow us: we shall give them a worthy welcome."

Jane, who was conversing with her sister, looked at her in surprise.

"What is happening?" she asked, slightly worried. "Who could be here at this hour?"

"I have not the faintest idea," replied Elizabeth.

She hurried to find her husband and clutched his arm. A long procession was formed and it slowly moved down the corridor, before descending the majestic staircase leading to the hall.

Large tables had been erected and laden with food. Elizabeth frowned, increasingly puzzled.

"What is happening, William?" she whispered.

"It is a surprise, a tradition that we celebrate differently here than in Hertfordshire, as I have discovered. I asked Mrs. Reynolds not to say anything on the matter... Can you guess what it is?"

He turned around, searching for Jane and Kitty, and beckoned them to join him at the front of the crowd so they could witness what was about to unfold.

There was something magical in the air outside.

A small crowd of people stood at the bottom of the porch, carrying torches that illuminated the night with a magical glow, studded with feathery snowflakes falling softly to the ground. All the Woolbert and Maesbury farmers were there, with their wives and children, warmly clothed and armed with pipes, tambourines and even a violin. They had not waited for the Darcys to step outside to sing their songs, but when they saw their masters, they doubled their efforts.

"Oh! The wassail!" Jane cried out behind her sister, clapping her hands.

In the crowd of dark silhouettes huddled together and sprinkled with snow, their joyful faces sang with enthusiasm in the flickering light of the torches. They unwittingly swayed to the rhythm, caught up in the infectious energy of the music. In the front row, where the youngest stood with their hats pushed down to their eyes and their coats pulled up to their noses, some even danced a few steps.

Elizabeth found the song so charming and the scene so poetic, that she felt deeply touched. She tightened her grip on her husband's arm.

In Hertfordshire, the farmers celebrated wassail in the orchards, throwing cider and offering food to the apple trees to ensure a good harvest in the upcoming year. The gentlemen, however, would never participate in something so heathen, so they simply drank a bowl of mulled cider with spices and exchanged wishes of happiness and prosperity. But at Pemberley things were different: the farmers did not turn to the trees for an abundant year, but to the master of the estate. They came singing at his door, promising blessings, goodwill and hard work, provided that he agreed to share part of his feast with them.

The farmers sang three different songs and, each time, they were warmly applauded by the guests. However, they were not dressed to stay out for long, which prompted Darcy to raise his hand and ask for silence.

"I thank you from the bottom of my heart, and I, too, wish you a happy year full of abundance and prosperity. God bless you! I would like to take this opportunity to tell you how happy I am to celebrate this Twelfth Night with you, especially as I am joined this year by my dear wife, Elizabeth. It is a joy to have her with us now and I hope she will attend many more wassails in future. And now, come in and enjoy the celebration! We have cake and punch for everyone!"

The young man beckoned everyone to come in as the crowd applauded.

In the hall, Weston, Mrs. Reynolds and a number of footmen were waiting next to the tables. The farmers approached, shaking the snow from their shoulders, and were handed figgy puddings, brioches and cakes. Large tureens of hot steaming punch were also opened. No guest was forgotten, and while most were still quite full from their dinner, soon everyone held a steaming cup. Elizabeth and her sisters, still astonished by this wassail which bore no resemblance to what they had previously known, were surprised to find that the punch was not cider but rather hot beer mixed with spicy apple puree.

But before the new Mrs. Darcy could help herself to a bowl, her husband grabbed her by the waist and guided her to a group of men.

"Lizzy, tradition dictates that masters and labourers must drink the lambswool together from the same bowl," he explained.

The bowl, which appeared to be a wooden cup belonging to one of the farmers, was passed from hand to hand, and more wishes of happiness for the New Year were exchanged.

"We have wished matrimonial happiness to Mr. Darcy for a few years now," said one of the farmers, his eyes already sparkling from the drink. "We can now change our tune!"

"Indeed," added another, "we shall now wish for you to be blessed with a child soon, madam! Seems to be the only thing missing!"

"Not just one! Well... one to start with, but then..."

Elizabeth was a little embarrassed and shyly uttered her thanks before dipping her lips to the bowl under Darcy's affectionate gaze.

~

At breakfast the following day, the residents of Pemberley looked a little worse for wear. There had been a great deal of drinking and dancing, and the guests had departed very late. Jane went upstairs twice to persuade Kitty to get out of bed, while Mr. Hurst came down looking puffy and red-faced, clearly not yet recovered from his excesses. Bingley himself, usually so full of good humour, was unusually quiet and drank several cups of coffee.

Margaret Gardiner had been the first to wake. Not because she suffered less of a headache, but because she had to bravely face her parental duties. The little ones had been playing in the corridors since dawn while they waited for the adults to awaken and they made such a frightful noise that the poor woman rushed to take them downstairs before they woke the rest of the household. The children had much to be excited about: the Epiphany followed Twelfth Night and presents would soon be exchanged.

In the large dining room, where all traces of the party had already disappeared, Darcy gave the signal to exchange gifts. For some time, there was a merry agitation around the table, full of joyful exclamations and embraces. Then, while the children, who had already eaten, went to play with their new toys in the drawing-room, the adults sat down at the table. They were not hungry enough to eat the ham or the eggs, but were tempted by the fragrant, freshly baked brioches. As the coffee and tea were being served, they discussed the events of the previous night along with the rest of the festivities, which were coming to an end.

"Poor Mr. Moore was really quite comical yesterday, even if it was unintentional..." said Elizabeth. "It would seem that being made king was a terrible matter of conscience for him. Did you see how uncomfortable he was in front of William? He did not know how to act!"

"What a shame, for I would have loved to see Darcy bow to the whims of the king," teased Bingley, winking at his friend.

"I would have done so willingly," Darcy replied, undeterred. "I am more spirited than you think."

"In the meantime, what a pity our friend dared not take advantage of his privileges. If I had been king, I can assure you that I would have made the most extravagant requests!"

"No one doubts that, my friend," Darcy returned with amusement.

"And I thank the heavens that it did not happen," laughed Elizabeth. "God knows what state my house and my guests would have been in!"

They also gently laughed at Grove, the valet, who had found himself queen for the night and who, like Mr. Moore, had been rather uncomfortable with the situation. He had used the wassail as an excuse to escape.

"Inviting your servants to share the Twelfth Night cake with us was an elegant touch, Mr. Darcy," Mr. Gardiner pointed out. "I know many who would not have gone to the trouble."

"Georgiana and I have often spent Christmas in London," the young man replied. "Since we were finally celebrating at Pemberley, it was only fair to respect the tradition."

"We shall do it again next year, William, shall we not?" his sister cried out. "I did not think that Pemberley could be so cheerful during Christmastide. I now wish to remain here each year!"

"If it pleases you so, we shall certainly stay here next year," Darcy replied kindly.

Elizabeth, who was seated right next to Georgiana, leant over and whispered,

"And by then I am sure that you will have been out and that your brother shall allow you to participate in all the festivities, without exception..."

This did not escape Kitty. She had not yet acquired her sister's discretion and began to giggle.

"Come now, Lizzy! Don't you know that by next Christmas, Georgiana will not only be out already, but also no doubt married? I am also fairly certain that Jacob would find no objection to this!"

"Kitty!" Jane and Elizabeth both cried out, glaring at their sibling.

"What are you saying, miss! Miss Darcy was well behaved all evening, I can attest to this!" protested Mrs. Annesley, shocked.

But the damage was done. Poor Georgiana did not have to wait for the look of suspicion her brother gave her and instantly flushed red. Darcy then turned to the Bennet girl.

"Mr. Jacob Langhold is a very pleasant young man, of course, but you must understand, Kitty, that a lady, even once she is out, has many other things to think about than agreeable men," he declared, sternly.

Elizabeth, embarrassed by her sister's misplaced familiarity, both towards Georgiana and the young man in question, whom she had referred to as 'Jacob' as if they were close friends, attempted to temper the situation.

"William is right," she said. "Georgiana will have a great deal to discover before even thinking of marriage as it is the last thing one would want to rush into. Nothing good can come of blindly following the first man who presents himself, believe me..."

Apart from the young Darcy and her companion, everyone around the table was very familiar with Lydia's case and it was clearly understood that Elizabeth was referring to her. Indeed, Caroline could not help smirking, but composed her features when her brother gave her an insistent glance.

"In the meantime," Elizabeth continued in a lighter tone, "I find that Georgiana was very well behaved all night, do you not agree?"

"Yes, I heard nothing but praise about her," Mrs. Gardiner pointed out. "And we had great fun playing cribbage together, did we not, dear child?"

Still crimson with shame, the adolescent nodded without saying a word. Jane continued the diversion, helped by Mr. Gardiner who deftly redirected the conversation to another subject. Darcy pushed down the anger that had risen in him by swallowing his coffee in one gulp, and then he stood up and began to take down the decorations, putting them in the fire with help from Bingley.

"What a pity it is to burn these wreaths and garlands after going to so much trouble crafting them!" sighed Louisa.

Out of politeness, no one mentioned that Louisa was the last person who could claim that she had gone to any great trouble, since she had hardly participated in their creation. Instead, Darcy retorted acrimoniously, "The decorations are to be hung up on Christmas day and taken down on the Epiphany, as intended. You would not want to bring bad luck upon this house by keeping them up any longer."

Elizabeth dared not look up and remained focussed on spreading jam onto the buttered brioche she prepared for Georgiana, in an effort to console her.

A moment ago, they had mentioned Lydia and Wickham's disadvantageous union, and now they spoke of misfortune potentially befalling Pemberley. Was it a premonition? She preferred not to believe it.

~

There was a peaceful silence in the parlour. Sitting at her secretary, Elizabeth wrote a letter, while Jane sewed by the fire. Further in the house, the Hursts and Caroline could be heard in faint conversation, along with the soft padding footsteps of the servants passing by in the corridor. Darcy and Bingley had gone to the stables with Mr. Gardiner, to see a mare, who had foaled the night before.

The festivities had come to an end and throughout the house, things were gradually going back to normal. Freed from their various social obligations, the guests spent time in their rooms or else gathered together according to each person's inclination. The children were taken out every day to play in the snow and it was a source of endless joy for them. They would come back inside eyes shining, with red cheeks and runny noses, to warm up with a bowl of hot milk before going to play in a room that had been set aside for them.

Kitty and Georgiana were a little at odds with one another after Kitty's maladroit revelation regarding Jacob Langhold, but their friendship rekindled when they discovered their mutual passion for theatre. They now spent their afternoons sifting through the plays, which they found in the library, rehearsing scenes they would then perform in the evenings in front of the other guests. It was a charming occupation and Darcy approved of it as much as Elizabeth did, for it allowed Georgiana to further express herself and gave Kitty the means to better channel her energy. The two girls, having limited means, proved surprisingly creative when presenting their excerpts. On one occasion, Kitty even made the audience laugh heartily when she entered wearing a soup bowl on her head in lieu of a helmet..

As for the elder Bennet sisters, they made sure to spend some quiet time together. Elizabeth's parlour became their preferred place for idle conversation.

Jane gave up on her sewing for a moment and watched her sister who was focussed on her work.

"Is it not hard to manage such a large house, Lizzy?"

Elizabeth smiled mischievously.

"That is indeed what everyone keeps telling me," she replied.

"You must admit, there is much to be intrigued about. I was astounded when I saw your servants all lined up like soldiers on Boxing Day. You have so many! And I see you either spend all your time at your secretary, or with Mr. Weston or Mrs. Reynolds giving them instructions..."

"Do you not do the same at Netherfield? You too, have servants to lead, have you not?"

"Of course! But I rely a great deal on my housekeeper, she is the one who handles the finer details."

"The 'finer details'?"

"Yes, confirming that there is wood in the reserves, that the pantry is filled, which good wines are served at dinner... That sort of thing. She is in charge of it all and she does it very well, for I never hear anyone complaining."

"Does this mean that you have never looked at the accounts?"

The young Mrs. Bingley looked guilty.

"Come now, Jane, you are going to have to do it. It is your responsibility!" exclaimed her sister. "Charles is rich, to be sure, but what would you say if, one day, this fortune withered away because you were unable to keep an eye on the household funds?"

"I know, but it all seems so complicated... As I have told you, Charles is thinking of buying Netherfield. We enjoy it very much. If that were to happen, I shall certainly have to get started."

"Indeed. If you want my advice, you should not wait until you become landowners."

Jane nodded. She resumed her work.

"You know," Elizabeth continued as she finished her letter, "if I were in your place, I would no longer wait to purchase property. It is the best investment one can make. But I would not advise you to buy Netherfield."

"Why is that? It is such a pretty house!"

"That is true, but the country is vast and there are many more beautiful homes in England that would suit you perfectly. Do you really want to spend your entire life accommodating our mother every week? Wait until you and Bingley have children. She will not leave you in peace! You should have more ambition, love..."

"You have always had a great deal more of it than I," Jane pointed out.

Elizabeth shrugged. She rose, put away her papers, and then locked her secretary. She slipped the little golden key in her pocket.

"What are you making? A shirt?" she asked, sitting beside her sister.

"Yes, for Charles. He regularly damages his own and his valet is always mending them. So, I am making him a new one in advance."

"You husband is an active man full of energy, to say the least," Elizabeth teased with a smile.

"Indeed! But I don't mind. I rather enjoy caring for him. And you? Will you also make shirts for your husband?"

Elizabeth laughed out loud at the idea.

"Certainly not! I have never been as talented a seamstress as you and this is unlikely to change, for I have not touched a needle since our wedding. My poor William would have rags on his back if I were tasked with making his clothes. No, thank heavens he already has all he needs: an excellent tailor in London for his coats and trousers, and a seamstress in Lambton for his small clothes."

She sank back into the sofa and sighed contentedly. These moments alone with her sister felt endlessly familiar and comforting, even if the topics had nothing to do with their previous lives in Longbourn.

"Could I borrow your writing box later, Lizzy?"

"Of course! Use whatever you need."

279

"I should like to write to Charles' sisters. If I don't do it, he will not either."

"Are you referring to the younger ones who are in boarding school?"

"Yes. Those poor girls spend their entire lives there... Can you imagine, they did not even join us for Christmastide! Charles sent them to an old cousin of his in Kensington. I have been married for two months and I have yet to meet them!"

"Why not ask your husband? You could spend a few days in town and visit them."

"It is one of the first things I asked, if you can believe that! He told me that it would not be necessary as he planned to bring them to Netherfield next summer. But that is a very long time away! Those poor girls must be terribly bored if they never see their family!"

"I admit that it must seem rather long to them... What do Louisa and Caroline say?"

"They simply don't care. You know how they are."

Jane made the face she always did when she disapproved of something. It was the most striking sign of reproach she was capable of. She returned to her sewing.

"I love Charles with all my heart, but I find him rather distant with his younger sisters. I wish the family were more unified," she added.

"Then you should tell yourself that you are there to encourage him in that direction," Elizabeth comforted her. "Since neither he nor Louisa or Caroline are very focussed on family affection, it is up to you to make up for this."

"Do you think so?"

"Yes, of course! Are the characters of a husband and his wife not meant to complement each other so as to simultaneously improve both?"

Jane smiled. Her face softened.

"You are probably right," she admitted.

"It is something I have also noticed with the Darcys," her sister continued. "William never really behaves as a brother should towards Georgiana. He is attentive to her needs that is certain, but ultimately he spends very little time in her company. Before I arrived, the poor girl had only Mrs. Annesley to converse with and rarely left Pemberley. And as you saw, William still refuses her the pleasure of coming out."

"There is a big age difference between them, Lizzy, which may explain why they are not very close. And Georgiana is still young, it is understandable that your husband wishes to keep her at home."

"But she is seventeen years old! Kitty's age! Do you not see an incredible difference between the two of them?"

"That is true, but Kitty is not always a good example to follow, as you well know," Jane tempered.

Elizabeth laughed.

"Oh, the poor darling... Always wanting to be the centre of attention. That said, she is rather calmer now that Lydia is not here to goad her."

"Indeed. She doesn't know how to hold her tongue at times, but apart from that, I do believe she has not had a fit of temper since we have arrived!"

"A significant milestone..."

The two sisters continued their ironic remarks a little longer as they recollected some of Kitty's more memorable outbursts.

"You spoke of Lydia just now," Jane continued. "Have you received any news?"

"No. I wrote to her when I was in London, and twice more since our arrival at Pemberley, but I have received no response."

"Me neither. She did write to Mamma, though."

"And what did she say?"

"That she is having an awfully good time, but that she would like to visit Longbourn more often."

"Poor Lydia... I shall ask Charles to invite her to Netherfield, as soon as Wickham obtains permission."

Elizabeth did not respond. This did not escape Jane's notice, and she looked up from her work.

"He is not welcome here, is that so?" she asked, candidly.

"He never will be. I even advise you against speaking of it to William."

"Is it that dreadful? But then... will you ever be able to see Lydia again?" worried Jane.

Her sister was quick to reassure her.

"No, no, only William is in conflict with Wickham. Lydia is not affected, I assure you. He is entirely happy to receive her here, provided she comes alone."

Appeased, Jane resumed her sewing.

"Don't you want to try and change his mind?" she asked.

There was another silence. Elizabeth bit her lip.

"I am not certain that I wish to make that effort," she replied, candid as always. "Wickham disappointed us all, me in particular, as you know. Either way, even if I wanted to, there is not much I could do. On this subject, as with many others, my husband is quite headstrong."

"It seems to me that you have found your match in this regard..." said Jane, eyeing her sideways.

The two sisters laughed cheerfully.

CHAPTER 11

The Gardiners returned to London at the end of January.

The house felt suddenly empty without the children scampering about from dawn until dusk. Only the Hursts and Caroline seemed to prefer this newfound quiet. They settled back into the more familiar routine they had become accustomed to in previous years at Pemberley.

The young Mrs. Darcy made an effort to stay a few afternoons with the remaining guests who took refuge next to the fire in an attempt to escape the cold. They whiled away the time as best as possible, most often by engaging in repetitive conversations, while keeping their hands occupied with some activity. Louisa possessed a certain talent for embroidery when she focussed her attention on her task instead of gossiping. Elizabeth noticed with some irony, however, that Caroline did not appear to possess the level of accomplishment she had so rigorously required of others, namely Elizabeth, in her social circle. Regardless of the occupation she chose to pursue, she lacked the patience to follow through. She angered easily when she failed to achieve the desired effect and gave up on her work entirely instead of persevering and seeking improvement. Elizabeth, who did not possess any notable artistic talents herself, was tempted to tease her, but she showed some restraint. She was now the lady of Pemberley and that was retribution enough.

At least Caroline had ceased making spiteful insinuations. In general, the mistress of the house attracted everyone's good graces and it was impossible to openly criticise her, so she turned her attention to Georgiana instead, upon whom she lavished loving attention. Caroline did the same with Darcy. Since his sharp rebuke over Christmas, her behaviour towards him now could only be described as exceedingly polite. Darcy responded, as always, with polite indifference.

For Elizabeth, these long afternoons spent in such company would have been as burdensome as Lady Fitzwilliam's visit, if it had not been for her sister. Sweet Jane, whom everyone loved, unwittingly served as an ambassador. To Elizabeth, she was still a Bennet, but to the Hursts and Caroline, she had become a Bingley and they had adopted her as their own.

"How sad that we no longer hear the children gambolling about!" Jane sighed one afternoon, when the atmosphere in the drawing-room had become a little dreary. "I miss them already!"

"You are very patient, my dear, as always," replied Louisa. "On the contrary, I find that your uncle and aunt ought to hire a governess in order to avoid having the children constantly underfoot. I can assure you that when Mr. Hurst and I have children, we shall hire the very best governess."

Caroline intervened.

"I have heard that the French are excellent. Is it not your friend, Mrs. Varnham, who always gushes about her governess, Louisa?"

She then continued with a little smile, "I do believe that to avoid perpetual chaos, they are essential. Do you remember Christmas...? I don't understand how Mr. Darcy could tolerate so many children amongst us. I could not count them all if I tried! There were more than a dozen! All that agitation was rather intolerable!"

"But how equally delightful!" Jane objected. "I can conceive that other people's children leave you indifferent, Caroline. You might perhaps change your mind when you have your own nephews and nieces in your arms. This 'agitation', as you call it, will then seem utterly charming."

Caroline shrugged. She preferred to change the subject and turned to her brother-in-law.

"Edmund! Would you like to join me for a game of piquet?"

As they walked away to the other end of the room to sit at a game table, Louisa immediately gave up on her sewing to follow them.

"You speak with such confidence, my dear... Are you eager to have children?" Elizabeth said, lowering her voice and glancing mischievously at her sister.

"Yes, and I am not ashamed to say so. Is it not the kindest thing one could wish for newlyweds? Don't tell me that you have not thought about it too!"

In truth, Elizabeth had not. She knew that she would fall pregnant one day, it was inevitable, but she did not know when and she was in no hurry. She liked the idea of having her husband to herself.

"It will come with time, I suppose," she replied, thoughtfully.

Then, her eyes wrinkled in laughter.

"But it cannot happen soon enough for Lord Fitzwilliam. Did I ever tell you that he considers me to be a broodmare, only useful for birthing?"

"Do not be vulgar, Lizzy..."

"I am merely reporting what he said. I believe his exact words were 'a healthy looking filly'. And he said so before the entire family. William was seething with rage, as you can imagine!"

She began to laugh and described the scene in detail. As she spoke, Jane's mouth made a shocked 'Oh!'.

"Lord Fitzwilliam has eleven children and I am sure that because of it, he has much disdain for his sisters. Lady Anne only had two, and Lady Catherine has but one, a daughter, no less. He will therefore only be satisfied when I have also given my husband a dozen children thus ensuring the longevity of the Darcy name..." she concluded, somewhat sarcastically.

"And why not? Your house is certainly large enough to welcome as many, isn't it?" replied Jane.

Elizabeth looked at her in horror.

"Is that truly what you would wish for me?"

"It is certainly what I would wish for myself," Jane answered serenely. "I don't believe I could ever grow tired of being surrounded by children."

"In that case we do not have the same opinion on the matter. I do want children, without a doubt, but not a dozen. Never!"

"If it is the will of God, what can you do to change it?"

"Oh, Jane, don't say that! Would you not rather want to limit the number of children you have in order to take the time to truly desire and love each one of them? Should a woman not have a say in such things? When I think of these ladies who are so exhausted from having to endure all that successive lying in and know of nothing else to talk about than their offspring... No, forgive me, but I should not like to be like that."

"Neither of us is in that position yet. Let us begin by having our first baby. We shall then see in due time."

~

Every evening, they gathered in the big sitting room. Once more, the group prepared to watch excerpts from plays, which Kitty and Georgiana had rehearsed with great delight. Inspired by the children's performances over Christmas, they also used the double doors leading to the small sitting room as a stage. This allowed the girls to maintain an element of surprise, as they could hide behind the closed doors until the last moment before suddenly appearing in front of the audience.

The scenes they chose to enact were always ghastly. Heroes called by duty and torn away from their homes, vengeful gods, the humiliation suffered by spurned lovers, death and madness concluding every story, and a great many cursed love affairs... As with all girls their age, Georgiana and Kitty were fascinated by darkness and tragedy which, while it amused Elizabeth, made Darcy raise a dubious eyebrow more than once. He did not utter any criticism, but he clearly felt that innocent young ladies would do better to explore a softer subject matter. Fortunately, the scenes were shortened, sometimes even rewritten, and they never lasted more than a few minutes, or else he may have objected.

Over the last few days, the two girls had started to explore Shakespeare. The audience had been treated to scenes from *Othello*, *Romeo and Juliet*, *Titus Andronicus* and *Macbeth*, all terrible tragedies. That night, they announced *Hamlet*, a play which also did not promise great joy.

"Silence! Silence, please!" requested Kitty as she looked out from behind the double doors. "Is everyone ready?"

Elizabeth, who had just finished serving tea to her guests, hurried to take her seat. There was silence followed by the three ritual knocks that rang out from the adjacent room. Then, the double doors opened wide.

The girls always took great care when setting the scene and had shown a great deal of imagination in the past. But that night far exceeded anything they had previously attempted.

Draped in a large sheet with a paper crown resting on her head, Kitty appeared slowly, looking serious. She pointed a solemn finger at an imaginary character and began to speak.

"'One woe doth tread upon another's heel,
So fast they follow; your sister's drown'd, Laertes.'"

She proclaimed, dramatically.

"'There is a willow grows aslant a brook,
That shows his hoar leaves in the glassy stream;
There with fantastic garlands did she come
Of crow-flowers, nettles, daisies and long purples,
Our cold maids do dead men's fingers call them:
There, on the pendent boughs her coronet weeds
Clambering to hang, an envious sliver broke;
When down her weedy trophies and herself
Fell in the weeping brook. Her clothes spread wide;
And – '".

Concentrated on her part, Kitty had come forward, revealing a long table behind her. She was soon interrupted by Bingley's laughter. Next to him, Elizabeth and Jane also began laughing, not knowing whether to be amused or offended.

The others were far less entertained.

"She is thoroughly wet!" began Louisa.

"Miss Darcy!" exclaimed Mrs. Annesley, quite appalled.

Unhappy about the interruption, Kitty was about to resume when Darcy stood up in a hurry.

"I do apologise. There will be no performance tonight. Georgiana, do go up to your room at once and change your clothes!" he hissed.

Behind the Bennet girl, stretched out on a table with her hands crossed on her stomach and her eyes closed, Georgiana was the epitome of a drowned Ophelia.

It looked as though she had stepped fully dressed into a basin before receiving several pitchers of water upon her head. Her white dress was roughly wrung out, and still dripped upon the table and the rug. Her hair, also drenched, hung loose. It rested on her shoulders in long tangled waves, dotted here and there with twigs and dried flowers, which the girls had likely found in one of the vases scattered around the house. She wore no shoes, only stockings, which were soaked like the rest of her, and gripped a long ivory rosary between her fingers.

The guests barely had time to catch a glimpse of Georgiana as she sat up on the table before the doors were slammed shut by Darcy. He controlled himself, but it was clear to everyone that he was furious.

"Forgive me, I'm afraid these young ladies have taken too many liberties this evening," he said, apologetically. "Mrs. Hurst, would you like to play us some music instead? I believe we have not heard you play in quite some time..."

Mrs. Annesley had leapt to her feet. She barely took the time to curtsy before dashing off to recover her charge. She could be heard vigorously reprimanding Georgiana, too shocked by what had transpired to control the volume of her voice.

"Miss Darcy! What were you thinking? Go upstairs at once! It is inconceivable that you could have even entertained the thought of presenting yourself to us in such a manner! I do not recognise you, miss! Rest assured, I am very, very disappointed in you!"

The rest was lost as they walked away down the corridor. Bingley attempted to soften the unease in the room.

"Well, I found our young friends to be rather creative. These little performances have continued to surprise and amuse me, tonight more than ever! But someone ought to tell me what happens in *Hamlet* for I am not certain to have understood all of it!" he said, punctuating his remark with a laugh.

"Oh, Charles, you never think badly of anything..." Caroline retorted, drily. "I told you that nothing good would come of these recitals. Did I not say so, Louisa? Mrs. Annesley must regain control over her charge to prevent events such as these from happening again. Georgiana needs a firm set of rules, something her companion is clearly not providing her with. Can you imagine, Mr. Darcy, if others had been present here tonight? How scandalous!"

"Scandalous, indeed!" repeated Louisa.

Momentarily stilled by her husband's reaction, Elizabeth came to her senses.

"Excuse me, ladies and gentlemen, I will go and speak with the girls. I am convinced that they meant no harm and surely do not entirely understand why we cut short their performance."

"I shall accompany you," said Jane, also standing.

"Would you please inform them that we shall only see them again if they are presentable, Lizzy," Darcy added dryly.

The young woman nodded, curtsied to her guests and left the room, Jane on her heels.

~

Ultimately, neither Kitty nor Georgiana reappeared in the sitting room that evening. The first was awfully upset that all her efforts had gone to waste in such a seemingly arbitrary fashion, and the second was mortified and could not bear the thought of one day having to even speak to her brother again. She was in tears, wanting to die, or at the very least remain in hiding forever. Elizabeth struggled to console her and had to ask Mrs. Annesley to leave several times as her scolding only made matters worse.

Once the girls had composed themselves, their sisters went downstairs. In the staircase, Jane confided:

"I do think your husband was a little harsh, this evening. I agree that Kitty and Georgiana's idea was rather daring, but then again, we are family, not the court of St. James's! If they cannot indulge in innocent games within their own homes, where else can they do so?"

"Nowhere, that is the problem. William tends to believe that the excellent education all young ladies are to demonstrate in society must necessarily preclude the spontaneity that ought to be allowed within the privacy of their homes. If it were up to him, Georgiana would spend the rest of her life playing music and smiling gently. He cannot imagine that she might want anything else from life."

"I wonder what he would think if he were to learn that it was Georgiana's idea, and not Kitty's, to get drenched from head to toe in order to make her Ophelia more dramatic..."

"I, too, wonder. I do not, however, want to be the person to tell him. He would certainly be appalled."

"Then I shall tell him! I know that our Kitty does not always behave as she should, but she is a good girl. She should not be made solely responsible for what has occurred."

Elizabeth glanced tenderly at her sister. It was rare to see Jane in high dudgeon but that evening, her sense of family and justice had suffered a blow, and she spoke with the passion of one who prepared to ride into battle.

Yet it was Elizabeth, alone, who faced Darcy's disapproval, once the house had retired for the night. He joined her in her room much later than usual, as if reluctant to begin the inevitable conversation.

"Are you not asleep?" he asked, seeing his wife sitting up in the bed.

"I was waiting for you."

"So I see."

He slid under the blankets and pretended he wanted to sleep. Elizabeth waited a minute, but upon realising that he would make no effort to address the matter, and that they were bound to disagree, she began:

"I regret what occurred tonight, William. The girls were devastated to have caused such a reaction. It was not their intention."

"I know. You said so in the sitting room earlier."

"Nevertheless, I cannot help but think that our reaction was somewhat disproportionate to the offence. Georgiana interpreted a character in a play and quite naturally, she wished to do the part justice."

"The choice to interpret a mad and suicidal adolescent is rather questionable to begin with, even if it is Shakespeare's Ophelia. But to present herself as she did in front of all our guests, drenched from head to toe, now that is an eccentricity that I shall not accept from my sister."

His tone was so categorical that Elizabeth hesitated on the best way to pursue the conversation without further antagonising him.

"The play does not specify whether Ophelia killed herself or if it was an accident..." she objected.

Her argument was so clumsy that she regretted it as soon as it was uttered. Darcy breathed a justifiably exasperated sigh.

"Do you really wish to debate this sort of thing?" he asked gratingly.

"No, I don't... Forgive me, that was rather silly. I am simply attempting to understand why you chose to punish her."

"Do you endorse this sort of behaviour? Unless this is your attempt at protecting Kitty, which I could understand. But if you approve of Georgiana's behaviour tonight, then we will certainly be having more of these vigorous conversations regarding which attitude we ought to adopt when raising our own children. What sort of education would you give them, Lizzy, I wonder!"

Thereupon he turned away, ending the conversation. Distressed, Elizabeth eventually lay down under the sheets, but it took her a long time to fall asleep.

She had wished to remind him of the little crayfish catcher and Lady Anne's tender smile, which had never failed to make his childhood mistakes seem less dramatic. She had failed.

~

As a result of this incident there was no more theatre in the evenings.

Mortified by what she now considered to be 'unbelievably inappropriate behaviour', Georgiana remained as discreet as possible. Mrs. Annesley took the opportunity to firmly resume her role and, as a result, the adolescent became a shy, timid creature once more. She no longer dared to take part in conversations when her brother was present and became a shadow of herself. In an attempt to make her more comfortable, Jane and Elizabeth showed her as much affection as they could, but she had completely withdrawn.

Kitty had lost her friend. From time to time she sought to pick up their conversations, but Georgiana was so hesitant in her replies, constantly turning to Mrs. Annesley as if to confirm what she could or could not say, that Kitty, wounded, eventually drifted away. Since she had never been capable of distracting herself, she quickly grew bored and sought the company of her older sisters.

The opinions of each differed on the matter. For a few, it was merely an innocent game, for others, it was dreadful misconduct, so each avoided bringing it up altogether. A few days passed and Elizabeth, although sad to see Georgiana so withdrawn, eventually grew convinced that all would improve with time. Then, one morning around the breakfast table, the imminent arrival of a travelling circus was brought up in conversation.

"What a strange idea to travel in winter!" remarked Caroline. These people go to a great deal of trouble... And for a town as small as Lambton! They must earn a pittance."

"I rather agree, dear sister," returned Louisa. "To live life on the road all year like that, both in summer and winter... These performers are quite courageous!"

"Or quite mad!" said her sister with a small laugh.

"Unless they simply do so to earn a living," Elizabeth chimed in. "As for myself, I have never been to a circus and I would be quite happy to encourage them."

"Mrs. Darcy, you shall no doubt be amazed by what you see," Mr. Hurst joined in. "We have been to Astley's and to Hughes' in London a few times and they are the best theatres for this type of show. The horseback acrobatics are quite impressive! Of course, a simple travelling circus will not achieve the same quality, but if you have never seen anything like it, you will certainly enjoy it. As for me, I shall gladly go see what those acrobats are capable of. It is rather dreary having to stay inside all day, I must say."

It was the longest tirade Edmund Hurst had ever delivered in the presence of Elizabeth and she was momentarily startled.

"Then we shall all go together," she concluded, giving him a broad smile.

"Will there be performing animals?" asked Kitty, who was delighted by the prospect of seeing a circus.

"I do believe so," Darcy answered. "As well as clowns and gymnasts. They will be inside the public hall, while the acrobats on horseback will be stationed out front to perform on the square. Something tells me that you will be amongst those ready to brave the cold just to see them..."

Kitty smiled with pleasure. She was not easily intimidated by anyone – Lydia had set a fine example in that regard – and even though Darcy had been quite angry with her after the *Hamlet* debacle, they had quickly resumed civil relations with each other.

"Do you hear that, Georgiana!" she said, turning to her friend. "Clowns and acrobats! How wonderful it will be!"

"Unfortunately, I do not believe Miss Darcy will be joining you, Miss Bennet," Mrs. Annesley immediately intervened. "She has been feeling a little unwell of late. It would be unwise for her to go outside."

Kitty's smile turned into a frown of disappointment.

"But she seems perfectly fine! Is that not so, Georgiana?"

The Darcy girl lowered her eyes in silence. Oddly enough, in that moment, she bore a striking resemblance to Anne de Bourgh, a half-faded shadow greatly affected by her companion. In order to avoid the conflict that might arise, Elizabeth attempted to calm tempers.

"Why not wait a few days until the circus has arrived before we decide?" she suggested. "Georgiana may be better by then."

"I do not believe it is a good idea to allow Miss Darcy to see such a spectacle, madam," Mrs. Annesley insisted. "It is rather vulgar."

"Vulgar? Do you think so?"

"Yes, I do. These spectacles are designed to shock and excite the crowds, stoking our most vile senses. Not to mention the noise, the looks, the jostling... It will be full of dawdlers, who cannot be depended upon to defer to a young lady of good breeding. I would not be doing my position any justice if I consented to letting Miss Darcy attend and witness such a show. It seems to me that she has been sufficiently exposed to unwelcome influences!"

Elizabeth was left speechless.

Around the table, everyone fell silent.

Realising the full impact of what she had just said, Mrs. Annesley suddenly blushed and began babbling an excuse. She reiterated that she was very attached to her charge and that Miss Darcy's well-being was of the utmost importance to her. This loyalty occasionally led her astray. She then spoke of the circuses and travelling theatres that she had seen in the past, and earnestly appealed to her neighbours to confirm that those types of events sometimes led to unpleasant disruptions.

When she finally fell silent, the unease remained. Darcy did not flinch. Jane and Bingley looked at Elizabeth in dismay. As for the latter, she pretended to ignore the condemnation and took a sip of tea, seeming utterly serene.

Outwardly, at least.

~

Elizabeth was seething when she followed her husband into his study. She closed the door with a great deal more force than necessary.

"Could you please enlighten me as to what happened earlier at the table?" she asked angrily.

"You should lower your voice, my love, you will be overheard," Darcy replied impassively.

"William! You heard Mrs. Annesley as well as I did! How could she utter such things? Georgiana is exposed to unwelcome influences? Mine, I imagine? And my sister's?"

"That is not what she said."

"And yet, that is what everyone heard! How could you not react to it?"

With a sombre expression, the young man bit his lip in uncharacteristic fashion. He eventually sat down at his desk.

"Mrs. Annesley came to find me this morning," he explained. "She worries that Georgiana's behaviour has greatly changed over the last few weeks and she is not the first to come to this conclusion. Of course, there were the festivities, it was quite normal to give Georgiana more freedom than usual, but Mrs. Annesley says she has increasingly less authority over her. She no longer knows how to keep her under control."

"'Keep her under control'? Do you hear what you are saying, William?" Elizabeth exclaimed indignantly. "We are not referring to a puppy in need of training or to the sudden proliferation of an invasive weed. We are referring to your sister! There is no need to 'control' her!"

"You cannot deny that she has greatly changed, can you?"

"I cannot, but if you wish to know my opinion, I find that this change has done her a great deal of good! Georgiana is more lively and resourceful than ever!"

"I agree, I have noticed it too. However, my sister cannot forget her position. She was born a Darcy and it is her duty to honour her family. Her conduct should be impeccable and as of late, it has not been so."

"That is where our views on the matter differ. We were not in public, we were amongst family, at Pemberley. Yourself, myself, the Bingleys, Kitty. We are her family. Do you really believe that Bingley or Jane would fault Georgiana? All they see is a lovely young woman of seventeen who is finally having a little fun. But perhaps you doubt their judgment? Would you prefer to listen to Caroline and Louisa's concerns? I do recall that, not so long ago, you did not seem to think highly of either of them!"

"Lizzy, do not start..."

"You are right, let us leave the Hursts and Caroline aside for a moment. They are merely relatives of our friend Bingley and simply not worth the candle," retorted his wife bitterly. "Let us speak of Georgiana and her behaviour. William, as her brother, you know her better than anyone. Apart from the various concerns raised by others, what are your thoughts on the matter?"

Sinking into his chair as Elizabeth furiously rounded on him with no intention of standing down, Darcy sighed.

"I do acknowledge that she is more lively, joyful and enthusiastic than usual..."

"Ah! There it is!"

"... but she also tends to test the boundaries of acceptable behaviour," he finished. "She may not have done anything detrimental to her reputation yet, although I would have preferred that she not drink as much as she did during the Christmas dinner, but if I allow her to continue in this fashion without any objection, one day or another, something more serious will happen and it will be too late for regret."

Elizabeth thought for a second. She composed herself and softened her tone.

"Perhaps it is because she simply does not know how to conduct herself..."

"What do you mean?"

"I am saying that with the life that she has led here, the poor child has never really had the opportunity to encounter others! I am convinced that she is not yet fully aware of what she can and cannot do in order to preserve her dignity and rank. She has never been in contact with the real world, except perhaps since I have arrived and encouraged her, unlike you, to mingle with people. Do you not think it is entirely normal for her to test these limits? It is up to you and I, then, to teach her the appropriate social graces..."

"It seems to me that Mrs. Annesley is here expressly for this reason," replied Darcy, vexed at being told that he may have failed in his brotherly duties.

"Oh, heavens! Must Georgiana's education solely revolve around learning Italian, playing the harp and receiving advice on how to lower her eyes with elegance to avoid being spoken to in society? When I arrived at Pemberley, she could not utter a word or make a gesture without Mrs. Annesley lecturing her! It is not by locking her up in a big house, suffocated beneath protocols and endless instructions, that she will flourish!"

"As I understand it, you believe I am too exacting? Georgiana has never complained about this to me!"

"That is hardly surprising, since she fears you!"

Seeing Darcy's astonished expression, Elizabeth realised that she had gone a little too far. This discussion was once again proof that she and her husband shared the same obstinate temperament, neither wishing to concede to the other, which only served to make matters worse.

She breathed deeply to regain her composure.

"Forgive me, William, I spoke carelessly. I should have said that you intimidate her, rather. You are the first to acknowledge that she is too shy and that she would benefit from behaving a little more freely with others, but you do not allow her the possibility to be more familiar with you. She sees you more as a father than a brother. When you are around her, she seeks only to please you and to endear herself to you. It would do her a great deal of good if you showed her a little more affection."

The young man remained quiet so Elizabeth continued, proceeding as gently as possible after their initially heated exchange.

"Don't deny her this chance to visit the circus with us, I beg you. Do not imprison her once again in Mrs. Annesley's shadow. Georgiana is a wonderful, loving and intelligent person, but you should stop looking upon her as a child, and give her more liberty. She needs to spend time with ladies her age, and to go out so she may know the world and sharpen her wit. She needs to judge for herself which conduct is acceptable in various circumstances. I know that you seek only to protect her, and that more than anything, you fear another incident such as Ramsgate, but, believe me, it is precisely because she is too sheltered, too isolated from the world, that she will be easily manipulated. That well-spoken wicked young man had little merit, for she was easy prey."

Elizabeth knew that she had touched on a very sensitive subject. She was not surprised when Darcy raised his hand to interrupt her.

"Let me stop you there, Lizzy. We have said a great many things to one another and I do follow the point you are making, but I wish to be alone now. Please. I must think about this in peace."

She gave him a long look before taking her leave and leaving the room, this time closing the door very gently behind her.

She suspected that she would not see her husband much that day. He might not sleep in her bed that night either. But as she walked away down the corridor, she felt much lighter.

This time she had managed to lay her heart bare. That was all that mattered.

~

Fresh snow had fallen the night before and all the paths had disappeared under its immaculate mantle. There was no trace of human activity. Even Stevens, known for exploring the woods in all weather, had stayed home.

Darcy guided his horse at a walking pace down the road leading up to the hills. He had passed Woolbert some time ago and headed towards the chapel. He was alone. Bingley, who was always ready for an outing, had offered to accompany him, but the young man had declined. He needed solitude to reflect on the frosty conversation he'd had with Mrs. Annesley that morning, along with the more heated one with Elizabeth later that day.

He was in a quandary.

He remembered Elizabeth's first visit to Pemberley, not so long ago, when she was not yet his wife and there was no indication that she ever would be. He had quickly recovered from his surprise at finding her there, unannounced, and his first instinct had been to present her to Georgiana. His feelings had been muddled. Even though Elizabeth had rejected him and he could not hope that she would change her mind, he had wanted her to meet his sister, his only immediate family, in a vague attempt to strengthen their ties. The inevitable had happened. As he watched her in the drawing-room, taking such sweet care of the shy girl, he had once again started dreaming that she might one day live at Pemberley for good.

That said, he could not have imagined that it would completely upset the existing family order. Affectionate and sensible, Elizabeth had quickly taken her sister-in-law under her wing and had begun turning the tide. The delicate adolescent who dared only open her mouth to acquiesce to what she was told and who blushed as soon as she was asked an unexpected question, had been transformed.

Darcy was a little ashamed to admit that he was only just beginning to discover his sister's temperament. Having never really lived together, the siblings socialised without really knowing one another. He knew her to be an excellent musician, of course, and gifted at drawing, but he had always believed her to be less cultivated than she actually was. More than once he had been surprised to find that once she overcame her shyness, she revealed a quicker wit than he had thought her capable of.

All this had been magnified when the guests arrived for the festivities. Elizabeth's family were in her image: affectionate, discerning, caring. Darcy quickly noticed that Georgiana, although more familiar with the Hursts and Caroline Bingley, whom she had known for years, had spent most of her time with the Gardiners and Jane. As for Kitty... He was forced to admit that having a true friend had greatly benefitted his sister. Kitty certainly lacked decorum, but she was also kind, loyal and sincere. Indeed, their friendship was an asset to them both, for while the youngest Darcy was encouraged in her spontaneity, the Bennet girl was learning greater self-control.

Darcy was pulled out of his reverie when he noticed that the sound of his horse's footsteps had changed. They had arrived on the hillside, where the wind swept the road, revealing the frozen stones. Now that his mount no longer sank into the snow, Darcy spurred him into a trot for some exercise.

They soon arrived at the chapel. He tied his mount to a tree a short distance from the entrance and headed to the cemetery to pay his respects. It was too cold to linger outside for long, however. He made sure that his mare, warmed up by the physical exertion and sheltered from the wind, could wait outside, and entered the chapel.

He noticed two pretty candles, placed in the centre of the small altar, and instantly recognised them. Adorned with little angels and ribbons, they were part of the decorations they had made for Christmastide. Elizabeth – for it could only have been her – had been thoughtful enough to place them there in memory of Darcy's parents.

The young man smiled fondly. He could not resist the urge to light them, gazing at the little flame for a moment, before shaking his head incredulously and smiling again. He eventually sat down on a pew.

He usually never troubled much with tributes and did not care for cemeteries. But although he had made an exception that day, it was not coincidental. Up on the hill and far from the guests who occupied his house, it was as if he had taken a physical step back to better evaluate his situation at home. It suddenly seemed easier to compare his parent's era with his own now that he was beside their grave.

Unlike his sister, Darcy clearly remembered life at Pemberley when their mother was still alive. Until the age of thirteen, he had explored the woods and the hills, learnt how to ride, played and studied with Wickham by his side, accompanied his father on hunting excursions, and trailed his mother on walks along the river banks. As a cosseted only child, he had received a rigid education befitting of his rank, somewhat softened by his mother's tenderness.

If, in London, it was her husband who took the lead as master, everyone knew that at Pemberley, it was the lady who took the reins. The beautiful and elegant Lady Anne always had a kind word for everyone, no matter their status, although no servant ever wished to be summoned to her parlour for a private meeting. As an accomplished mistress, she ran her house with both a smile and a firm hand. She was the one in charge of orchestrating the succession of visitors and grand receptions, and the rooms were always bustling with people. Parents, friends, a bishop, or a visiting lord... At that time, the Hastings did not yet live in the county: the Darcy's ranked highest, and Lady Anne was considered first lady of the environs. Everyone crowded around her. Darcy remembered all the evenings he was asked to greet their guests before going to bed, the music, the laughter, the merry figures and turns of the dancers. How many times had he escaped his governess's watchful eye, sneaking down the staircase to try and catch a glimpse of the festive lighting that shone through the half-open doors! He loved the fireworks that were sometimes set off in the valley near the bridge. On those evenings, he was allowed to stay up late to watch them from his bedroom window.

Then Georgiana was born. Lady Anne had endured the difficult pregnancy with philosophy, carried forward by the joy of finally having another child, a blessing she had dared not hope for after so many years. But Darcy's golden era had come to an end. Young Georgiana was barely a year old when he was old enough to go to boarding school. He was to spend many years at Eton. His time at Pemberley was shortened to just a few weeks in the summer, during which he reunited with his friend Wickham and warily observed his ungainly younger sister as she thrived in their parents' nearly undivided attention.

He was seventeen and still at Eton when he was informed of his mother's death via a letter from his father. His world collapsed. No one had told him that she had fallen sick a few months prior and the young man perceived this silence as a terrible betrayal. Although his father later explained that it was to protect him, Darcy had developed a deep resentment. He had been kept away and treated like a child who was unfit to handle family crises. It was something that, to this day, he was unable to forgive.

He made a trip in time to attend Lady Anne's burial, in this very cemetery, before returning to Eton to finish his year of college. Afterwards, things followed their course. First university, where Wickham joined him, although their relationship quickly deteriorated, then friends and life in London... Since he was accustomed to living far from home, he only visited a few months a year, mostly for the planting season in spring or the harvest in autumn, for his father continued to prepare him for the responsibilities he would one day inherit. As for Georgiana, she was only a child. Their interactions remained limited and they were not close.

Without Lady Anne there were no more visits to the large family home, or receptions and dances. Even after a period of mourning, George Darcy ceased to send out invitations. He neither possessed his wife's talents nor her desire to bring those around him together. The large gatherings of people were reduced to only a few close friends, and his son, finally a man who was allowed to attend, had the unpleasant impression that he had missed out on a golden era.

Left to himself, Darcy's father became increasingly temperamental. He insisted that no object be moved in order to respect his late wife's decorative arrangements. He also sent the dogs to the stables saying only that he was fatigued by their barking, and forbade his daughter to play music when he was in the house. Gradually, Pemberley slipped into a steady routine, illustrated by the hustle and bustle of servants who compensated for Lady Anne's absence by tirelessly repeating the activities they knew best. Of course, there was still much splendour and elegance, the food was exquisite and the servants numerous, but, deprived of any real family life, the large house became quieter and colder. It was another reason for Darcy to spend his time in livelier places such as the city or with friends.

Surprisingly, the young man had become accustomed to this routine and when he inherited the estate a few years later, he made no changes to it. On the contrary, maintaining old habits was a way of protecting himself and finding comfort in the face of all the responsibilities that were now incumbent upon him. He therefore placed his sister in boarding school as soon as she was of age, while he continued to live in the city. Pemberley had become a splendid empty shell, used only in the summer, when Darcy decided to spend some time there with a few friends.

Elizabeth's presence, however, changed everything. There were now people who congregated in the sitting rooms, laughing and celebrating, children bickering and playing on the carpets, music that could be heard down in the great hall, and Georgiana whose eyes shone with joy. This festive season had by far been the happiest period that Darcy had experienced in a long time, and while he had considered returning to the city in order to enjoy the season, he was amazed to realise that he no longer had the slightest desire to leave. He felt good at Pemberley. He felt at home again, like he had when he was a child.

He then remembered the decision he had to make.

He stood up, blew out the candles and left the chapel without looking back.

~

"Oliver, would you be so kind as to bring me the pie?" Elizabeth whispered to the footman leaning over her shoulder.

He nodded and moved quietly to the other end of the table to fetch the dish.

"Mrs. Annesley has not yet come down?" asked Louisa. "She is usually never late. I hope she is not ill!"

"If she is, it cannot be too serious. She was quite well yesterday. We shall send someone up just now to see if there is anything we can do to help..." Caroline replied with relative indifference.

Unsurprisingly, it was Bingley's sisters who remarked upon the glaring absence that no one, out of discretion, had dared to mention. A few glances were thrown in Elizabeth's direction, but since she appeared equally unaware, the group turned to Darcy instead.

Impassive, he took the time to finish his sip of coffee before answering.

"Mrs. Annesley is no longer with us. She has been dismissed."

Georgiana let out a small exclamation. Elizabeth, like the others, stared at him in surprise.

"Why is that?" Bingley exclaimed naively. "She was quite competent!"

"Indeed, she did take very good care of Georgiana. Nevertheless, I do not appreciate anyone calling into question the manner in which my wife runs this house and family. Mrs. Annesley's attitude yesterday was quite improper, so it seemed right that she should find a place more suited to her talents and tastes."

Silence followed his words. Darcy glanced at his wife, seated at the other end of the table, and gave her a little nod, before drinking his coffee as though nothing had happened.

Elizabeth was taken unawares. She had not had the opportunity to speak privately with her husband the night before. As expected, he had preferred to sleep in his own room. She knew he had much to ponder after their conversation and she had not been gentle with her words, but she never suspected he would take such drastic action. She was flattered that he supported her and happy for her sister-in-law who would be gaining some of her independence but at the same time, she panicked that she was to blame for the dismissal.

Georgiana also worried.

"What is to become of her?" she asked, shyly.

"Rest assured, everything will be well," replied her brother, inscrutable. "Mrs. Annesley will not be cast out. She will leave in a few days, when she has found a new place to stay. She had informed me that her sister would no doubt be able to accommodate her. As for myself, I shall gladly write her a good reference so she may easily find a new position."

"Does this mean that Georgiana will come with us to the circus?" asked Kitty, eyes bright.

"Of course, it does."

The two girls exchanged glances. Georgiana seemed not to believe her luck and feared rejoicing too soon. After all, was she not supposed to bitterly regret the departure of her faithful companion?

"You seem quite resolute, Mr. Darcy," Caroline stated, mouth pursed. "I hope you do not come to regret it."

"And why should he regret it?" Bingley asked, annoyed. "I believe Darcy may do as he pleases in his own house. Who are we to judge his decisions? His attitude is commendable. It demonstrates his affection for both his wife and his sister. If I had a glass of wine instead of tea, I would raise it in a toast!"

Caught off guard, Caroline did not answer.

It was the first time that Bingley, patient as he was, had managed to silence her.

~

Elizabeth and Jane were sitting in the parlour when Darcy appeared.

"I have just received a letter from your cousin, Mr. Collins," he said. "He announces the birth of his son."

The two women hurried to read the letter.

William Collins wrote of the arrival of his son, who bore his name and whom he had personally christened. His letter was as long as it was pompous, full of the affected phrases he so often used, even if a sincere exaltation could be perceived in his words. In his delight, he lost himself in endless metaphors expressing his praise, although a certain amount of curiously phrased sentences betrayed his distress. Elizabeth could easily imagine poor Collins bewildered by the cries that now resonated within the parsonage, and his haste to see the infant grow as quickly as possible into a more reasonable individual.

The rector invoked all the blessings of heaven upon Charlotte, for whom he also had the highest praise. He wrote that the birth had been difficult and that she was still recovering, prompting them to hire a wet nurse to care for the baby. The wet nurse currently lived with them, but there was a possibility that she might soon return to the neighbouring farm where she lived, taking the little one with her until he was weaned. Unsurprisingly, Charlotte was strongly opposed to this, and so Collins had not yet made a decision.

"What is he thinking?" Jane exclaimed, offended. "Charlotte has just given birth to her first child and he wishes to give him to a wet nurse? Poor darling! I cannot imagine how I would feel in her position!"

Elizabeth agreed, but she was not too worried. Collins was rather compliant and sensitive to flattery, as well as the opinions of others, and Charlotte would not find it difficult to make him do what she thought was best.

Life continued. Gone were the days when the ladies of Longbourn and Lucas Lodge visited each other to share gossip from the neighbourhood. They were no longer young girls. Their conversations now turned to their husbands, their homes and their children.

Elizabeth found it to be a strange feeling.

~

The roads were still very snowy when the Bingleys and Hursts left Pemberley. The journey would be arduous, but they refused to impose themselves upon their hosts any longer, especially since the season was about to begin in London. Louisa was already wholeheartedly looking forward to it.

"All the dinners, the shows, the balls... Truly, do you not want to join us in town, Mrs. Darcy? Everyone will be there!"

"Louisa does have a point," admitted Jane. "It would be an opportunity for your husband to present you to all the people you do not yet know."

But Elizabeth declined the offer without an ounce of regret. Unlike Bingley's sisters, she was not an avid city dweller. The Derbyshire country seemed infinitely more attractive to her than the constant bustle of receptions, especially after the busy festive season she had just hosted. She aspired only to enjoy some peace and quiet and to take care of her house, for which she nurtured many plans, as well as maintaining her relationships within Lambton society, and showering poor Georgiana, still a little unsettled by Mrs. Annesley's departure, with affection.

Nevertheless, saying goodbye to her sisters proved to be difficult. There were a great many tears along with promises to visit each other soon. Charles and Jane planned to return to Netherfield in the early summer and it was not inconceivable that the Darcys would join them, especially since Elizabeth would also be able to visit her parents.

They finally waved goodbye once everyone was reassured that they would soon see each other, promising to write regularly in the meantime.

CHAPTER 12

In March, the snow melted and was replaced with dreary rain. Despite the occasional frost, Cox and his sons were already preparing the park for the approaching summer months.

Darcy wandered aimlessly between the library and his study. It was the first time he had spent an entire winter in Derbyshire and, away from the entertainment the city had to offer, he became spiritless. The bad weather dissuaded everyone from going outdoors much. There had been no visitors in weeks, and the invitations exchanged within the Lambton society bore a sense of déjà vu. More than ever, Pemberley revealed its status as a country residence. Albeit a family home, it was also quite isolated from the rest of the world.

The young man had suggested they go to London a few times, but Elizabeth had too much work to do. Unlike her husband, who spent his days next to the fire whiling away the hours with books, Pemberley's new mistress was working very hard.

It was a charming sight for Darcy. He watched her with both great curiosity and admiration.

The first three months of their marriage had taught him that his wife needed fresh air at least once a day. The following three months he had learned that she needed time to herself, without him and Georgiana present to distract her. Darcy had noticed that since Mrs.

Annesley's departure, Georgiana demanded much more attention; so he took it upon himself to explain to her that Elizabeth needed time on her own in order to feel rested when she was with them.

Even so, there was not much to worry about in that regard, for since the festivities, the mistress had truly taken charge of her new surroundings. Once the kitchen inventory had been completed, she carried another out for the rest of the items in the house. It was an enormous task that had mobilised the servants for a fortnight and she followed their progress so closely that she was now intimately familiar with each room and its objects. She knew the names of each servant, had memorised their positions and seniority in service of the family, and knew who was on leave or sick. Far from merely giving Mrs. Reynolds orders to carry out, she often asked her to entrust particular servants with a specific task.

Her commitment never ceased to surprise Darcy. He wished to give his mother-in-law due credit for having adequately prepared her daughters to run a household, however Mrs. Bennet's knowledge was limited to Longbourn. With its six rooms and its handful of servants, it could hardly be compared with Darcy's stately home. He had therefore assumed that due to her lack of experience, Elizabeth would have relied more heavily on Weston and Mrs. Reynolds. After all, following Lady Anne's death, they had looked after the house for almost fifteen years since neither he nor his late father had ever interfered in domestic affairs. He could not fault their work and would have gladly left things as they were.

But that was before he had taken Elizabeth's character into account. She arrived at Pemberley as a stranger, a little unsettled at first, but quick to recover. She was keenly aware that she had married both Darcy and the legacy he carried with him, so she set herself seriously to work and, with sensibility and great determination she was managing rather well. Darcy realised that she was even more spirited than he had imagined. She asked relevant questions, was fully aware of wider contexts without getting lost in countless details, easily combining a wealth of information, retaining only the most important elements that enabled her to make decisions accordingly.

She also possessed the essential ability to handle everything with tact. She was patient, respectful of even the most humble servants and she paid attention to the manner in which she communicated orders to avoid appearing contemptuous. On the contrary, she valued their experience and opinions, with great consideration for them. Having observed the way she worked for some time, Weston could only commend his mistress. As for Mrs. Reynolds, she had found Elizabeth's interference in what had previously been her realm, a little harder to accept, but after a time, the two women eventually found a balance, which suited them both.

Moreover, Mrs. Annesley's dismissal had somewhat shaken the servants. Although she had not actually been one of their own, they knew that her dismissal was a direct result of a disagreement with Mrs. Darcy. Word had spread: the young mistress was proving to be more demanding than her husband had been and obedience was preferable to provocation.

But Elizabeth's curiosity about Pemberley's interests soon spread beyond its walls.

"When do you depart for your quarterly tour?" she asked Mr. Moore one evening.

He had been invited to dine with them after a whole day spent working with Darcy.

"In a week, madam. I believe this tour will be a little longer than usual, as your husband has given me instructions that somewhat disrupt the seedling preparations."

"Really? How so?"

"Last year's harvest income was not as satisfactory as we had hoped," Darcy explained, "so I asked Mr. Moore to change our crop ratios. The livestock are not affected. The price of wool, meat and milk have never been better, but when it comes to cereal crops, we must adapt to the market. If towns now call for more wheat than barley or oats, then we must provide the wheat."

"Do we have wheat fields?" Georgiana asked in surprise. "I thought the rest of the estate consisted of hills and flocks, much like in this valley."

A fatherly smile danced upon Mr. Moore's lips as he turned to the girl.

"If only you could imagine, miss... Pemberley is vast, and covers a wide and varied territory. Indeed, for the most part it is home to cattle and sheep, but I can assure you, your family's land produces quite a number of goods. It is one of the secrets to its success."

Elizabeth raised an eyebrow. She was about to express her surprise that Georgiana knew so little regarding the extent and nature of the estate that made up her family's wealth, but she remembered that since the girl did not even know the inner workings of her own home, there was little chance that she had been shown the rest of the territory.

"Would you not like to see it with your own eyes one day, Georgiana?" she suggested. "For my part, I should be very eager to visit the estate in its entirety. It would give me a better understanding of the affairs you manage with my husband, Mr. Moore. Perhaps I could one day accompany you on one of your tours? And meet our farmers and tenants beyond Lambton?"

The good man could not hide the look of bewilderment on his face.

"You wish to tour the estate, madam?"

"Why, yes! I should like to see the farms, the livestock and the wheat fields you mentioned earlier... So that I may put faces to names and see the land parcels that Mr. Darcy has told me about but which I have so far only glimpsed on a map. And I would gain a better understanding of how you manage the crops, which would perhaps enable me to speak on behalf of my husband when he is not available."

Mr. Moore seemed troubled, reducing the cheese pastry before him to crumbs.

"Forgive me, Mrs. Darcy, but you should know that the quarterly tour is a matter of numbers, annual projections, rents, taxes, negotiations and, more often than not, involves farmers who are rather uncouth. It will be insufferably tedious for a lady of your standing! Not to mention that such an expedition would last about a fortnight."

"If that is the case, I shall see it as an educational excursion! Besides, I need to learn more about the estate's affairs, as I am quite ignorant on the subject. In fact, I laughed when I asked Mr. Darcy one day, out of curiosity, to explain how the annual taxes for the estate are calculated. Well, did you know, Georgiana, that we pay a tax based upon the amount of windows in the house? Is that not an amusing way of counting? The mere thought is enough to make me laugh again! Not to mention the taxes on each of our servants, our carriages and even our hounds... I discovered a great deal that day, but I should like to never feel so ignorant again. Therefore, this tour is a most wonderful idea, isn't it? What say you, Mr. Darcy?"

A small smile had appeared on Darcy's lips when he remembered the bemused expression on Elizabeth's face as he explained the incredible amount of taxes he paid each year for Pemberley and Chalton House.

"I reckon it is a good idea," he acknowledged. "After all, I too accompanied my father and the late Mr. Wickham when I was younger, in order to learn how to manage our affairs."

"It seems only natural, since the estate belongs to you," retorted Moore. "Having said that, I do not think it necessary for your wife and your sister to concern themselves with such matters."

"Yet, Mrs. Darcy has a point: what would happen if, one day, I were not available to respond to an emergency? I would feel reassured knowing that she could intervene on my behalf. Believe me, dear friend; my wife shares my desire to act for the good of the family. She has proven thus every day since her arrival."

Elizabeth smiled at her husband from across the table, then added:

"I should like to add that it would be beneficial for Georgiana to accompany us."

"Do you think so?" the latter asked, looking rather unconvinced.

"Of course, I do! As a member of this family, you ought to know exactly what that entails, in order to better understand your place in the world."

Elizabeth's allusion was subtle, but from the look Darcy gave her, he understood.

Despite the progress she had made in recent months, Georgiana was still vastly unaware of her situation. She had lived in isolation, with no real notion of her family's wealth and no means of comparing herself to others, which made it difficult for her to consider herself an heiress. If she were able to see the grandeur of the estate for herself, she would finally understand how it could make her an object of prey for fortune hunters when she finally entered society, and hopefully this knowledge would incite her to remain cautious.

The young woman remained silent, but her expression betrayed a distinct distaste for the idea of spending several days traversing fields and farms. Detecting her unhappiness, Darcy added:

"Did you know that our mother also knew everything about the estate? She would certainly approve of this idea. You are still young, of course, but understanding how to manage such an estate is essential and will serve you well when you undertake the imposing duties of a mistress yourself."

This was an argument that both Georgiana and Moore could not fault.

"In that case, ladies, it may be difficult to plan such a journey with only a few days' notice," the steward defended weakly. "But perhaps you could join us on the following tour at summer's end?"

Elizabeth agreed and apologised for all the trouble it would cause. She pointed out that the matter was by no means urgent and could be discussed at a later date. Georgiana acquiesced out of habit, not entirely sure what to make of it all.

As for Darcy, he watched his wife with a look of satisfaction.

~

Mrs. Vaughan had retired. Lying on her bed, Elizabeth waited, eyes fixed on the ceiling.

After what seemed like a very long time, she finally heard footsteps in the passage followed by the familiar sound of the dressing room door opening and closing, and a few quiet words exchanged with Mr. Grove.

The dressing room was located on the other side of her husband's quarters, but the doors connecting their two rooms beyond the little boudoir had remained wide open, enabling her to hear the sounds quite clearly. In the stillness of the house, she easily made out the muted thud of boots falling onto the rug, and recognised, by its distinctive creak, which of the two wardrobes Mr. Grove opened. She even managed to detect the sound of the brush he used to remove the creases from his master's clothes before putting them away.

Suddenly, Elizabeth rose from her bed.

~

Darcy was shirtless, leaning over his washbasin and rinsing himself with a pitcher of water, when the door opened. His wife looked in.

"You may leave us, Mr. Grove, thank you," she said.

Surprised to see the lady of the house enter a room where she did not belong, the valet looked at his master cautiously. But since the latter indicated that he should comply, Grove bowed gravely and disappeared without a word.

"I believe you may have frightened him," said Darcy, amused.

"I grew tired of waiting for you..."

With a mischievous smile, she took a towel and drew nearer to help him dry off. Darcy raised an eyebrow in amusement, delighted at the idea of what would follow.

He welcomed the fact that their married life was progressing so well. In London, at the very beginning of their marriage, he had struggled to control his passion. Despite his noble resolve not to rush his bride, he was unable to resist the urge to invite himself to her bed every night. However, some time later, at Pemberley, things changed when Elizabeth had dared to push him away. At the time, Darcy was so disconcerted that he had almost left her bed to return to his room. It had taken a great deal of patience on her part to make him understand that she took equal pleasure in simply falling asleep next to him. Darcy had been vexed, of course, and similarly embarrassing moments like this one had followed, but he eventually showed more restraint and Elizabeth had appeared satisfied.

Now, the young woman seemed bolder. She understood that she, too, could seek out attention should she desire it, and it certainly pleased her husband. He had wished for her to be more playful and was happy to realise that she was becoming increasingly intrepid.

313

The towel was only an excuse. Soon, her fingertips caressed his abdomen with confidence.

"Lizzy! What has come over you?" he exclaimed in a falsely shocked tone.

"I'm fairly certain you know the answer to that," she replied, giving him a little side-glance that had its intended effect.

He lifted her in his arms and kissed her passionately. As they caught their breath, entwined in each other's arms, an unexpected thought crossed his mind.

"Did you know that Lady Catherine has finally responded to me?" he whispered.

"William!"

She pulled away slightly with a peal of laughter.

"You are impossible! What a time to bring up your aunt!"

"Forgive me, I thought it might please you..." he responded with irony.

Still laughing, she threw the towel onto a chair and wrapped her arms around Darcy's waist, attempting to collect herself.

"Why did you not mention it earlier at dinner?" she asked.

"I did not want to have to explain anything in the presence of Mr. Moore."

"And what does your aunt say? Has she finally forgiven you for your intolerable silence?"

"Pardon me, but I have written to her twice since the beginning of the year and she chose not to respond. There is blame on both sides," Darcy promptly defended himself.

"I know, my love. Let us rejoice in the fact that, because of you, contact has been restored between Pemberley and Rosings..."

Elizabeth was being indulgent and her husband knew that if contact had been restored, it was due to her efforts and not his.

"She proposes to visit us for a month at the end of May," he explained.

"How wonderful!"

"Do not rejoice so quickly. You know her, she will quite likely continue to be disparaging towards you."

"That is true, but at least I shall have the opportunity to show her that Pemberley has lost none of its grandeur since I have made it my home."

Elizabeth nestled against him once more.

"I suppose she will come with your cousin and Mrs. Jenkinson?"

"That is correct."

"So many women at our table! You may feel rather alone, my poor friend! Do you not wish to invite Colonel Fitzwilliam? He would be a good addition to our party. He possesses a gift for deflecting the more indelicate comments of your relations."

"I guessed you might make such a suggestion. I shall write to him tomorrow."

"In that case, might we consider this matter closed, at least for tonight?"

With a teasing smile, Darcy tightened his grip around her.

"Forgive me, my dear! Where are my manners? With all these digressions, I forgot to enquire as to why you came all the way to my dressing room. Do you require my assistance in some way?"

~

While preparing for Lady Catherine's arrival, Elizabeth made a show of being in good spirits, but in truth, she viewed the impending arrival with increasing anxiety.

She had not forgotten that their last meeting in autumn had been disastrous. Accustomed as she was to being obeyed, Rosings' mistress had not tolerated the Bennet girl standing up to her and so had left Longbourn in a state of deep fury. But Elizabeth was far less concerned about Lady Catherine's scathing remarks towards her than she was about the possibility of sharp exchanges between aunt and nephew. They were equally resentful and she knew that her husband had not yet forgiven Lady Catherine for her insulting words regarding their marriage. Given the situation, it would not be easy to renew courteous relations.

The next few weeks promised to be tense. But regardless of everyone's apprehensions, it was too late to reconsider the matter, for the guests arrived as planned at the end of May.

When Weston announced that their carriages had been glimpsed across the valley, Darcy gave his wife a long look.

"So it begins..." he sighed, as though suddenly bearing the weight of the world.

Outside, the weather was splendid. Warm sunlight illuminated the façades, the gardens were in bloom and the greenery features that Cox and his sons had arranged around the entrance of the house produced the most beautiful effect. As usual, the butler had lined the porch with a dozen servants in formal attire. The estate was at its best and Elizabeth had much to be proud of.

When the first carriage stopped in front of the steps, Darcy went down and opened the door in person. His smile was a little tense, but the tone of his voice was steady.

"I am pleased to see you again, aunt. Welcome to Pemberley."

Lady Catherine alighted from the carriage with exasperating slowness. Far from making as much of an effort as her nephew, she wore a contemptuous look that clearly reflected her state of mind.

Elizabeth had hesitated for days on how best to welcome her new aunt, and she concluded that being too familiar with her might further antagonise her. The young woman therefore refrained from walking towards her and stayed by Georgiana, smiling amiably as she waited for Lady Catherine to approach of her own accord. Only then did she make a curtsey.

Thankfully, the older woman was not alone, which alleviated the proceedings somewhat. Following closely were Anne and Mrs.

Jenkinson, and then Colonel Fitzwilliam who was delighted to return to Pemberley. They greeted one another with the utmost courtesy.

"Where is Mrs. Annesley?" exclaimed Lady Catherine. "Has she not been called down?"

"Mrs. Annesley is no longer with us," answered her nephew.

"No longer with you? But who looks after Georgiana now?"

"Myself and Elizabeth, of course."

"Good gracious! I have yet to set foot in the house and I am already met with change!"

"Lady Catherine, I assure you there are not as many inside," Elizabeth continued with a gentle smile. "Would you like to gather in the drawing-room? We have prepared refreshment. You must be very tired from such an exhausting journey."

"I would prefer a change of clothes first," Lady Catherine replied, drily.

"Of course. Your rooms are ready. Mrs. Reynolds? Would you please accompany these ladies?"

The guests were then led away by the servants, disappearing up the staircase.

"Well, my love, you may regain your habitual calmness! The hardest part is done..." whispered Elizabeth with a small smile as she took her husband's arm.

But inwardly, she heaved a deep sigh to soothe her own agitation.

~

Pemberley, once so austere, immutable and rigid in its solemn rituals that had not changed since Lady Anne's death, now entered a lively era. Admittedly, dinner was still announced at the same time, and the same number of maids and footmen were still required to clean the rooms and serve the meals, but both the changes established by the new mistress, and the succession of guests who had stayed since her arrival, had somewhat disrupted the course of daily life.

This did not escape Lady Catherine's notice. Moving with ease through the rooms as if she were at home, she gazed sharply at everything, pursing her lips, before voicing her opinion – which more often than not, was critical. During the first few days, she seemed almost permanently suspicious of Elizabeth, which made the atmosphere as tense as the latter had dreaded it to be. Darcy hastened to shield her, diverting his aunt's attention as soon as she ventured to make a reproach. He was helped in this regard by his cousin, Colonel Fitzwilliam, whose amiable smile never seemed to falter.

Elizabeth accepted these thinly veiled admonitions unflinchingly. She had the patience of an angel and calmly tolerated the constant reminders that she was an inexperienced bride. Occasionally she justified herself by explaining that she compensated her ignorance with her common sense and sensible mind, and that she would fare increasingly better as time went on. But Lady Catherine did not seem interested in these arguments and went so far as to interrogate Mrs. Reynolds about her mistress. She was disappointed, however, not to find any ground upon which to base her criticism. The housekeeper had nothing but praise for Elizabeth and expressed how delighted she was to have such an intelligent young woman at the helm of the house.

To please their distinguished, yet difficult guest, the Darcys hosted several dinners. Quite a few within Lambton's society knew Lady Catherine and were flattered to be invited. Viscount Hastings, the widow Langhold, the Nortons, Mrs. Keen and other respected people thus came to visit, which served to ease her sharp tongue for a time. For Elizabeth, it was a step towards a much hoped for acceptance.

But while her mother, who clearly appreciated being the centre of attention, eventually became less churlish as the days went on, the same could not be said about Anne de Bourgh. She remained utterly impervious to Elizabeth's attempts to befriend her. She was even more reserved than the shy Georgiana had ever been. She did not leave Mrs. Jenkinson's side, even for a moment, only speaking to her in whispers, and when she finally answered a question directly addressed to her, it was in a somewhat plaintive voice, which irked Elizabeth. She wavered between pity for the poor girl, and a desire to shake her in an attempt to elicit some kind of reaction.

"Good Lord, as far as I know, your cousin is not destined to live in a convent!" she exclaimed one evening to Darcy. "She has been out in society for years! She must have learnt the basic rules of courtesy and acquired enough conversation to make a good impression in drawing-rooms, but makes no effort to employ them!"

Her husband laughed and shrugged.

"Anne has never been able to emerge from my aunt's shadow. You accused me once of being too protective of my sister but as you can see I am certainly not the worst. Simply follow my lead and ignore her. Leave it to Colonel Fitzwilliam to be pleasant to her from time to time. In this matter, he knows exactly what to say."

Darcy was not wrong. The colonel was the only one who occasionally managed to make the young de Bourgh smile. Elizabeth pouted a little, upset that, for once, her talent for cultivating friendly relations had failed.

"It is hardly surprising that she is still unmarried, in spite of her fortune. I pity the poor man who might one day be persuaded... But I pity her even more! Heaven's, what a sad life! A sad life indeed!"

~

Days soon turned into weeks. Disappointed that she could not find any dreadful fault with the new Mrs. Darcy – apart, perhaps, for her habit of speaking with too much candour –, the formidable woman slowly allowed herself to be placated.

Elizabeth felt her soften for the first time when she invited the ladies for tea in her parlour instead of the usual drawing-room. The older woman immediately noticed the portrait of her sister hanging opposite the beautiful mahogany secretary. In this intimate and sentimental setting, she spoke more openly.

Catherine de Bourgh loved talking about her past. Nothing pleased her more than being asked about her youth, which she recalled with a fair amount of emotion. Thus, she recounted her childish bickering with her brother, the Earl Fitzwilliam, her marriage with Sir Lewis at the age of eighteen and the misfortune of having lost no less than four children at birth or at a very young age. Not to mention her constant concerns about the health of her youngest daughter, Anne, who was the only child to have survived early childhood.

It was the first time that the woman had displayed any kind of genuine sensibility, the greatest proof of which was her infinite devotion towards her sister, Lady Anne. It surpassed even the praise she had for her late husband, Sir Lewis. She therefore strongly approved of the fact that her niece looked up to the previous Mrs. Darcy in an effort to be a worthy mistress for Pemberley.

"You could not ask for a better model, madam," she told Elizabeth. "Moreover, that portrait should never leave its place, so you may always remember who made this house so prosperous."

"I shall be sure to remember it, Lady Catherine," answered the young woman, who felt that the portrait was a way to initiate a rapprochement between the two women. "On this subject, would you like to accompany me tomorrow to the chapel? As Georgiana mentioned before, with the amount of rain we have had this spring, the plants have grown into a veritable jungle and it is high time we looked after the graves, otherwise they may soon disappear!"

The expedition, which was organised the following day, bore fruit far beyond Elizabeth's expectations.

Darcy and his cousin had found other business with which to occupy themselves, leaving the ladies to head to the chapel alone, accompanied only by a coachman and a footman. Elizabeth had prepared a few gardening tools, and, while her puzzled guests wondered what attitude to adopt, she led Georgiana to the graves to begin removing the greenery that had invaded them.

"Do you really intend to do all this yourself?" Mrs. Jenkinson asked in surprise. "Could you not ask your footman to do it for you? You shall dirty yourself!"

"Well, that seems quite likely," replied Elizabeth undaunted, "but a little soil on one's hands never hurt anyone. Is it not up to us to look after our dearly departed? I would never entrust such a task to a servant. The responsibility befalls us, as their relations."

The woman fell silent. As for Lady Catherine, she made no comment.

Elizabeth tended to George Darcy's grave first, ripping out the weeds with her bare hands and using a billhook when the stems were too rigid, giving Georgiana instructions as they progressed. Within a short time, the stone was relatively cleared and the girl, armed with a brush, began cleaning the moss that had grown in here and there. Meanwhile, Elizabeth moved on to the late Mrs. Darcy.

"Would you join us, Miss de Bourgh?" she ventured.

Poor Anne appeared flustered. It was her godmother's grave, but Mrs. Jenkinson's earlier comment had made her uncomfortable. Sensing her hesitation, Elizabeth attempted a different approach.

"I have a better idea! Perhaps you could pick some beautiful flowers to decorate the graves and place on the altar. What say you? There are some pretty wildflowers along the path."

"With pleasure," Anne replied, relieved that she could participate in an activity that was more suited to her mother and her companion's expectations.

"I shall accompany you," said Mrs. Jenkinson.

"Be careful not to pick yellow flowers!" returned Lady Catherine. "My sister hated yellow!"

Elizabeth thought of the pretty golden drawing-room at Chalton House, which Darcy had mentioned was his mother's favourite room. Lady Anne hated yellow? Nonsense! But the young woman made no comment. Her aunt was merely ceding to her usual impulse for authority, expressing her views even if they were without solid grounds. It was better not to respond. Indeed, Lady Catherine spent the rest of the excursion alternating between the two workers at the graves and the flower pickers, providing advice and criticism, as was her wont.

Finally, perspiring slightly from the effort, Elizabeth and Georgiana went to wash their faces and hands with water from a pitcher that the footman had fetched from a stream nearby, before returning to the other ladies. They had created three beautiful bouquets of flowers and grasses, tied with ribbons. One was placed inside the chapel, replacing the Christmas candles, and the other two were placed on the Darcys' graves. The group then paid their respects for a short while.

In the carriage on the way back, Georgiana, whose nails were black with soil, could not help fiddling with her fingers. Feeling her aunt's imperious gaze upon her, she hid her hands under a fold in her dress.

"Forgive me..." she said, blushing. "I should have worn my gloves."

"There is no need to justify yourself, child," replied Lady Catherine. "What you and Mrs. Darcy have done today is all to your credit, for there is nothing nobler than caring for the deceased."

Elizabeth smiled.

She was on the right path.

~

The atmosphere was peaceful in the drawing-room. A meal consisting of sandwiches, cold meats, cheeses and fruits had been served to perk up the group after their long walk in the park. Georgiana had taken a plate with her to the next room and practised her music between mouthfuls, while Darcy and Colonel Fitzwilliam kept the rest of the women company. Elizabeth had quietly slipped away to read a letter, which had arrived during her walk.

"Well, Darcy, where is your wife?" asked Lady Catherine, growing impatient. "She should have joined us by now! What is this letter that keeps her away from us?"

"I am certain that she shall be with us any minute," he replied with his usual composure. "Would you like more tea?"

And indeed, a minute later, Elizabeth's footsteps resonated in the passage. When she entered the room her face was radiant.

"Jane is with child!" she cried out.

Upon hearing the news, Darcy and his cousin exclaimed in turn, followed by Georgiana who had rushed in.

"She writes from London," Elizabeth continued. "She says that she had suspected she was with child for a few weeks, but wished to be certain before announcing it to the family. The child is expected in November and apparently she is already starting to show."

"Exactly one year after the wedding!" observed Colonel Fitzwilliam. "What a joy it must be for your sister!

"I shall write to Bingley to congratulate him. Knowing him, he must be brimming with excitement..." teased Darcy. "Are they still in London?"

"No, Jane wrote to me on the eve of their return to Netherfield. They plan to stay there until the birth, and no doubt longer."

"In that case, it will be an opportunity for us to visit them this summer. But if you will excuse me for a moment, I shall ask Weston to serve some Madeira. A toast is in order, I think!"

Even though Lady Catherine had never met Jane, she could not bear to be left out of the conversation any longer and took advantage of this interruption to speak up.

"Don't forget to congratulate your sister on my behalf when you answer her letter, madam. My wish for you is that you may soon follow her lead as it is never too soon to fill a house with children."

Elizabeth, who had rejoiced upon hearing the news without thinking about her own situation, immediately felt the responsibility of having married Darcy like a weight upon her shoulders, and remembered what the earl had reminded her of with so little discretion: she was to provide her husband with heirs. Colonel Fitzwilliam must have thought the same thing, for he gave her an uncomfortable look.

She knew she was not yet with child. Indeed, the months passed without her having given it much thought, and she was convinced that it would all happen in due time. But she now realised that Jane's pregnancy put her in an awkward position. Since both girls were married on the same day, they would undoubtedly be compared to one another. People would rejoice as soon as one gave birth while condemning the other for not following suit. From this day forward, the longer it took Elizabeth to announce a pregnancy, the more people would ask, with increasing indiscretion, if she and Darcy were struggling to conceive.

No sooner had the thought occurred to her that Lady Catherine chimed in.

"You need not become distressed about such matters," she said complacently. "Everyone will tell you the same thing: nature will take its course. Nevertheless, if ever it takes longer than it should, do not hesitate to call upon me. You will no doubt be offered countless suggestions, but believe me, the best you can do is to take the waters. Bath is very good, but I do have a preference for Tunbridge Wells. By the way..."

Fortunately, Darcy's return interrupted his aunt, otherwise she would have begun listing the countless suggestions she had just belittled.

~

It was so beautiful that day that Elizabeth had set up a table and chairs in the gardens, in the shade of a large sycamore, so the ladies could enjoy the breeze. Anne and Mrs. Jenkinson sat there to work on their embroidery, while Elizabeth read. Georgiana was seated a little further away on a blanket laid out on the grass, with a box of watercolours and the firm intention to paint one of the little ponds filled with water-plants. Lady Catherine joined them after her nap. Seated on a chair, hands idle, she made incessant conversation and stood up occasionally in order to examine Georgiana's progress.

"The gentlemen will regret having missed out on such a beautiful day. We shall have to tell them so at dinner. Have I not always said that May is the most pleasant time of the year to be at Pemberley? Of course, Rosings is best for summer's end, when the roses are in full bloom. You shall come visit, Mrs. Darcy. You simply must see it, along with Georgiana. And I suppose that Mrs. Collins will be delighted for you to meet her little boy. He was but a newborn when I saw him. Nothing out of the ordinary, but I am convinced that he will quickly become a very pleasant child. It seems to me that being born into an honest family of rectors always guarantees a good education..."

Lady Catherine may have been a woman of strong character, but she was not subtle. The topic of conversation could always be relied upon as an indicator of her state of mind. When she began to extol the virtues of her estate or talk of heirs, two subjects she particularly valued, it meant that she was in a splendid mood. And Elizabeth had not failed to notice that, amidst the chatter, her aunt had slipped in an invitation to visit Rosings. She refrained from smiling in triumph.

In the middle of the afternoon, she asked Mrs. Reynolds to serve biscuits and lemonade. But when the footman appeared, arms laden with a big tray, she could not help but notice that he appeared unusually hasty.

"Madam," he said, laying the tray down on the table, "there are guests at the door."

"Visitors? Who could it be?"

"Does it matter? Bring them here! The garden is vast, we have more than enough space to receive them," added Lady Catherine, with her usual authority.

The footman grew flustered.

"Mr. Weston wishes you to know that you are awaited on the porch, madam," he stammered before bowing to his mistress.

Elizabeth frowned. The butler knew that they could still receive guests at this hour. There was surely a reasonable explanation as to why he had not escorted them to the garden himself. Why all the mystery?

"Forgive me, ladies," she said with a smile, "if you will excuse me for a moment. Don't wait for me to taste the lemonade, I can attest that it is delicious."

She then followed the servant. She ventured to ask a few questions about the identity of the visitors, but the man refused to answer, merely repeating Weston's message. Increasing their pace, they passed the western terrace, crossed the inner courtyard and reached the great hall, after which the man slipped away.

Elizabeth had just entered the passage when she recognised the voices that rang out. At once, she understood.

"Lydia! Mr. Wickham! What a surprise!" she said, appearing on the porch.

In front of her, Weston, Mrs. Reynolds and three footmen stood in a half circle around the couple, whose carriage waited in the pathway. At a glance, Elizabeth noticed that it was loaded with trunks. It was clear that they did not intend to stay for mere refreshment.

"Lizzy! There you are at last!" cried Lydia, flying into her arms to kiss her. "What a splendid surprise, is it not? You see, George, we were right to come unannounced! I do think there is nothing more wonderful than a surprise! Look at her face!"

"Mrs. Darcy," greeted the ensign, bowing with the utmost respect. "It is a pleasure to see you again and I am delighted to see you so well. I hope you are enjoying Pemberley! You must be well settled by now."

"Indeed, thank you... But... Forgive me, to what do I owe the pleasure of this visit?"

"As I was just explaining to Mrs. Reynolds, I am on leave for a few weeks. Mrs. Wickham and myself have come directly from Newcastle."

"It was a dreadful journey! Imagine, Lizzy: three long days on a stagecoach, with people we did not know... And two horses died along the way! It was only once we arrived in Lambton that we rented this post chaise and I must say, I never wish to travel in a public coach again!"

With a smile frozen on her face, Elizabeth remained as composed as she possibly could to hide her dismay. What had the two of them been thinking? Did they truly believe they would be welcomed with open arms? Was it Lydia's carelessness that had led them to her doorstep, or else was Wickham attempting to use his wife as a battering ram to force his way in?

Next to her, Weston stood stiff as a board, his face impenetrable. Elizabeth noticed that behind him, the footmen conspicuously barred access to the entrance hall. It was the housekeeper who appeared to be most at ease, smiling affectionately at everything Wickham said. Obviously, the ensign's charm still had an effect on her, despite everything the good woman knew about him.

"But now that we have arrived, all is forgotten. Spending a few weeks at Pemberley will do us the greatest good, I am sure of it," continued Lydia, as cheerful as ever. "Believe it or not, Lizzy, I have a surprise for you. Look!"

Simpering, the girl turned to the side to flaunt her rounded belly.

This time, Elizabeth lost her composure.

"You are with child?" she breathed.

"I am indeed! Is it not wonderful? Go on Lizzy, congratulate me! I shall be a mother before you, before Jane, even! The baby is due in September. It is indeed fortunate that I still have some time, for I have not quite become accustomed to the idea that I shall have to look after it! Ah, what a feeling it is to have one's first child!"

She laughed heartily.

"But, could we talk about all this inside? In my current state, I must rest often, you know..."

Mrs. Reynolds was about to intervene when Weston stopped her. He gave his mistress a perplexed look.

"I...," stammered Elizabeth.

She paled when she realised that she was to handle this situation alone. In Darcy's absence, what was she to do? Receiving Wickham at Pemberley was out of the question, but could she deny Lydia as she was? She began to feel most alarmed. She could no longer think clearly.

There was an endless silence. Everyone awaited her instructions.

The ensign looked at her with an amiable smile. Elizabeth almost wished he would openly taunt her, but alas, he wore a look of utmost innocence.

"Well, Lizzy? Will you not let us come in?" Lydia insisted, as the silence grew.

"Well, well, what is all this about?" queried a voice.

The ensign's smile faded. Behind him, in the sandy path, Lady Catherine came into view. Driven by her insatiable curiosity, she had walked around the house to come see the visitors for herself. If her expression was anything to go by, she was not disappointed.

"Mr. Wickham, I did not think to see you here again," she said. "I almost did not recognise you in that uniform."

The man bowed.

"Lady Catherine, if I had known I would have the honour of finding you here at Pemberley..."

"And this must be your sister, Mrs. Darcy. Will you introduce us?"

Elizabeth, who no longer knew what to make of this surreal situation, reacted mechanically.

"Lydia, this is Lady Catherine de Bourgh, Mr. Darcy's aunt."

"Lady Catherine," Lydia curtsied in turn. "I am honoured to meet you. I have heard much about you. I am ver–"

"I have also heard of you, child," said Lady Catherine, cutting her off, "and I see that your character was aptly described to me, since you saw fit to present yourself without warning."

"It was a surprise..." stammered Lydia, blushing up to her ears, vexed to have been called a 'child'.

"It is a surprise, indeed, and I am amazed that your husband did not attempt to dissuade you," Lady Catherine continued, coldly. "Do you not have some unresolved quarrel with my nephew, Mr. Wickham?"

The question was so direct that the group felt it like a slap.

Confronted thus openly by a woman whose imposing presence was well known, Wickham was alarmed. He made an effort to regain his composure before replying.

"'Quarrel' is a strong term. There has been a disagreement of sorts, but it shall soon be resolved. Darcy and I have been like brothers since childhood and, as such, we have had both arguments and reconciliations. I come with a peace offering and I do not doubt that he will accept it."

"Your effort is commendable, sir, unfortunately my nephew is away for the day and neither his wife, nor myself may decide on his behalf," retorted Lady Catherine, undaunted. "Would it not be better to await his return?"

"Of course. Mrs. Wickham was just saying that she..."

"In that case, why not go pay your respects to Mrs. Keen? It so happens that she and I were talking about you not too long ago. She recounted the charming memories she had of the time you and my nephew were her pupils. She has not forgotten your mischievous tendencies and the way you struggled to concentrate on your lessons, but she spoke of it with such emotion one could easily see her affection for you. She told me that your departure greatly saddened her, so I am convinced that she will welcome you with tremendous joy. It will be another great surprise!"

Wickham would have liked to respond, but under the older woman's unflinching gaze, he lacked any argument. Lydia, who did not understand what was happening, followed the discussion looking a little foolish. As for Elizabeth, she was silent, bewildered at seeing the ease with which Lady Catherine had taken control of the situation and the direction she was heading with it.

"So, this matter is settled then," continued Darcy's aunt when no one responded. "We shall inform Mr. Darcy of your visit as soon as he has returned and tell him to meet you at Mrs. Keen's house."

Then, without waiting for an answer, Lady Catherine extended her hand to Mr. Wickham to signal that the conversation was over. The young man blindly took the offered hand and bowed, then grabbed Lydia by the arm and dragged her to the carriage.

"But... Are we not going in? What is happening?" stammered the girl, finally understanding that she was being sent away. "Lizzy...? Lizzy!"

Led by her husband, she climbed into the post chaise, her eyes wide with stupefaction. Her sister attempted to feign some semblance of normality by waving and smiling affectionately but Lydia failed to return the greeting.

~

Back in the garden, Lady Catherine resumed her chatter with remarkable calm as though nothing had happened, commenting on the acidity of the lemonade, the birds singing and the warmth of the breeze. Anne and her companion reacted with the utmost indifference upon learning who the visitors were. If they were surprised at the fact that Elizabeth had not welcomed her sister to stay, they hid it well. Georgiana, however, found it harder to hide her emotions. She composed herself and refrained from asking any questions, throwing her sister-in-law anguished looks instead. 'Wickham was here?' her eyes seemed to read. 'Will he come back? Will I be able to see him? Why was I not called to greet him?'

As for Elizabeth, she continued her efforts to hide her inner turmoil. As a worthy hostess, she smiled and refilled glasses and plates, but it was truly an ordeal for her, and she could not stop thinking about what had just unfolded on the porch.

She did not last half an hour. When the footman came back to remove the lemonade tray, she took the opportunity to retire.

"If you will kindly excuse me, ladies, I have letters to write. Enjoy the garden as long as you wish, we shall see each other at dinner."

She took refuge in her parlour. There, at least, she no longer had to maintain appearances and could surrender to her distress.

It was the first time that she had seen the Wickhams since the few days they had spent at Longbourn, after their wedding. Lydia only wrote to their mother and it was through Mrs. Bennet's letters that Elizabeth kept abreast of her younger sister's adventures. Finding her today on her porch had been a shock that was then exacerbated by the news of her pregnancy.

Wickham was capable of extraordinary boldness! What was it that he sought by coming to Pemberley? Money, no doubt, as it was the only thing that had ever inspired him. Was he still not able to live decently now that he held a position and some income from his marriage to Lydia? He knew that Pemberley was not within his reach and yet he still tried to pry the door open, without concerning himself with how it might put Elizabeth in a delicate position.

And Darcy was not there! Was it just a coincidence, or had Wickham planned this on purpose? Had he been relying on Elizabeth's weakness and their relationship as sisters to assert himself? It was likely. And the least enchanting aspect of this most unfortunate situation was that he had almost succeeded. For how could she not welcome her own sister into her home? Without Lady Catherine's intervention, Darcy would have likely found his adversary in his sitting room, and Elizabeth dared not imagine his reaction, let alone how he would have resented her for it.

Above all, Georgiana was to be protected. Although almost two years had passed since she had been seduced by the handsome Wickham's sweet words, the girl still thought of him most tenderly. She knew that the elopement they had planned together was reprehensible, and had accepted her brother putting an end to it, but she still believed that Wickham had truly loved her. Seeing him so unexpectedly, and in the company of his pregnant wife, would only revive painful memories.

Poor, innocent Lydia, who was still so unaware of her own situation, also had to be kept in mind. Ten months of married life did not seem to have had much of an effect on her. She still said whatever came into her head and her conduct was objectionable, for she acted as though she had the standing of a great lady, taking liberties everywhere she went. It was an attitude that Elizabeth was not proud of. Even as she congratulated herself on having won over her husband's formidable aunt, the arrival of her sister served only to confirm the disastrous image that Lady Catherine had of the Bennets.

And yet, the older woman had swiftly evaluated the situation and found the ideal compromise. Elizabeth could not have been more grateful. It was unlikely that Lady Catherine was aware of Georgiana's misadventure at Ramsgate – Darcy was far too cautious to have taken the risk of making this matter known, particularly to his aunt –, but luckily, the mere fact that Whickham was both a gambler and in debt, was enough to render him a disgrace in the eyes of Lady Catherine and to warrant his dismissal. The ensign was no match for her and had submitted, abashed. Elizabeth might have laughed if she had not been so anxious.

An agreement had thus been made. But that did not mean the matter was resolved. What would people say if they found out that Pemberley's mistress had gone to Mrs. Keen's to meet with her sister, after the latter had appeared at her door? Elizabeth could count on Weston and Mrs. Reynold's discretion, but what about the footmen who had been present? Not to mention Lydia herself, who would delight in telling everyone in the neighbourhood that her sister had refused her hospitality in her condition.

This brought Elizabeth back to the impending arrival of a niece or nephew.

There was, of course, nothing extraordinary about a young bride making such an announcement. Elizabeth knew that it was the opposite that made people frown. But she could not imagine her little sister with a child under her care. Lydia was herself scarcely out of childhood! She was younger than Georgiana! She was frivolous, careless, irritable... How could she undertake motherhood? Mrs. Bennet, who had been so pleased to marry one of her daughters off at such a young age, had never broached the subject. Perhaps she had concluded that married life would come to her naturally. Elizabeth, however, could only foresee trouble.

She paced up and down her parlour until she finally heard the sound of her husband in the passage. Judging by his footsteps, Darcy was aware of what had transpired.

He burst in without knocking.

"Lizzy! What is this I hear about Wickham appearing at our doorstep?"

She nodded miserably.

"He arrived two hours ago."

"That scoundrel..." uttered Darcy, properly irritated. "I expected him to contact us sooner or later, but how dare he show himself after the promise he made me? Has Georgiana seen him?"

"No, but she knows of his arrival."

"And what did she say?"

"Nothing. What could she say?"

He appeared relieved and somewhat calmer.

"Weston tells me that he was accompanied by Lydia? Where are they now?"

"With Mrs. Keen."

"Mrs. Keen! I am afraid I do not follow. You did not receive them?"

332

Elizabeth sat him down and briefly told him of the conversation on the porch and Lady Catherine's intervention. She then fell silent and let the information sink in.

The young man stood up abruptly and began pacing pensively.

"I will admit, he knows how to play his cards," he grumbled. "I certainly did not expect him to use his wife's condition as a way to invite himself here... And for a few weeks no less! He certainly does not lack gall!"

"Do you mean that we are to receive them? William, if we do so, Wickham will believe he can do as he pleases!"

"You are absolutely right, which is why I shall remain steadfast in my decision. Your sister is welcome here, but without her husband. I shall not allow him to have the upper hand."

"Do you think he will agree to this? What will happen if he refuses?"

"He shall leave with his wife and go anywhere else it pleases him."

Elizabeth was speechless.

"Rest assured, Lizzy, we will find some sort of justification. I will not allow anyone to say that you turned your sister away. Now, tell me, where are the ladies? I suppose they have gone up to change?"

"Yes, they have..."

"In that case, I shall tell Colonel Fitzwilliam to attend to them. They will dine without us. Get ready, we will go see Mrs. Keen."

~

The widow lived in a charming little house in the heart of Lambton. She was about to commence dinner with Wickham and Lydia when her servant announced the two newcomers waiting in the drawing-room.

"Mr. Darcy! Mrs. Darcy! I am honoured to receive so many visitors! Will you dine with us?"

The couple accepted, unable to refuse without appearing discourteous.

333

"If I had known I would be receiving visitors, I would have ordered some venison or pies to be prepared. I hope you do not mind if the meal is not as copious as you are used to at Pemberley!"

"We are the ones who should be apologising for all the trouble, madam," Elizabeth reassured her. "You are very kind to receive us."

"Not at all! It is delightful to have so much company. It does not happen very often! And my dear Wickham, whom I have not seen since his departure for the military... He could not have made me happier than by knocking on my door!"

"I could not pass through Lambton without paying you a visit, dear madam," he replied with a pleasant smile.

Mrs. Keen chuckled with delight, then excused herself to give the kitchen their instructions. The guests remained there by themselves.

"So, you are back in the environs, sir," Darcy began coldly, turning to his former friend.

"Indeed. Perhaps you are already aware, but I have been granted leave for a few weeks. Mrs. Wickham has long been requesting that I show her where I spent my childhood. I could not help but to submit to her wishes, particularly in her condition..."

"Forgive me, dear madam, I have not yet had time to congratulate you," added Darcy, bowing to Lydia. "Like Elizabeth, I rejoice for you."

The girl was flattered.

"I suppose it will soon be your turn," she replied. "Is that not so, Lizzy?"

"'Good things come to those who wait,'" answered her sister. "What is true in marriage is just as true in motherhood."

Darcy and Wickham both glanced at her sharply. Lydia, who was the only one who did not understand that the criticism was aimed at her, only shrugged and teased Elizabeth for being as sanctimonious as Mary.

~

The dinner unfolded in the most pleasant way imaginable, given the circumstances.

Lady Catherine had been right. Mrs. Keen was delighted to see the man she had known as a little boy. Wickham's charm continued to have an effect and it infuriated Elizabeth to see him banter with his former preceptor. He always knew which words to use, how to make her laugh, remind her of fond memories, or enquire about her charity work, all with such artfully feigned interest that the good lady spent a marvellous evening. She had even placed him at her right, a seat of honour that should have been given to Darcy, given his higher rank, which showed just how highly she regarded the young ensign. Evidently, news of Wickham's wrongdoings had never reached her ears.

Darcy observed it all and occasionally exchanged a knowing glance with his wife. But he was careful not to make any unwelcome remarks.

It was the first time that Elizabeth saw both men in the same room, seated at the same table and participating in the same conversation. She could see that her husband clearly did not possess the same natural ease as his childhood friend. Wickham showed delightful humour and spontaneity in addition to his devastating smile, whereas Darcy held himself upright, only speaking with carefully chosen words and betraying nothing of his emotions. The young woman had to admit that, in this regard, her husband did not rank favourably.

Mrs. Keen asked a great many questions, and the ensign gladly spoke about his life in Newcastle. He mentioned that he was stationed at Fenham but thankfully did not reside there.

"It is merely comprised of rows of barracks for the soldiers, containing only the most rudimentary comfort," said Lydia. "Thank God the officers do not live there! We have a small apartment in town. Having said that, I eagerly await the day that Mr. Wickham shall become a lieutenant, then captain or major, so we may live more amply."

"In that case, you shall have to be patient, my dear, for these things take time," Mrs. Keen said, with indulgence.

"Oh, but my friend's husband became a lieutenant-colonel just a month ago, and he is not much older than Mr. Wickham!"

Lydia did not seem to understand that army ranks were purchased at a high price.

"It is true that being a simple ensign offers few advantages. I confess that, as a start, I would quite like to become a lieutenant," continued Wickham. "The rest will follow with time, as you say, madam..."

If it was even the slightest hint that Darcy should contemplate buying the ensign a higher rank, he pretended not to have heard it.

~

After dinner, as Mrs. Keen asked her servant to serve coffee in the drawing-room, Darcy suggested they go to the garden instead.

"It is still rather mild and the sun is just setting. Would it not be more pleasant for our travellers since they spent such a long time aboard a coach?"

The motive was well argued and so the group headed out to the garden. The lovely grounds extended lengthwise, surrounded by a tall enclosure. Well-kept flowerbeds and a few fruit trees made it quite pleasant indeed.

Coffee was served and conversation continued. Then, Darcy turned to Wickham.

"Would you care to take a walk with me? I believe that we have a number of things to discuss since we last saw each other."

The ensign had no choice but to nod and the two men walked away, leaving the ladies seated around the table. But Darcy had only taken a few steps when he turned around.

"Would you join us, Elizabeth?"

Elizabeth rose and before her sister could open her mouth to request that she, too, join them, she said:

"Would you keep Mrs. Keen company, Lydia? I shan't be long."

She then joined the two men.

Thankfully, the garden was relatively large. As soon as they were far enough and could thus no longer be overheard, Darcy, who had been contemplative since the beginning of the evening, launched an attack.

"Wickham, I believe that now would be a good time to finally show your hand. What possessed you to show yourself here, knowing you were not welcome? Money problems, I presume?"

The ensign threw an alarmed glance at Elizabeth.

"You need not concern yourself with my wife," Darcy added, "she knows everything."

"I am on leave, as I said before," Wickham repeated. "Given Lydia's condition, we thought it might be beneficial for her to breathe some fresh air. The air in Newcastle is filled with smoke. I did not realise that our presence would be such an inconvenience."

"Do not ridicule me, sir. I do not want to have to remind you of the last conversation we had which occurred, I believe, only a few minutes before you entered the church. We had an agreement that day."

"I do not deny it. That said, Lydia's condition changes a number of things..."

"When you married her, you never imagined such an eventuality? She is your wife and your responsibility now!"

Seeing that Darcy was becoming angry, Elizabeth tried to temper the conversation.

"When are you due back in Newcastle?" she asked.

"In mid-July, which leaves us with ample time to visit the country. If my wife is not welcome in Derbyshire, I suppose that we shall go to Hertfordshire. She misses her family a great deal."

Elizabeth raised a sceptical eyebrow, but did not comment.

"Lydia is more than welcome to spend these weeks at Pemberley. I shall gladly welcome her," she said.

But as Wickham began to smile, Darcy interrupted.

"Only Lydia. I told you that you would never set foot in Pemberley again and I shall keep my word," he declared firmly. "I have no doubt that many of your friends would be delighted to welcome you during your leave..." he added, sarcastically.

"But..."

"I'm afraid becoming my brother-in-law does not afford you any additional rights, Mr. Wickham," Elizabeth retorted. "You shall have to respect my husband's wishes. Now, gentlemen, if I may, I shall go tell Lydia that she is coming home with us later."

"And where am I to sleep this evening? I cannot in all decency impose myself upon Mrs. Keen, especially if I am alone. She is sure to wonder what is happening."

Darcy glared at him. Then, with a sigh, and taking care to turn his back to the house so that no one could see him, he took out a five-pound note.

He did not say a word. Wickham pocketed the money silently. Elizabeth decided to return to the ladies.

She was already seated next to her sister and Mrs. Keen when the men finally joined them, Wickham amiably commenting on the garden's beauty.

~

On the street, when she finally understood that the Darcys were taking her to Pemberley without her husband, Lydia began to resist strongly. It was not what she had been promised! Elizabeth had all the trouble in the world to reason with her. It was only once she had promised her sister many enchanting outings and encounters, assuring her that time would pass swiftly, that she succeeded in getting her into the carriage while Darcy took care of her trunk.

Contrary to all expectations, Wickham proved quite persuasive in convincing his wife to stay at Pemberley. Considering Lydia's difficult temper, he was hardly subtle in his efforts, switching between an authoritative tone and tenderness to convince her that this was for her own good. Darcy and Elizabeth looked at each other, wary of this change of attitude. After being offended at being denied access to Pemberley, the young man could not hide his haste to rid himself of

Lydia. It was hardly surprising. He was probably rejoicing in the fact that, for a few weeks at least, he had finally regained his freedom, no longer needing to endure his petulant young wife's company.

Nevertheless, Lydia clung to him until the very last moment, bursting forth in long romantic expressions that eventually exasperated everyone. Darcy flagged down a coach in the street so as to load Wickham's luggage and send him off to the first inn that came along – or to hell, as far as he was concerned. The scene, more ridiculous than it was heartbreaking, ended with Lydia in tears. Once Darcy's carriage finally set off, she fell completely quiet, her silence punctuated by small sobs.

While Elizabeth was disappointed in her sister's behaviour, she felt relieved. The situation had been resolved in the best possible way.

For now, at least.

CHAPTER 13

"My dear Georgiana, would you be so kind as to fetch me my shawl? I believe I may have left it in the drawing-room."

"Oh, Georgiana, you played us such a wonderful Italian tune last night. I would love to hear it again! Would you be so kind as to play it once more?"

"My dear friend, when you are married and in my condition, I truly hope you never suffer as much as I do! I feel so heavy that I fear that my feet may soon no longer carry me! What a pain it is to have to endure so much for the simple pleasure of having a child to pet."

"Really, you never use rice powder? Nor carmine? But how do you intend to attract a husband if you do not lend nature a helping hand? Of course, you must be subtle so as not to resemble one of those painted women – that would be quite unseemly. But I do think you would do well to brighten yourself up a little..."

"How sad that your brother prevented you from attending the dinner hosted by the Blackmores. We had a splendid evening! We played lotto and commerce, and I won three pounds from Sir Norton! I do not think he expected me to be quite so good at playing cards... It serves him right! Besides, I broke my fan last week so the timing could not have been better. Will you accompany me to Lambton to buy another?"

"Ah, that visit to Mrs. Moore was frightfully tedious! Do you not agree, Georgiana? It is a pity that my sister is not surrounded by young people. All her relations here are old! I almost miss Newcastle. I assure you that one does not grow bored there! Most of my darling Wickham's friends are not yet twenty-five. We have great fun with them, indeed! There is always someone available to offer you a dance or a game, and to celebrate with you! It is entirely different from these pompous visits where one has to sit straight, drink tea and have dreadfully dull conversations..."

It had taken very little time for Lydia to make herself comfortable at Pemberley. She demanded everyone's attention, using her condition as an excuse. Georgiana, who was barely older than her and who did not possess the temperament to resist such ill-treatment, became her favourite target. Inundated with frivolous requests, impulsive behaviour and criticism, the poor girl no longer knew what to think. She would have loved nothing more than to maintain a courteous relationship with the newcomer, perhaps even form a sort of friendship, but her hopes were dashed: confronted with such an obtrusive personality, Georgiana felt as she had in her boarding school days, when she had been taken advantage of by her classmates who unapologetically exploited her innocence. She retreated behind a pitiful wall of silence. While Kitty's presence had been a generally positive influence, Lydia's was considerably less so.

Thankfully, Mrs. Wickham had enough common sense to mind her manners when Lady Catherine was present. The latter was increasingly contemptuous of this young woman whom she deemed to be an awful relation. She stared at her with an implacable gaze that would make anyone want to withdraw, and instructed her daughter to speak to her as little as possible.

As for George Wickham, Lady Catherine did not hesitate to share her thoughts.

"I never trusted that boy. I saw him as nothing but a rogue, even as a child, and I always wondered why my sister and her husband were so fond of him. So, when I first heard of his nasty gambling habit and the debt he incurred everywhere he went, I told my nephew that pursuing any kind of relationship with him was out of the question. Thank heavens, he heeded my advice!"

Lady Catherine avoided referring to Wickham's objectionable character in Lydia's presence as a matter of common courtesy. Both were extremely wary of one another and saw to it that they never found themselves in the same room. When that could not be helped, they were careful never to speak to one another directly.

As for Elizabeth, she was well aware of the damage her younger sibling could inflict, and so she watched her as best she could. As soon as she heard that one of the card tables had played for money during the Blackmore party, she sought out Sir Norton to ask him not to do it again, even for the smallest of sums, so as not to encourage any bad habits. She also made a habit of always sitting by her sister when they were in society, in the hope of preventing any foolishness. She sometimes interrupted her or nudged her with an elbow, something that Lydia never failed to complain about once they were alone.

"Stop treating me like a child, Lizzy!"

"I don't treat you like a child, but you forget that this is not your home. Derbyshire is not Longbourn, and I would ask you not to behave so freely in front of my friends."

"How tedious you are, acting like a duchess! Do you truly believe they care about what I have to say? I am just expressing what I think as I think it. It is of no consequence!"

Elizabeth refrained from slapping her. Lydia did not realise how spiteful her words could be. Deep down she was not wholly without education, but given how she trespassed on the patience of those around her, it was easier to give up in despair than to reason with her, which only encouraged her insolence.

And yet, Elizabeth soon realised that something in their relationship was changing.

At Longbourn, having almost no neighbours apart from the Lucases, the Bennet girls had always been very close. The result was a tender affection for one another but, as Darcy had once pointed out, it had also led to a kind of competition, each one seeking to distinguish herself from the others. Because of this, Elizabeth had developed an incisive mind and a wit that made her a popular addition to any conversation. Lydia, however, the youngest who had been suffocated by their mother's overbearing love, had instead developed the need to appear older in order to overshadow her sisters. Nothing made her happier than showing her superiority and proving that she had lived through more than they had. Marrying before Jane and Elizabeth – even by two months – had been a great victory for her.

While she still lived in Newcastle, Lydia had been under the illusion that she was still one step ahead. At Pemberley, however, she was forced to compare herself to Elizabeth once more and found her own situation wanting.

"Why do they all bow and scrape? How ridiculous! They seem to take you for Queen Charlotte!"

"I don't know how you find your way around all these servants... One bumps into a footman or a maid at every turn. They are everywhere! Don't you feel as though you are constantly under observation? If I were you, I would dismiss half of them, just to have a little peace!"

"It is a beautiful house, I must admit, but far too big. I would certainly not feel at home in such a place!"

"From what I can see, your husband is very wealthy. I fail to understand why you don't make the most of it and buy yourself more dresses. If I were you, I would own at least ten ball gowns, each with matching shoes, and I would order a new muslin dress every week!"

These comments, each one more scathing than the last, betrayed Lydia's obvious jealousy as she observed her sister's new life. Of course, she was relieved that she did not have to handle the complicated planning of a large house, nor exchange pleasantries with acquaintances she cared little for. She also far preferred her own husband to Darcy, whom she found quite handsome, but far too dull for her liking. However, she could only envy Elizabeth's social position, with all its resulting material benefits, which contrasted so starkly with her own.

Outshone as she was in her self-imposed contest for status, the frustrated Lydia sought revenge by both posturing before Georgiana who was the only girl her age who was still considered a child, and calling attention to the only thing that still separated her from her sister: her first steps into motherhood.

"All the same, it is strange that you have not added children to your list of accomplishments, Lizzy. Is your husband not too disappointed in delaying thus? My beloved George is delighted! He has no sisters or brothers, you see, so the responsibility of passing on the Wickham name rests on his shoulders."

But Elizabeth, who had initially been hurt by these comments, soon had other matters to worry about which overshadowed Lydia's behaviour.

When the guests had been informed of Wickham's month-long leave, Colonel Fitzwilliam had frowned.

"On leave for a month? How odd..."

"How so?" asked Darcy.

"Well, I have never heard of a soldier taking such a long leave of absence, especially a low-ranking officer like Mr. Wickham, who is not likely to benefit from any privileges. Not to mention that we are at war. It would serve Bonaparte well if we allowed our valiant fighters to take one or two months of leave a year, don't you think?"

"Are you saying that we should doubt his word?"

"I don't know, dear cousin... In truth, I would be remiss if I raised unwarranted suspicions, purely based on the gentleman's history with the family. But if I may, I shall write to a few friends to find out. It all seems rather strange to me."

Ten days later, the Darcys had their answer and it was not encouraging.

George Wickham had indeed lied: his so-called leave concealed a temporary dismissal from the army, without pay, for disobedience. According to the information that Colonel Fitzwilliam had gathered, it was not the first time the ensign had drawn the wrath of his superiors. He was known for his lack of discipline and apathy towards his patriotic duty.

"A dismissal!" Elizabeth panicked. "But what will become of him? And Lydia?"

"Do not be alarmed, it is only temporary," Colonel Fitzwilliam assured her. "Wickham will return to his post in July, as scheduled. This incident will not have the best impact on his reputation within his garrison, but if he makes amends and carries out what is expected of him in future, all this will soon be forgotten."

"He has barely had this position for a year and he is already getting into trouble," grumbled Darcy. "Will the wretched man ever learn!"

At these words, Elizabeth bit her lip. The colonel noticed and threw a glance at his cousin, urging him to be mindful of his words in the presence of his wife.

The misgivings Elizabeth had had before her wedding were resurfacing and multiplying tenfold.

She could now see the problem that Wickham and Lydia represented for her husband. The young man was still every bit as deceitful and lacking in self-respect, continuing to claim undeserved benefits with confidence that would fill anyone else with shame. It was clear that since his pay had been suspended, he would soon be clamouring for money. He would soon have to care for two people in addition to himself, but it was also the best argument he had to apply pressure upon Darcy.

As for Lydia, her behaviour at Pemberley was consistent with the thoughtless young girl she had become in recent years. As a child she had not been without qualities: affectionate, mischievous and always ready to laugh, she had happily brightened dreary evenings. Elizabeth fondly remembered their younger years at Longbourn. However, Lydia had made her first appearance in society with the desire to frequent young men, hoping to marry before her sisters so as to taunt them. Since then, she had become a real nuisance and she showed no intention of settling down.

What influence was she exposed to now that she lived in Newcastle? Elizabeth could not say, but it was surely objectionable. Either way, she could feel Wickham's effect on her sister. Lydia had always liked to play games during social events and now she showed a growing interest in gambling. She complained that she did not own the dresses, ribbons, combs or trinkets she would have liked to have, and told anybody who listened that all this would surely change if she just won a fortune one night.

Worse still, she drank more than was desirable for a lady.

"What is the point of drinking if one does not become a little merry? How dull you are, Lizzy! You are becoming as tiresome as your husband!"

And so, Lydia no longer drank for the sake of elegance. She chased the effects of alcohol instead. It was certainly not the Bennets who had taught her this behaviour.

She was to spend three weeks at Pemberley. Elizabeth realised that this visit would require much more patience than she had previously imagined.

~

Darcy escorted his steward to the door, after they had spent nearly two hours locked away in his study. Together, they had taken stock of the crops in progress throughout the estate in preparation for Mr. Moore's departure, so he could carry out inspections in the northern part of the territory.

"... in that case, all that is left is to thank you and wish you a safe journey. I shall tell my wife to visit Mrs. Moore in your absence."

"She will certainly be very pleased with that."

"Would you like a carriage to escort you back to Woolbert?"

"You need not go to the trouble. With such lovely sunshine, it would be a shame to deprive myself of a little stroll... I wish you a good day, sir."

"And to you, too."

As the steward walked away down the sandy path with his ledgers tucked under his arm, Darcy turned to his butler.

"Tell me, Weston, do you happen to know the whereabouts of Mrs. Darcy? I see that she is not in her parlour."

"Indeed, sir. She left earlier to sit along the river, under the willow trees."

"And the ladies?"

"Lady Catherine is resting in her room, and Miss Georgiana and Miss Anne are in the garden, with Colonel Fitzwilliam. As for Mrs. Wickham, I do not know."

Darcy remained thoughtful for a moment. The butler added:

"We are about to serve refreshment in the garden. Would you care to join?"

"No, I shall join my wife. But refreshment is an excellent idea: would you ask Mrs. Reynolds to prepare a bottle that I may take along?"

"Very well, sir."

Darcy went upstairs to change. When he came down soon after, Weston was waiting at the bottom of the staircase with a little basket containing a bottle, two glasses and a few cakes, all neatly wrapped in cloth.

"Orgeat syrup and soda water, sir," he explained. "Mrs. Reynolds has added extra ice to keep it cold while you join Mrs. Darcy."

The weeping willows the butler had referred to were quite far from the house. They could be seen from the first floor, but it took a good ten minutes to cross the plain under the hot sun before reaching the pleasant shade of the trees – which was especially lovely in the heat.

The young man eventually caught sight of Elizabeth. She was perched on a large, flat rock, a book in her lap, her skirt rolled up and her bare legs dipping in the water. She was so absorbed by her reading that she did not hear him approach until he was almost upon her. She startled.

"William! Good heavens! You frightened me!"

"Forgive me, dearest. You were so absorbed that I did not wish to disturb you..."

She laughed.

"To what do I owe this visit? Were you not in an important meeting with Mr. Moore, this afternoon?"

"Indeed, but our discussion is over, Mr. Moore has returned home. May I join you? I come bearing gifts."

"Oh, what a splendid idea!"

He placed the basket next to Elizabeth who began rummaging through it, while her husband happily removed his hat, his linen frock coat and his waistcoat. Walking under the sun had made him hot enough to dip his handkerchief in the water and wipe his face.

"Sit down, my love, and come bathe your feet. It is such a treat!" said his wife as she made room for him on the rock.

"I do not doubt that for a second."

Once seated by Elizabeth, Darcy cried out in delight when he plunged his bare feet into the water. The rock was wide enough, so he lay on his back and breathed a sigh of contentment.

"How wonderful! I understand why you braved the heat to take refuge here, Lizzy. It is so peaceful..."

There was a very soft light beneath the willow trees, both from the rays of light that filtered down through the garlands of drooping leaves, and the bright reflections that bounced off the water below. The birds could be heard singing, along with the lapping water and the rustling of the trees as they stirred in the light breeze that picked up from time to time.

"You have discovered my secret retreat," whispered Elizabeth, mischievously. "Whatever you do, do not tell anyone!"

Shoulder to shoulder, legs cool in the water, the couple spent a moment observing the foliage above.

"You and I should come here more often," Darcy continued.

"I would like nothing better. But in order for that to happen, you need to stop riding out so often with your cousin and I should endeavour not to be so occupied with the ladies."

"A little more patience, my darling, my aunt's stay is coming to an end."

"I am delighted! Please understand, I am glad that she came to stay, and I dare believe that she likes me a little more today than she did before, but I must admit that I am beginning to feel exhausted. It will be good for us to spend some time alone together, don't you think?"

"I am sure of it. It is most understandable that you should feel weary, Lizzy. You have gone to great lengths to make my aunt feel welcome here, and you have done wonders, I must say. I did not expect her to like you so much."

"Come now, do not be so complacent..." replied Elizabeth with a small laugh that showed she thought nothing of it. "She likes me a little better, but I am certainly not a favourite!"

"Yet when I hear her mention her plans for the autumn and her insistence that we both come to Rosings, I am surprised at how far we have come!" Darcy said, firmly.

"Perhaps. Unfortunately, Lydia's arrival did not work in my favour. You should see the dark looks that your aunt throws at her from across the table!"

Darcy reached over and took Elizabeth's hand, bringing it to rest on his chest and stroking it gently.

"I married you in spite of your family, Lizzy, and I do not wish to speak ill of your sister nor any of your other relations. However, I hope I may reassure you when I say that my aunt is no fool. She is now quite capable of recognising your personal qualities."

This was wonderful praise from Darcy, and Elizabeth took it as such.

"Are you trying to tell me that you don't regret writing to her?" she asked, teasing.

The young man also smiled.

"You look like a lady waiting to hear: 'I admit that you were right'."

"In that case, will you tell me that I was right?"

"You ask for too much, my love," he whispered, smirking.

He then pressed up on an elbow to kiss her, before straightening up.

"So, how about some lemonade? Shall we taste it?" he suggested, to change the subject.

Elizabeth sat up in turn and took the provisions out of the basket. But as she took a big bite of moist cake that Hewitt had prepared, Darcy became serious again.

"Lizzy, I am thinking about my meeting with Moore earlier. We discussed the land at Leah's Pass again."

"Is there any news?"

"Yes, there seems to have been a breakthrough. According to Moore, it appears that the Bromley brothers are finally ready to sell. But they will not negotiate via correspondence, which means that I must go meet them in person. In London."

Elizabeth was silent, waiting for him to continue.

"As my aunt is about to return to Rosings, I thought that the easiest course of action would be to accompany her on her trip. I don't know how long it will take to close this deal – given the way that the Bromleys have behaved from the start, it seems like they enjoy being coaxed a little –, but I suppose that it will all be settled in about a fortnight."

"That is a good idea. Lady Catherine will surely be delighted to be escorted by her two nephews."

"There is something else... I am thinking of taking Georgiana with me."

"Really?"

Elizabeth swallowed some lemonade to wash down the mouthful of cake.

"Does this mean that you are leaving me alone here with Lydia?"

"We do not have much of a choice, since Wickham's so-called leave is coming to an end and he will soon be back to fetch her. You will therefore be on your own when he arrives, and I must confess, I do not find this very comforting."

"What do you think he could possibly do?"

"I don't know, but I have learnt to expect anything from the wretch. That is why I prefer to bring Georgiana with me. I would like to avoid any encounters between them."

"Not to mention that Lydia is a poor example for her."

Darcy gave her a look but did not say anything.

"Well now! Two weeks without you! Alone at the head of Pemberley!" continued his wife cheerfully. "I am honoured by the trust you place in me, my dear!"

"I trust you completely. I am only sorry that I have to leave you to face Wickham alone. Would you like me to ask Colonel Fitzwilliam to stay a few more days?"

"The poor Colonel! Everyone calls upon him at a whim... No, no, do let him go with the others, as planned. Mr. Wickham does not frighten me."

And with a broad smile, she placed a kiss on her husband's cheek before biting into her cake once more.

~

For the duration of her stay, Lydia received no news from her husband. Wickham had once again made a promise he did not keep, and no one knew where he was or what he was up to. Had he found refuge with friends? Was he in Bath, as his wife believed? Was he attending many balls and dinners? Without his wife there to burden him, he was as free as a bird. None would hazard a guess as to where his taste for adventure had led him.

Lydia defended herself in front of everyone, claiming that writing was a tedious and lengthy exercise, and that Wickham could easily tell her what he had done during his leave in person when they saw each other again. But her sister could see that this absence weighed increasingly upon her morale. Naturally prone to liveliness, the girl grew instead more irritable, and Elizabeth thought she heard her crying in her room on more than one occasion.

The departure came just in time to create a distraction. Lady Catherine spoke at length of Rosings, which she missed so dearly. Not a single day passed without a letter being sent detailing the instructions to be given to the servants in view of her return. Even Anne ventured to say how eager she was to be reunited with Sirrah and Altaïr, her beloved ponies. As for Georgiana, she looked forward to seeing London again. Her only regret was that Elizabeth would not be joining them.

"You shall surely be quite at a loss in our absence, Lizzy!" she told her sister-in-law.

"Why is that? I will have Lydia with me for at least another week."

"But it will only be the two of you!"

"Did you not live like this before, alone at Pemberley with Mrs. Annesley, while William was on a visit elsewhere? Come now, do not worry: Mrs. Reynolds and the servants will take it upon themselves to keep me busy..."

Elizabeth's jesting tone hid the fact that she was actually a little apprehensive about this trip. Moore was not far, of course, and she could turn to him in case she needed help, but she would indeed be quite alone in this great house, without Darcy's reassuring presence at her side. They would be separated for the first time since their wedding and the thought did not appeal to her.

"All will be well, my love," her husband whispered in her ear, while they were saying goodbye on the porch. "I shall write as soon as we are in town."

He waited until the visitors were not paying attention to them, and discretely kissed her lips, before climbing into the carriage.

The horses surged forward. And as Elizabeth waved a final goodbye, gesturing frantically in an effort to dispel the wave of emotion that threatened to overcome her, Weston approached.

"Would madam perhaps like some tea?" he offered gently.

"Good idea. Thank you, Weston..."

~

Darcy's absence had the most unexpected consequence: many ladies from around the neighbourhood called upon Elizabeth, guessing the sense of loss she must have felt without her husband at her side.

Mrs. Moore, Mrs. Munroe and Mrs. Keen were amongst the most diligent. They presented themselves in the mornings, alone or as a party. Mrs. Langhold, who lived a little too far away, made the trip once, but she wrote a few lovely little notes and sent over several books as a distraction. As for Judith Clarkson, she invited Elizabeth and her sister for tea or lunch with other neighbours, passing the time whilst chatting over some sewing or craftwork.

The young woman had finally been given her rightful place amongst the ladies of Lambton. Moreover, her sister's presence was a great help as she was now the one treated with a reserved courtesy, while Elizabeth was addressed as one who had always lived in the neighbourhood. After having fought for so long to prove that she had a place amongst them, she was astonished by their sudden show of friendship.

In order to mark this new state of affairs, she hosted a large dinner, inviting the Clarksons, the Munroes, Mrs. Keen, as well as Mrs. Langhold and her sons. In a friendly atmosphere they played cribbage and piquet. Music was also played, and Mrs. Munroe once again offered to accompany the younger guests on the pianoforte for a few dances. It was a most pleasant evening, which confirmed, beyond a doubt, that Elizabeth was quite capable of hosting without her husband's help and that if one wished to participate in such elegant receptions, it was best to be on good terms with her. Miss Norton understood the message perfectly: neither she nor her brother, let alone their cousin Sophie, were invited. The two women nevertheless presented themselves at Pemberley just a few days later to pay their respects to the mistress of the house and enquire after her health. Elizabeth smiled wryly when she noticed how much Miss Norton now fawned over her, especially when the latter had previously found it so easy to criticise her. However, she behaved like a perfect hostess and they ultimately had a rather pleasant time. In that moment, she wished to rejoice at having finally succeeded in gaining acceptance among her neighbours. Her long awaited acceptance as a member of Derbyshire society did not necessarily mean she had to appreciate all those who were a part of it, and there would be time later to maintain a certain distance from those whose company she least enjoyed. There was, however, a shadow that loomed: July was fast approaching, and Wickham had still not sent any news. He had neither written to Lydia, nor to herself, and Elizabeth feared finding him once more at her door at the most inopportune time.

She asked Lydia on numerous occasions to think about organising her trunks in preparation for her return to Newcastle, but the young girl merely shrugged.

"Will you stop insisting? I will have time enough later!"

Since the rest of the family's departure, Lydia had begun to feel quite at home at Pemberley. Without Lady Catherine or Darcy there to cast disapproving glances in her direction, she no longer feared leaving her belongings strewn across every room. She regularly ordered the servants to bring her a shawl or a bracelet she had forgotten somewhere, somehow always having an urgent need for the items in question. Her condition did not yet cause too much discomfort, but she nevertheless used it as an excuse to justify her laziness – or else merely for the enjoyment of being able to give orders.

Now that the venerable Lady Catherine had departed and there was no need to demonstrate any kind of ceremony, the sisters took their meals in the small dining room, which the Darcys usually occupied. Lydia had, of course, objected.

"You have a magnificent dining room and you no longer wish to use it? Really, my dear, you don't know how to enjoy your privileges!"

"I don't see the point of eating in a reception room made for forty people when there are just two of us. The regular dining room will do just fine."

"But it is so small!"

"Small? Lydia, it is twice as big as the one in Longbourn!"

The relationship between the two sisters, which had already been delicate, had not improved now that they were alone with each other. Although Elizabeth showed infinite patience, it never proved to be sufficient. Lydia had lost her natural cheerfulness and spent all her time complaining, and her sister hoped she would return home as soon as possible.

~

At last Wickham made his whereabouts known. Early one afternoon, when Elizabeth had retreated to her parlour, Weston brought her a letter.

My dearest sister,

You will be happy to know that I am back in Lambton. The excellent Mrs. Keen had the kindness to receive me for the night, without appearing surprised that I did not present myself at Pemberley instead. I told her that I had friends to see in town, which, as it happens, is true.

As you know, my leave is coming to an end and I must report back to Newcastle in four days, which gives me just enough time to make the journey if I leave tomorrow at dawn. However, before I take Mrs. Wickham into consideration, I should like to speak with you in private. Would you be so kind as to present yourself at Mrs. Keen's residence as soon as you have read my letter? I have notified her of your impending arrival.

Yours ever,

George Wickham.

Upon reading this, the young woman was initially disconcerted. But she soon remembered the character she was dealing with and composed herself.

If the ensign had arrived in Lambton the day before, Mrs. Keen would not have failed to mention that Darcy was in London. It was thus quite natural for Wickham to address Elizabeth directly. But why had he not written to Lydia to notify her of his return? And why should he wish to announce it in his wife's absence?

Elizabeth paced up and down her parlour for some time. She pondered, turning towards Lady Anne's portrait a few times, as if to ascertain what the late Mrs. Darcy would have done in such circumstances?

Finally, she went out into the passage and summoned a footman who was passing by.

"Prepare the carriage, I am going to Lambton," she ordered. "Would you let Mrs. Wickham know that I have gone out and will return shortly?"

After which she went upstairs to fetch her maid.

~

"Ah! Mrs. Darcy, we were expecting you... And I see you have brought a guest with you!"

Erring on the side of caution, Elizabeth had made arrangements so as not to meet Wickham alone. His mere presence in Mrs. Keen's residence was enough to cause comment. It was known that the widow was very fond of him, but what was he doing in her home while his wife waited at Pemberley? He should have rushed there to present himself as soon as he arrived. People would not fail to find this rather surprising and, as a result, would offer explanations of their own. Elizabeth wished to avoid the questions that would have been raised had she met her brother-in-law alone, without Lydia. When the mistress of Pemberley had lost her way in the woods and was found just in time by a shepherd, it had been quite a surprise to the inhabitants of the region: she had no intention of being caught off guard again in improper circumstances, especially with a handsome young man in uniform, who, incidentally, was her sister's husband.

In order to disguise this meeting as an innocent courtesy visit, Elizabeth made a detour to Woolbert, where she sought out Mrs. Moore to ask if she would like to accompany her. The steward's wife was very flattered that her dignified neighbour had thought of her and was delighted at the prospect of such a pleasant outing. She never suspected that she actually served as a chaperone.

When he saw that Elizabeth was not alone, Wickham frowned, but said nothing. He greeted Mrs. Moore with great elegance and took the time to enquire about Woolbert and the cottage where he had spent his childhood.

"So, you are the famous Mr. Wickham I have heard so much about!" the woman exclaimed. "It is a pleasure to make your acquaintance! My husband will regret not being here today, for I am certain that he also would have liked to make your acquaintance."

Mrs. Keen invited everyone to settle in the wicker chairs that were placed beneath the trees in the shade, and had tea and coffee served. The conversation was exceedingly genteel. The group enquired after Darcy's stay in London, Lydia's health, the various trips Wickham had undertaken over the last few weeks – he spoke so eloquently that Elizabeth could not tell whether he was lying –, as well as his future plans. They discussed his return to the garrison at Newcastle, the upcoming birth, and the likelihood that it would be a son, but also the difficulty of road travel and the unfortunate need for husbands to occasionally absent themselves from home, where their presence was nonetheless crucial.

At that point in the conversation, Mrs. Keen and Mrs. Moore embarked upon a long complaint about their lives as wives alone at home – the widow, who had been married to a travelling merchant, and the steward's wife whose husband often left her to undertake his rounds of the Pemberley estate. They were so engrossed that they barely noticed when Wickham rose and offered to accompany Elizabeth on a walk around the garden to admire the flowers.

She nodded, hiding behind a forced smile. It disappeared as soon as they left the older women.

"You said in your message that you wished to speak to me about something private, sir?" she confronted him without ceremony. "Forgive my surprise, but I expected you to contact your wife instead, so you could organise your return to Newcastle together."

"You know our Lydia... She is so young and heedless – that is, of course, what makes her so charming – that sometimes she simply forgets important matters. Which is why I preferred to speak to you, a person of reason, to determine what would be best for her future and that of the child."

"What would be best for her future? What do you mean?"

"Would you allow me, dear sister, to speak with the utmost honesty? You see, I worry a great deal for her and her health."

Wickham suddenly seemed preoccupied.

"I do not believe you know Newcastle as I do," he continued. "The air is not as it is here in Derbyshire, and the accommodation Lydia and I live in is not at all appropriate for her confinement. Not to

357

mention that she is very far from her family. We have, of course, acquaintances there. We often frequent the circle of officers at Fenham, but I fear that she might feel rather isolated at a time when, more than ever in her life, she needs to be surrounded and cared for. Busy as I am with my military engagements, I would not be available to provide the necessary care that she might need. I would hate it if anything happened to her while I was away. To tell you the truth, I would feel greatly reassured if I knew she was here, at Pemberley, or else with your parents..."

"I never thought that I would one day hear such words from you, sir," replied Elizabeth, her voice hard.

"The imminent arrival of a child changes a great many things in a man's life, believe me. Not only do I have myself to consider, but I also have my wife and child to think of. It is with a heavy heart that I consider this option, but I feel that it is the best one for all involved."

There it was. The ensign had shown his hand.

Elizabeth felt herself flush with anger.

Even though she had suspected something of the sort, she was no less outraged. Wickham had not returned to Lambton to fetch his wife: on the contrary, he sought to rid himself of her. And now that he had outlined his arguments, he waited, looking just regretful enough, as though to fully demonstrate the reluctance he felt at sending Lydia to live far away from him.

The young woman remained silent. She tried to gather her thoughts.

"Perhaps my request has shocked you?" Wickham persisted. "Maybe if you were to write to your parents, they would better understand my desire to ensure that Lydia is properly cared for?"

"What I understand is that you are leaving the matter of Lydia's future in my hands, while you return to Newcastle having only to worry about yourself," she replied when she was sure that her voice would not tremble. "You still intend to leave tomorrow morning, I suppose?"

The ensign grew slightly flustered at the rebuke, but he tried to mask it with a smile of apology.

"That is correct, do forgive me, but I cannot be late. My superiors would be most displeased."

"Indeed! As things stand, it seems they are already quite displeased with you, is that not so?"

There was no need to add anything more.

Surprised, Wickham gave his sister-in-law a long look. 'Was she aware? If so, how did she find out?' he seemed to wonder to himself. But the young woman made no effort to explain herself.

They continued to walk side by side, in silence. As the garden was not large, they walked in a circle and this was the third time they strolled past the same spot. Angered both by this turn of events and by the ensign's hypocrisy, Elizabeth had increased her pace without realising it.

"I hate to see so many responsibilities fall upon you, dear madam," Wickham continued, with civility. "I can see that this upsets you and I do regret it. If Darcy had been present, I would have dealt with him directly."

"I am quite as capable as my husband of handling this situation," Elizabeth retorted drily, "especially since it concerns my sister and not his."

"And Lydia could not be more grateful to have a sister like you to take care of her. But since we are talking about Darcy, do you perhaps know when he will return?"

"How does this affect you?"

"I would have liked to ask him... Forgive me, I do not want to bore you with such trifling matters concerning my travels. I had better write to him directly."

Once more, Elizabeth felt her blood boil. The condescending way in which Wickham addressed her made her all the more enraged, for she could not tell whether it was a form of manipulation, or whether he truly believed that she was too submissive to make decisions without her husband.

Although she had the painful sensation of being drawn into his game, she could not help protesting:

"Explain yourself, sir. As I said earlier, I am as capable as Mr. Darcy of handling matters that concern us."

The ensign hesitated for a second. Then, as he casually contemplated a delicately flowering laurel branch, he declared:

"I confess that I am not very comfortable speaking of these things with a lady, but since you insist... It so happens that my trip these recent weeks has left me in some difficulty. I incurred some unforeseen expenses which my meagre pay could not cover."

"Hardly surprising since it was stripped from you," replied Elizabeth with a small laugh.

This time Wickham glanced at her in alarm. The young woman had the satisfaction of seeing that she had unsettled him.

"You... You know?" he murmured.

"That you were not truly on leave? Yes, I was aware of it."

"Oh..."

Elizabeth inwardly rejoiced. She had managed to unsettle the man at last. She felt herself regaining control of the conversation.

"I don't know what you have been told, or how, but what was surely left out is that I was faced with a matter of conscience," he said, trying to justify himself.

"I do not wish to know what happened, sir. It remains your business."

"I was faced with two equally undesirable options, a true internal conflict," he insisted. "I cannot provide any details without betraying military secrecy, but please believe me: if I had to disobey the orders of my superiors, it was because those orders went against my personal moral code."

"Your personal moral code?"

Elizabeth almost laughed. She refrained from doing so, but the stunned way in which Wickham looked at her revealed that it had not gone unnoticed.

"You do not believe me..." he commented.

"I am surprised, that is all. I did not think you possessed any sort of moral code."

Judging from his expression, it was clear that he had not expected her to attack him in this way. Before he could speak again, she pressed her advantage:

"I have become acquainted with you, sir," she declared, "and I am sorry to find that you are so very different from what I could have imagined before and what I might have wished for my sister. Your actions and your words are sadly consistent with the reputation you built for yourself at Pemberley long ago. Despite the reservations that you have expressed, Lydia seems to be of little importance to you, so you will be reassured to learn that her family will now take on the responsibility of providing her with safety and care. But you should also be aware that it is not by addressing me in the absence of Mr. Darcy that you will obtain the help that he refuses to give you. If your pay is insufficient to cover the costs of your expenses, along with the dowry Lydia brought to this unfortunate marriage, wherever it may have gone, do not think that you can turn to us every time you find yourself in need. Pemberley is off limits to you, along with its resources. If you ever dare to use your marriage to my sister as a way to exert this kind of pressure again, I will happily destroy your reputation in every single one of our shared social circles. Everyone will know that you have abandoned your wife and, believe me, she will not be the one held responsible for it. And so, I wish you a safe journey back to Newcastle, sir. I shall tell Lydia that you wish her all the best."

After which Elizabeth curtsied and spun on her heels without waiting for a reply.

She trembled so much with rage that when she returned to the chairs where Mrs. Keen and Mrs. Moore were still chatting, she refused to take more coffee for fear of dropping her cup. She busied her hands by grabbing a fan, breathed in deeply a few times, smiled a great deal and very quickly took her leave, claiming that the heat was causing her some discomfort.

Wickham, who had joined the ladies shortly after Elizabeth, revealed nothing of the conversation they had just had, but he proved to be unusually quiet. She refused to look him in the eye, and bid him a cold farewell before leaving, followed by Mrs. Moore, who was a little disappointed to have what she considered a most charming visit, thus shortened.

~

The ensign left Lambton the following morning as planned, without reappearing at Pemberley. In order to avoid seeing his wife suddenly arrive at Mrs. Keen's and causing a scene, he waited until the very last moment before sending her a letter. He wrote succinctly and without mentioning his short stay at Lambton, explaining that he would return to Newcastle alone for he preferred to know that she was with her family for the duration of her pregnancy. He swore that he would write soon to enquire after her.

"Lizzy? I don't understand... George tells me that he is going home without me. How is that possible?"

The girl did not immediately understand that her husband was abandoning her. But when she turned towards her sister, seeking clarification, her eyes suddenly widened with the realisation. Elizabeth barely had time to rush to her side and take her in her arms. Lydia collapsed on the sofa, breathless and shocked.

Then, a terrible bout of tears ensued.

Elizabeth was moved by her distress. How could she not have been? Her sister could be exceedingly tiresome and her thoughtlessness caused nothing but trouble, but in that moment, she was just a panicked child.

"How could he? How dare he! I am his wife! I am carrying his child! And now he no longer wants me? He does not want me, Lizzy! Oh, my darling George... How could he do this to me... George... George!"

Between sobs, the reality of her situation revealed the most pressing and painful questions.

"But... Who shall care for me now? Where shall I live? With what shall I live? And what will people say, good Lord! What will people say?"

These emotions were not without merit. Elizabeth had often wished for Lydia to draw her own conclusions from her experiences so she could learn how to behave in a more appropriate fashion. But she found this particular lesson to be especially cruel.

She did her best to soothe her fears.

"You are not alone, I am here! I shall write to our parents. I am certain that they will be most happy to welcome you at Longbourn. It may perhaps be a comfort to you that you will have your child there, with Mamma, Jane, Mary, Kitty, and all our friends at your side?"

"But George was supposed to fetch me! Why did he not come? Is this child the reason he no longer wants me? He can no longer bear to see me so large, I am certain of it!"

Lydia had neither the maturity nor the hindsight to realise that by embracing the first handsome boy who had presented himself, she had made a disastrous choice, both for her family and for herself. But she needed to cling to something. If she did not question her husband's lying temperament – the extent of which was still unfamiliar to her –, she could very well conceive that Wickham might find her less pleasing at present. This explanation gave meaning to the suffering she was experiencing.

It also dealt a serious blow to the feelings she had for him.

"Must I really stay forever young, pretty and slender for my George to love me? How vile it is to cast me aside simply because my figure has changed! After all, is it not his fault that I am like this?"

The days that followed were tumultuous for the adolescent. Distress was followed by feelings of mortification, then anger – rage even –, resentment, occasionally resignation, before circling back to distress. What, she wondered, was to become of her? Lydia cried for hours in her bedroom, slamming doors, responding violently at the slightest irritation, yelling more than she spoke, or else remaining prostrate on her bed. She resented the baby, whom she blamed for Wickham's departure, and swore that matters would change as soon as the child arrived. Slender and beautiful once more, she would have no trouble seducing her husband again, and she vowed to make him suffer as much as she suffered now.

Elizabeth reacted with all the compassion she could muster. Meanwhile, she wrote to her father to explain what had transpired. A decision had to be made regarding Lydia and the most obvious choice was to send her back to Longbourn. There, at least, she would be in good company for her lying in, and time would tell whether Wickham would return. Elizabeth then sent a second letter to Chalton House, and a third to Netherfield.

Darcy was the first to reply. He stated that he was appalled by this sad turn of events and wished Lydia the greatest courage during this trying time. He would be going to Longbourn as soon as possible to offer Mr. Bennet his help and advise him on the best course of action. He agreed that it was for the best to return Lydia to her parents, although she was welcome to stay at Pemberley for as long as necessary.

Jane wrote the following day, distraught. She described her astonishment upon reading such news. Refusing to believe that Wickham could lose interest in his wife so soon after their wedding, she chose not to doubt his intentions entirely. In her eyes, the young man must have been subject to an imperative greater than his own will, and she was convinced that he would return to Lydia as soon as he could. In the meantime, she welcomed her little sister to Netherfield with open arms. They could enter confinement together and the experience would strengthen the affectionate bond they shared.

Mr. Bennet eventually sent a long letter expressing both his annoyance and his painful resignation. He had been too confident, wanting to believe that although Lydia was not well married, she would, in future, be under the responsibility of her husband. He could not hide his bitterness at the thought of her coming home under such circumstances. He never mentioned money, yet his concern was palpable behind every sentence. Mr. Bennet had been taken for a fool since the start. First by his youngest child, who had behaved most objectionably by eloping with a man, then by the man himself, who had shamelessly extracted all the money he could in exchange for a marriage that would redeem Lydia's reputation. And now, the girl was handed back to him, without her husband taking the trouble to support her himself, keeping the dowry and everything else, and leaving the family to care for her.

It was a bitter truth to accept. Mr. Bennet, who so enjoyed chuckling at the discomfiture of others and who had scoffed a great deal at the charming husband his daughter had found, no longer laughed.

~

Without invitation, Lydia entered the parlour, looking for her sister. The latter did not protest. On the contrary, she gently offered her a seat and ordered them tea.

"Does it not bother you to have this woman here observing you all day?" Lydia remarked after a few moments, pointing to the portrait of Darcy's mother.

"Not at all, especially since I was the one who requested it be placed there," Elizabeth explained.

"Were you lonely?" her sister smirked.

"Lady Anne's presence is a comfort to me. There was so much I needed to learn upon my arrival that I was happy to have an example I could follow."

"But she has long since gone!"

"Indeed, but her belongings, personal effects, notes, they all remained untouched. Many knew her and could tell me all about her, including William. There were also the servants, Mrs. Langhold, Mrs. Keen... and, of course, Lady Catherine. I found that all were of the opinion that Lady Anne was good, refined and well-loved."

Lydia observed the portrait, looking doubtful.

"We always speak well of the dead and are discouraged from speaking ill of the living. Perhaps we should..."

Lydia's words were heavy with resentment towards her husband. Elizabeth gave her a compassionate look.

"You never told me much about your life in Newcastle," she said. "Did Wickham treat you well, at least?"

The younger girl shrugged. The only times she had spoken about Newcastle was to vaunt its parties, gatherings and outings, depicting the pleasant life of a new bride and the elegant manner in which she was treated in society. On the other hand, she had not said much about her daily life.

"He was not there very often. And when he was... he was often absent."

"What do you mean?"

"George would lock himself away in his study and I was forbidden from entering. He would say that he had many responsibilities and was tired."

"And what did he do in his study?"

"He smoked. And drank. Sometimes he would invite a friend or two to play cards."

"Did the two of you... argue?"

Lydia shrugged her shoulder again, looking disenchanted.

"Apparently all couples argue at one time or another."

She spoke little, but suspecting that it might make her feel better, Elizabeth gently encouraged her sister to confide in her. It became clear that the young girl did not have the thick skin that she seemed to like flaunting.

Her elopement with Wickham had been the most exciting adventure she had ever had, even though, after believing they were headed to Scotland to get married, she had ultimately arrived in London with no plans. She had resented Darcy for having found them and precipitating the wedding, for it was then that everything had changed.

Her marriage had begun quite well. Her visit to Longbourn had been most pleasant, along with the beginning of their new life in Newcastle, where she and her husband were settled in a comfortable inn. They rented a large room with an adjoining parlour to receive guests, and took all their meals in the common room below. Before long, Wickham had made acquaintances amongst the officers of his regiment, which meant that Lydia had many occasions to go out. She had met new friends, most of them recently married like her, and had enjoyed the city's small pleasures as often as possible. It certainly was not London, but it was nevertheless livelier than Meryton.

After only a few months, Wickham announced that they had to leave the inn as it was too expensive. They settled for some time in the home of a widow who rented out rooms, but she eventually ordered them out, not liking the constant presence of people in the passage, along with the laughs and the music played late at night. Eventually they found a small apartment to rent, where they were finally masters in their own home. Lydia had dreamt of having a pretty townhouse but was quickly disillusioned. The young couple were on the third floor of a residence that only had four rooms, the kitchen being so small it could not even house a maid. Besides, Wickham saw no reason to hire a servant, despite his wife's incessant appeals.

Elizabeth could clearly imagine her sister's disenchantment. She pitied Lydia. She was experiencing the first difficulty in an ill-advised marriage and no doubt more difficulties would follow. The thoughtless girl would be forced to come to her senses one day and it would not be an easy process.

For now, at least, she was safe. Removed from her husband's harmful influence, there was even hope that she might improve somewhat.

"I wish to go back to Longbourn," sighed Lydia. "I want to see Mamma, and Kitty..."

Her sister was about to reply that she was waiting for a letter from Darcy or their father, announcing what would happen next, but she paused. She glanced at Lady Anne's portrait in its gilded frame.

"We could leave tomorrow," she suggested. "After all, no need to wait for Papa to fetch you. I can accompany you there myself. What say you?"

367

CHAPTER 14

The heat of the day was subsiding. The sun was still high on the horizon but the air had cooled, inspiring a chorus of birdsong from blackbirds, doves, robins and starlings.

In Meryton, market day was over. Farmers and small trinket vendors went down their different paths on their way home, carrying their unsold wares on carts or on the backs of mules. They walked slowly, bent over and feet dragging, dreaming of the moment they would be able to rest their tired bodies in front of the fire with soup and a thick slice of bread. The Darcys' carriage passed them by, also biding its time. It had been three days since they had left Pemberley: the horses were exhausted and the coachman refrained from pushing them too hard. Besides, there was no urgency.

Lydia waved at the farmers from the window, delighted to find herself back in familiar country.

"Look, Lizzy, I see Maria...! Maria! Maria! We have returned! Will you come see us tomorrow? Give our compliments to your parents for us!"

The young Lucas girl stood on the side of the road, watching over her brothers as they played in the thicket. But the carriage did not stop and her response was lost amid the sound of hoofs.

Elizabeth observed the scene in silence, a smile on her lips.

She was home.

Ever mindful of upholding his masters' prestige, Weston had suggested, when she had told him of her plan to return to Hertfordshire, that she travel with two carriages and three footmen instead of one, in addition to Mrs. Vaughan, the coachman and his stable boy.

"One never knows, madam. If a wheel breaks in a rut you will be most relieved to have more shoulders to push the carriage back onto the thoroughfare. Not to mention that they will also ensure your safety on the road and in the inns."

Therefore, it was a fine entourage that arrived at Longbourn shortly before dinner, frightening the hens and startling the Bragg sons who loitered in the courtyard. Inside, there was a commotion, and Mrs. Bennet burst forth, cheeks red and lips trembling.

"My darlings! My girls! You are here! Oh, what joy you bring me!"

While the Hills looked on curiously from the kitchen window, Mary joined her mother in the doorway and they all happily embraced one another. Alerted by the cries of joy, Mr. Bennet emerged from his study and joined them, looking a little astonished at receiving such a visit.

"My dearest Lizzy..."

The good man had tears in his eyes when he clasped Elizabeth in his arms. It was their first meeting since the double wedding at Netherfield and they embraced with emotion.

"Did you receive my letter, papa?"

"Just this noon. But I did not expect to see you here until tomorrow or the day after. What a journey you have had! You must be weary!"

"I thought it might be best to bring Lydia back myself, to spare you from such a trip."

"You did well, my dear, you did well... Good gracious, Lizzy, how you have changed! Look at you! What a beautiful lady you have become!"

The young woman blushed a little. She, too, had not failed to notice how the elegance of her clothes, the flawless upkeep of the carriages and the various people accompanying her, struck a discordant note with her more modest childhood home.

Her servants stood back while the heartfelt family reunion took place, awaiting their instructions. She told the coachman and his apprentice where they could rest the horses, and sent Mrs. Vaughan and the footmen to the kitchen to eat once they had taken Lydia's trunk up to her room.

"Is Mr. Darcy at Netherfield?" she asked.

"Indeed, he has been there for about a week," her father replied. "He came to visit us a few times – we saw him just last night, in fact."

"I am glad to hear it. I wrote to inform him of our arrival, but I did not await his response and feared that, in the meantime, he might have returned to Pemberley. Might I send word that we have arrived?"

"You will be staying for dinner, I hope?"

"Of course! Rest assured, papa, I am not ready to leave so soon!"

~

It had been a long time since the Bennets had had three of their daughters at their table, and the conversation was especially cheerful. Mrs. Bennet wanted to know everything about Lydia, Elizabeth and their stay together at Pemberley, and she prattled more than ever as she informed them of the latest news from the neighbourhood. Revived, Lydia seemed to have forgotten her anguish. She described the weeks that had gone by since her departure from Newcastle as though they had been a wonderful excursion, and spoke well of Wickham, though with a bit more reserve than usual.

In the midst of this deluge of words, Mr. Bennet showed infinite patience. He could not remain impervious to his youngest daughter's plight, her expanding waistline now forcing her to sit a little further

370

away from the table than usual. And so, whenever anyone praised his son-in-law, he kept his scathing remarks to himself. He merely exchanged a few glances with Elizabeth and shrugged. Lydia had come home and he could only resign himself to the fact.

As for Elizabeth, she spoke little, preferring to watch rather than participate in the conversation. She listened to her mother and sister's spirited chatter, observed the ever discreet Mary, smiled at her father, and basked in all the familiar smells and sounds she had so dearly missed. At first she had the comforting sensation that nothing had changed at Longbourn. Every object and every piece of furniture was still in its place, and the flowers in the vases were similar to the ones they had always picked in the garden or on the roadside. She eventually noticed several details, however. Her mother's dress was new, Mary had changed the way she tied her hair and her gloomy expression had been replaced by a softer look, her father's old dog was gone – she remembered a letter saying he had died the previous winter – and, through the window, the sparse clump of trees that had always been there had been cut down.

Time had passed here as elsewhere.

More than anything, she noticed how Hill's behaviour towards her had changed as he went about his usual task of serving them. Throughout the meal he treated her with great civility, referring to her as 'madam' whenever he addressed her. This seemed absurd to the young woman and she almost teased him about it a few times. She had grown used to being treated deferentially by her people at Pemberley and at Chalton House, but Hill was different! She had known the man her entire life, jumped on his lap when she was a child, walked with him when they both followed her father on a hunt and had endured his numerous scoldings when she had been caught poking about somewhere she had no right to be. Seeing him that night, humbly lowering his eyes each time she addressed him was proof that there was a new distance between them. She would never have the freedom she had previously enjoyed with her parents' servants ever again.

~

The setting sun filled the drawing-room with a warm glow as tea was served to everyone. Once they were finished, Elizabeth asked for the carriage to be readied.

371

"Please visit us tomorrow, my dear," urged her mother. "I'm sure you have not finished sharing all your news from Derbyshire! I shall relate it all to Lady Lucas. She will be most surprised to learn that you have finally returned!"

While the horses trotted towards Netherfield, Elizabeth gazed out at the countryside, painted almost black by the night, and guessed at the shapes more than she actually saw them. On a few occasions it was she who directed the coachman, as he was not familiar with the area.

The roofs of Meryton appeared and she was flooded with memories of the last time she had made this journey, on her way to London. She remembered her tears and the distress she felt at the time, her joy at being married mingling with the apprehension and heartbreak of having to leave her home. Nine months later, she was there again, and the distress had become endless gratitude.

She felt good. She was simply eager to arrive.

~

Darcy's first impulse when reading the note sent from Longbourn was to jump on a horse and gallop there as fast as possible. He then decided against it. His wife was not a child. She did not need him and would join him in due course, once her family dinner was over.

However, the young man still burned with impatience.

He had not seen Elizabeth for almost three weeks, which had suddenly felt much longer once he learned of the debacle Wickham had caused. At the time, Darcy was infuriated at not being able to instantly transport himself to Pemberley so he could embrace his wife and reassure her.

He soon realised, however, that she was doing very well without him. He did not know the exact words exchanged with the ensign – she had not been able to describe the whole story in her letters –, but evidently she had managed to reject his incessant demands. Darcy finally understood that he had nothing to concern himself with: Elizabeth was handling the matter. In fact, just a few days later, she had sent another letter, confirming that it would be futile for him or Mr. Bennet to make a round trip to Derbyshire as she would accompany her sister back to Longbourn herself. And, without waiting for his approval, or that of her father, she set off.

Darcy recalled, not without some amusement, their conversation with Mr. Moore, when the latter had almost choked when the young woman asked to participate in the financial affairs of the estate. Since her arrival, Elizabeth had gracefully taken charge of every aspect of her new life and its responsibilities. There had indeed been some hesitation at first, but she gradually gained confidence. Far from merely taking on the responsibility of leading the household with skill and discernment, she had swiftly revealed her determination to participate on equal footing in matters that were usually a man's responsibility. She was just as committed as he was to ensuring that the household and the estate were properly managed, and she intended to take her own actions without having to refer to him. The former Bennet was beginning to understand the extent of the freedom that her status as a married, privileged woman granted her.

This display of independence could have offended Darcy. There were many who would have taken umbrage. Accustomed to being the sole master and decision maker, he might have felt somewhat annoyed that his wife challenged him on his own territory. After all, were not women generally thought to be at the service of their emotions and was it not best to keep them from making important decisions?

Surprisingly, however, the opposite happened. Darcy saw no reason to prevent Elizabeth from acting as she pleased. Not only did he take pride in having married a sensible woman, but even felt unexpected relief: he was no longer alone and could now share his burdens with his wife. Of course, this was not something he would have done with anyone, but the young woman was intelligent, and even if they were not always in agreement, he knew that she would always make sure no harm befell the Darcy name. She had his trust.

How he looked forward to seeing her again...

After dinner, he drank his tea with impatience at the window so he could watch for the arrival of the carriage. Bingley was quick to tease him.

"Your wife informed you that she would not be here before nightfall, my friend. Prowling at the window like that will not make her arrive any faster. Why not join us instead!"

But Darcy continued his silent vigil, incapable of tearing his eyes away from the sandy path that stretched out before the house, except when he glanced at the clock on the mantle nearby.

His patience was eventually rewarded, for he was the first one to catch sight of the horses turning the corner of the path.

"She is here!" he suddenly exclaimed.

He rushed outside, not bothering to take formal leave of the group on his way out.

~

They met at the bottom of the stairs, Elizabeth emerging from the carriage without waiting for the coachman to unfold the steps, and Darcy hurtling down the stairs after having bumped past the servants.

"Lizzy!" he cried out.

She opened her arms, laughing in surprise at her husband's unusual eagerness.

Darcy had never held her so tight.

He immediately buried his nose in the warmth of her neck and breathed in. He could smell the sweet orange blossom scent she now wore since Mrs. Vaughan had begun assisting her with her toilette. It mingled with her clothes, her hair and her skin. He found her soft, almost tender in his arms. They were precariously balanced on the steps and he felt her lose her footing and so caught her by the waist. Forced to end their embrace, they held each other's hands instead.

"What a reception, dearest!" Elizabeth whispered, her eyes sparkling. "I gather that you missed me?"

"You have no idea..." he whispered in return.

But he was not yet satisfied. Despite two footmen descending the staircase with lanterns, and Bingley, Jane and the others who congregated on the porch, Darcy took his wife's face between his hands and kissed her passionately.

He blushed a little when he let her go, embarrassed that so many people had witnessed their kiss, but he hid his discomfort behind a broad smile and hastened to offer her his arm as they climbed up the steps.

The joyful cries that greeted the young woman created further diversion.

~

Once Elizabeth had removed her coat, hat and gloves, she was invited to sit down in the drawing-room, where a fresh cup of tea awaited her. She immediately felt at home. Since Caroline Bingley and the Hursts were away, visiting cousins in Bath, she was amongst people whom she loved and had not seen in far too long.

"I will not ask how Papa and Mamma are faring, since we visited them just yesterday," said Jane. "But you, dearest sister, how are you? And how is poor Lydia?"

Elizabeth quickly described her journey and gave a rather brief account of her discussion with Wickham, endeavouring not to make him sound like the wicked man that he was in Georgiana's presence.

"Lydia has found herself a husband who is as fanciful as she is," she concluded with a deliberately well-intentioned smile, "I believe that we can certainly expect a few more surprises! They will undoubtedly lead a rather adventurous life, but I am certain they will find happiness, one way or another."

Only Kitty and Georgiana seemed to believe her. The others simply nodded their heads in silence.

"Since we are discussing marriage and unexpected arrangements," added Kitty, whose face had suddenly lit up, "you deserve quite a scolding, Lizzy! We learnt something, a few days ago, that left us quite speechless, and we are rather vexed that you never told us about it!"

"You wish to scold me? But I have only just arrived! What could I have done to warrant your wrath?" asked her sister, amused.

Kitty had spoken impulsively and began to stammer when she realised that what she wanted to reveal was more of an intimate confidence than a subject suitable for drawing-room conversation.

She became even more flustered when Darcy looked at her, intrigued. She eventually explained herself.

"Well, it would appear that everyone in Meryton is aware that you rejected a certain proposal last year. Mamma certainly wishes she had known. It would have saved her from feeling a little silly when our aunt Phillips boasted about it in front of the neighbours!"

"Poor Mr. Collins? But you were all there! The only surprise is that our aunt knows about it too – although I have no doubt about who informed her..."

Bingley's eyes creased with laughter.

"Kitty is referring to our friend Darcy's first proposal, which you rejected," he clarified.

Elizabeth's lips parted in a silent 'Oh!'. She then glanced at her husband, only to find that he had retreated behind his most impenetrable air, and laughed heartily.

She suddenly understood. The colourful scene with Caroline and Louisa on the day of their wedding had borne fruit: news that Elizabeth Bennet had taken the liberty of refusing a generous offer, from a gentleman far above her station, had indeed spread most swiftly.

"Good Lord! Whatever shall become of me now! People must think me a truly contemptuous person..." she sighed, looking falsely upset.

"I do not think so, no!" Bingley continued, a twinkle still in his eye. "We actually hear nothing but praise for you. Imagine: a young lady refusing such an advantageous match merely because she did not like him... A most commendable woman! You have become quite the darling here, Elizabeth!"

"Indeed!" said Jane. "If you only knew how Mamma and our aunt speak of you! And Mrs. Lucas! We always mention you as the best example to follow!"

Elizabeth's eyes widened further and, this time, her surprise was real.

She had never been of great importance in Meryton. Many of the ladies came from better families, they were wealthier and prettier than she was, and, in comparison, Elizabeth had little value on the marital chessboard. And yet she had by far surpassed them. She suspected that the matrons were praising the ingenuity she had shown in having secured the match, for if Elizabeth had neither status, nor fortune, nor beauty, then she must be rather clever indeed!

Now, things seemed to go even further. Her reluctance lent her a certain integrity. Marriage was all good and well, but not under just any conditions, for even if the suitor was extremely wealthy, what was fortune without love.

The young woman smiled to herself. They would probably not think so highly of her if they had witnessed the pitiful proposal, which had taken place in Hunsford. Between Darcy's arrogance and Elizabeth's harsh words, there had been very little merit on both sides... Thankfully, people would never know. Besides, she was no fool. She was only admired because a marriage had eventually taken place. Had she remained unmarried, she would have been chastised for this same reluctance.

"How respectable I am now!" she said a little later, as the evening drew to a close and she headed to her room in the company of her husband. "My dear... Are you not too embarrassed that everyone in the neighbourhood knows of this now?"

"Not in the least. You will recall that I am primarily responsible for it," Darcy replied. "I gave Caroline and Louisa my blessing to spread this rumour. I sought only to silence their gossiping tongues."

"Indeed, you silenced Caroline and Louisa, but in doing so you created an equally important problem..."

"For your greater glory, my dear. You are the one they celebrate, now!" teased her husband.

~

Mrs. Vaughan was always very prepared. She had requested that a tub and pitchers of hot water be brought up to Darcy's dressing room so that her mistress could wash away the journey's fatigue. Darcy made no objection to granting the women full access to his dressing room. He undressed in his room instead, aided by his valet, and was the first to climb into bed.

Amidst the sheets, eyes half closed, he listened. He heard Elizabeth conversing with her maid in a low voice, and guessed what she was doing from the various noises. Water splashing, then drying, hair untied and brushed thoroughly, the rustling of linen and clothes... It had been a few weeks since he had heard these familiar noises and it brought him solace. It was proof that Elizabeth was with him once more.

A delicate fragrance soon wafted through the air. He smiled. When she applied lotion, it meant that she was almost done. The peaceful chatter between the two women continued.

"There is not much left, Mrs. Vaughan. We shall have to make some more."

"Yes, madam."

"Do we have enough dried flowers? What a pity. If I had thought of it sooner, I could have asked Mr. Darcy to bring some back from London..."

"I shall check when we return to Pemberley, madam."

"It will not be anytime soon! We have just arrived! But if we do indeed run out, we shall find a solution... My mother has an excellent recipe for lotion. She makes it with flowers from the garden. I shall ask her."

Soon after, Darcy heard the door leading to the dressing room open and close, and Elizabeth's hushed footsteps approaching. She held a candle, her hair gathered in a large braid over her shoulder.

"Why do you stare at me so, my love," she teased him. "Only a few weeks apart and it appears you have become unaccustomed to seeing me in your room!"

"I assure you that I am quite accustomed to it and I firmly intend to keep it that way," he retorted. "I was merely wondering how your stay without me at Pemberley went. How were you able to sleep alone all those nights? Were you not afraid?"

The young woman raised a wry eyebrow to indicate that his teasing had no effect on her.

"I was doing quite well. The bed merely took a little longer to warm up..."

Darcy smiled.

"In that case, you will have no use for me tonight," he sighed. "I asked Grove to open the windows as it has grown hot in the evenings."

"Indeed. I am actually surprised that you have chosen to keep your shirt on. Would you mind if I removed mine?"

Darcy's smile grew.

Elizabeth had become aware of the effect she had on her husband and no longer hesitated to use it to her advantage. Tonight, the game was particularly easy, as they were both so eager to be reunited.

Sitting on the edge of the bed and bathed in the glow of the candle that rested on the bedside table, the young woman pulled her shift over her head with deliberate slowness, pausing to rub her neck a little, before giving Darcy a seductive look over her shoulder. He stretched his arm out, unable to resist, and trailed his fingers down her back to her waist, and lower. She was magnificent and, evidently, she liked the feel of his hand on her skin.

"Lie down, Lizzy," he whispered.

Still silent, Elizabeth lay down on her stomach, pushing the sheets out of the way so her husband might continue his ministrations. She closed her eyes and sighed deeply.

Darcy trailed his hand up and down, from her neck to her lower back. She arched a little and sometimes shuddered when he touched her on the sides – he knew she was sensitive there – but she let him continue, clearly enjoying herself.

"If I had known, when I was in this room last year, that one day you would be sleeping here with me..." he said.

"Who said anything about sleep?" she murmured. "Kiss me, instead..."

The young man, now fully awake, had no difficulty complying.

~

At first, Darcy had only planned to be in London for a fortnight, with the intention of completing the purchase of land from the Bromley brothers and then returning to Pemberley. Subsequent events had disrupted his plans, but now that Lydia's problem had been at least temporarily resolved, that Georgiana was thoroughly enjoying her time with Kitty and that Elizabeth had joined them, he was in no rush to return home. Besides, the Bingleys would hear nothing of it. They were all too happy about this visit and insisted on keeping the Darcys with them until the end of summer. Mrs. Reynolds was thus sent a letter with instructions to send a few more trunks, and the group settled down for what promised to be a most joyful stay, with visits planned between Netherfield and Longbourn every second day.

Mr. Bennet was delighted to have his five daughters reunited once more. Although he was generally rather uninterested in social events, he proved quite motivated to plan a large dinner at his home, inviting the Lucases, the Phillips, the reverend of Meryton and other neighbours, in addition to his daughters and his sons-in-law. He spared no expense and even hired additional servants.

"There are certain things I can afford, now that my children no longer need me," he whispered to Elizabeth. "Although, with Lydia's return, I shall have to watch my purse once more, lest my wife and youngest spend it all!"

The dinner opened the floodgates: from that day forth, Elizabeth and Darcy received an impressive amount of invitations from families in the region. Formal dinners along with outings, teas, hunting excursions and other distractions.

"Really, I did not know I had so many friends!" remarked the young woman, with some irony.

Her parents, on the other hand, were endlessly proud that their daughter was held in such regard. Mrs. Bennet, in particular, held her chin high and was quick to greet everyone in the streets of Meryton. She announced to whosoever would listen that her daughter and son-in-law had been present at this or that reception, or which forthcoming events they would likely be attending. Her memory was impressive and she was able to recall even the most insignificant details. For her, the Darcys' social activities were an endless source of news to be peddled, and she took it upon herself to inform everyone of the exact contents of their calendars.

Elizabeth, at first unsettled by everyone's sudden interest in her, graciously accepted all the invitations. She was very aware that her newly acquired status aroused people's curiosity. She had left her home for Derbyshire, a faraway county if ever there was one, to settle in a prestigious house and family. It was only natural for people to think that she returned with fascinating stories to tell.

Which she gladly told. She recounted her time at Pemberley with her usual talent and wit. Her audience was composed of her parents, her uncle and her aunt Phillips, the neighbours she was well acquainted with, along with those who were less familiar. It became clear that her transition to becoming the mistress of a large estate had not rendered her arrogant in the slightest. She entertained her audience with the same kindness and desire to be agreeable, relating common anecdotes of her daily life: her first difficulties with the servants; her small errors before London's high society; the time she lost her way in the woods; the beautiful receptions they had organised and attended over the festive season; the imposing presence of Lady Catherine de Bourgh, whom she had appeased with great difficulty; her beloved Georgiana, for whom she hoped to be a good example... And then, from time to time, amidst the laughter that her stories prompted, Elizabeth met Darcy's gaze.

Amused. Tender. Enamoured.

At Longbourn, nothing remained of the era when footsteps, laughter and bickering rang out amongst the five Bennet girls. Only Mary stayed with her parents, surrounded by a solitude and calmness that suited her best. She had initially been frustrated by Lydia's return, apprehensive of her restless disposition but that had not lasted very long. Indeed, Lydia soon realised that the most pleasant distractions were unfolding further away. So, after barely a week, she requested to live at Netherfield with the others – which the Bingleys, with their usual kindness, quickly granted her.

However, the young Mrs. Wickham hesitated to fall back into the old life of a blithe adolescent with her lifelong companion, Kitty. Two obstacles lay in her way: her increasingly large belly on the one hand, and the fact that Kitty had found a new friend in Georgiana, on the other. As Lydia now only spoke of her husband and her future child, the relationship between the formerly inseparable sisters could not be rekindled. Too many things lay between them now. Unfortunately, it was Georgiana who paid the price for the jealous spats that ensued, until Lydia eventually decided to gravitate towards her older sisters, who were more patient with her.

With their little group finally united, everyone was in good spirits as the weeks wore on. What had once been two pairs of young fiancés seeking privacy as they courted, had now become a solid group of friends who planned their time around common activities. They often ventured out, on foot or by carriage, and as the days became hotter, they also planned picnics at the edge of the stream that ran through Netherfield Park. Barefoot in the water, Kitty and Georgiana took great delight in moving large stones to build makeshift dams.

In the evenings, if they were not invited for dinner with an acquaintance, they would enjoy spending time in the garden. Meals were served on the terrace and everyone lingered outside as late as possible, covering themselves with shawls or blankets when the air grew cool. Bingley and Elizabeth got along famously. To them, balmy summer evenings were not for playing card games, reading, or embroidery. One of them always suggested a game of battledore and shuttlecock, which, at the moment, was their favourite activity. Jane sat close by to encourage the players and was usually accompanied by Darcy who staunchly refused to pick up a racket. He saw no reason to chase after a silly shuttlecock, which changed its trajectory at the slightest gust of wind. He much preferred to converse with his sister-in-law. Lydia, too, did not participate, but it was her condition rather than a lack of motivation that kept her from joining the players. Her frustration at not being able to participate often darkened her mood. As for Kitty and Georgiana, neither was very accomplished and they quickly grew tired of losing, so Bingley eventually invited Maria Lucas and her oldest brother so they would have enough players.

They never mentioned Wickham. Or rather, only Lydia mentioned him. The girl repeatedly asserted that her husband was a valiant soldier who was torn between his military duty and his love for her. As dramatic as it sounded, patriotic duty came before family. Positioning herself in the role of the heroine was a way for her to find some solace, like Penelope, patiently and virtuously waiting for her husband to return. But more importantly, it was the only way she had found to protect her reputation in Meryton as it provided an explanation as to why, less than a year into her marriage, she had returned to her parents. Whether or not people were convinced, they soon accepted her version of events. The lonely young wife was provided with much encouragement and well wishes for the impending arrival of her first child.

For those who knew about the real nature of their relationship and the abandonment Lydia faced, the wisest course of action was nodding with kindness and allowing her to express herself. She did not believe a word of what she said, but she put so much effort into maintaining appearances that it would have been cruel to constantly remind her of what had really transpired. And so, when a large trunk from Newcastle containing all her belongings was delivered to Longbourn, the girl hid upstairs to weep, yelling that she would not open the door for anyone. When she came downstairs again, even Mrs. Bennet pretended not to have noticed a thing. Jane put a comforting arm around her shoulders and the conversation continued.

Wickham had not even bothered to attach a letter. As far as they could tell, he was shirking all of his responsibilities as a husband, and there was no indication that he would ever be willing to take her back again.

All that remained was to hope that the birth of their child would change his mind.

~

Lady Catherine got wind of the Darcys' presence in Hertfordshire through Charlotte Collins. She wrote to her nephew at once, inviting them to visit Rosings at the beginning of September, as she wished to present them to other guests of hers. She made the assurance that while the ladies enjoyed the park and its sumptuous rose garden, Darcy would be a considerable asset to the small party of gentlemen and their hunting excursions.

"What do you think, Lizzy? Would you like to go to Rosings or would you rather return to Pemberley?"

"Since your aunt has extended such an eager invitation, it would be quite unseemly to refuse. Let us go to Rosings in September! Why don't we make a stop in London on our return journey? Charles spoke of a visit he made to the royal menagerie some years ago, and Georgiana was quite excited at the prospect of seeing all those strange animals. We could take her there. It would be quite diverting for her I should think."

"As it would be for you, too, I suppose..."

Elizabeth chuckled when she caught the look Darcy gave her, and continued in the same tone:

"Indeed! See how well I have managed things for expedient's sake? Apparently there is a grizzly bear... Would you not be curious to see such a creature?"

Darcy shrugged, teasingly. Elizabeth did not need that many arguments to convince him.

It was therefore agreed upon that they would visit Lady Catherine in September, and then stop in London for a few weeks before returning to Pemberley for the festive season. And, in order not to separate Georgiana and Kitty, the latter would be joining their party.

However, before they could focus on their plans, another event occupied everyone's minds in August: a public ball in Meryton had been announced.

"Do not wait to buy your tickets, girls, otherwise there will be none left! Summer balls are always most popular, especially with all the seasonal visitors in the county," warned Mrs. Bennet.

Hence, Bingley had rushed to obtain tickets for everyone, which sparked a new debate at the table.

"Darcy, how can you still be so hesitant to allow your sister to join us? I recall having the same conversation with you when we were at Pemberley, last year!"

Jane's husband was in this rare instance somewhat displeased with his friend. As a personable man accustomed to facilitating fun and festivity around him, he greatly disliked the idea of leaving a member of their party behind.

"Georgiana ought to be allowed to attend balls like everyone else!" he declared.

Bingley, however, could not engage Darcy further in a direct confrontation. Elizabeth took it upon herself to do the rest.

Seeing her husband's face harden at his friend's reproach, she swiftly changed the subject. Experience had taught her that Darcy did not like it when his authority was questioned in front of the family, and it was best to wait until they could discuss this sensitive matter in private.

This time, their conversation was far less heated than the one prompted by Mrs. Annesley after Christmastide. Darcy had been able to come to terms with the idea that, sooner or later, Georgiana would have to step into society, and constantly delaying this event was useless.

"The Meryton ball would be the perfect opportunity," Elizabeth argued. "You are the first to admit that the society here in Hertfordshire is not so elegant as elsewhere – no, don't try to contradict me, we both know that this is the opinion you hold! For once, think of it as an advantage: if Georgiana makes her entry here, amid more provincial circles, she risks nothing more than having a delightful evening. Everyone will be far too occupied to judge whether she adheres to the standards of conduct appropriate to her rank... Which she will, of course, but you are familiar with Georgiana's shyness and her marked desire to do well by us. In Meryton, she will be accompanied by Kitty, surrounded by people whose opinion matters little to her, and she need not concern herself with what she is allowed to say or do. I assure you that Jane will join me in ensuring that everything goes well. Don't you think that this would be a wonderful opportunity?"

Darcy remained dubious.

He had dreamt of a more striking entrance for his sister. When Mrs. Keen had mentioned the elaborate parties held at Pemberley in the past, he had imagined one of them becoming a prestigious, unforgettable event, where Georgiana would be presented with great ceremony to the rest of society, to the immense pride of the family. After all, she came from a line of earls: at the same age, their mother, Lady Anne, had appeared at Court and had met the King in person!

But it was a great deal to ask of Elizabeth. She had only been at Pemberley for a year. Planning events of that magnitude just to shine a light upon her younger sister-in-law was a huge responsibility to bear. Besides, he had to acknowledge that Georgiana's shyness did her no favours. While she was indeed learning to assert herself within the family circle, it was clear that putting her on display in such a fashion to be scrutinised by everyone – would be quite taxing. By contrast, a cheerful and friendly public ball, held in a small country town, seemed more appropriate.

The young man eventually relented.

While he deliberated, Georgiana awaited her brother's decision with some apprehension, determined to submit to her fate, whatever that might be. Therefore, when Darcy announced that she could accompany them to the ball, and that henceforth he would ensure that she also participated in the receptions they were invited to, she beamed with joy.

"Oh, dear brother! I am so delighted! I don't know how to thank you!" she exclaimed, throwing her arms around his neck to kiss him.

The rest of the family fully approved of this decision, and Bingley declared that he was pleased to see his friend's stubbornness come to an end at last.

As for Darcy, he felt relieved. Admittedly, he would now have to keep an eye on the young fellows who would not fail to hover around Georgiana. But, in that moment, seeing her eyes shine bright with excitement really meant the world to him.

~

When she first arrived at Longbourn, Mrs. Vaughan made no comment at all. She did not frown, nor purse her lips, nor peer about with a knowing look. Her manners were impeccable as she impassively observed what she had suspected from the start: her mistress came from a very modest background, far removed from the splendour of Pemberley.

The maid adapted. Without receiving the slightest instruction to do so, she kept the most conspicuous jewels in their boxes, and offered Elizabeth elegant yet sober ensembles instead, so she would not look glaringly out of place amongst her neighbours. Contrary to Louisa and Caroline who had, in their time, done everything they could to distinguish themselves from the local residents whom they scorned, this was Elizabeth's home. Flaunting her newly acquired wealth would not have been tactful. On the evening of the Meryton ball, with her elegant hairstyle and tailored, yet unostentatious dress, the former Miss Bennet felt quite at ease and ready to dance all night, both with the gentlemen and the merchants, or anyone wealthy enough to afford a ticket. The only big difference with the last ball she had attended there was that she was now accompanied by her husband.

Elizabeth knew him well enough now. Darcy would grant her a few dances at the beginning of the evening, but would then arrange to spend time with Mr. Bennet or Sir William Lucas. He had a talent for slipping past crowds and pretending to be too caught up in a conversation to notice that a new quadrille was about to begin. And since he could always count on Bingley's tireless motivation, he had no qualms about letting him lead the ladies on the dance floor.

As the little party from Netherfield entered the room and began to pair up for a dance, Elizabeth rose on her tiptoes to whisper in his ear:

"Offer the first dance to Georgiana. She will be delighted!"

"Do you think so?"

"Of course! This is her first ball! Who do you think she would rather dance with other than her brother, to whom she owes the honour of finally being out?"

"In that case, whom will you dance with?"

"Well! Do not concern yourself with me, I am sure my dear papa will do me the honour..."

Darcy did as he was bidden. She saw him approach Georgiana, ceremoniously inviting her to dance with him. His sister acquiesced as pure delight lit up her face.

Elizabeth sighed with satisfaction. Then she turned to Mr. Bennet with an affected air.

"My dear father, see how my husband abandons me. The ball has not yet begun and I am already without a partner!"

"Poor child!" replied Mr. Bennet in the same tone. "Am I to understand that you, too, must look to your father when you find yourself in a difficult situation?"

"That is because you are my refuge, papa, as you well know..."

"Well, it would appear that our fate as parents is to care for our children for as long as life allows us to do so... do take my arm, child, and let us see if I am still able to caper about as I did in my youth!"

Georgiana, whose expression indicated that she did not know whether to feel intimidated or excited, performed her first dance with her brother, the second with Bingley, and then Mr. Bennet, and finally with Sir Lucas. She then did not leave her small group of friends, comprised of Kitty, Maria, the eldest Lucas brother and two other young neighbours, who made sure she laughed and spun about the dancefloor until she was exhausted.

For her part, Elizabeth joined her husband for the second dance, and then was led by Bingley and again by Mr. Bennet. After which she spent quite some time seated at a table, chatting with Jane, until Lady Lucas and their uncle and aunt Phillips joined them. They were quite surprised to learn that Jane had already danced three times.

"Do not become too agitated, young lady," advised Lady Lucas, in a maternal tone. "In your condition, it is best to be careful."

"Rest assured, I am in perfect health!" Jane retorted. "I am still able to move with ease, and my husband leads me with such tenderness that I never grow tired while we dance..."

"Wait until the tempo accelerates once the musicians have had more in the way of refreshment!" Mrs. Philips said. "You know how these things progress: for now, the dancers cut a fine figure, but soon, they will return perspiring, red-cheeked and breathless as though they have run three miles!"

But Jane protested that her condition could not prevent her from having a delightful time at the ball. As if to confirm her assertion, Bingley, who had not left the floor since the start of the evening, soon returned to fetch her for another dance.

"Darcy is in the other room, Elizabeth," he said as he walked past her. "Would you like me to fetch him for you? Or, if you wait for this dance to finish, it will be my pleasure to invite you again."

"No, no, by all means, enjoy dancing with your wife. I shall fetch Mr. Darcy myself, even if I have to drag him by the collar!"

Bingley laughed cheerfully and disappeared with Jane. Elizabeth followed her own advice. She slipped through the crowd into the next room, where refreshments were served and people gathered to escape the din of the music. Darcy was there, engaged in a debate with Sir Lucas and a few other gentlemen.

"Would you do me the honour of joining me on the dance floor?" said the young woman quietly as she drew near to her husband. "I fear that I have been sitting for far too long."

"Where is Bingley?"

"He is presently dancing with his wife in the other room, as any good husband is wont to do..."

A little smile appeared on Darcy's face at this veiled rebuke.

"You mean to say that I am neglecting you, Lizzy?" he whispered.

"Indeed, terribly so! Quick! Ask me to dance before I wither away forever!"

Laughing, the young man excused himself from the conversation, citing his husbandly duties. He led Elizabeth away.

Mrs. Phillips' prediction had proven right. The tempo had accelerated, much to the delight of the dancers. Eyes sparkled and everyone laughed. The ladies fanned their necks with their hands and the gentlemen patted the sweat on their brows with as much elegance as they could muster. Everyone was red-cheeked and out of breath.

Sixteen couples rallied and the quadrille began. Darcy proved to be a good sport. No matter how much he balked at the idea of dancing all evening as Bingley did, once on the dance floor and accompanied by the right partner, he knew how to make the most of it. Keeping an eye on Georgiana who danced a short distance away with the Lucas boy did not prevent him from focussing on his steps, and he occasionally let out a laugh or a wink. Elizabeth, in turn, enjoyed herself tremendously.

But after only a few minutes, while Darcy was leading her around, the young woman was suddenly taken by a wave of dizziness. The room around her began to spin and she almost lost her footing.

Darcy, who felt that something was wrong, put a hand on her waist to steady her.

"Lizzy? Is everything all right?"

She wanted to say something but a sudden surge of nausea kept her from doing so. She simply nodded.

She finished the movement as best she could and took her place in the line of dancers facing one another. But as the music continued and the ladies began to spin again, she remained motionless, confused and seeking only to maintain her balance. She felt the colour drain from her face.

Upon seeing this, Darcy leapt towards her and passed an arm around her waist to prevent her from falling. He apologised to the Bingleys who danced next to them, before helping her off the dance floor.

"What a pity... How will they continue the quadrille if there is a couple missing?" she stammered.

"Do not concern yourself with the dance, Lizzy! You are white as a sheet!"

He guided Elizabeth to the back of the room and sat her on a chair. Once seated, the nausea subsided.

"How do you feel, my dear?" Darcy asked, kneeling before her. "Would you like some refreshment? Tea, perhaps?"

The thought of drinking anything sweet made her stomach churn. She shook her head forcefully, and immediately regretted it as the room spun again.

"What can I do to help?" he asked again.

"Nothing, I assure you. Let us wait another minute for it to pass. It is nothing serious."

Indeed, once she was calmly seated, with Darcy's reassuring presence at her side, the dizziness faded.

"You see? There is nothing to be worried about. It was probably just the heat. Or perhaps the dance was too lively. Give me another minute and we may return..."

That was out of the question, of course. Darcy summoned a footman and asked for a cup of tea, sitting by his wife while she drank.

To her relief, Elizabeth felt better after unfolding her fan and taking a few sips. She gathered her wits and colour returned to her cheeks. She then glanced around and laughed.

"How far we have come!" she exclaimed.

"What do you mean?" asked Darcy.

"Well, it so happens that I am very familiar with this particular bench. I was seated here when I overheard the unfortunate conversation which long compromised our relationship."

Elizabeth looked at her husband mischievously before continuing:

"Do you recall when we first met? I found you very much to my liking and I gladly would have ventured to know you a little better. But just as Bingley suggested that you invite me to dance, you told him you did not find me pretty enough to be tempted in any way."

Darcy's face darkened.

"We should not keep revisiting the past. Especially when there is no pride to be taken in it," he grumbled.

But Elizabeth stroked his hand fondly.

"Rest assured, my love, I do not seek to rekindle bad memories, nor elevate myself for having overcome your initial reluctance. I am simply surprised to see how far we have come since that mishap. I was offended and resented you for a long time, and yet here we are. I am your wife and I love you."

She had rested her head against his shoulder and now lifted it to kiss the corner of his lips. The young man smiled and discreetly returned the kiss.

391

"I vividly remember what I said that night, but I am not proud of my conduct," he admitted in a low voice.

"Especially since you knew that I had overheard you."

"Indeed, I was unforgivable. It is not how I was raised. Only..."

He paused.

"Only...?" insisted Elizabeth, curious.

Darcy looked uncomfortable.

"Would you hold it against me if I explained the reason behind my actions? Believe me, I do not seek to absolve myself."

"Pray, do tell me, my dear! I look forward to it!" Elizabeth teased him again.

But, as was often the case when she attempted to make him laugh in order to defuse the situation, her husband answered with utmost seriousness.

"Keep in mind that at the time, everyone was most anxious to see me married," he explained. "Truth be told, as soon as my father passed away, I was frequently introduced to young ladies and then admonished for not being able to make a decision. According to them, I was overly fastidious. I was given to understand that I was selfish, that it was essential for me to have a wife and children, if not for my own happiness, then to honour my family. It was as though, without my father there to advise and guide me, everyone felt compelled to compensate for his absence."

He paused for a brief moment, lost in thought, before continuing.

"At Pemberley, London, Rosings, Bath and all the places I visited, I would always hear the same injunction. Bingley was the only one amongst my friends who left me in peace. Busy as he was admiring the ladies who gravitated in and out of his circle, he never seemed bothered about my situation. That is to say, until that fateful night. I suppose he was influenced by his having just met your sister and wished for me to experience the same joy. However, I was annoyed that he, too, was now reciting the same speech I had so often heard, that I roundly dismissed him."

"Do you mean to say that your remarks were directed at Bingley rather than at me?"

"Of course. And if I had been more courteous, you would have never heard my comments."

He smiled awkwardly before continuing.

"To be perfectly honest, it is true that I did not immediately admire you on the first night. You were – according to my tastes, at least – no more and no less pretty than all the other young women that had already been introduced to me. It was only after hearing you speak, and witnessing the intelligence and finesse you are capable of, that I allowed myself to be seduced. And now, I cannot imagine a life without your laughter and your fine eyes..."

Enamoured, Elizabeth listened in silence. She smiled blissfully. Darcy was not one to speak so freely, and when he did, his sincerity always surprised her.

Jane and Bingley interrupted their moment of intimacy. The dance was over and they had come to enquire after Elizabeth.

"What happened, my dear?" worried her sister.

"Nothing at all, as you can see! I believe the dance was a little too spirited for me. Unless, of course, it was my husband's handsome features that made my head spin...? But as you can see, I am quite well now, and determined to dance again as soon as possible!"

Her plans were foiled, however. First by Darcy, who preferred to see her rest and eat something, and secondly by Georgiana, who came seeking comfort from her family. She was alarmed when a strange young man had boldly asked her to dance with him. Having not been introduced to him beforehand, she was caught off guard, unsure of which attitude to adopt. She had blushed crimson and stammered an unintelligible response before fleeing towards Elizabeth and Darcy.

The poor girl was most agitated.

"Who is this young fellow?" Elizabeth asked, upon hearing the tale.

"I have not a clue! I am not even certain that Kitty or Maria know him... He was rather bold addressing me as he did! Was I right not to accept his invitation?"

"Indeed, yes... Would you like me to enquire after him? I am sure that we will be able to make introductions, after which you can return to the dance floor."

Georgiana's anxiety grew.

"Oh no, Lizzy, I truly would be too frightened to see him again after having appeared so foolish! No, no, I would rather stay with you for now. I have danced enough for tonight..."

Elizabeth did not insist, realising that Georgiana's timid nature was resurfacing. She took her by the hand and together they went to fetch a glass of punch before joining her parents, Jane and Sir Lucas.

Mr. Bennet was unapologetically criticising the night's events along with his neighbours' state of inebriation.

"Look at him... Yes, yes, the man who just passed before us... Do you see how he staggers? I give him less than half an hour before he collapses somewhere, all the more so because he seems determined to empty yet another glass. Someone should tell him to refrain from blowing out his own candle before he goes to bed, or else he might set the house on fire!"

Georgiana smiled at this, finding her good humour once more. However, she did not leave her party for the remainder of the evening.

~

It was late when Elizabeth opened her eyes the following morning. She was awoken by Lydia's voice ringing out in the passage.

Darcy was already up, so she was able to enjoy the entire bed. She dozed off but woke up again when she heard Mrs. Vaughan discreetly fussing about in the dressing room next door.

Elizabeth coughed and moved a little to let her know that she was awake. Her maid entered the room a few minutes later, with a tray laden with tea and biscuits.

"Did madam sleep well?"

"Wonderfully... What time is it? Where is Mr. Darcy?"

"It is just past half nine. Mr. Darcy came down about an hour ago. I believe he and Mr. Bingley have gone out with their horses."

"Already! Good gracious, I must get up if I am to join everyone for breakfast!"

As she spoke, Elizabeth lifted the sheets and stood up. But she fell back down on the bed almost immediately. Her head was spinning so much that she had lost her balance.

"Madam? Is everything all right?"

"Yes, yes, I'm just a little light headed. I stood up too quickly."

The maid, who had been pulling the curtains back and opening the window to air the room, gave her a long look.

"Are you quite certain?" she enquired, delicately.

Elizabeth, who was waiting for her head to stop spinning, leant over her cup of tea and took a sip without answering. She was about to get up again when she met Mrs. Vaughan's scrutinising gaze.

"Well, what is it?" she asked.

"Your husband informed me earlier that you had a similar episode yesterday evening."

"It was hot and I was spinning about a little too much, that is all. There is no mystery to it! In fact, I was quite well afterwards."

But Mrs. Vaughan had a little smile on her lips. She continued:

"I beg your pardon for insisting, madam, but I wish to remind you that you have not bled for some time. Your light-headedness may well be an indication of happy news, don't you think?"

Puzzled, Elizabeth wondered for a moment what the maid was alluding to.

Then, her lips parted and her eyes opened wide.

"Do you think so?" she blurted.

Mrs. Vaughan's smile widened.

~

Elizabeth descended Netherfield's grand staircase at an unusually slow pace, as though walking in a dream. She counted the steps distractedly, listening to the thud her footsteps made on the marble. Beneath her hand, she felt the polished shine of the wooden handrail as she trailed her fingers from the top of the stairs to the final spiral at the bottom. She turned right, into the passage, and then walked through the second door to the left, into the dining room.

At the entrance she paused, as if intimidated.

Nothing was out of the ordinary in the scene before her. The family was preparing to sit down to eat, before making the most of another beautiful summer day.

"Good morning, Lizzy!" Jane cried out gaily as she, too, came down the passage, gently stroking her arm as she walked by.

Without pause, the young Mrs. Bingley headed to her place, at the head of the table. She let out a sigh of contentment as she sat down, and rubbed her belly before reaching out towards a large teapot.

At the other end, across from the ham, the bread and fruit baskets, the cheeses, scrambled eggs, muffins, and a leftover candied fruitcake, stood Bingley. As head of the family, he was busy cutting a big loaf into slices, and greeted his wife with an affectionate quip about how tired she looked. Lydia was late, but Georgiana and Kitty were there, seated next to one another. It appeared they had spent an eventful evening, as they now exchanged confidences in low voices, giggling together.

Darcy, too, was there, seated with his back to the large windows through which light flooded into the room. He rose to greet Jane as she entered and was about to sit down again when he saw Elizabeth standing in the doorway. He smiled at her, then raised an eyebrow, a little surprised to see her there, motionless.

As their eyes met, Elizabeth suddenly felt her heart beat faster.

396

She wondered how she would tell him.

OTHER BOOKS BY THE AUTHOR

« La cantatrice » serie:

- o *La jeunesse d'Emma Albani*, Les Éditeurs Réunis, 2011
- o *Le triomphe d'Emma Albani*, Les Éditeurs Réunis, 2012

« Les filles de joie » serie:

- o *Le Magnolia*, Les Éditeurs Réunis, 2013
- o *L'heure bleue*, Les Éditeurs Réunis, 2013
- o *La grimace du tigre*, Les Éditeurs Réunis, 2014

« La renaissance de Pemberley », self-publishing, 2019

---

www.liseantunessimoes.com

 Lise Antunes Simoes - Auteure

Printed in Great Britain
by Amazon

49773900R00244